NIGHT OF THE
LIVING DANDELION

A FLOWER SHOP MYSTERY

NIGHT OF THE LIVING DANDELION

KATE COLLINS

KENNEBEC
CHIVERS

This Large Print edition is published by Kennebec Large Print, Waterville, Maine, USA and by AudioGO Ltd, Bath, England.
Kennebec Large Print, a part of Gale, Cengage Learning.
Copyright © Linda Tsoutsouris, 2011.
The moral right of the author has been asserted.

The text of this Large Print edition is unabridged.
Other aspects of the book may vary from the original edition.
Set in 16 pt. Plantin.

LIBRARY OF CONGRESS CATALOGING-IN-PUBLICATION DATA

Collins, Kate, 1951–
   Night of the living dandelion : a flower shop mystery / by Kate Collins.
  — Large print ed.
     p. cm. — (Kennebec large print superior collection)
     ISBN-13: 978-1-4104-3833-1 (pbk.)
     ISBN-10: 1-4104-3833-3 (pbk.)
     1. Knight, Abby (Fictitious character)—Fiction. 2. Florists—Fiction. 3. Women detectives—Fiction. 4. Vampires—Fiction. 5. Large type books. I. Title.
     PS3603.O4543N54 2011
     813'.6—dc23   2011021310

BRITISH LIBRARY CATALOGUING-IN-PUBLICATION DATA AVAILABLE

Published in 2011 in the U.S. by arrangement with NAL Signet, a member of Penguin Group (USA) Inc.
Published in 2012 in the U.K. by arrangement with the author.

U.K. Hardcover: 978 1 445 86556 0 (Chivers Large Print)
U.K. Softcover: 978 1 445 86557 7 (Camden Large Print)

Printed in the United States of America
1 2 3 4 5 6 7 15 14 13 12 11

*Dedicated to the memory
of my beloved husband
and soul mate, Jim.
I will always love you.*

ACKNOWLEDGMENTS

I'd like to thank the following people for helping this book come to life:

My technical experts: Harry E. Ramsey, MD, and James V. Tsoutsouris, Esq.

My editorial team: Nancy Cergizan and Jason Eberhardt

My promotional teams: Julie Eberhardt; Barbara Ferrari; Nulita, owner, Love in Bloom, Key West, Florida; Jennifer Badry, 7 Artists Studio, Key West, Florida

Valparaiso University SPARK team: Kevin Brown, Ryan Roman, Pete Volmut, and Professor Bonita Neff

Author, friend, and psychologist Mary Kennedy

My Cozy Chick buddies: Deb Baker, Lorna Barrett, Maggie Sefton, J. B. Stanley, Leann Sweeney, and Heather Webber

My editor: Ellen Edwards

My agent: Karen Solem

"We don't accomplish anything in this world alone . . . and whatever happens is the result of the whole tapestry of one's life and all the weavings of individual threads from one to another that creates something."

— Sandra Day O'Connor

All my stories come from the weavings of individual threads — some from past events, newspaper stories, overheard conversations, and brainstorming sessions with friends and family, and the rest from the meanderings of my imagination. Some information is made deliberately vague to fit the purpose of the plot. Nevertheless, I strive for accuracy and apologize for any errors I may have made.

As with all my books, this is a collaborative

effort. I thank all of you for your continued help and support.

CHAPTER ONE

Monday

Of course I could handle the flower shop for fifteen minutes. It was my shop.

Or so I said to Lottie, my assistant, who needed to deliver floral arrangements to the funeral home before five o'clock. Still, she was hesitant to leave me alone, and not out of fear of a burglary. Bloomers couldn't have been in a safer location. The courthouse was directly across the street, the police station a block away, and my fiancé's bar, Down the Hatch, two doors north.

No, Lottie's fear was of someone causing me physical harm — that someone being me. Because of an ankle sprain I'd suffered two days before, I'd been ordered to stay off my right foot for two weeks, forcing me into an existence ruled by crutches and a wheelchair. So far, I'd slipped twice; fallen once; gotten wedged halfway inside the shop's front door, unable to move in or out;

crushed half a dozen fresh Red Beauty roses; and toppled the towering dieffenbachia in the corner near the glass display case. That was on crutches — in my first two hours at work.

So I'd ditched the crutches and switched to the wheelchair when I was inside the shop, for obvious reasons, and had thus far banged into three doorjambs, run over Lottie's foot, *and* mangled Grace's new eyeglasses. Hence Lottie's hesitation. "I'd feel better if Grace were here," she said from the back of the shop.

"I'd feel better if I hadn't broken her glasses. Thank goodness she was able to get her new ones before Eye-Caramba closed today."

Grace Bingham was my other assistant, a slender sixty-something Brit who had been a legal secretary in a law office where I'd clerked during my only year in law school. Grace had retired just before I bought Bloomers, then decided she was bored and came to work for me as the hostess of our coffee-and-tea parlor. Both Grace and the parlor were big hits with our customers.

But the parlor was empty now, and I'd be closing up shop soon anyway. "Lottie, I'll be fine. Don't worry about me."

"It's not you I'm worried about, sweetie.

It's Bloomers." She winked.

Lottie Dombowski was a big-boned Kentuckian with a soft heart, brassy curls, and a penchant for pink. She had a true gift for floral design and was in the process of passing on her knowledge to me. Lottie had owned Bloomers until her husband's health problems had nearly forced them into bankruptcy. And there I was, freshly booted out of law school and in need of employment. So I used the remainder of my grandfather's trust fund to make a down payment on the shop, hired Lottie and Grace to work for me, and the rest was, well, owned by the bank.

"That Marco has a lot of making up to do for this," Lottie said. "I hope he's taking you somewhere special for dinner tonight."

"No, thanks. Going somewhere special for dinner is how I sprained my ankle in the first place."

Well, to be fair, it wasn't the *going* that had caused the sprain. It was Marco accidentally bumping me, causing me to trip in my new bargain-find-of-the-century five-inch spike heels. To think my only desire had been to be fashionable — and taller — which hadn't seemed unreasonable, given that I was twenty-seven years old and stood a mere five feet two inches. The ER doctor, however, hadn't shared my feelings on that subject. He'd seen too many women with sprains and broken bones caused by stepping off ridiculously high heels.

I'd worn the sexy shoes only once before, to a disastrous dinner thrown by the parents of the girl Marco's brother wanted to marry. I'd ended that evening by walking barefoot to the car and freezing my toes rather than taking a chance of slipping on the ice in those treacherous heels. This time I'd landed in the emergency room of County Hospital and waited three hours for a diagnosis. The high heels had landed in a donation box.

Marco was taking full responsibility for the accident and had been doing everything possible to make it up to me. He'd even rented the wheelchair and bought the crutches. And while I didn't mind the pampering, I did mind my loss of independence. With my right foot in a boot built for Frankenstein's monster and miles of Ace bandage wound underneath, I couldn't fit it in the driver's side of my old yellow Vette to work the pedals. Even drying my hair, which involved either propping my injured foot on the bathroom counter or squeezing a chair into our tiny bathroom, was a test of endurance. But it explained why my do looked

14

more like a pile of red matchsticks than a sleek bob.

The worst part of all was that Marco was supposed to check in at the army base in three weeks, and I'd be spending two of those three immobilized. But at least we *had* three weeks. We'd feared his departure was imminent.

I still went cold all over when I recalled the moment he'd shown me the letter. It was from the Department of the Army, addressed to Lt. Marco Salvare, RA 55667591.

Dear Lt. Salvare:

You are hereby notified that the current shortage of manpower mandates that we redeploy those individuals who have been previously discharged but are still committed to a six-year term. Accordingly, you will be receiving notification shortly and a set of orders as to your next assignment as an active-duty officer.

Sincerely,
Gen. I. M. Bragg, Undersecretary
Dept. of the Army

Marco had served with the Army Rangers for two years, but until his full six-year commitment was up, he was subject to recall. I'd never imagined it actually happening, especially on the eve of our engagement, and now that it had, I was faced with the very real possibility of losing him. It was a thought so frightening that I struggled daily to block it from my mind.

For that reason, Marco and I had decided to let only a select few in on the news, swearing them to secrecy until we knew exactly what the army's plans were. We didn't want our parents to worry needlessly or call incessantly to see if we'd heard anything, and my mom did incessant better than anyone. For those who knew about the letter, Marco's brother and my assistants included, it was as surreal and shocking as it had been to us. No one cared to talk much about it.

The creak of rusty hinges on the back door as Lottie let herself out jerked me into the present again. The shop was quiet, so I wheeled myself to the big bay window to look outside, where a fine mist, overcast skies, and approaching dusk seemed to cast a pall of gloom over the town square. Even the stately limestone courthouse across the street seemed more of a ghost image than an actual building.

Suddenly a figure separated itself from the

gloom and strode up the sidewalk in my direction. Because of the dark hair and black coat, I thought at first it was Marco, who favored his black leather jacket no matter what the weather. But now I could see that this man wore a long black trench coat, the collar turned up against the damp, his dark hair, slicked back by the mist, a sharp contrast to his pale skin.

When I realized I was visible through the glass, I grabbed the wheels of the chair to back up — I didn't want him to think I had nothing to do but stare outside — but before I could move, his gaze met mine through the glass. Not only had he caught me, but he was also headed straight for the shop. Abashed, I pretended that I was actually watching something across the street, just over his shoulder, in fact, and, oh, was that my phone ringing? Pardon me while I checked.

I did a quick pivot and raced away from the window. When the bell jingled, I was arranging the floral display on a table in the center of the room. I turned around, expecting to see the man standing at the front counter. Instead, he was in front of me, so close I could see the droplets of moisture on his coat. I craned my neck to look up at him and stared straight into a pair of pale

17

gray wolf eyes that were gazing back at me as though I were dinner.

I tried to back up but hit an armoire behind me. With nowhere to go, I found myself wishing I hadn't been so hasty in sending Lottie away. And when the stranger stepped closer and reached into his coat, all I could think was that he was going for a weapon.

I glanced around to see what artillery lay within my reach. A pair of small ceramic doves? A silk posy? Pink candles?

Get a grip, that inner voice of reason whispered in my ear. *He's a customer!*

"Can I help you?" I said, my voice coming out in an embarrassing squeak.

He smiled, revealing a set of even white teeth, except for the canines, which were longer than the rest. Wolflike, in fact. "You must be Abby."

How did he know my name?

He removed a folded piece of paper from inside his coat. "I'm told you have a good selection of houseplants. In particular, I'm looking for these specimens." He handed me the paper. On it was a list of neatly printed plant names: bloodwort, Dracula orchid, devil's tongue, wolfsbane, strangleweed, mistletoe, voodoo lily, bat flower.

Was he serious? The only thing missing

18

from that ghoulish list was a Venus flytrap. "I don't have any of these plants in stock, but I'm sure I can order them from my suppliers."

"How soon would they arrive?"

He had a mere hint of an accent, but I couldn't place it. Czech perhaps? "Usually in three to four days."

"That will do."

"They may be expensive."

He shrugged. "Cost isn't a factor."

"I'll need to take down your name and phone number." I pointed to the cashier's counter, seizing the opportunity to put some distance between us. "My order pad is over there."

Instead of moving, he studied me with those icy wolf eyes. "Irish or Scottish?"

"Excuse me?"

"Red hair, green eyes, light skin, and freckles. You have to be Irish or Scottish."

"Irish. And English — mother's side." Why was I telling this stranger my background?

He crouched in front of my chair and picked up my injured foot. "Bad sprain, eh? Did you break the skin?"

"No." How did he know it was a sprain?

"Good. Always a risk of a blood infection when the skin is broken. Get some staphylococcus in there and you're in for a rough ride."

Who *was* this guy?

I removed my gigantic booted foot from his grasp. Being in a vulnerable position made me extremely edgy — not that he was giving off any bad vibes. Quite the opposite, in fact. He was strikingly good-looking, virtually thrumming with virility and sex appeal, reminding me very much of my fiancé, Marco.

"Do you want me to order those plants?" I asked, trying not to betray my jitteriness.

He smiled again as he rose. "You don't know who I am, do you?"

The bell jingled and Marco walked in, looking undeniably male in his black leather jacket, lean jeans, and black boots. Steely-eyed and iron-jawed, he swept the room with his dark gaze, gauging the stranger's close proximity to me, no doubt assessing my immediate danger.

I was so relieved to see him that I wanted to leap out of my wheelchair and hop across the room to throw myself in his arms. "There you are," I called, maneuvering my chair around the stranger.

Marco gave the clock behind the cashier's counter a quick glance. "Am I late?"

"I'm early," the wolfman said. "I wanted

to order some houseplants for my apartment."

Early for what?

"Ah. Then you've already met Abby," Marco said.

"We haven't been formally introduced," the man said, giving me a dazzling smile.

"Abby Knight," Marco said, "this is Vlad."

Wait. What? *This* was the man Marco was training to take over the bar? His foxhole buddy when he was in the army? The guy he described as *average*-looking?

Vlad walked up to me and bowed from the waist. Then he took my hand, removed his list from my tightly clasped fingers, pocketed it, and brought my hand to his lips. "Vladimir Serbanescu, at your service. Vlad Serban, to make it easy." He pressed his lips against my fingers. "Or New Chapel's resident vampire, if you'd prefer."

That was an introduction that demanded an explanation, but judging by the chortle Vlad's comment elicited from Marco, I was apparently the only one not in on the jest. So in order to preserve my self-respect, I laughed, too, though there is obviously no such thing as a human vampire. I'd just have to get to know Vlad better so I could understand the joke.

To that end, I suggested that Vlad join us for a light dinner at the Down the Hatch Bar and Grill. Ten minutes later, we had regrouped there, Marco and me on one side of the booth, Vlad and my crutches, which I had fondly named the Evil Ones, on the other. Over a meal of burgers and fries, I observed Vlad while he and Marco discussed their latest drink concoction, a house specialty that Marco had dubbed the Hatch Match. The ingredients were secret, except for the last one — a matchstick to light it on fire.

Vlad was tall, broad-shouldered, and lean, with jet-black hair combed away from his face, arched black eyebrows over light gray eyes, a handsome nose, dimpled chin, and skin so light and pure it glowed like fine porcelain, with just a hint of a five o'clock shadow to define his jaw. He wore a white button-down shirt, neatly pressed black pants with a crease in them, and immaculate black shoes, a nerdy look on anyone but a sexy guy. And Vlad was certainly that, emitting an undeniably powerful male charisma, which is undoubtedly why every woman in the bar had her eye on him.

Seated with two of the hunkiest males in town, my foot wrapped like a mummy, my hair a bundle of red hay, I felt like the joker between a pair of aces.

It wasn't easy to draw Vlad out — it seemed to be a trait shared by men in the Special Ops division of the military — but he did reveal that he was single, had no family in town, a brother in Florida, and parents in Romania, where he'd been born, thus explaining his accent. He had completed his six-year tour with the army and had already received an honorable discharge. He had a master's degree in biology, was a trained phlebotomist, and had last worked as the manager of a blood lab in a Chicago hospital.

That was my aha moment. As in, *Aha! So that's why he made a joke about being a vampire. He drew blood for a living!* Although he did resemble the stereotypical Hollywood vampire. Was that intentional? Was that why Marco had laughed?

Vlad had come to New Chapel after deciding he needed a career change, something completely different from his routine nine-to-five job. Marco had suggested he might enjoy owning his own bar and grill, and offered him the opportunity to get hands-on training. Intrigued, Vlad had agreed to try it, so three days ago he'd started as Marco's intern, where he was currently learning how to be a proper bartender. And since I knew interns didn't make much money, I had to infer that the income wouldn't be a problem.

"So, Vlad," I said, as I dipped a crunchy fry in ketchup, "you weren't serious earlier about wanting those houseplants, were you?"

He stopped chewing to focus those striking eyes on me. "Why? Is there something wrong with them?" He pronounced *wrong* as *vrong.*

Okay, so he *was* serious. "Not wrong . . . per se."

Marco glanced at me, clearly as puzzled as Vlad was. "Are they hard to grow?"

Be tactful, Abby. "Well, you could say that about some of them."

At that moment, a slender yet curvaceous brunette stopped by the booth to bat her eyelashes and say in a breathy voice, "Hi, Vlad." Her girlfriend, a slender yet curvaceous blonde, echoed the eyelash batting and the breathy voice. "How's it going, Vlad?" They both giggled shyly when he turned his intense gaze on them.

"Hello, Lara. Hello, Holly." He smiled, flashing those long white canines, causing them to moan in ecstasy as they glided away to join friends at another booth. I watched them whisper together, then turn to gaze at

24

him longingly.

"I have an excellent green thumb," Vlad said, showing me his digits, ignoring the girls' avid interest. "I collect unusual houseplants. I even have plant lights and a humidifier."

Poor guy. He was doing his best to convince me. "I'm not doubting your green thumb, Vlad. It's just that some of the plants on your list are kind of . . ." How could I explain? Tact was not something that came easily for this redhead.

Vlad pulled out the list, smoothed the wrinkles, and turned it so both of us could see it. "Which ones?"

"Okay, take bloodwort, for instance," I said. "It'll cause a skin irritation if you touch it, and it's semipoisonous if you ingest it."

"Do you have a pen?" Vlad asked.

I took one from my purse and handed it to him. He made a note next to *bloodwort.*

"Now the Dracula orchid is a strange-looking plant that prefers to grow in shadow," I said. "It also likes cold temperatures, which probably wouldn't make your other plants happy."

Vlad noted that, too.

"You also have to be careful what species of devil's tongue you get, because some can grow up to five feet high, a foot across, and weigh in at twenty-two pounds — not exactly houseplant material, in my opinion."

"Duly noted," he said.

"Hi, Vlad," said a thirtysomething auburn-haired woman in a revealing sweater, giving him a "come hither" glance.

"Hi, Shari," Vlad said without missing a beat. He smiled at her; she grew breathless; I glared at her; she moved on; Marco nudged me.

"Then there's wolfsbane," I said, ignoring Marco's nudge, which was meant as a reminder to be nice to his patrons. "Wolfs-bane gives off a highly unpleasant odor, probably not something you'd want in your house, especially if you plan to entertain."

Yet, given the way women were fawning over Vlad, I doubted whether they'd notice his plants, stinky or not. "On the other hand," I said, "if you need to ward off any werewolves, wolfsbane is your go-to flora. I hear werewolves are highly sensitive to smells."

I waited for Vlad to chuckle — or at least to smile. Instead, he wrote it down. I glanced at Marco and gave him a non-plussed look. He merely shrugged.

Okay, then. I'd saved the worst for last.

"Strangleweed is a parasitic vine," I explained. "It's also known as devil's guts, witches' shoelaces, and dodder vine. It starts out as a tiny tendril with no roots or leaves, then, like a skinny green snake, starts searching for a sweet-smelling host plant. Once it finds its victim, it wraps itself around the stem, sinks its fangs in, and starts drinking the sap. Sounds like a vampire, doesn't it?"

Marco put down his beer with a clunk. Vlad stopped writing. Neither one chortled at *my* vampire reference.

"You seem to know a lot about these plants," Vlad said.

"I'm a florist," I said with a modest shrug. "It's what I do. I also take online courses. In fact, I learned about these particular specimens in a course called Scary Plants."

Marco rested his arm along the back of the booth so he could face me. "Scary plants?"

I nodded.

Vlad appraised me for a moment, then pointed to his list. "What about the others?"

"Mistletoe is also a parasite, but its victims are usually trees. You definitely want to avoid it. Some species can hurl their seeds up to thirty or forty feet away. The berries stick to the tree trunk — or another plant — and send out shoots that penetrate the poor victim's innermost core, where its vital sap is sucked dry. Yet another type of vampire." I paused to arch one eyebrow for effect. "And to think we view mistletoe as romantic."

Both men stared at me. Was I creeping them out?

"But the voodoo lily and bat flower are okay," I offered. I had to give Vlad something. "They require a bit more care than the average houseplant, but that shouldn't be a problem for someone with a green thumb."

Vlad crossed off only one — mistletoe — then pushed the list toward me. "Would you order those, please? And make sure the devil's orchid is one of the short varieties."

"Sure."

"One more thing. Would you add dandelions to that list?"

He had to be joking this time. "I don't think I've ever seen them offered by any of my suppliers, but hey, my dad has some in his yard. I'm sure he wouldn't mind parting with them."

"How many?"

He wasn't joking. "I don't know, a dozen perhaps? My mom went green this year to keep all those toxic pesticides out of the water supply, so they have to dig up the

28

weeds by hand."

"Your dad wouldn't mind if I helped myself?"

"He'd be overjoyed. Let me know when you want to pick them and I'll alert my parents."

"Terrific. Is there any way you can procure a few flats for me now?"

"Flats? I'll have to look into it."

"I appreciate that. My supply is low. And now I believe it's time for me to tend bar." Vlad rose and gave me a slight bow. "Thank you for inviting me to dinner. It's been a pleasure."

He gave Marco a nod and left us.

I watched him walk around behind the bar and bump knuckles with the other bartender. As though they'd been waiting for a signal, women from every corner rushed up to the counter and began clamoring for Vlad's attention.

"He's a great guy," Marco said, observing his intern at work. "One of those men you want guarding your back — or your bar."

"Why would he want dandelions?"

"Why would Vlad want any of those plants, Abby? He collects unusual specimens."

"Two flats of dandelions isn't a collection. It's a crop." I propped my chin on my fist

29

and watched him flirt with the women. "I wonder if dandelions contain toxins. Vlad was in your outfit in Iraq, right? Did he work with toxic nerve gases or anything?"

"No. He just likes odd plants. Believe me, you get to know what a guy is really like in those circumstances, down to the nitty-gritty." Marco paused to take a pull of beer. "You were a little heavy-handed with those vampire references, weren't you, considering the situation?"

"What situation?"

"The rumor going around about Vlad being a vampire."

I paused to stare at Marco, a french fry halfway to my mouth. "I didn't hear any rumors about Vlad. You mean he was serious when he introduced himself?"

"He wasn't serious. He was making a joke *about* the rumor. I'm surprised you haven't heard it from Jillian, or that she hasn't stopped by to pump you for information about him."

That *was* odd. My cousin was always on top of the latest town gossip. Why *hadn't* Jillian stopped by? "Seriously, Marco, I haven't heard a thing about Vlad, but I can understand how someone might get that impression of him. He has that classic movie star Count Dracula look."

"He's not a vampire."

"I'm not saying he *is*, Marco. I'm sure he's completely normal."

Except for wanting weeds and life-sucking vampire plants in his house.

CHAPTER TWO

"Hey, look who's here!"

At the sound of the familiar male voice, I glanced around to see our friend Sean Reilly, a sergeant on the New Chapel police force, and his girlfriend, Sara, a nurse at County Hospital, heading toward our booth.

"Hey, man," Marco said, rising to shake his hand. "Good to see you. Sara, how's it going? You guys want to join us?"

"As long as you'll tell us to leave when you want to be alone," Reilly said. They slid in opposite us and took off their coats while Marco went to get menus.

Sergeant Sean Reilly had been a rookie cop when my dad was on the force. Reilly trained under my dad, then, as coincidences go, later took a rookie by the name of Marco Salvare, fresh out of the military, under his wing. Reilly was about forty years old, divorced, father of a young teen, and an upstanding cop. He was our go-to guy for information and had helped us out many times. He was nice-looking, too, with brown eyes, short brown hair, and a tall, sturdy build.

Sara was his girlfriend, also divorced, also tall and brown-eyed, with abundant auburn hair. We'd hit it off immediately, and I had a feeling she was *the one* for Reilly.

Now she leaned across the table to say quietly, "What do you think about Marco's new bartender?" She raised an eyebrow, as if to say, *Have you heard the rumors?*

Was I the only one who hadn't?

At that moment, Marco returned with their beers and menus. Reilly handed Sara one of the beer mugs, then picked up the other and held it aloft. "Here's to a short separation and a speedy reunion."

"Hear, hear," Sara said, as we clinked glasses.

"Thanks," Marco said.

"We're still trying to absorb the news," I said with a wistful sigh.

Marco reached for my hand under the table and entwined his fingers in mine, bringing a film of tears to my eyes. I blinked them away, unable to wrap my mind around the idea of him being gone. I couldn't imagine my life without Marco in it.

Reilly and Sara didn't know that we were

engaged. In fact, we hadn't told anyone but my friend Nikki. Since she was my room-mate, in addition to my closest friend, it would've been impossible to keep it from her.

We'd hoped to announce our engagement after we knew for sure whether Marco was going to be deployed. But my eagle-eyed cousin Jillian had spotted my engagement ring under my sweater and decided to spread the word herself. I persuaded her to let me tell the family at our next Friday night family dinner, and she had agreed, as long as it was in just one week. That was as long as she could keep it in. Until then, I kept my ring on a chain around my neck, close to my heart.

"Is it a done deal?" Reilly asked. "You're sure you're going overseas?"

Marco lifted a shoulder. "It's the army. Who knows? I have to plan as though I am."

As Reilly and Sara ordered their sand-wiches, and Marco and I sipped our beers, I found myself wanting to freeze the mo-ment: good friends enjoying each other's company, all healthy in body and mind. I squeezed Marco's hand. Sensing my thoughts, he put his arm around my shoul-ders, drew me closer, and changed the sub-ject.

"What's new down at the police station?"

"It's crazy," Reilly said. "People calling to ask if it's safe to go out at night. Senior citizens, mostly, but also parents with little kids, worried about vampire attacks."

"You wouldn't believe how many people came into the ER today, asking to be checked for vampire bites," Sara said, laughing. "Main complaint? Feeling light-headed — as though someone had drained their blood while they were sleeping."

A man that I recognized as my postal carrier, also one of Marco's regular customers, stopped at our booth to say to Marco, "Hey, man, are you serious about letting that new guy make drinks? Everyone's saying he's a vampire."

"Everyone's wrong, Bob," Marco said. "Hey, I'm sitting across from a cop. Would *he* be calmly drinking a beer if I'd hired someone dangerous to bartend?"

A frown flitted across Reilly's face, as though he wasn't at ease with Marco's statement.

Bob had the decency to look embarrassed. "Yeah, you're right. Sorry to bother you."

After Bob left, Sara leaned forward to say to Marco, "So what *do* you know about Vlad?"

"He's intelligent, capable, and dependable," Marco said. "That's all I need to know."

"He served with Marco in Iraq," I added.

Sara studied Vlad. "He's sure got that sexy Ranger confidence." She turned to me and asked eagerly, "What else do you know about him?"

"Sara!" Reilly said, as though offended.

"Oh, don't worry," she said, linking her arm through his. "I think you're sexy, too. So go ahead, Abby. You were saying?"

"Vlad's a phlebotomist. He ran a blood lab in a Chicago hospital."

"A phlebotomist?" Sara asked, giving me a wink. "Is that perfect or what?"

Reilly leaned in. "You're telling me Vlad gave up a career in science, living and working in the Second City, to come to a small town and tend bar? Listen, Marco, army buddy or not, you haven't worked with him in a few years, so check the guy out thoroughly. He could be running from someone — loan sharks, an ex-wife, the IRS . . ."

"I ran him through all my sources," Marco assured him. "I'm satisfied with that."

Reilly didn't look convinced.

A cheer went up from all the women gathered at the bar as Vlad lit a Hatch Match. Judging by the number of scowling guys in the room, they were less than thrilled with Down the Hatch's new boy wonder.

"Where is Vlad from?" Sara asked. "He's so exotic-looking."

"Romania," I said.

Sara's eye grew wide. "Transylvania's Romania? This just gets better and better."

"Now you see what I've been dealing with all day," Reilly said to Marco, putting an arm around Sara. "Honey, let's drop the subject, okay?"

"I'm sorry," Sara said. "I don't mean to be rude, but I think the rumor is funny. Vampire books and movies are so popular that people here in New Chapel *want* a vampire to claim as their own." She shifted her gaze back to the subject in question, who was still bedazzling the women. "Poor Vlad fits the bill whether he likes it or not."

"I'm pretty sure poor Vlad likes it," I said. "Look at those women. They're falling all over themselves trying to hold his attention."

"The men, on the other hand," Sara pointed out, "don't seem all that happy."

"Can't say that I blame them," Reilly said, leaning back to sip his beer.

"Hey, Marco," another bar regular said, stopping at the booth. "Tell me it's not true about that guy up there."

"Come on, Kyle, not you, too," Marco said.

"Kyle, you're an EMT, buddy," Reilly said. "Don't you dare say you believe in vampires."

The tall, doughy, balding paramedic said with an embarrassed grin, "Don't razz me, Sarge. I hear strange things in my job. You know how people talk in this town."

"It's talk started by idiots who have nothing better to do," Marco said testily.

Kyle glanced around as though to make sure he couldn't be overheard. "I hear what you're saying, but I gotta tell you, last night we transported a patient to County Hospital who claimed she was bitten by a vampire. And you know what was really freaky? She had two small wounds in her neck. Just saying . . . Anyway, I'd keep an eye on Vlad, if I were you."

"Thanks, Kyle," Marco said, then rolled his eyes as Kyle went back to his booth.

"A paramedic worried about a vampire," Reilly said with an impatient sigh. "I'm telling you, this town is going bonkers."

At that moment, I caught sight of a coppery head just coming in the door. "Oh, no!"

"What?" Marco asked, trying to see what had alarmed me.

"The queen of bonkers just walked in." I ducked behind a menu.

"Too late. She spotted us," Marco told me.

"Who?" Sara asked, turning for a look.

"Abby's cousin Jillian," Marco said, eliciting a groan from Reilly.

The bane of my existence.

Jillian Ophelia Knight-Osborne was my first cousin on my father's side, my blood relation, which was the only thing we had in common — besides the missing tact gene. Being a year apart, we'd grown up as close as sisters — and fought like it, too. Like me, Jillian had inherited the trademark red hair and freckles. Unlike me, Jillian's freckles were a bare sprinkling of cocoa, and her hair was a silky copper waterfall.

She was also tall, gorgeous without makeup, fashionably dressed even on weekends, and married, although she had jilted four men at the altar first. In fact, jilting fiancés had been something of a hobby of hers until she met the bank account of her dreams, Claymore Osborne, son of one of the wealthiest families in New Chapel.

Coincidentally, I'd been engaged to Claymore's older brother, Pryce, while I was in law school. Both school and my fiancé had been unmitigated disasters and both had given me the boot. At that thought, I shifted my twenty-pound mummified foot beneath the table. Apparently, the boot was a recurrent theme in my life.

"Hello, hello!" Jillian called to people she knew, as she dragged Claymore toward us. Seeing me, she cried, "Oh, Abs!" and sank onto the small space at the end of our bench so she could wrap her long arms around me and give me a hug. "I heard about your accident, poor baby, and had to come right over to see how my wittle cousin was doing."

I hated when she talked baby talk. "My accident happened two days ago, Jillian. What's your rush?"

She pulled back to look at me, her lips in a pretty pout as she shook her head and clucked her tongue. "You're going to have to stick with flats from now on, Abs. Clumsy people shouldn't wear high heels. It's one of the first rules of fashion sense."

I leaned close to her ear and said in a low voice, "Clumsy people shouldn't let others sit beside them on a bench either, because sometimes they *accidentally* push people off!"

Jillian rose from the bench like a graceful swan and swept back her long hair, which couldn't have looked like hay even if she'd stuck her head in a thrasher. As she tightened the belt of her Burberry trench coat, she suddenly noticed Sara, and her eyes lit up.

"I don't believe we've met. I'm Jillian Knight-Osborne, owner of Chez Jillian, a personal shopping service that I'm sure you've heard about. This is my husband, Claymore, a prominent CPA. And you are?"

Reilly stepped in. "This is Sara Jorgensen."

Sara smiled and extended her hand toward my cousin. "Nice to meet you."

As Jillian took her hand, she gave Reilly a perplexed look. "What happened to your other girlfr—" She gasped as I kicked her shin with my boot. When it came to tact, Jillian made me look good.

"Very nice to meet you, Sara," Claymore said. He pulled a slender purple camera from his coat pocket and handed it to Jillian. "Here, darling. Take your photos and let's leave these people to their dinners."

"Photos of what?" I asked.

"The vampire," Clayton said quietly, casting a discreet glance over his shoulder.

"He's not a vampire," Marco said firmly.

"That's not what I heard," Jillian said.

"You heard the rumors and didn't tell me?" I asked.

"I was going to stop by, but then I heard about" — she lowered her voice to a whisper — "your accident."

"I didn't sprain my ears, Jillian. Why are you whispering?"

She turned to aim the camera at Vlad, but couldn't get a clear shot. "I wish he'd stop moving! Would someone go up there and ask him to pose for me?"

She pushed the button and the flash went off. "Never mind. I got him that time. Oh, wait. That's odd. Look at this, Claymore. Everyone but Vlad came out. Let me try it again."

"Jillian," I said in a whisper, "that's enough. People are looking at us."

She took two more pictures and put the camera away. "I'll check them when I get home. Nice to meet you, Sara." She pointed her finger at me. "Remember what I said about high heels." And then she sailed through the crowd with Claymore trotting behind her.

"Sorry," I said to Sara. "Jillian is family. I have to tolerate her."

Reilly's cell phone chimed. He flipped it open and read the message, then put it back in his pocket. "I've got to get back to the station. There's a situation." He shrugged, as though he couldn't say anything more.

Sara scooted out of the booth. "It's been fun almost having dinner with you."

"Hold on," Marco said. "I'll have your food wrapped so you can take it with you."

Reilly waited until Marco was on his way to the kitchen, then said to me, "Do me a favor. Make sure Marco actually did that background check on his friend Vlad. Something tells me there's more to that guy than meets the eye."

Rumors about Vlad continued to spread all week. By Thursday, every person who walked through Bloomers' door seemed to be buzzing with speculation about him. Since it was assumed I would have answers because of my connection with Marco, I was inundated with questions, until I finally decided to stay in the back room and work on orders while my assistants waited on customers.

I instructed them to assure people that Vlad was a regular guy who simply happened to be of Romanian extraction and to remind them that human vampires were merely folklore.

Unfortunately, it didn't seem to make any difference. The women who came into Bloomers were thrilled at the prospect of having a real-life Count Dracula in town.

The men either dismissed the rumors as nonsense or made angry comments about what nerve the vampire had to show up in their peaceful burg.

During a brief midafternoon lull, I ventured out of my inner sanctum to grab a cup of hot tea and bask in the delights of my shop. I wheeled to the cheerful yellow frame door, with its old-fashioned beveled-glass center and brass bell over the top, and then turned around to take in the scene.

Bloomers occupies the ground floor of an old three-story redbrick building, which still has its original tin ceiling and wood floor, both refinished. The retail side of Bloomers has a cash counter near the front door, a glass-fronted display case on the back wall, various shelves and tables, and an armoire for gift items. A wide doorway in the side wall opens into the coffee-and-tea parlor, a Victorian-inspired room featuring white wrought-iron ice-cream tables and chairs, rose-patterned china, and a coffee counter at the back for the various machines.

Both rooms have big bay windows filled with lush plants and silk arrangements, and views of the courthouse square. The window in the parlor is a favorite with customers who like to drink coffee and watch the happenings on the square.

A curtained doorway at the back divides the shop from the workroom, my personal paradise, redolent with all the colors and sweet scents of greenery and blossoms. It holds containers in every shape and size, silk flowers in big buckets, drawers filled with florist's tools, my desk and computer station, and the two giant walk-in coolers where our fragile flowers are kept.

Beyond the workroom are a tiny bathroom, a kitchenette, and a fire exit that opens onto the alley. A staircase by the rear exit leads to the basement, where we keep large bags of potting soil, giant clay pots, and supplies too bulky for the workroom cabinets.

Filling myself with good karma, I wheeled to the parlor, where Grace was straightening chairs.

"Did you need some tea, love?" she asked.

"A cup of mint tea, please."

"Coming right up." She paused to glance out the window. "A group of ladies is headed this way. Shall I bring the tea to the workroom, do you think, so you can avoid more questions?"

"Good idea." I turned the wheelchair around and banged the footrest against the doorframe, nicking the white paint. I backed up and knocked over a chair.

"Perhaps you could just send Lottie to get your tea next time," Grace said.

Back in the workroom, I plucked an order from the spindle on my desk and studied it. The client wanted a fragrant arrangement done entirely in shades of peach, so I wheeled myself to the second cooler to see what was available. I found blossoms of sweetpea, snapdragon, Prima Donna roses, mini carnations, Gerberas, and tulips. For my accent color, as well as for fragrance, I pulled stems of Pelargonium graveolens, or "Lady Plymouth," pale green leaves with frilly white edges that were known for their sweet scent. I decided to use a square glass vase filled with white gravel in order to make a crisply modern, yet peachy soft statement.

I was stripping thorns from the rose stems and humming with carefree abandon when my thirteen-year-old niece, Tara, came through the curtain with her friend Jamie. Tara is the daughter of my younger brother, Jordan. Because she and I share the same hair color, height, and freckles, people meeting us assume we're sisters. All Tara lacks to be my twin is fourteen years, twenty pounds, and a generous bust-line. If only I could give her half of mine . . .

"Guess what, Aunt Abby!" Tara exclaimed. "We made a Web site for the New Chapel vampire. We call it We Heart Vlad dot com. Show her, Jamie."

Jamie, all legs, arms, and big brown eyes, with cocoa-colored skin and a long black braid down her back, climbed onto a stool, opened her backpack, and removed a sleek pink laptop.

"Are you Wi-Fi'd?" she asked. "Oh, never mind. I found a free connection." She typed a string of letters into the SEARCH box and then swiveled the computer to show me. "See?"

"How do you know you *heart* Vlad?" I asked the girls, gazing at the pink hearts, white bows, and photos of movie actors that played vampires. "Have you met him?"

"We've seen him through the front window of Uncle Marco's bar," Tara said. "Besides, we've never met the Jonas Brothers either, but we *heart* them, too."

"News flash," I said, tickling Tara's chin with a rose petal. "Vlad is not a vampire and Marco is not your uncle."

"Vlad *is* a vampire, Aunt Abby. Why else would he go out only after dark, eat bloody meat, and sleep in a casket?"

"How do you know what kind of meat he eats?"

47

"Crystal's mom saw Vlad eating raw steak at a restaurant," Tara replied.

"And Vlad has fangs, too," Jamie said. "My aunt saw them up close. She visits Down the Hatch every evening now to watch him."

"Don't listen to those rumors," I said, going back to my arrangement. "Vlad goes outside during the day, and his eyeteeth may be a little longer than the rest, but they're not fangs. Your mom probably saw him eating steak carpaccio, which is served raw. As for sleeping in a casket, that's just silly."

"Have you *seen* Vlad outside during the day?" Tara asked.

"Yes, I did," I said. "He came down to Bloomers on Monday to order houseplants."

"What time?" Tara challenged.

"A little before five o'clock."

"That's dusk," Jamie said, shredding a leaf with her fingers. "That counts as night-time."

"What kind of plants did he buy?" Tara asked.

As if I'd tell her now. "What is this? An inquisition? You shouldn't spread these rumors, girls. They're hurtful."

"We're not the ones spreading them," Tara said. "We're trying to undo the damage. Jamie, show her the other site."

48

Jamie typed in the URL and at once the background on her screen turned black, with a border down each side made of silver stakes, silver bullets, and silver knives tipped with red. Across the top, in red letters that resembled dripping blood, was the name: HOW TO KILL A VAMPIRE, with the Web site URL www.howtokillavampire.com.

If that wasn't alarming enough, in the middle of the page was a sketch of a man who looked like Vlad. Beneath the sketch was the heading HOW TO RECOGNIZE A VAMPIRE. Under it was a list of vampire lore with check marks next to each item that allegedly matched up to Vlad.

On the right was the image of a tombstone on which had been printed RIP, with a link that said CLICK HERE. The link led to a page that listed various ways to get rid of vampires, such as the traditional stake through the heart or a silver bullet. From there they became even more gruesome.

My stomach lurched. It was a Web site devoted to murdering Vlad.

CHAPTER THREE

"Whose Web site is that?" I asked Tara.

"Not mine! Don't get angry at *me,* Aunt Abby. I'm only the messenger."

"I'm not angry. I just want to know who put up that trash."

Jamie was searching the site but finally shook her head. "There's no contact info."

I grabbed a pen and tablet from my desk and wrote down the URL. "I'll have Marco find out. He'll know who to contact about having it taken down before it inspires someone to hurt Vlad. In the meantime, maybe you can spread good things about Vlad, such as that he was an Army Ranger, and was the head of a Chicago hospital's blood lab . . . On second thought, scratch that last one. Let's not add more fuel to the fire."

"This goes way beyond spreading rumors," I told Marco, as he looked over the HOW

TO KILL A VAMPIRE Web site. "Someone has it in for Vlad."

Marco had his chin propped on his hand as he viewed the page. He was seated at the sleek black and chrome desk in his office at Down the Hatch. I sat across from him in one of the two leather sling-back chairs, with the Evil Ones on the floor by my feet. I'd insisted that Marco take a look at the site before we ate supper.

Decorated in modern shades of gray, black, and silver, Marco's office is in sharp contrast to the bar, which still has the olive green, burnt orange, and dark wood that the original owner installed in the sixties. I've been pushing Marco to redecorate — he's owned the bar for nearly a year — but the customers are so used to it that Marco fears they'll revolt if he changes anything.

"This is the work of a coward," he commented, studying the Web page, "someone who fears Vlad but doesn't have the courage to face him. It was obviously done to instill fear. I'll contact the service provider for this site and see if I can get it taken down."

"You don't seem too concerned."

"The Internet is full of trash like this."

"It doesn't help that Vlad fits the part. Can you talk to him about wearing a pair of jeans and a Down the Hatch T-shirt instead of dressing like he's going to a funeral?"

"That's who he is, Abby. Vlad has always dressed differently. In fact, after we'd been in the military for a while, he started wearing his Goth-style clothes when he was off the base, and was immediately called down for it. I felt that was wrong and went to bat for him. So I can't very well tell him not to wear them now. Besides, he's in compliance with my dress code."

What dress code — shirts and shoes?

Marco shut off his computer and came around the desk to help me out of the chair and onto the crutches. "I'm not going to waste these next few weeks worrying about Vlad's choice of clothing or some idiot's Web site when I'd much rather think about you."

He put his arms around me and kissed me, causing me to totter on the crutches until he steadied me. "You don't have much of a sense of balance, do you?"

I shrugged. My crummy sense of balance was why I'd never thought about modeling — well, that and the fact that I'm half a person too short. "You know what else we should think about?" I pulled out the chain I wore beneath my blouse to dangle my engagement ring in front of him. "Our wedding plans."

He locked his hands behind my waist, keeping our bodies together, and said in a sexy voice, "What are we planning?"

"Nothing yet. That's the problem. Once we announce that we're officially engaged, our families will want to know the details, like when, where, and how, and the only thing we can tell them is who."

"That's the only detail that matters to me," Marco said, rubbing his nose against mine.

"So," I said, catching his romantic mood, "are we talking about eloping?"

Marco pulled back to give me a quizzical glance. "Eloping? Why? Do you want to elope?"

"I actually hadn't thought about it until now. Do *you* want to elope?"

"I hadn't thought about it either, but maybe we should think about it. Imagine the money we'd save."

"And the parents we'd hurt."

"Let's hold this discussion later. I'm hungry."

So was I, but not for food. "We could get something to go," I said, giving him a flirtatious glance, "if you can slip away from the bar for an hour."

His mouth curved up at one corner, and this time he pulled me against him so I couldn't fall. "I can make that happen," he murmured, his lips against mine. Then he gave me a long, hot kiss to whet my appetite. As if it needed more whetting.

We waited for our food in "our" booth, the last one in the row opposite the bar, where we watched the five thirty newscast on the closest TV. I noticed Vlad performing a glass trick for a bevy of women, some seated on stools, others standing three-deep in places, while the men who'd been crowded out sat in booths grumbling and glaring.

I studied the men, wondering if one of them was the culprit who'd put up the Web page. "You know," I said to Marco, "you might want to suggest to Vlad that he shouldn't play to the ladies so much. He's not making any friends among the guys."

Marco turned to glance at the men in question, but their attention had suddenly shifted to the televisions mounted on each end of the bar, where crawling text at the bottom of the screens read: PARKVIEW HOSPITAL DIRECTOR OF NURSING LORI WILLIS REPORTED MISSING WEDNESDAY. ATTEMPTS TO REACH WILLIS AT HOME UNSUCCESSFUL. POLICE ARE SEARCHING FOR HER 2007 GREEN HYUNDAI AND SEEKING INFORMATION FROM ANYONE WHO

SAW WILLIS AFTER 5 P.M. TUESDAY.

"Hey, Vlad," one of the guys called, "wasn't that Willis woman one of your admirers?"

Vlad grinned but didn't respond.

Another called, "Didn't we see her here Tuesday night slipping you her phone number?"

Still with a smile on his face, Vlad merely shook his head and went about his business.

Then a guy called, "What did you do with her, Vlad? Tuck her in the meat locker for a midnight snack?" He followed it with sucking sounds.

Several women turned to glare at him, but that only made the others join in.

"Hey, guys, cool it," Kyle, the EMT, called from his booth.

"Shove it, Kyle," one of the hecklers said. "You can't stand the dude either."

"Calm down, guys," the mailman said, rising. "This is a friendly bar."

"Those jerks are just jealous, Vlad," one of the women said loud enough for them to hear.

That caused more grumbling among the men.

"I'll be right back," Marco said quietly, then slid out of the booth and walked calmly through the crowd of women to join Vlad and the other bartender behind the bar. He made eye contact with several of the loudmouths, as though reminding them who the alpha male was. The room grew quiet, then after a few minutes, conversation began again without further heckling.

Marco had a quick word with his buddy, filled two glasses with draft beer, and returned to our booth.

"What did you say to Vlad?" I asked.

"To cool it with the women until the guys get to know him better. There's some kind of turf war in progress right now."

"It doesn't help that the women are practically drooling over him." Not that I could fault them for it. There was simply something tantalizing about Vlad Serban.

Marco kept an eye on the crowd from our booth. "I hate to do this, Sunshine, but I'd better stick around here this evening."

Although I understood Marco's decision, the thought of going home alone saddened me. I feared I'd be doing that soon enough. "I'll stay, too."

"I'm sorry to ruin our plans," Marco said, reaching for my hand.

Forcing myself to appear cheerful, I said, "You didn't ruin anything. As long as we're together, I'm happy."

He turned my hands over and traced the lines in my palms with his thumbs, then raised his eyes to mine and studied my face with such wistfulness that I knew immediately he was thinking about our parting.

Gert, the waitress who'd been at Down the Hatch since the sixties decor was new, chose that moment to deliver our pulled pork sandwiches and sweet potato fries in two big takeout containers. "Here you go, lovebirds," she said in her gravelly voice.

"Thanks, Gert," Marco said. "We've decided to eat here."

"Good idea," Gert said quietly. "We've got some restless males in the room tonight."

As I unpacked the food, Marco's younger brother Rafe made his way past the people at the bar and slid onto the bench beside me. Without so much as a hello, he put his chin in his hands and sighed with such misery that I halfway expected him to burst into tears.

Great. Another long face. If we kept it up, we'd drive the customers away.

Rafe reached for one of my fries, chewed and swallowed, then sighed again. When he reached for another, I asked, "Want to order some food?"

He sighed again. "No, thanks. I don't have an appetite." Then he took another fry.

Raphael Salvare was the youngest of Marco's siblings, and at the age of twenty-one, looked like a lankier version of his thirty-one-year-old brother. And while he had inherited the handsome Salvare looks, he didn't seem to have his brother's drive or common sense.

Rafe had quit college a semester before graduating, then lazed around his mother's house in Ohio, claiming he needed to find himself. After a few months of watching Rafe search for himself via cable TV, Mrs. Salvare, a widow, had driven him to New Chapel and handed him over to Marco to be molded into a responsible human being. Or so her theory went.

As one would imagine, Marco was ever so grateful. He'd put Rafe to work doing basic janitorial work, hoping his little brother would grow tired of it and go back to school. Instead, Rafe had taken a job in a nearby city working as a bartender trainee at Hooters. There he'd met the girl of his high school fantasies, Cinnamon Howard, and had impetuously proposed.

Marco's mother had nearly killed Rafe when she learned that Cinnamon was only nineteen. On top of that, Cinnamon's father had insisted the wedding reception be held at his gentlemen's club, which had turned out to be a sleazy strip joint. In the end, Mrs. Salvare had been spared the agony of the ill-suited marriage when Cinnamon's parents called it off, claiming that the Salvares weren't up to their standards. Rafe had been left with a broken heart.

Now he slumped against the back of the booth, looking bereft and friendless.

"Rafe, you can't go on this way," I said. "You'll make yourself sick."

"I am sick — sick at heart. Every time I walk into Hooters, I expect to see Cinnamon."

"Doesn't she work there anymore?" I asked.

"Her mom made her quit. Now whenever a girl with red hair walks in, my heart pounds so hard I want to puke."

Hello-o-o. My hair was red. Cinnamon's was neon orange. But now was not the time to, well, split hairs.

"You knew her for a week," Marco said. "Get over it."

"Two and a half weeks," Rafe corrected.

I gave Marco a frown to let him know he wasn't helping. "Why don't you get a new job, Rafe?"

"No one's hiring right now," he said, taking another fry. "I could've worked *here* as a bartender, but no. Someone *else* got *that* job." He nodded in Vlad's direction.

"You went to Hooters because you didn't want to work for me," Marco reminded him.

"I didn't want to be your janitor," Rafe said. "You never offered me the bartender's position."

"Because you have to learn the ropes first," Marco replied.

"Did *that* guy learn the ropes first?" Rafe nodded again at Vlad and reached for a piece of pork that had fallen out of my bun.

"*That* guy has a master's degree," Marco said.

"In bartending?" Rafe asked.

Four to three. Rafe was ahead by one. I smacked his hand when he reached for another fry. There was a limit to my charity.

"I need someone smart and reliable to run the place if I have to go overseas," Marco explained. "Vlad ran a lab at a Chicago hospital for five years. He has managerial skills."

"Are you saying I'm not smart enough to handle things here?" Rafe asked.

"You're not experienced enough."

"Then train me. Give me the experience."

Marco glanced at me for support, but I was staying out of that argument.

"Wouldn't you rather leave the bar in a family member's hands," Rafe posed, "instead of in the hands of someone half of your customers dislike?"

Score another point for the younger brother.

Gert stopped by the table to say to Rafe, "I suppose you're gonna want something to eat, too."

"Yes, he would," I said.

"What can I get you, handsome?" Gert asked him, ruffling his dark, wavy hair.

"I could really go for a big, juicy cheeseburger," Rafe said, gazing at her with his liquid brown eyes, "if it wouldn't be too much trouble."

She wrote down his order, then turned to Marco. "Boss, you need to bring this kid back. We miss him here." She winked at Rafe and left.

Marco glanced at me and I shrugged. He put his hands on the table, leaned in, and gave his brother a searching stare. "Do you really want to work for me?"

"Yes!" Rafe answered, then added, "As a bartender."

Marco sat back. "Show up tomorrow morning at eleven."

Rafe's eyes got wide. "Are you serious? That early?"

Before Marco could lay into him, he said, "Just kidding. I'll be here at eleven sharp."

Rafe extended his fist to give Marco a knuckle bump. "Thanks, bro. I'm going to go get myself a beer. Either of you want anything?"

After Rafe sauntered off, I said to Marco, "It was very nice of you to take him back."

"He won't last," Marco said. "He hates taking orders from me."

"Then you won't give him a shot at being your manager, in case Vlad doesn't work out?"

"Sunshine, mark my words. Rafe will quit before he puts in a full week."

Marco and I ate breakfast in front of the television the next morning, a habit I'd developed in college, being a morning talk show junkie. It wasn't Marco's usual routine, but since he was staying with me for his remaining few weeks, he was adjusting. As long as I kept the volume down, it didn't bother Nikki, who worked the afternoon shift as an X-ray tech at County Hospital and liked to sleep until nine o'clock. But I'd forgotten that Nikki's white cat, Simon, loved oatmeal, and since that was also Marco's breakfast of choice, Simon assumed they would share.

"We could eat at the kitchen table," Marco said, as I shooed Simon away for the second time. He hissed at me. Being a feline, Simon didn't take kindly to being told no.

"I can't see the television from there."

"Do you *need* to see the television?"

"No, I *want* to see it. Simon, get down!" I put aside my toast with peanut butter and sliced bananas, and scooped him onto my lap. "Okay, fat boy, you've been warned. It's off to the bedroom for you. You'll just have to amuse yourself by threatening squirrels from the window."

At that moment the TV anchor said, "In local news, the green Hyundai belonging to Lori Willis, a New Chapel woman missing since Wednesday, was discovered in the parking lot behind the Casa Royale Apartments early this morning. There has been no sign of the missing woman, but police are hopeful that her car will hold clues to her whereabouts."

Marco muttered, "Damn."

"What?"

"Casa Royale is where Vlad lives."

"Maybe the woman lives there, too."

"Whether she does or doesn't, it'll still start a whole new round of rumors." Marco took his bowl to the kitchen, so I released Simon, who was wiggling in my arms.

63

The little furball gave himself a shake, licked his paw, then sashayed after Marco, his long white tail curled into a question mark. "Don't feed Simon," I said. "He's had his tuna."

"Sorry, buddy," I heard Marco say. "The queen has spoken."

Marco returned with the coffeepot to refill our cups.

"What time did you get in last night?" I asked. I'd crashed before midnight and only vaguely remembered Marco coming in.

"Twelve thirty," he said. "The hecklers were gone, and Rafe was there, along with Bob, Kyle, and some of the other regulars, so I figured Vlad would be okay."

Marco's cell phone buzzed. He pulled it out of his pocket, snapped it open, and answered with a crisp "Salvare," as he walked into the kitchen. He talked quietly for a few minutes, and when he came back to the living room, he looked grim.

"That was Reilly giving me a heads-up," he said as he sat beside me. "The cops found the Willis woman's purse in her car with her phone and wallet still inside, money and credit cards intact, so it doesn't appear to have been a robbery."

"An abduction, then?"

"Looks that way."

"Why are you frowning?"

"Because inside the purse was a piece of Parkview Hospital stationery with Vlad's name and number on it. He's now officially a person of interest."

CHAPTER FOUR

"The cops have been trying to reach Vlad since they discovered the car, but he's not answering his door or his phone," Marco told me, scrolling through his cell phone's address book. He punched in a number, then held the phone to his ear and said to me, "Reilly asked me to make sure Vlad gets in touch with them."

"Poor Vlad. Once he gets in the cops' crosshairs, he's doomed."

Marco listened for several seconds, then said, "Vlad, it's me. Call as soon as you get this." He closed his phone and tucked it away. "Reilly should be able to persuade calmer heads to prevail until the evidence can clear Vlad. The forensic team is still processing the car, and the cops are going door-to-door in the apartment building and to all the houses in the neighborhood to see if anyone witnessed anything. Something will turn up. I'm sure of it."

"Are you one hundred percent sure Vlad isn't involved? I mean, other than the time you served with him in the army, how much do you really know about him?"

"Sunshine, believe me, there is nothing in Vlad's background that would make me suspect him of stealing a pack of gum, let alone abducting someone. It's just a matter of time until he's cleared."

"Is there anything we can do to speed it up?" I asked.

"Pray that they find the woman soon." Marco put his arm around me and drew me against him. "And here's another thing you can do." He tugged on one end of the velour belt that tied my robe and tugged until it was loose. "Tell me how much time we have before you have to leave for work."

"I think there's enough time for what you have in mind."

That was all the encouragement Marco needed. He swept me up in his arms and carried me to my bedroom, closing the door before Simon could scurry in after us.

When Marco pulled up in front of Bloomers at two minutes before eight that morning, Lottie hadn't arrived, so Grace held the door open and then helped me switch to the wheelchair. She had already started a pot of her special blend of coffee and had set out cups and saucers, and her home-made scones, so I headed straight for the parlor.

"You've a lovely blush in your cheeks this morning," Grace said, bringing the coffeepot to the table. "This brisk spring weather must agree with you."

Brisk weather was one explanation.

The bell over the door jingled as Lottie let herself in. "Mmm! I smell blueberry scones," she called. She came into the parlor rubbing her hands together. "Let me at 'em. I could eat a horse this morning."

"A deplorable Yank saying," Grace said. "No one could eat an entire horse. The thought of it is revolting."

"I could say the same about kidney pie," Lottie said, pulling out a chair at the front table.

"Pork rinds," Grace said with a shudder.

"Black pudding," Lottie said.

"Speaking of black," said Grace, who was the mistress of segues, "those houseplants you ordered for Vlad will be delivered Monday, Abby. There was a message waiting this morning. Apparently the supplier was having some difficulty getting the voodoo lily."

"Speaking of Vlad," Lottie said, who loved

topping Grace's segues, "have you heard the latest on the missing woman? The news on the radio this morning reported that her car and belongings were found behind the apartment building where Vlad lives."

At least we were off the subject of disgusting food. "How did you know Vlad lived there?"

"It was on the radio," Lottie said, selecting a scone. "You should've heard what people were calling in to say about Vlad. As I see it, if Vlad did abduct that woman, he'd have to be pretty dumb to leave her car behind his building."

"Or exceedingly clever," Grace said. "He could be trying to make himself look so guilty that no one could possibly believe he was the abductor."

"I hope Marco's business isn't affected by all the hoopla," Lottie said.

"I doubt it'll matter," I said. "Marco is one hundred percent behind Vlad."

"Let's hope he isn't disappointed," Grace said, then cleared her throat and lifted her chin, a sign that she was about to share a quote. "As George Washington said, 'Be courteous to all, but intimate with few; and let those few be well tried before you give them your confidence.' "

We clapped. She acknowledged our applause with a regal nod, then went to refill the coffeepot at the back of the parlor. Lottie whispered, "She just got done putting down Yank sayings. Then she turns around and quotes Washington."

"If you want to point that out to her, go ahead," I whispered back.

"Heck, no. She'd probably chop down my cherry trees."

The phone rang and Lottie went to answer it as Grace returned to freshen our cups. "What is your impression of Vlad, Abby?" she asked.

I popped a bite of scone into my mouth and thought about her question as I chewed. "He's polite. Beguiling. Handsome. Different . . ." I ran out of adjectives.

"Different," Grace mused. "Do you mean he's odd?"

I blinked at Grace, not wanting to cast aspersions on Marco's buddy. "Can't we leave it at different?"

Lottie came into the parlor with the handset. "Sweetie, it's your mom."

Speaking of different. I glanced at my watch as I wheeled out of the parlor to take the call. It was eight thirty. What was Mom doing phoning me now? "Mom? Aren't you teaching today? Is everything all right?"

"Everything is fine, honey. The class is

having an art lesson now. Jillian texted me earlier to remind me to remind you about our family dinner tonight. She wants to be sure you and Marco will be there."

I'd get Jillian for siccing Mom on me. "We'll be there. Don't worry."

But as soon as I hung up, a thought struck me. Given Vlad's situation, would Marco feel confident enough to leave the bar for the whole evening? I couldn't imagine making an engagement announcement without him, and I certainly didn't want to be alone when I told the family that Marco might be going overseas. So as soon as I hung up, I wheeled into the workroom to phone Marco, only to get his voice mail.

I didn't leave a message. It could wait until I saw him at lunch.

We opened Bloomers at nine o'clock to a handful of customers, most of whom headed for the coffee-and-tea parlor to gobble down Grace's scones. With Grace covering the parlor and Lottie manning the retail side, I stayed in my cocoon of peace and handled orders that had come in overnight.

My blissful cocoon burst shortly after eleven o'clock, when Grace came in to alert me that she'd spotted my cousin Jillian through the bay window, heading for

Bloomers.

"This will help you brace yourself, dear," Grace said, placing a cup of tea beside me.

"The only thing that would help me now is a potion to ward off evil spirits."

"I'm afraid it's only chamomile, love." Grace headed for the curtain. "I'll see what I can do about the potion."

Did she think I was serious? "Wait, Grace," I called after her. Sometimes she was so efficient she scared me.

The curtain parted and Jillian swept in. She wore a rich, colorful paisley scarf over the shoulders of her white wool coat, with brown leather boots and a matching beret that brought out the highlights in her coppery red hair.

"Look at this picture," she said, thrusting her tiny camera at me. "Tell me what you see."

"I see people standing around the bar at Down the Hatch."

"Now tell me who's not in the picture."

"How am I supposed to know who's not in it?"

She huffed in exasperation. "Remember when I stopped at the bar to take Vlad's photo? Well, do you see him in the photo?"

"Here's an idea, Jillian. Say, 'Look, Abby! Vlad's not in the picture.' "

Frowning, she said in a monotone, "Look, Abby. Vlad is not in the picture. Now tell me *why* he's not in the picture."

I examined the screen. "Here's your problem. Your thumb was on the lens."

Jillian clicked a button on the camera to forward it to the next shot. "He's not in this one either." She clicked again. "Or this one."

I had to admit it was odd that she hadn't managed to capture even one shot of Vlad, but I wasn't about to give her the satisfaction of agreeing with her. "Maybe you should have asked Vlad to pose instead of trying to take his picture through the crowd."

Jillian put her hands on the sides of my face and bent her knees so we were eye to eye. "Abby, hello! Don't you get it? He isn't in the photos because vampires can't be photographed."

"Let go of my face."

She tucked a lock of hair behind my ear. "Have you ever thought of flipping your hair? Remember when you were fourteen and I did a makeover on you? We were at your house over spring break — it was March twenty-sixth, at one seventeen p.m. — and you —"

I pulled away from her. "Vampires aren't real, Jillian."

73

"You don't believe me?" She narrowed her eyes. "Then I'll just have to get more proof." She slipped the camera into her purse and started toward the curtain. She'd forgotten all about dinner at the country club.

Then she paused, turned toward me, and tapped her chin. "There was something else . . ."

I held my breath.

Lottie peeked through the curtain. "I'm gonna take my lunch break now, sweetie. The shop is quiet and I need to get home to start my dinner for tonight."

"Dinner!" Jillian said, brightening. "That's it! Thank you, Lottie."

"You're welcome," Lottie said, giving her a puzzled glance before she left.

Looking smug, Jillian returned to the worktable and leaned on both elbows to smile at me. "You were hoping I'd forget, weren't you?"

"Listen, Jillian, about the dinner."

She pointed at me. "I agreed to keep quiet about your you-know-what for one more week, and that week is up tonight. So if you don't show up, I get to tell."

Where was Grace with that potion?

"I don't understand why you're making a big deal out of our news," I said.

"And I don't understand your need for

74

secrecy," Jillian countered. "This *is* a big deal, Abs! After waffling for months, you're finally going to tie the knot. You should be delighted to share that with family. Imagine the fun you, your mom, Marco's mom, and me and my mom will have planning your bridal events and shopping for your wedding accoutrements. Seriously, who could possibly be better qualified to help you shop for a wedding gown than *moi?*"

"That's because you bought five of them."

"I *meant* because I shop for finicky Chicago women all the time. And, FYI, I returned four of those gowns. But just think, Abs. We can make an entire day of it in Chicago. No, a week! Fire up your charge card, cuz. Magnificent Mile, here we come!"

Which was exactly why I'd been keeping our engagement a secret. In fact, an elopement was starting to look pretty darn attractive. "Grace?" I called. "The potion? Hurry!"

"There's a new rumor spreading about Vlad," Lottie reported upon her return from lunch. "The gossip is that he set up a secret rendezvous with the Willis woman so he could drink her blood, and in his bloodlust craze, he left her car and belongings behind."

"That's absurd," I said.

"Maybe so, but people are eating this stuff up, sweetie, and that doesn't bode well for Vlad. You might want to call Marco and alert him."

"I'll tell him in person. I'm heading down there for lunch now anyway."

I exchanged the wheelchair for my crutches and waited while Lottie opened the door for me. Outside, people were once again huddled on the courthouse lawn, but many more than before, with cops in patrol cars watching from both ends of the block.

I felt hundreds of eyes on me as I laboriously made my way up the sidewalk — *step-hop-step-hop.* I managed to wave to a group of women from the clerk's office, regulars at our coffee-and-tea parlor, but they pretended not to see me. At Down the Hatch, I tapped on the big window and waited until Gert let me in. Marco was working with Rafe behind the bar, and as soon as he saw me, he came around to help. There were a few customers sitting in booths and two at the counter; otherwise the place was empty.

"Hey, Buttercup," Marco said with a smile. "You're just the tonic we need."

"I need to talk to you privately," I said in a whisper.

"Sure. Let me finish up with Rafe. Then

I'll meet you in my office."

"Hey, Rafe," I said, passing by the bar. "How's it going?"

"Ask my brother," he answered with a grimace.

"Rafe's doing well," Marco said.

"That's not what you said earlier," Rafe countered. "You said I couldn't even —"

"That was an hour ago," Marco cut in. "You're improving."

"Improving?" Rafe asked. "How can I improve when you're always criticizing me?"

"It's not criticism," Marco said. "It's instruction."

I left them arguing and crutched down the hallway to Marco's office, sinking gratefully into one of the sling-back chairs that faced his desk.

Minutes later, Marco came in and closed the door. "What's up?"

"Two things. First, you need to know there's a nasty new rumor going around."

"About why Vlad abducted the Willis woman?" Marco sat down in the chair next to mine. "I've already heard it."

"Lottie says everyone is talking about it, and after seeing all the people across the street, I believe her. It was unnerving walking down here, like I was on the set of *The Birds*."

"Sorry, babe," he said, taking my hand. "Until the cops clear Vlad, we're stuck with it."

"It's not us I'm worried about. If people work themselves into a frenzy, they'll turn against Vlad. I'll be very surprised if he wants to stay in New Chapel after he hears the latest."

"Vlad is free to go whenever he chooses. I'd be disappointed, though. I think he'll do a great job running the place — if I have to leave."

"*If* you have to leave. Let's not jump the gun. And that brings me to the second thing. Today is Friday."

Marco gave me a blank look.

"*Friday,* Marco. Dinner with the family. The night we make our announcements."

"Ah," he said.

I threaded my fingers through his. "I want us to announce our engagement together, and then have you explain about your letter, because I know there will be lots of questions. But I know you're not going to feel comfortable leaving the bar this evening, so I'm not sure what to do. If we don't attend the dinner, I'm not sure I can get Jillian to keep quiet for another week."

There was a rap on the office door.

"Hold that thought," Marco said, and got

up and opened the door. I turned to see Reilly standing in the doorway in his police uniform. He looked unusually somber.

"Hey, Sean, what's up?" Marco said.

"I just wanted to stop by and check on a few things."

"Come in and have a seat," Marco said, indicating the chair he'd just vacated.

Reilly sat down, his thick leather belt and gun holster creaking. He pulled a five-by-seven glossy color photo out of a manila envelope and showed it to Marco, who was leaning one hip on the corner of his desk. "Do you recognize this woman?"

Marco studied it. "Is this the missing woman?"

"Her name is Lori Willis," Reilly said. "Ever seen her in the bar?"

"She looks familiar," Marco said, then passed the photo to me.

At first glance Lori Willis appeared to be in her late forties. She had long ash blond hair, bright red lips, and brown eyes rimmed with heavy black liner and glittering purple eye shadow. She wore dangling crystal earrings, a matching choker necklace, and a low-cut silver evening gown. A more careful look revealed heavy bags beneath her eyes and more than a few crow's-feet in the corners. It also showed over-processed hair, a nose obviously shortened and pinched in just above the tip, and lips fattened by injections. I revised her age upward about ten years.

"It looks like one of those glamour photos," I said, handing it back.

"Parkview Hospital supplied it," Reilly said.

That was her personnel file photo?

"Have you heard from Vlad yet?" Reilly asked Marco.

"No. I don't expect to. He doesn't start until five o'clock."

Reilly took off his hat, smoothed his hair, and put the hat back on, a sign that he wasn't pleased with what he was hearing. "Vlad still isn't answering his door or his phone, and he hasn't responded to any of the messages we've left. From what we can tell, he doesn't own a car — no registration listed at the BMV — so we can't even use that to indicate whether he's home."

Marco folded his arms over his chest, which was the equivalent of Reilly's hat signal. "Is there a reason the detectives can't wait until five to talk to him?"

Reilly scratched his nose. Another signal. It translated to: *Yes, there's a reason, and now I'm going to lie as to why.* "We want to make sure he's safe."

"Ha," I said.

"We received a tip that there might be trouble," Reilly added, giving me a frown.

"What kind of trouble?" Marco asked. No signal for me to interpret.

"Rumors of vigilantes out to catch a vampire. We're taking that to mean Vlad."

Marco studied his friend for a moment. "Are you working the abduction case?"

Reilly leaned back in his chair, clearly trying to play it cool. "Yeah, why?"

"Because maybe I wouldn't have told you some of the things I did. Why didn't you say something at the start?"

Reilly shrugged. "You know how it is, Marco. We're friends, but I've still got a job to do. And besides, if the guy really is in trouble, I'm doing you a favor."

Marco let it pass, but his body language showed that he was now on his guard. "Any validity to the rumors about the vigilante group?"

"We believe they're just a bunch of hotheaded males who don't like the female attention Vlad's been getting. Might even be some of your regular customers. We're taking the threat seriously in any case. No one wants a posse in town."

"Why did you want to know if the Willis woman had been here?" Marco asked.

"We think Vlad made contact with her before she disappeared."

"Do you have a reason for thinking that?" Marco asked.

Reilly studied Marco for a moment, then sat forward, hands on his knees. "Okay, what I say here doesn't leave this room." He glanced at me. "Got that?"

I nodded. Women's signals were much more straightforward.

"In going through Willis's PDA," Reilly explained, "we found a dinner engagement at the Calumet Casino boat's Tumbling Dice Restaurant at nine o'clock on Tuesday evening. We contacted the restaurant, but they couldn't tell us anything because the reservation hadn't been made under her name. We got a list of patrons who'd dined there that evening and contacted them, but they're all clean.

"However, there was a party of two that didn't show up Tuesday — a Mr. Vlad Serban and guest. And the phone number listed for that reservation was not in service. So you can see why it's imperative that we talk to Vlad ASAP."

Marco was scowling as he walked around his desk and sat in his chair. "In the first place, Sean, whether Vlad knew the Willis woman or not, he wouldn't have made a reservation for an evening he was on duty at the bar. And I can vouch for him being here Tuesday evening."

"Did he take a break?" Reilly asked, pulling out his notebook and pencil.

"Of course he took a break," Marco said. "For thirty minutes. He ate a sandwich and went back to work. Secondly, if Vlad had made a dinner reservation, how can you assume his guest was Lori Willis? It could've been anyone. And last, the woman is a little long in the tooth for a healthy thirty-year-old male."

"When was his night off?" Reilly asked.

Marco typed something into his computer, watching the monitor. "Wednesday."

Reilly took off his hat, smoothed his hair, then put the hat back on. "Wednesday was the day Willis was reported missing."

Marco's jaw muscles tensed. "Do you have anything that positively implicates Vlad? Fingerprints? DNA? A witness?"

"We've lifted several sets of prints but haven't identified all of them," Reilly said tersely.

"So the answer is no," Marco said.

"What do you want me to do, Marco? Ignore the connections to Vlad? Is that what you'd do if you were in my shoes?"

I'd kept quiet until this point, but as both

men seemed to be taking their argument to a higher level, I decided to jump in with my two cents.

"Let's look at the big picture," I said. "The woman's car was abandoned behind Vlad's building with her purse inside containing a piece of hospital stationery with Vlad's name and number on it, and her PDA containing a restaurant reservation that had been phoned in by a person claiming to be Vlad. Doesn't that smell like a setup to you, Reilly? I mean, how many more ways could someone try to pin the blame on the poor guy?"

Reilly did his hat trick again, meaning he was annoyed with me. "I guess that remains to be seen, doesn't it?"

I looked at Marco and gave him a shrug. I'd tried.

"Vlad needs to get himself printed right away if he wants to clear his name," Reilly said, standing up. "He's not doing himself any favors by being MIA today."

"He's not MIA unless he doesn't show up for his shift," Marco said.

The men glared at each other.

"Just make sure Vlad gets in touch with us," Reilly said. "Maybe he can tell us who might be trying to frame him. And be sure to caution him to watch his back."

After Reilly left, I said, "I've never heard you guys argue like that."

"Reilly should've been straight with me from the beginning," Marco grumbled. "I don't like being grilled under the pretense of having a favor done for me."

"Maybe it wasn't a pretense, Marco. Even though Reilly is officially on the case, he's still your friend. Sure, he's suspicious of Vlad, but he is a cop. It goes with the territory. As he said, he can't ignore the evidence. And stop looking at me like I'm siding with Reilly. I'm just trying to understand where he's coming from."

Marco picked up the phone, dialed a number, and waited a long minute before slamming down the receiver. "Where the hell is Vlad?"

He pocketed his car keys and rose.

"Where are you going?" I asked.

"To find my AWOL buddy."

CHAPTER FIVE

The Casa Royale had been a church in its first life. After a century of use and a lot of structural disintegration, it had been sold to an enterprising developer who gutted the insides and remodeled it into modern apartments. The Gothic-style building was located four blocks north of the square, normally a nice walk from Bloomers. Because of my injury, however, Marco drove us there, which gave me the opportunity to discuss the family dinner with him.

"I'm sorry, Sunshine, but I don't think I should leave the bar this evening. Let Jillian tell the family we're engaged. I'm sure they're all expecting it. We can let them know about the letter next Friday."

"Having Jillian make the announcement is not how I want my parents to find out. Imagine how hurt your mom would be to hear from my cousin that her son is getting married."

"Won't be a problem. I forgot to invite her."

"Marco!"

"I'm sorry, babe. With everything going on, it slipped my mind. Look, call your mom right now and tell her. As soon as I park the car, I'll call mine, too."

"My mom is in class — and don't tell me to leave a message."

"Then call your dad."

I sighed. He didn't understand mothers and their need to have firsthand information. "Never mind. I'll think of something."

"I have to be honest with you, Abby — I'm not too concerned about how our families find out. They're not children. They'll be happy for us no matter who tells them. And if not, what's the worst that can happen? They boycott our wedding?"

"My mom would sooner be dragged naked through town than miss my wedding."

"So elopement is out, then."

"I don't know, Marco. I'm so confused. Maybe we shouldn't make any plans about the wedding until we know what the army wants with you."

"You know, that's probably a wise move."

"I'll have to work on Jillian, then. When we were kids, I always managed to get her to do what I wanted."

"How?"

"Bribery." But Jillian had everything now. What could I use? Nikki's advice would be to ask the universe for help. So far, though, that route had been nothing but a black hole.

My attention was drawn to a large crowd of people standing on the sidewalk across from the apartment building. Some were taking photographs and others were waving signs that read NO VAMPIRES IN NEW CHAPEL. A short distance up the street, cops watched from patrol cars.

"I'm ashamed of our townsfolk," I told Marco as we passed the cops. "They've judged Vlad based on stupid rumors. If I were Vlad, I'd leave and never come back."

Marco turned a corner and headed up an alley to the parking lot behind the church. "You have to understand Vlad, Abby. He doesn't care what people think of him. Those signs won't bother him. He's a very focused guy."

"Maybe so, but it's still unfair."

"It is what it is."

That was Marco's way of ending a conversation. He pulled into an empty parking space and shut off the motor. "I'm going inside to see if Vlad answers his door. Want to wait here or come with me?"

"Come with you." My desire to see where Vlad lived was greater than my fear of having a mishap with the Evil Ones. I opened the passenger door and waited for Marco to help me.

"Is this the lot where Lori Willis's car was found?"

"Yep." Marco pulled the crutches from the backseat and held them so I could balance on my good foot and get the crutches under my armpits, and then he followed me up the sidewalk to the rear entrance.

I saw steps ahead and had second thoughts about my decision. "You'd better go on without me. I don't even want to attempt stairs."

"Not a problem. I'll carry you."

After toting me, the crutches, and my purse up five concrete steps, then having to maneuver inside while holding a heavy wooden door open, Marco may have regretted his gallant offer. While he caught his breath, I rebalanced on the crutches. "That was way too easy," I said.

"No, it wasn't."

"I meant getting into the building. There's no security."

"The contractor probably cut corners."

"A contractor cutting corners? Hard to imagine."

"Vlad's apartment is on the lower level, number four," Marco said, consulting a slip of paper. "Let's take the elevator."

We rode down, then walked along the central hallway until we reached the last door, marked with a brass numeral. Marco knocked several times, called Vlad's name, then tried to reach him on his cell phone, but we didn't hear any ringing from the other side of the door.

Outside the building, Marco walked along the back of the old church until he found Vlad's ground-level windows, but he couldn't see in because the shade was closed.

"Maybe Vlad left New Chapel after all," I said, as we headed toward Marco's green Prius.

"He wouldn't leave without letting me know. I'm sure there's a good reason why he isn't answering his phone."

For Marco's sake, I hoped so. But I kept remembering Reilly's words: *Something tells me there's more to that guy than meets the eye.*

By the time we got back to the square, more people had gathered on the courthouse lawn. When they saw the Prius stop at the curb in front of Bloomers, they waved signs at us and chanted, "No vampires in New Chapel!"

Marco ignored them as he came around to help me out of the car. Grace took over from there and held the door while I peg-legged it inside, where Lottie was waiting with the wheelchair. It took a village to get me into the shop.

"We have to get an automatic door opener for Bloomers," I told my assistants as Lottie stowed the crutches. "I never realized what a pain it could be to open a door while trying to balance on chopsticks. I don't know how I'd make it through in a wheelchair."

"An automatic door opener is a splendid idea," Grace said. "Shall I get estimates?"

"Yes, please."

"Big bunch of people across the street," Lottie said, peering out the bay window. "Seems like most everyone in town is waiting for Vlad to — Uh-oh. Here comes trouble with a capital *J*."

Both of my assistants scattered. The door opened, the bell jingled, and in flew Jillian, a look of panic on her face. "Abs, I need to talk to you."

She grabbed the handles of my chair and pushed me as fast as she could through the curtain. Then she turned my desk chair around to face me and sat down. "I need a really, really big favor," she said.

Sometimes the universe actually listened. "Good. We can trade favors."

She gripped the arms of my wheelchair. "Clayton's boss is going to make him a partner. Isn't that fantacious?"

"*Fantacious,* Jill? Would you stop making up words? You're not twelve anymore."

"Did you hear what I said? Clayton is going to be a *partner!* He found out forty-two minutes ago. His boss invited us to dinner at their house to make it official." She pressed her hand to her heart. "Abby, the dinner is going to be *catered!* Do you understand how much money it takes to get a dinner catered at the last minute?"

"Way more than I'll ever make."

Jillian sighed dreamily. "Someday I'll be able to have dinners catered at the last minute." She sniffled, as though she was about to cry.

"I'm happy for you. What's the favor?"

"Hold off on your announcement for a week."

I tugged on my ears. "I'm sorry. What?"

Jillian gripped my wrists. "I have to be there when you tell the family, Abs. I *need* to see their reactions. *Promise* me you'll wait until next Friday to make your announcement."

"I promise. Stop squeezing. I'm losing feeling in my fingers."

She stood up, beaming. "Perfect."

If she only knew.

"So what favor did you want from me?"

I blinked at her. "I forget."

"If you're going to ask me to escort Vlad home again," she said, "you're out of luck."

"Why would I ask you to escort Vlad home?"

"Didn't he tell you how I helped him escape last night?"

"What are you talking about?"

Jillian sat down, crossing one long leg over the other. "Clayton and I and some friends were at Down the Hatch, and right before closing time, this group of scuzzy males claiming to be members of the Garlic Party came in looking for Vlad."

"The Garlic Party?"

"Haven't you seen them across the street? They wear garlands of garlic cloves around their necks. They're a group of extremists who believe the youth are being corrupted by vampire books and movies. Their goal is to drive a stake through the heart of anyone who claims to be a vampire or who looks like a vampire. Their leader claims to be a reformed vampire.

"Anyway, they were obviously looking for

trouble. One of the bartenders told them to leave, so they did, but then they waited outside. That's when I had the brilliant idea to have Clayton slip out the back and bring our car through the alley so we could take Vlad home."

She flipped back her long hair. "Vlad was so appreciative that while we waited for Clayton, he kissed my hand to show his gratitude. Seriously, Abby, what guy does that these days? But if he asks for my help tonight, I won't be there." She glanced at her watch, slid off the stool, and started toward the curtain. "Anyway, thanks for holding off on that announcement. Gotta run. Hair appointment in eight and a half minutes."

"What announcement is that?" Grace asked, gliding into the workroom seconds later.

Thank goodness Jillian hadn't been specific, because Grace had ears like a bat. "Jillian's husband is going to be a partner in his CPA firm."

"How lovely. Do congratulate them for me." Grace handed me a sheet of paper. "I've brought you three estimates for automatic door openers."

I looked over the numbers and heard the *whoosh* of money as it flew out of my bank account. "Two thousand dollars is the lowest estimate?"

"Shall I get a few more estimates to see if I can find something a bit less costly?"

"Please."

Grace started toward the curtain, then paused. "Abby, dear, I'm puzzled. Why would you have been the one to make Clayton's announcement?"

"Make Clayton's announcement about what?" Lottie asked, walking in behind her.

"He is to become a partner," Grace said. "And Jillian has asked our Abby to hold off making the announcement."

"Why would you be the one to make their announcement?" Lottie asked me.

I glanced at the phone on my desk. Now would be a great time for it to ring.

"Because," I said slowly, "Jillian and Clayton can't make the family dinner tonight to make the announcement themselves."

Grace and Lottie exchanged puzzled glances and then Grace said, "Jillian didn't ask you *not* to make it, only to hold off."

Okay, *now* would be a great time for the phone to ring.

Still nothing. "Jillian has always liked the way I make announcements."

Grace started to say something, but the

phone rang at last. Really. Was that so hard?

I picked it up at my desk and said, "Bloomers Flower Shop. How may I help you?"

"Abigail," my mom said, "are you aware that Marco's new employee is a vampire?"

It took ten minutes to convince my mom that Vlad was merely the victim of malevolent rumors and that I was perfectly safe at Down the Hatch in the evenings. It took another five to repeat it all to my dad. Then I had to break the news that Marco and I wouldn't be at the family dinner. They were both on the line at that point, so it got a little confusing because they talked over each other, but I hung up feeling that they were okay with it.

I'd just returned to the floral arrangement I'd started earlier when Tara and her friends Jamie and Crystal came darting through the curtain in breathless excitement. "Have you heard about the Most Hunkable Vlad abducting a mortal?" Tara asked as her friends climbed on stools.

"Hunkable?" I asked.

"That's Aunt Jillian's word," Tara explained. "It's a mix of *hunky* and *adorable.*"

I should have known. "Tara, Vlad didn't abduct anyone. Someone is spreading false rumors about him again."

"It's those crazy vigilantes," Crystal said.

"So we formed a girl posse to protect his MHVness," Jamie said proudly.

All three girls removed their coats to show me their black T-shirts with WE ♡ VLAD inked on the back in puffy, heart-shaped red letters, with their Web site URL beneath. Then they held out their hands to show me their black nail polish. "We've got black lipstick and eye shadow, too," Jamie said, "but we're not allowed to wear it at school."

"Aunt Jillian said the Garlic Party believes dressing Goth means we've gone to the dark side," Tara said. "So to show our support of Vlad, we've gone Goth."

"What do your parents think about that?" I asked.

The girls glanced at each other; then Tara said, "They're fine with it."

Right.

"We're not going to let any vigilantes harm one hair on MHV's head," Crystal declared, proving that even young teens were susceptible to his charm.

"Where did you hear about the Garlic Party?" I asked.

"Someone posted it on Facebook first," Tara replied. "Then everyone was tweeting about it, so I asked Aunt Jillian. She's a vampire expert. She's read every vampire book out there."

"That's noble of you to want to help Vlad," I said, "but you can't stay out all night."

"Some of the girls in the posse are older," Jamie said, "and they've volunteered to take over for us at nine o'clock."

"We're going to form a human chain around almost-Uncle Marco's bar," Tara said.

"No one will get to Vlad unless they go through us."

"Exactly how many girls are in this posse?" I asked.

"Six" — Tara stopped to count in her head — "seven dozen."

"Seven dozen girls?" I was stunned. "There aren't that many girls in the entire middle school. Did you have to import them from Maraville?"

"Okay, not seven dozen," Tara said. "But a lot. You can do just about anything using Facebook and Twitter."

Tara's phone chirped. She read the message, then motioned for her friends to follow. "Time for action."

"Tara, what about the family dinner tonight?" I asked.

Tara made a face. "Bor-*ing.* Nothing ever

happens at those dinners."

Wait until next week, I wanted to say. Things would be happening then.

"Tara," I called, wheeling after the girls, "do your parents know what you're planning?"

She glanced back at me and put her fingers to her lips.

"Tara!" I called. "You have to tell them!" But the girls slipped out the door faster than I could get through the shop without tearing down the doorframe on my way.

I rolled to the bay window and watched as Tara and her friends joined with more girls in Goth clothing and headed up the sidewalk. The crowds across the street watched curiously as at least three dozen girls formed a semicircle around the front of Marco's bar.

A news van pulled to a stop across the street, and a reporter and cameraman from the local cable channel got out and walked toward them. Uh-oh. Tara was going to be on the evening news. If my brother and sister-in-law didn't know what Tara was up to, they would shortly.

My phone rang again. I checked the caller ID, then answered. "Yes, Marco, I know what Tara and her friends are doing, and I'm sorry about it, but it wasn't my idea. If you don't want the girls there, tell them to go away."

"I appreciate that, Abby, but it wasn't why I phoned. Have you had any harassing calls this afternoon?"

"No. Why?"

"We've had a number of them here from someone claiming to be the leader of the Garlic Party, whatever that is, with threats to harm Vlad if he shows up for work. I was hoping they hadn't called you, too."

"The Garlic Party is what the vigilantes call themselves, Marco. Tara said they wear garlic cloves around their necks."

"In any case, I called the police and asked to have a tap put on our line. We'll see if they cooperate. Actually, the media outside may be doing us a favor. I doubt anyone would harass Vlad with dozens of young women and a news crew watching."

"In that case, you're welcome."

At ten minutes after five, I hop-stepped up the sidewalk toward the chain of girls, who cheered when Tara announced me. Marco was waiting at the door to let me in, and he got a cheer, too. There were still quite a few people standing across the street wearing garlic garlands and carrying signs, but the news crew had departed, having finished filming for the evening broadcast.

"I hope the Goth squad isn't keeping customers away," I said to Marco.

"No worries there." He stepped back to let me inside, where I saw a packed room. Apparently Tara and company were good for business.

And that wasn't the only surprise. Marco pointed toward the bar, where Vlad was mixing drinks, to the delight of the women filling every seat along the counter.

"Where was he?" I asked.

"Let's get you seated first," Marco said. "Then I'll explain."

"Vlad took the train to Chicago?" I asked, as Marco brought two beers back from the bar and slid into the booth across from me.

He nodded. "Took a cab to the station early this morning, then rode the seven-thirty train into the city to see an old army friend. He got back at four thirty this afternoon, showed up here at four fifty, and was shocked when I told him the police had been looking for him."

"Didn't Vlad get their messages?"

"Nope. He forgot to charge his cell phone last night. He didn't realize it was dead until he got to Chicago and tried to use it. He was completely unaware of what was happening here."

"What was his reaction?"

"Alarmed. Concerned. He was going to go straight to the station to be fingerprinted, but I talked him into calling Dave Hammond instead. And it was a good thing I did. Once Vlad explained the situation, Dave put a halt to any thoughts he had of giving the cops any help. As he told Vlad, either the prosecutor has a case against him with what he already has, or he doesn't. And fortunately he doesn't."

"Did you tell him about the threatening calls?"

"Yep."

"And Vlad still wants to work here?"

Marco nodded. "He said he enjoys the work and isn't going to let a few idiots ruin that for him. A news reporter tried to get an interview from him, but he wouldn't agree to it. He doesn't want the publicity. I had to guard the door to keep more reporters from coming in."

"Was there a mob scene out front when Vlad arrived?"

"He saw them and came in the back way."

"I hope he realizes that will only work a few times before they figure it out. Anyway, I've got some good news. Jillian asked me not to make our announcement because she and Clayton can't be there. I didn't have to bribe her after all."

Gert stopped at our booth. "What's for dinner tonight, lovebirds?"

"Ham and cheese on rye," I said.

"Same, please," Marco said. "Would you bring fresh beers, too?"

"Sure thing, boss," Gert said, and hurried away.

"What happened when you told your parents we weren't coming to dinner?" he asked.

"The usual. Dad was understanding, and Mom was disappointed. I had to promise three times that we'd be there next week."

"You got off light."

"Not quite. Mom told me she was going to drop off her latest work of art after school on Monday and asked if I'd hang it in a prominent place. What could I say?"

Marco reached across to squeeze my hand in sympathy. "Did she say what it was?"

"Does it matter?"

My mom's art was infamous around New Chapel. She thought of herself as an *avant-garde artiste,* but in reality she was a week-end hobbyist with a talent for combining the ridiculous with the outrageous. Her baby bassinet was a good example. It was literally a bass-in-a-net. Then there was her hatrack — a man-sized bowling pin with a bowler hat on its head and hooks on which to hang hats down each side.

"I hope she's not using mirrored tiles," Marco said. "I still can't go into her house without cringing. Covering the inside of the toilet seat lid was way over the top."

"The tiles were last summer, right before the giant beads. Then came the . . . I forget. But now she's back at her pottery wheel. I just hope that whatever she made, it's not too —"

A dark shadow fell across the table. I gave a start at the man with gleaming white fangs and slicked-back black hair — Oh, wait. It was Vlad with our drinks.

"Sorry to interrupt," he said with a smile, setting the bottles down. I smiled back, completely forgetting what I'd been saying. There was simply no denying the raw male magnetism Vlad emitted. It was a powerful draw that even I wasn't immune to.

"I hear you talked to Dave Hammond," I said. "How did you like him?"

"I liked him well enough to retain him," Vlad said.

"Did he warn you about not talking to the cops?" I asked.

"Yes. He told me the police have a tendency to leapfrog over other information to arrive at the conclusion they want, which was a luxury we weren't going to give them." Vlad grinned. "I like the way he phrases things. And I understand I have your niece Tara to thank for my circle of friends outside."

"I'll pass along your thanks. And by the way, your houseplants and dandelions will be in on Monday. Sorry for the delay."

"You found a supplier for the dandelions, then?"

"I sure did." And it hadn't been easy. A florist from Georgia had tipped me off that dandelion greens were popular as a side dish in some cultures, so I was able to track down a farmer who sold them to markets. Thank goodness for the Internet.

"That's great, Abby. I really appreciate it."

"I don't mean to be nosy," I said, "but I can't help wondering why you need so many."

Marco cleared his throat, then said quietly, "Abby, that's Vlad's business."

Vlad winked. "Exactly right. Enjoy your dinner."

I watched him return to the bar, then said to Marco, "Why didn't you let him answer? Don't you want to know?"

"Doesn't matter. If he wants us to know, he'll tell us."

"Did you tell him about Tara forming the posse?"

"I mentioned it, yeah."

"Did you tell Vlad her name?"

"No, it never came up."

I tried hard to stay awake that evening — every hour I got to spend with Marco was an hour to treasure — but finally I had to give in to my heavy eyelids. Marco drove me home, helped me to the door, then returned to the bar to stay until it closed so he could be sure Vlad made it home safely. Why Vlad didn't move somewhere else was a puzzle.

When he slipped into bed in the wee hours of the morning, I snuggled against his firm, warm body, still damp from a hot shower. "Any problems after I left?" I asked, still half asleep.

"Nope. Not even a hint of trouble."

"Did the girl posse stay outside?"

"Yep. Someone brought an MP3 player and speakers, and they had a party. When the younger girls left, the older ones took over, rotating in and out of the bar until closing time."

I yawned and snuggled closer. "Maybe this will be the end of Vlad's problems."

Since it was my Saturday to work, I let Marco sleep in the next morning while I dressed and had breakfast. I moved quietly, stumbling only once, but stepping on Simon's tail in the process. I tried to make it up to him by giving him an extra helping of liver in gravy, but he still eyed me warily as he ate, as though I'd forever lost his trust.

I had just rinsed my breakfast dishes when Marco's cell phone rang. He'd left it on the kitchen counter, so I picked it up. "Hello?"

"Is this Abby? It's, um, Evan."

Evan was Marco's dishwasher–janitor–substitute waiter, an easygoing college kid Marco had hired after Rafe quit and went to Hooters. Today, however, he sounded uptight.

"It's Abby. What's up, Evan?"

"I need to talk to Marco. I just took a bag of garbage out to the alley and, well, there's a dead woman in the bin."

CHAPTER SIX

I hopped as fast as I could into the bed-room, sending Simon fleeing for his life. I shook Marco's shoulder and whispered, "Marco. Wake up."

He was deep in slumber but came awake with a start. "What?"

"Evan wants to talk to you." I handed him the phone.

He put the phone to his ear. "Salvare," he said, then started listening. I watched his expression go from sleepy to full alert.

"Did you call the cops?" he asked, sitting up. "Did you touch anything? Anyone else there? Okay, I'll be down in ten minutes."

Marco flung back the covers and grabbed his jeans and T-shirt as he headed for the bathroom. "Did Evan tell you about the body?"

"Just that he found it in the garbage bin," I said, maneuvering toward the kitchen. "I'll pour you some juice."

Marco joined me minutes later and drank down the OJ. "Cops should be there by now. We'd better go."

"I don't suppose Evan recognized the woman."

Marco grabbed his keys and jacket and opened the door for me. "I didn't even ask."

"I have this horrible feeling that it's the missing nursing director."

"Me, too."

"And that she was put in your garbage bin to implicate Vlad."

Marco didn't reply, but I could see he was preparing himself for that eventuality.

Patrol cars and police barricades blocked both ends of the alley behind Franklin Street to keep out a growing crowd of curious passersby, so we parked on the side street behind an ambulance. Another police car was parked in the alley closer to Down the Hatch, with an emergency rescue van behind it. Crime scene investigators were already taking photographs and measurements, and searching the gravel for evidence, while Marco's nervous employee stood just outside the rear door of the bar talking to Sergeant Reilly and Al Corbison, a detective I recognized from past cases.

"Are you sure you don't want me to take

you down to Bloomers first?" Marco asked. "I'll have to be here a while."

"And miss this? No, thanks." I opened the door.

"They're not going to let you get close, Abby. And how are you going to maneuver on crutches in the gravel?"

"Fine," I said with a sigh. "I'll wait here."

Marco got out and strode up to the barricades. He stood there for a few minutes until he caught Reilly's attention. Reilly waved him through; then he, Reilly, and Corbison huddled together in conversation. Damned sprained ankle! I wanted to be in that huddle, too. I had questions!

Two EMTs stood beside the blue and red rescue van, watching as a police photographer took pictures of the interior of the garbage bin. When one of the EMTs walked in my direction to take a call on his two-way radio, I recognized him as Kyle from the bar. He signaled to the other paramedic, then started toward the ambulance.

I rolled down my window and called, "Hey, Kyle. Can you talk for a minute?"

"Hey, Abby," he said, coming up to the glass. "I've got another emergency call."

"Just two seconds, Kyle. Have the police identified the body?"

"Yes. It's the nursing director from Park-view."

My gut feeling was right. "How did she die?"

"It hasn't been determined. They haven't even removed the body."

"Did you take a look?"

"Well, sure."

"Can you make an educated guess?" I smiled.

"I shouldn't. I could be wrong by a mile."

"I won't hold it against you. Please?"

Kyle glanced over his shoulder to see if anyone was around, then bent down to the window. "I could be mistaken, but it looks like she was exsanguinated."

I had to run through a list of medical terminology before I figured it out. "She was drained of blood?"

Kyle started toward the ambulance. "As I said, I could be mistaken."

"How?" I called from the window. "Were her wrists cut?"

He paused outside the vehicle to curve two of his fingers, fanglike, and tap them against his throat. Was he saying she was bitten?

When Marco returned to the car several minutes later, his jaw was clenched. "It's the Willis woman."

"I know. I just talked to Kyle. He said she appears to have been drained of blood."

Marco checked the side and rearview mirrors, then pulled out.

"Did they have an idea as to when she died?" I asked.

"The paramedics estimate sometime before midnight. They're still waiting for the coroner to arrive. He'll have a better idea."

"If she died last night, then she was held for several days before being killed."

"That's what seems to have happened."

"Did Vlad's name come up in the conversation?"

"Right away. Corbison said he wants to bring Vlad in for more questioning. I told him to talk to Dave Hammond."

Now I knew why Marco's jaw was clenched. "It has to be obvious that your garbage bin was used as the dump site to implicate Vlad."

"I didn't have time to get into that with them, but I'm going back after I drop you off. I want to see what other evidence they find."

"I hate to sound pessimistic, Marco, but if Reilly and Corbison are talking about questioning Vlad again, they're not going to share information with you."

Marco was silent. I could tell he was concerned.

"I can try hitting up Morgan for the info," I said. "He's surely forgiven me by now."

Greg Morgan was a young, good-looking deputy prosecuting attorney who always bragged about how his finger was on the town's pulse. I'd had the hots for him in high school, but he hadn't even been aware of my existence. Now he was dating Nikki, which should have been a plus in my favor, except that his boss, Chief Prosecuting Attorney Melvin Darnell, had found out that he'd leaked information to me and called him on the carpet for it.

"He hasn't forgiven you," Marco said. "When I ran into him last week, he said Darnell was still watching his every move."

So Morgan was out. Reilly was out. Who did that leave?

I pondered the matter as we circled the block to get to Bloomers. "I can't think of anyone else to ask, Marco. Can you?"

"Mmm."

That was Marco's answer when he didn't want to answer. And when he didn't want to answer, it was often because he knew his answer would lead to a debate, and Marco hated debates. I, on the other hand, relished them. Probably because I usually won them.

He pulled up in front of Bloomers and came around to help me out. As I balanced on one foot, waiting for him to pull the crutches off the backseat, I said, "What aren't you telling me?"

He nodded toward the flower shop. "Grace is waiting at the door. We can talk later."

I tucked the Evil Ones under my arms but didn't move. Instead, I studied Marco's face, trying to work out the answer for myself. What had happened in the alley? Had Reilly told Marco to stay out of his way? Had the cops already discovered something in that bin that implicated Vlad? Was Marco having to acknowledge that his Ranger buddy might be the killer?

All of the above or none of the above, it didn't matter. Because I'd just spotted a glint in Marco's eyes that I knew all too well. "You're going to do your own investigation."

Marco's lips twitched, meaning I'd guessed correctly. And now I knew why he hadn't wanted to tell me. "Marco, you said you weren't going to take on any more PI work so we could spend your remaining days together."

"If this were any other case, Abby, I wouldn't take it. I want to be with you, sweetheart, but this is important. It concerns my army buddy. It could be a life-or-death situation for Vlad."

"That's why he hired Dave. You're not in the Rangers with Vlad anymore, Marco. You're here with me — for only a short time."

"Look, babe, I know it's hard for you to understand. You haven't been through what Vlad and I have, but there's this" — he glanced around, as if searching for a tool to help him describe his feelings — "this tie, this connection that forms among soldiers who fight together that's as strong as any blood bond. You witness death and devastation and sights so gut-wrenching, you hope to God you never see them again. You'd do anything to protect each other."

Marco put his hands on my shoulders. "I need to help Vlad, Abby. If I don't get involved, the police investigation will stall right on his head. Then the media will catch the fever, and we'll have a three-ring circus on our hands. Vlad wouldn't stand a chance for any real justice. That's not how I want to leave things. I *won't* leave things that way, and I need you to be on my side on this, Sunshine."

I hated references to his leaving. They were like a fist in the gut.

115

Step back, Abby. See the problem through Marco's eyes.

I took a deep breath. Although I couldn't relate to all of his experiences, I did understand having such powerful feelings because that was how I felt about him. "I will always be on your side, Marco."

He gazed into my eyes for a moment, then hugged me against him, being careful not to throw me off balance. "Thank you, sweetheart. It means a lot to have you with me."

"Good, because I'm also going to help you investigate."

He pulled back with a frown, holding me by the shoulders. "Abby, no. That wasn't what I meant. Look at you. You can barely make it from the car to your shop. If we're dealing with a killer, there's no way I'm going to put you in danger."

"I don't have to run a marathon to help you. I can do other things — computer searches, phone calls, accompany you on stakeouts . . . We have thirteen days left, Marco. Want to know how many hours that is? I'm not spending them away from you."

"I don't want to spend them away from you either, Abby. It just goes against my better judgment."

"You'll get over it. We're a team now, Marco. Partners."

He looked as though he was going to argue, but then he sighed and shrugged. "Okay."

"Great! So what do we do first, partner?"

"Not so fast. We need to set some ground rules."

My turn to frown. Following rules didn't come naturally to a Knight.

"You have to promise to abide by my instructions."

"I love it that you're so protective, Marco, but don't I always abide by your instructions?" *Always* meaning when I felt like it.

"You also have to promise not to argue if I say something is too risky for you."

"Define *risky.*"

Marco put his hands on either side of my face. "This is for your safety, Abby. If you don't intend to do exactly as I say, then thirteen days or not, I'll do it without you."

The stubborn part of me wanted to fold my arms and tell him to stop being so bossy. That wasn't how partnerships operated. But the logical part of me knew he was acting out of love. And besides, how could I look into those intensely passionate eyes and deny him anything? I loved Marco with every molecule of my being, and I wanted as much time with him as possible. If that meant abiding by his rules, then so be it.

"I promise," I said solemnly.

"I don't want you to discuss this case with anyone either. That includes Lottie and Grace. The fewer the people who know what we're doing, the less likely it is that the cops will find out and interfere. So mum's the word. You don't know anything about the murder."

That last promise was going to be tricky. "Got it." I gave him a salute, then nearly lost my balance.

Marco caught me and kissed me right there in full view of Grace and anyone else watching. I felt such an overwhelming love for him that I dropped the Evil Ones, wrapped my arms around his ribs, and kissed him back, clinging to him to keep from falling.

Unbidden, one of Grace's sayings jumped into my mind: *All good things must end.* And just like that, my connection to Marco felt as tenuous as a thin rubber band stretching toward that thirteen-day mark and the murky future beyond. I hugged him tighter, wanting to hold on to him and the moment forever.

"Will you call me as soon as you work up a plan?" I asked.

"You know I will." He picked up the crutches and helped me position them.

"You don't need to escort me to the door," I assured him. "I can manage." I started forward, hit a crack in the sidewalk, and tottered backward.

Marco caught me again, only instead of kissing me, he looked troubled. I vowed then to practice on those darned crutches until I mastered them. No way did I want Marco thinking I'd hold him back. I rebalanced myself and hobbled forward alone.

Grace held the door for me. "Is it true what Lottie heard? That a body has been found in the bin behind Marco's bar?"

I'd made Marco a promise five minutes ago and was already being tested. Figuring I was safe with gestures, I nodded.

Lottie held the wheelchair while I settled in. "I heard the news on the radio," she said, taking the crutches from me. "They're saying it's the Willis woman."

"Lottie, why are you here on your Saturday off?" I asked.

"Are you kidding?" Lottie said, pushing my chair into the parlor. "With all of this hullabaloo, we'll be swamped with customers. You'll need help."

"She doesn't want to miss any of the excitement," Grace translated.

We sat at a table near the window, where

Grace had already set out a basket of fresh scones. I put one on my plate and broke off the end. Yum. Pecan raisin.

"What else did you hear about the woman's death?" Grace asked Lottie, filling our cups.

"Most of it was speculation," Lottie said. "They said she wasn't the suicidal type or much of a drinker, and rarely took a day off work. A person like that doesn't disappear for a few days, then reappear to dive into a garbage bin and die."

"So it was clearly murder," Grace said.

"Yep. Murder," Lottie said.

What was murder was playing dumb. I bit into the scone, hoping they'd tire of the subject.

"Did you hear whether the police have any suspects?" Grace asked.

"One," Lottie said, then gave me a side-long glance. "Vlad."

"That was on the radio?" I asked.

"You don't even want to know the things people called in to say about him," Lottie said, then proceeded to tell me. "They're calling him the vampire killer, and saying he drained her body of blood."

I swallowed the bite of scone with some difficulty. "Thanks for the image."

Lottie patted my arm. "Sorry, sweetie."

"Vampires," Grace said, shaking her head. "What rubbish."

We drank coffee silently for a few minutes; then Lottie said to me, "So how did Marco find out? Did the cops call him?"

"One of his employees found the body and phoned," I said. No harm in revealing that.

"That poor woman," Grace said. "Stuffed in the trash like yesterday's fish."

"I saw the alley is blocked off," Lottie said. "Has Marco been back there to take a look at the scene?"

"Yes," I said, busying myself with putting clotted cream on the scone.

"Was he able to talk to the cops about what happened?"

"Yes."

Both women gazed at me expectantly. "And?" Lottie asked.

"They're investigating."

"Do they know how she was murdered?" Grace asked.

"The coroner hadn't been there yet when we left."

"So you were there, too?" Lottie asked.

"Yes, but I waited in the car while Marco went to see what was happening. I couldn't see anything."

They studied me for a moment; then

Grace said, "Are you feeling all right, love?"

This was never going to work. They knew something was up. How could I withhold information from them without hurting their feelings? Lottie and Grace had seen me through many crises. I trusted them with my life; I knew I could count on them to keep mum. But I couldn't break my promise either.

Giving myself a few seconds to compose my response, I put the scone down and wiped my fingers. "All I can tell you is that the police are investigating."

"That's all you can tell us?" Lottie asked.

I said carefully, "Yes. That's *all* I can tell you." I raised my eyebrows, hoping they'd pick up on the hint.

They exchanged glances; then Lottie said to Grace, "Looks like someone told Abby not to discuss the murder with us."

"I'd have to guess that somebody is Marco," Grace said, "and that he is undertaking a private investigation and has sworn our Abby to secrecy."

They both looked at me. With a smile, I popped the last bite of scone in my mouth and rolled my wheelchair out of the room. My work there was done.

The three-ring circus started sooner than

Marco expected. By nine o'clock, four Chicago TV news crews and the local cable crew had camped out in front of Down the Hatch. They couldn't get in because the bar didn't open until eleven. After that, I could only imagine how Marco would be bombarded with reporters shoving mics in his face.

The news about the gruesome discovery also brought out even larger crowds of curious bystanders, as well as vendors selling hot dogs, soft drinks, and even pickled peppers left over from the last Picklefest. The only good thing that came of the hubbub was that Bloomers made all kinds of sales.

By ten o'clock, the radio newscaster announced that the body discovered in the bin was Lori Willis, director of nursing at Parkview Hospital, and that the police had no suspects at that time.

By eleven o'clock, the newscaster reported that the police considered Vlad Serban a person of interest and that his attorney had refused their request for an interview.

By eleven fifteen, Marco had given statements to four television reporters and one newspaper journalist.

By eleven thirty, Marco's news sound bite had already been shown on two of the four

TV stations, with the others to air at noon, Marco had heard nothing from Vlad, and I had finished my seventh floral arrangement and was working on two more for a pair of customers waiting up front. The coffee-and-tea parlor was so full, people were standing at the coffee counter in the back and a line of people waited to pay at the cash register in the shop.

Which was probably why, at eleven forty, Lottie wasn't able to warn me.

One moment, I was humming peacefully in my private slice of heaven, carefully placing pink Veronicas, purple "Monaco" snapdragons, white spider mums, and green bells of Ireland in a bed of wet foam. The next, the curtain swept back and Jillian lurched in, looking wan despite the cheerful lime trench coat she wore.

She pulled out a stool at the worktable and sank onto it, propping herself up on her elbows as though she didn't have any strength left. "Did you hear the horrible news?"

"About the body found behind Down the Hatch?"

"Dear God, Abby, what other horrible news is there?"

I eyed the wet foam, imagining the *splat* it would make when it landed on Jillian's head. And speaking of her head, what was that awful odor coming from her hair?

"To think I gave him a ride home," she said.

"Who?" I sniffed her hair. Nope. That wasn't the source. "And what's that smell?"

She pushed me away. "Stop it! I'm talking about Vlad, okay? I told you yesterday how I helped him get away. What was I thinking? I could have been his next victim."

"Don't be silly. Vlad didn't kill anyone." I sincerely hoped.

"He kissed my hand, Abby." Jillian thrust the palm of her right hand in front of my face and pointed to two red bumps on it. "Look at these marks and tell me what you see."

I examined her hand. "Insect bites — mosquito, maybe."

"In April? Please. You don't have to cover for Vlad. Your loyalty to Marco doesn't have to go *that* far."

She pulled a necklace from beneath her coat and removed it from around her neck. Dangling from the chain was a stainless-steel tea infuser. She opened the infuser and shook out pieces of raw garlic. No wonder she smelled.

"A lot of protection *that* offered," Jillian said, dropping the pieces into the waste can beside the table. "If Clayton hadn't driven up with our car when he did, I shudder to think what would have become of me."

"Okay, before you go all loopy on me, Jillian, where *exactly* did Vlad kiss your hand?"

She shifted uneasily. "Does that matter?"

"The palm is not where a gentleman kisses a woman's hand to thank her for something. If Vlad had bitten you — and I'm *not* saying he did — the bite would be on *top* of your hand." I turned her hand over and indicated the smooth flesh. "Nothing there. See?"

Her forehead wrinkled as she turned her hand over again to study the bites. "It's such a blur now. Maybe he did kiss my palm. Do I feel cold and clammy to you?"

I put my hand on the back of her neck. "No."

She felt her forehead, then her neck. "Yes, I am. I'm cold, clammy, and utterly exhausted. And that's another strange thing. I couldn't sleep at all last night. But now that it's daylight, I can't keep my eyes open. What does that tell you?"

"That you need coffee. Stay here."

I wheeled into the crowded parlor and managed to nab a cup of Grace's strongest brew. I balanced the cup and saucer on my lap and made my way slowly back to the workroom only to find Jillian asleep with her head on a pile of Veronica stems.

Lottie bustled through the curtain, headed toward our walk-in coolers, but stopped when she saw Jillian. "Good Lord, what happened to her? Is she okay?"

Jillian wasn't *okay* when she was okay. But did I want Lottie to know just how crazy my cousin was? "She's just tired, Lottie. She'll be fine." I found Jillian's cell phone in her purse, located Clayton's number in her directory, and called him. "Clayton, come get your wife. She's sound asleep on my worktable."

"I'm not surprised," Clayton said. "Jillian drank a pitcher of cola yesterday evening, then couldn't sleep all night. The caffeine in that soda could keep a bear from hibernating."

I cupped my hand around the phone. "She thinks she was bitten by a vampire."

Clayton sighed. "I know. She told me. I'll be down in fifteen minutes."

I put the phone back in Jillian's bag and returned to my flower arrangement.

"No, I'm definitely cold and clammy," Jillian said suddenly, lifting her head.

"Have some coffee." I scooted the cup

toward her and swept up the crushed Veronicas.

She peered at the strong black liquid, sniffed it, then made a face and pushed it away. "I can't even stand the smell, and you know how I love coffee."

Her chin quivered and her eyes welled with tears. Then she held out her arms for a hug.

Right. Like I wanted to hug that.

"Abby, I'm turning into a vampire!"

CHAPTER SEVEN

Jillian insisted that Clayton pick her up at the back door, claiming the alley was dark and out of the sun, which now hurt her eyes. Lucky for Jillian, the cops had finished their work on the crime scene two buildings down. Once she was gone, I took my lunch break, using the alley to reach Down the Hatch. It was risky on a bed of gravel, given the tricky nature of the Evil Ones, but I preferred that to fighting the throng that now filled Franklin Street.

The girl posse had returned — those who weren't in school. The news crews were still there, too, as were seemingly hundreds of bystanders waiting with their cameras ready. Members of the Garlic Party had lined up on both sides of the street, carrying signs that read VAMPIRE GO HOME! DEATH TO VAMPIRES! And of course the cops were out in force. Everyone was waiting for the alleged vampire to make his appearance. If

Vlad showed up today, I'd be floored.

As I hop-stepped up to the big fireproof door at the back of Down the Hatch, I noticed that the bin where the body was found had been removed and another one put in its place. Otherwise, there was no sign that anything untoward had ever happened. Not even crime scene tape remained.

Inside, I found Marco's office door closed, so I headed down the hallway to the bar. Through the crowd, I caught sight of Rafe standing at the door, obviously posted there to keep the news crews out. It was too noisy for him to hear me, but I managed a quick wave hello without toppling over, then maneuvered a 180-degree turn and found Marco behind me.

"Is Rafe your doorman now?" I asked, talking loud to make myself heard.

He nodded. "Reporters are driving us crazy. Come on back. We can have lunch in my office. I'll put in our orders now."

"I'll have a turkey burger," I said. "Hold the fries."

"What kind of fries?" Marco asked, cupping a hand around his ear to hear my reply.

"No fries!" I yelled. My jeans were feeling a bit too snug in the thigh area, probably because I hadn't been able to take my morning power walks.

Marco opened his office door for me, then headed for the kitchen. He returned just as I lowered myself into a chair. "Pretty wild stuff going on out front," I said. "Picketers, cops, reporters, vendors — I'm waiting for the parade. Any word from the star of the show?"

"Nope. I've tried to reach him several times." Marco sat down at his desk and picked up a yellow legal pad. "I'm not worried. He'll show up."

I admired the confidence Marco had in his buddy. I wished I had it.

Marco tapped his pen on the pad. "I've been doing research, trying to give our investigation some direction, so I looked at who might be trying to frame Vlad. I went back into his work history, but I couldn't find anything to suggest he had made any enemies. I even called the hospital in Chicago where he worked last and talked to the current manager of the blood lab. As I expected, he had only good things to say about Vlad. Conscientious, courteous, reliable, no reprimands, and no employee complaints against him."

"What about someone from Vlad's personal life? A girlfriend, ex-wife . . . maybe even someone from your military days?"

"No marriages, no lawsuits, and nothing

from our army days that I'm aware of, except for the one run-in over his clothing. Vlad was an exemplary soldier. I asked the manager of the blood bank what he knew about Vlad's personal life, but all he could tell me was that Vlad was a private person whom he saw occasionally outside work, mainly at one of their favorite hangouts, but never with a steady girlfriend — or 'never with the same woman' is how he phrased it."

Marco sat back. "I've accounted for everything except for eleven months following his discharge from the army. I couldn't find any work history for that period. Maybe he took time off to get his head together. A lot of guys have to do that after they get out."

"Did you?"

"I joined the police force."

No comment there. "Are you going to ask him about those months?"

"If I need to."

"If it's no one from Vlad's past," I reasoned, "then it has to be someone from the present. I wonder if he's seeing anyone in New Chapel."

"With working the late shift and being new in town, when has he had time?"

"Mornings. Afternoons. A lot of women here at the bar are just waiting for a signal

132

from him. Who knows? Maybe Vlad is out with someone right now. And maybe that someone has a boyfriend. That could make some guy want to go after Vlad in a big way."

"It would take a sick mind to go as far as murdering an innocent party for revenge."

"We've seen some sick people in New Chapel, Marco."

"We're talking about an abduction and brutal killing, Abby. I'm sure you understand that Lori Willis had to be alive to have the blood drained from her body. That speaks of someone who had a deep hatred of her."

"Or needed a supply of blood."

Marco frowned at me. "No vampire theories."

"How about a ritualistic killing? I've read about cults who drink blood."

"If that was going on in our area, we'd see a pattern of that type of crime."

"Unless this is the start of a new pattern."

"Let's keep that theory in reserve and stick with the simplest explanation first. So let's take a look at who might have wanted to kill the victim."

"Let's call her by her name. *Victim* sounds too impersonal."

"You're right. It's a habit. I'll try to watch that." Marco pulled his legal pad closer and

133

began to read from his notes: "Lori Willis. Sixty years old, never married, no criminal record of any kind, not even a traffic ticket. She worked as a licensed practical nurse, then went back for a four-year nursing degree from Purdue. Moved to New Chapel from West Lafayette, Indiana, to take a job as an RN at County Hospital. Spent several years on the oncology floor. Taught nursing classes in the evenings. Promoted to nursing supervisor, then when Parkview opened three years ago, she left County to take a position there as director of nursing."

Marco leaned back. "Thoughts?"

Just one. *When was our food coming?* My stomach was starting to eat itself.

"Thoughts. Okay. Judging by her upward mobility, Lori must have been considered quite competent, especially to be offered the position of director of nursing. Nikki said that was a position with a lot of power."

"And people in power make enemies. Why don't you see what Nikki can find out about how the victim — I mean Willis — got along with the staff at County? Anyone with a grievance, any reprimands she might have given out, that kind of thing. Also whether she was seeing anyone or had broken up with anyone. I'll take a trip across the street to the county clerk's office to see if the vic

134

— if Willis was ever involved in any malpractice litigation."

"Sounds good," I said.

"Moving in a different direction, how about a trip out to the Tumbling Dice Restaurant after supper tonight?"

"Sure. Why?"

"If you remember, Reilly told us that Willis's PDA showed an appointment there Tuesday night. I want to see if the night manager can tell us whether she showed up and who the other party was. The manager won't be in until four o'clock, so we can eat first and then be on our way." Marco leaned back. "That's all I have. Anything you want to add?"

"Are you going to talk to Vlad about the murder?"

"If the facts lead us there."

That was his second avoidance answer. "I realize it's awkward for you, Marco, but to be fair, the evidence does point to Vlad. Yes, it's circumstantial, and someone might be trying to frame him, but don't you think we should know whether he had any prior contact with Lori Willis? At least to keep us from being blindsided by the detectives, in case he did have?"

"What kind of contact do you mean? I know he wasn't at the restaurant with her.

And besides, Willis was sixty years old."

"Come on, Marco. Haven't you ever heard the term *cougar?* Lori was a single woman. Why wouldn't she date? You saw her photo. She was trying very hard to look like a forty-year-old. She wouldn't be the first older woman to date someone a lot younger."

"Thirty years younger?" Marco shook his head. "You've seen the women lined up at the bar. He could have his pick, and I'm telling you, Lori Willis wouldn't have been it."

"Maybe not for you, but do you really know Vlad that well? It's been a few years since you and he were in the military. A lot can happen in even one year. Look at us. A year ago we didn't even know each other. You need to talk to him, Marco. Remember when Nikki was a suspect in a murder case? I had to ask her tough questions, too."

Marco tapped his pen on the desk as he studied his notes. I could tell he was softening, so I kept working on him. "It's the fair thing to do. The just thing to do. As you're fond of reminding me, an investigator has to remain objective."

He studied me for a moment; then one corner of his mouth quirked, as it always did when he was mildly amused. "For a new partner, you're awfully pushy."

I gave him a sidelong glance. "Like you didn't know that going into this."

"All I can say is, it's a good thing I like pushy women."

"*Woman.* Not *women.* And I prefer the word *enterprising.*"

At a knock on the door, Marco said, "Come in."

The door opened and both Rafe and Gert entered. Gert carried a tray with our food on it. Rafe brought a scowl with him.

"Here ya go, kids," Gert said, putting the plates on the desk. "Anything to drink?"

"Water for me," I said, reaching for a plate. Marco held up two fingers.

"Two waters it is," Gert said. She elbowed Rafe on her way out. "Go get 'em, tiger."

I bit into my burger as Marco pulled his plate forward and shook out the napkin. "What's up?" he asked his brother.

"How long do I have to play bouncer boy? I've been there for hours."

"Switch with Evan, then."

Rafe immediately brightened. "Thanks!" He started toward the door, then stopped. "Wait. Evan is clearing tables."

"And?" Marco asked, picking up his burger.

"I want to work behind the bar."

"Rafe, you're in training. You have to be

able to do everything. So clear tables for a few hours, then work behind the bar." At that, Marco took a bite.

Rafe watched Marco for a moment, his lips flattened together just like Marco's when he was trying to suppress an angry reply. Then he spun on his heel and walked out. He would have slammed the door, but Gert came in just then with our water.

"Got it worked out with the cub?" she asked Marco after Rafe had gone.

"For now," Marco said, opening his bottle and taking a swig.

Gert merely shook her head and pulled the door shut behind her.

I swallowed a bite of burger and washed it down with water. "Why *did* you put Rafe on door duty?"

"I needed someone to keep the media people out."

"You know what I mean. Why not Evan? That fits in more with his duties, doesn't it?"

"What difference does it make?"

It wasn't like Marco to be so uncaring about his brother. Was he testing Rafe?

Marco's telephone rang. He picked up the receiver. "Down the Hatch. Salvare."

I finished my turkey burger while he conversed with someone on the other end and took notes. When he hung up, he said, "My source at the coroner's office just told me the coroner's preliminary report lists the cause of death as exsanguination."

Just as Kyle had thought. I remembered him making two fangs with his fingers and asked, "Anything about how the blood was drained?"

"Two small puncture wounds in both jugular veins."

"In both veins? Why would it be necessary to tap into each side twice to drain blood?"

Marco drummed his pen on the pad. "Maybe the killer didn't hit the vein on his first try."

"That doesn't sound like someone who's experienced." I used my tongue to feel the distance between my eyeteeth. "Did your source mention how far apart the marks were?"

"About two inches."

A shudder ran up my spine. Were we looking for someone who knew how to draw blood — or suck it?

CHAPTER EIGHT

"Our killer could be a doctor, nurse, medic, lab technician — basically anyone who knows how to perform a phlebotomy," Marco said.

Which would include Vlad. Despite Marco's confidence in him, the evidence against Vlad was compelling enough that I had to put him on the list, though I wouldn't tell Marco that. Not yet. It would be better to let him come to the conclusion himself. Then again, with those twin wounds in Lori's neck, maybe Vlad needed to be a suspect in a category all his own.

"Once we start digging into Lori Willis's medical history," Marco said, "suspects will emerge."

I reflected on the coroner's report as Marco ate his burger, and finally had to speak my mind. "I can't get past those double puncture wounds, Marco. If our killer is an experienced medical person, he or she should be able to hit the jugular vein on the first try, right? Especially if you take into account that his victim must have been restrained."

"The killer could have been in a hurry, gotten careless. Remember, we're talking about a murder, not a hospital procedure."

"But two tries on both sides of the neck? Doesn't that seem odd?"

"What are you saying?"

Marco wasn't getting it and I wasn't about to blurt it out. Maybe if I tried a different approach. "Are you positive there were two wounds on each side?"

"I'm only telling you what my source said, Abby. I've asked for a photo of the body so we can see the wounds for ourselves."

"Who is your source, by the way?"

"Someone who knows people at the coroner's office." Marco paused for a drink of water.

I hated when he wouldn't tell me things; it only heightened my desire to know. "Is your source a female?" Okay, why did I ask that?

He put down his mug, a little smile appearing at one corner of his mouth. "Do I detect a hint of jealousy?"

I gave him a look that said, *Don't be ridiculous.*

"Wouldn't matter if it was a female," Marco said. "I've got all the woman I need right here in this room." And on that romantic note, he took another big bite of his burger.

"Well, all-the-woman-you-need wants you to treat her like all-the-partner-you-need, too."

"Is it *that* important to know?"

This man had a lot to learn about intimacy.

"I'm teasing you, fireball." He wiped mustard off his mouth. "It's Kyle."

"The EMT?"

"I've used him for several months now. Kyle's in and out of the coroner's office all the time, talking to the staff, picking up bits of gossip . . . That's the kind of contact every investigator cultivates. Remember that for the future, *partner.*"

I didn't like the way he kept planning for my future, as though he wasn't going to be around. It spooked me. "If we're looking for someone who's experienced at drawing blood, that would include Kyle. How do you know you can trust him?"

"I don't know that I can trust him, which is why I'm going to run a background check on him. But until I can find a new source, I don't have a choice."

142

"Fair enough. Was that all the information Kyle had?"

"That's all there is at the moment. A final report will be issued when the toxicology results are in, which won't be for a while."

I glanced at my watch. "I'd better get back to Bloomers. We've been so busy, I hate to leave Lottie and Grace there to manage things for too long." I paused at the door. "The notoriety may not be good for Vlad, but it's sure been good for the flower business."

It was almost two o'clock when I got back to the shop, an hour before Nikki started her shift at the hospital. Grace was occupied in the coffee-and-tea parlor, and Lottie was helping a customer, so I parked myself at my desk in the workroom and called Nikki at the apartment.

"Hey, Nik, I have a favor to ask."

"Sure. I have a favor to ask you, too."

"You go first."

"Okay. Remember when you gave Simon strawberries the other morning? Don't do that anymore. It does bad things to his intestines."

"I thought they would be good for him."

"If you want to clean out the litter box after he's eaten strawberries, be my guest."

"Oh, those bad things. Got the message, Nik. Have you had the news on today? Did you hear that Lori Willis's body was found behind Marco's bar?"

"Yes. In the garbage bin. How awful! Everyone at the hospital is talking about what happened. A lot of the nurses knew Lori."

"Okay, here's my favor. Would you see if you can find out whether Lori had been seeing anyone, or whether she'd made any enemies or received any reprimands while she was at County?"

"Sure. I'll ask around today."

I knew she'd help me. When we were kids, we used to pretend we were Sherlock Holmes and Watson. I was always Holmes, naturally.

"Did Dave hire you and Marco to investigate?"

"No. I'm just curious."

"Right. Okay. Good-bye."

"Come on, Nik. Don't be offended. I'd tell you if I could, but I made a promise."

"Who is the *only* person you told about your engagement? Me. Have I said a word to anyone? No. So, what's the problem? You know I won't blab."

"The problem is my promise."

"You promised not to tell anyone that you

144

and Marco are investigating?"

"Right."

"Did you promise not to play Sherlock Holmes and Watson?"

"What are you talking about?"

"You didn't, trust me. So this time I'm Holmes, okay? Now play along. And don't make fun of my British accent." She cleared her throat. "Someone hired the two of you to investigate Lori's murder, right?"

"No. And yes. And I'm not sure I should be answering."

"Shut up, Watson. By your waffling answer, I deduce you weren't hired, yet are still investigating, meaning that someone close to you is involved. Taking into account the rumors going around, I conclude that Marco doesn't want Vlad to be accused of Lori Willis's murder and is undertaking to find the killer himself. With your help, of course."

"Spot on, Holmes. Good show. Plus it allows Marco and me more time together."

"Why does it have to be a secret?"

"Because Reilly is assigned to the case, and Marco is afraid that if it gets out that we're helping Vlad, the cops will try to interfere."

"Do you seriously think Reilly won't find out?"

"Hey, it's Marco's call. I'm just along for the ride."

"Now, was that so hard, Watson? I'll phone — I mean send word — as soon as I have some information."

At three thirty, Tara and her friend Jamie bopped into the workroom. "Guess what," Tara said, showing me her notebook. "We got His Most Hunkableness's autograph."

I glanced at the neat script on the inside cover: *Tara, thanks for being a friend. Vlad.*

"Isn't that awesome?" my niece asked. "He even knew my name."

"Mine, too." Jamie showed me where Vlad had written to her below her giant balloon letters that said *I ♡ Vlad.* "Isn't he totally adorable?"

"That dark hair, those long fangs . . ." Tara fanned her face. "Vampires are so sexy."

"Stop!" I said. "Vampires are fictional characters! And *never* say the *s* word in my presence again. You're too young."

"Too young to say *sexy?*" Tara asked.

I put my fingers in my ears and began to hum. The girls looked at each other with saucer eyes, then burst out laughing.

"You sound like Grandma," Tara said through her giggles. "How old are you?

Eighty?"

"I'm twenty-seven. I do not sound like Grandma. And fine. Say *sexy* all you want. I'm totally cool with that."

For some reason, that caused more giggling.

"We've got to get down to the bar," Tara said, trying to stifle her chortles as she gave me a hug.

"Be careful. Oh, wait. I'm stuck. Would one of you pull my wheelchair out from under the table?"

They laughed so hard, I could hear them gasping for breath as they left Bloomers.

With only twenty minutes to go until closing time, Marco phoned me at the shop. "Hey, Sunshine, can you talk in private? I want to bring you up to speed on the investigation."

I was alone in the workroom, but with Grace's superhuman power of hearing, that was no guarantee of privacy. "Let's just say I can listen in private."

"Starting with Kyle — I found out he was enrolled in the nursing program at County a few years back but was dismissed because of charges brought against him by the nursing supervisor. Guess who the supervisor was."

"That's too easy. Lori."

"Yep. She accused him of stealing drugs and had him tossed out. The charges were later dropped, but Kyle never reapplied for the program."

"That gives Kyle a motive. We have our first suspect, Marco. I hope you've lined up another source."

"I'm still working on that."

Not having Reilly on our team was really putting a cramp in our style.

"Next," Marco said, "I went to the county clerk's office to see what I could find about Lori Willis and hit pay dirt — a medical malpractice suit filed against her and County Hospital five years ago. Willis was blamed for injecting a patient with heparin, a blood thinner, in an amount ten times greater than what was prescribed, causing the patient to have a stroke and die. The patient's husband sued Willis and the hospital, and after a two-year battle, he got a large settlement.

"Here's where it gets interesting. I spoke with a doctor who worked at County Hospital at the time and remembered the incident well. He said the patient's husband demanded that Willis be fired, but the hospital refused to put that in the agreement. The husband was so outraged that he refused to accept their offer as long as Willis was employed there. Eventually he capitulated. A year later, Willis left County to take the position of director of nursing at Parkview."

"Wow, Marco. Lori made a fatal error, then not only didn't get fired but landed a better position. I'll bet the patient's husband was enraged."

"His name is Jerry Trumble. He's a pharmacist now at Dugan's Pharmacy. I checked his background and found out that he worked as a veterinary assistant during college, so I called the clinic where he worked and was told one of the duties of an assistant is to —"

"Let me guess. Draw blood?"

"You got it."

"We have another suspect."

"You bet we do. After we talk to the manager at the Tumbling Dice this evening, we'll stop at Dugan's. Trumble is on duty from two to ten p.m. Tuesday through Sunday."

It was going to be a busy evening.

"I have to put you on hold, Abby. There's some kind of trouble outside the bar."

A minute later Marco came back on the line. "Gotta go, babe. Don't come down until I let you know it's safe."

"Wait, Marco! What kind of trouble?"

149

"Vigilante trouble."

Oh, no! Tara and her friends were outside Marco's bar!

CHAPTER NINE

I tossed the handset onto the desk, wheeled through the doorway, and got caught in the purple curtain.

"What is it, sweetie?" Lottie asked, as I freed myself with a muttered curse and headed toward my crutches.

"Marco said there's trouble at the bar," I said. "Tara is down there with her posse."

"You're not gonna make it through the crowd on crutches," Lottie said, grabbing her jacket. "I'll go."

She was out the door before I could thank her. As I rolled to the big bay window, Grace poked her head out of the parlor.

"Where did Lottie run off to?"

"She went to check on Tara for me. Marco said there was trouble at Down the Hatch."

"Good heavens. You'd think this was the Wild West."

For a while I sat at the window, hoping to see what was going on two buildings down, but there were too many people on the sidewalk. At least I hadn't heard any sirens.

Finally, I gave up and turned away from the window. "Let's close up shop, Grace. It's almost five o'clock."

Before Grace could flip the sign to CLOSED, Lottie hurried in, locking the door behind her. "Whew! What a madhouse! Tara and the girls are fine, but there are cops all over the place. Seems there was a dustup in the alley behind the bar when Vlad showed up for work. Several members of a group calling themselves the Garlic Party were hauled off to jail, but apparently Vlad is okay. Tara said he waved to her from the window. I tried asking a cop for details, but he was busy dispersing the crowd and didn't want to chat with me."

With a sigh of relief I said, "Thanks, Lottie."

"Perhaps Tara's parents should be advised of the situation," Grace said. "They may wish to remove her from the posse."

"Oh, they'll find out," Lottie said. "TV crews were there shooting film for the evening news. I pointed them out to Tara. She was texting her mom when I left."

The phone rang, so I wheeled myself to the cash counter to answer it.

"Abby, it's me," Nikki said. "I've got some

152

info for you on Lori Willis."

"Just a minute." I put Nikki on hold and said good-bye to my assistants, then went to the workroom and picked up the handset I'd tossed onto the desk. "Go ahead, Nikki."

"I've got good stuff, Abby. Do you remember me telling you about Dr. Sebastian Holloway, that gorgeous cardiac surgeon who could pass for George Clooney?"

"No, but go on."

"You have to remember him, Abby. Early fifties, salt-and-pepper hair, tanned, fit, arrogant, an ego the size of Texas. I pointed him out at the hospital picnic at the Indiana Dunes last summer. Think buns of steel and blue Speedo."

"Oh, him!"

"Yeah, him! Lori Willis walked in on Dr. Speedo and a young nurse in the utility room, catching them in a *compromising* situation. It happened before I started here, three or four years ago, when Lori was a supervisor. Anyway, instead of turning a blind eye to it, which is what most people here do — you wouldn't believe how much of that goes on — she *fired* the nurse and reported Dr. Holloway to the chief of medical staff, which got him a — wait, I want to read this to you — a 'reprimand for improper behavior on hospital property and with a hospital employee.' "

Wearing that Speedo at the company picnic should have earned him another. "That is good stuff, Nikki!"

"There's more. When Holloway's wife found out, she dumped him in a long, nasty, bitter divorce that dragged on for two years and cost him tons of money."

"Wow! I can only imagine how he felt about Lori Willis after that."

"No kidding. Then she went to Parkview."

"Leaving behind a doctor with a life and a career in tatters, and a young nurse with no job."

"So if you're looking for someone with a motive, Ab, you found two of them."

And they both knew how to draw blood. I grabbed a pen and had Nikki spell both names for me. "You did a great job, Nik. Thanks so much."

"No problem. If I find out anything else, I'll let you know."

Four suspects in a matter of hours. Not a bad start.

While waiting for Marco to give me the all clear, I pulled an order from the spindle and went to work. No sense letting the time go to waste.

The arrangement was for a fiftieth birthday party, and the person who ordered it wanted a centerpiece with fifty button mums in it, the birthday girl's "fave" flower. I pulled all the mums I had, all in bright spring colors, and went to work. I didn't want just a boring old mound of flowers, so I cut thick slabs of green foam to form a layer cake, with white mums for the frosting, green mums for the piping around the base and the top edge, pink mums to spell out the name Barb, and yellow mums for a border of flowers, accented by dark green leaves.

The phone rang just as I finished, and I was relieved to hear Marco's voice at last, telling me everything was fine. "The cops chased everyone off the sidewalk, even Tara and her posse."

"What happened? Lottie said people were arrested."

"Several guys waylaid Vlad when he turned the corner into the alley. They told him they were his escorts out of town. Luckily, Evan opened the back door about that time to take a sack of trash to the bin."

"Was Vlad hurt?"

"He's going to have a few bruises. I suspect the guys got as good as they gave."

"Have you talked to Vlad about Lori Willis yet?"

"Haven't had a chance. If you're ready, get your coat on and I'll be right down."

Down the Hatch was so busy that people were standing four-deep at the bar, every booth was occupied, and more people were waiting at the door. So Marco and I found ourselves eating in his office once again, while Vlad and two other bartenders struggled to keep up with the demand for drinks.

I filled Marco in on the two new suspects Nikki had uncovered as we dined on hearty beef stew and crusty bread. "That gives us four so far," I said. "I hope Lori didn't make many more enemies. We don't have all that much time to work on the case before . . ." I realized where that thought was headed and decided not to go there.

Marco didn't comment.

I reached into my purse and pulled out a piece of paper with the doctor's and nurse's names on it. "Dr. Holloway is still at County," I said. "The nurse lost her job there, so she may be a little harder to find."

Marco set aside his empty bowl and went to his desk. "Spell her name. I'll do a search right now."

I read the spellings of her first and last names and waited while the search engine did the work. "Two Courtney Anne O'Keefes in the state," Marco said. He typed in another command and watched the screen. "But only one from New Chapel. She works at Loyola Medical Center in Chicago."

In a minute, her information printed out, and Marco put it into a folder. "I'll give her a call Monday morning. Dr. Holloway will be harder to pin down. Cardiac surgeons are usually either in surgery or running back to their offices to see patients in between surgeries."

"Dr. Holloway found time in between surgeries for Courtney Anne." I fingered the top button of my sweater. "He might find time to talk to me."

"I'm sure your crutches will make quite an impression, especially when you tell Holloway he's a suspect in a murder investigation."

Rats. "Then I'll have one of my brothers set up a meeting with him. He wouldn't refuse a fellow surgeon's request." I scrolled through the address book until I found Jordan's name, hit the green button, and put the phone to my ear. "Jordan will help me," I assured Marco.

Marco leaned back in his chair while I explained what I needed to my brother. Jordan and I had always been closer than Jonathan and I, because Jordan was the closer to me in age. He was also Tara's father. "So would you set up a meeting between us and Holloway?" I asked.

"No freaking way, Ab. I'm the new surgeon on the block here. I keep a low profile around seasoned veterans like Holloway. Mentioning Lori Willis would be a bad move on my part. All the doctors know what she did to his career. In fact, if you're going to call to set up a meeting, I highly recommend you not mention her name either."

"But I told Marco you'd come through for me," I whispered. "Don't embarrass me."

"Sorry to disappoint you, Ab, but I'm not asking Holloway for any favors. Why don't you pretend you're a heart patient in need of a consult? Tell him you've heard he's the premier heart surgeon in the country, and I'll bet he'll see you ASAP. Just don't use our last name. Do you remember any of your high school French?"

"*Oui.* Why?"

"You're a heart patient from Paris. And be sure to show up in something low-cut."

Was there ever a doubt that Jordan was my brother? "Way ahead of you on that one, bro." I thanked Jordan for the suggestions and immediately dialed Nikki's number.

"Who are you calling now?" Marco asked.

"I need to leave a message for Nikki, *s'il vous plait.*"

When Nikki's voice mail kicked in, I said, "Would you talk to whoever sets up Dr. Speedo's appointments and make one for Gabriella La Cour? Gabriella needs a second opinion from the top heart surgeon in the country. She's flying here from France and will be in town tomorrow. Thanks, Nik."

Marco was sitting on a corner of the desk, the crutches leaning against his legs. "Who is Gabriella La Cour?"

"That was my name in high school French class. Gabriella, or Gabby, was as close to Abby as we could get."

"Gabby. Yeah, I can see that. And La Cour?"

I got up, wedged the crutches beneath my armpits, and started toward the door. "I'd rather not talk about it. Ready to go?"

Marco got there first and put his hand on the doorknob. "I'll open the door if you tell me what La Cour means."

"It's just a French name."

"I could look it up online."

"Fine. I'll tell you if you promise to never tell anyone else. Nikki is the only one who knows."

"You mean other than your entire French class?"

Like they'd even remember me. "It means *the short one.*"

Marco rubbed his thumb over his lower lip, trying not to smile. "It sounds better in French."

"Can we go now?"

He opened the door to let me through. "You know, I think I'd like to meet Gabriella. What is she doing around midnight?"

"If you're lucky, *le cancan.*"

The Calumet Casino Boat was docked on the Little Calumet River, about a forty-minute drive from New Chapel. Compared to big-name casinos like Blue Chip or Horseshoe, it was small, but that didn't stop people from all over the area from flocking to it.

Marco circled the full parking lot and stopped in front of a covered boat ramp, waving off the parking attendants. He helped me out of the car, then went to find a place to park while I tried to navigate the ramp. It was tricky enough trying to keep the triangle configuration on a level surface — crutches, foot, crutches, foot — but throw in an incline and I had a whole new set of problems. Finally, one of the parking attendants took pity on me and followed me up the ramp, one hand on my back to keep me from falling.

While I waited in a line inside the reception area, I noticed a surveillance camera pointed in my direction. It was a eureka moment. If Vlad had come onto the boat, he would show up on the security video.

When Marco came in and joined me in line, I pointed to the camera, and he nodded. We stepped up to the counter to register and show our IDs, then entered a gigantic room filled with slot machines, roulette wheels, craps tables, and more slot machines. The room was noisy, with bells going off and people laughing and talking, and one-armed bandits clanking, so Marco merely pointed toward a marquee for the Tumbling Dice Restaurant at the far end.

We made our way through the crowded casino into an area Marco said was for high rollers. Beyond was the restaurant, where a brunette in a revealing black dress, gargantuan silver hoop earrings, and silver heels stood at a podium just outside the entrance.

"Would you like to dine with us this evening?" she asked, as we walked up.

"No, thanks. I'm here to see the manager," Marco said. "I phoned earlier."

"Just a minute." She stepped into the

161

restaurant and came back a few moments later with a trim, fortyish man in a snazzy gray suit and an orange-and-purple tie. Marco stepped forward and held out his wallet to display his PI license. "Marco Salvare. This is my assistant, Abby Knight."

"Grant Gambol," the manager said, extending his hand to Marco.

That was a fitting name for a casino employee. Had he felt compelled to work there?

"As I explained on the phone," Marco said, "we're working on an investigation and would appreciate ten minutes of your time." He flashed a fifty-dollar bill, then tucked it back in his pocket. "Somewhere private."

The manager immediately showed us to an elegantly appointed private dining room with walnut wainscoting, gilt-framed paintings, and a crystal chandelier. He offered us drinks, but we turned them down. When Marco was in his PI mode, he wouldn't let anything ruin his focus. I simply wasn't thirsty.

We were sitting at a white linen–covered table for eight, with burgundy crushed velvet chairs, flatware rolled inside burgundy linen napkins, and a crystal bud vase in the center of the table with a single stem in it. I identified the flower as an alstroemeria, a standard in every florist's shop, and thought the restaurant management could have done a single calla in blush pink, given the money they'd put into the decor.

Marco touched his knee to mine under the table, apparently noticing my wandering attention. He had taken an envelope from the inside pocket of his leather jacket and laid out a newspaper photo of Lori Willis and a photo of Vlad from his army days. With a low, flat building in the background, Vlad was standing beside a tan jeep, one shoe on the bumper, a rifle in his arms. Although the photo wasn't recent, Vlad's distinctive good looks hadn't changed a bit.

"Do you remember seeing either of these two people here Tuesday evening?" Marco asked.

Gambol tapped the black-and-white photo of Lori. "I heard about her murder. What a shame. She used to come to the boat quite a bit to play the slot machines. But to answer your question, I know she wasn't in the restaurant Tuesday evening. I checked for the detectives when they came around to talk to us."

"Was she on the boat at all that evening?" I asked.

"For that, you'd have to talk to the casino staff."

"What about this man?" Marco asked,

163

moving Vlad's picture forward.

"Ah. The vampire." Gambol shook his head. "He wasn't here. I'd remember him."

"Would you be willing to sign a statement to that effect?" Marco asked.

"I don't have any problem doing that," Gambol said.

"Do you have a security camera inside the restaurant?" Marco asked, putting the photos away.

"No. But the cameras in the game rooms cover a wide area."

"What would it take for us to be able to review the security videos taken Tuesday evening?" Marco asked, sliding the fifty-dollar bill toward Gambol, but not releasing it.

"I can set that up for you. It'll have to be during the day, when Paul Van Cleef, the head of security, is here."

"How about on Monday, half past twelve?" Marco asked, taking his hand off the money.

"I'll take care of it." Gambol pocketed the money; then they shook hands.

Back in Marco's Prius, I worked my finger beneath the layers of Ace bandage around my ankle, trying to reach an itch. "It should be simple to prove that Vlad wasn't here

Tuesday evening by looking at the security video."

"The video might prove he wasn't here," Marco said, "but if Willis's death occurred after Vlad got off work, it won't prove he didn't kill her. And we won't know the exact time of her death until the coroner releases his official report. So I'm hoping the tapes show Lori leaving the casino with one of the other suspects."

"If they *do,*" I said, "we can show them to Reilly and get Vlad off the suspect list."

"I won't do that until I can tell Reilly who really killed Lori Willis. Never tip your hand too early. Remember that for the future."

His "future" reminders were making me nervous, as though he'd had a premonition.

"There's a Starbucks ahead," Marco said. "Want to stop for coffee or anything?"

"No, I'm fine. I'd like to come with you Monday to see those surveillance tapes, though."

Marco reached over for my hand and gave it a squeeze. "That's why I made the appointment for twelve thirty, so it would be during your lunch hour."

That deserved a kiss. I waited until the light turned red, then leaned toward him. Our lips met and lingered; then we reluctantly parted when the light changed.

"Thanks, partner," I said.

He gave me a scorching-hot look. "You can thank me more tonight."

"Count on it." My cell phone rang. I checked the screen and saw Nikki's name.

"What's the word, Nik?"

"I have to hurry," she said. "I'm not supposed to be taking a break now but I wanted to tell you two things. First, Mademoiselle Gabriella La Cour has an appointment for a consult with Dr. Holloway this coming Tuesday afternoon at two o'clock."

"A Tuesday appointment with Dr. Holloway," I repeated for Marco's benefit.

"And I've got another person for your suspect list. Her name is Diane Rotunno. *R-O-T-U-N-N-O.* She was up for the director of nursing position at Parkview, but Lori Willis got it instead. And from what the nurses told me, Diane was out for blood when she heard the news."

"Nurse Diane Rotunno. Got it. Good work, Nikki. And very quickly, were you able to find out whether Lori was seeing anyone?"

"I forgot all about that. I'll see what I can do."

"We've got a new suspect," I told Marco as I put away my phone. "A nurse with a grudge."

■ ■ ■ ■

Dugan's Pharmacy was a small chain operation that had stores throughout northwest Indiana. In New Chapel, the store was located at the busy intersection of Lincoln Street and Concord Avenue, a five-minute walk from the town square. When we arrived, there were only a handful of cars in the parking lot, so Marco was able to pull in close to the door.

Leading the way on my crutches, I headed for the window marked PATIENT CONSULTATIONS, where we saw a man in a white short-sleeved lab coat with a brass pin on the pocket that read JERRY TRUMBLE, PHARMACIST. He was on the phone taking down a prescription order, giving me a chance to study him.

He had a shaved head that showed a pear-shaped skull, a brown unibrow, deep-set eyes, and a broad nose that had a dent in the middle. He had the huge neck of a weight lifter, and his sleeves bulged with overdeveloped arm muscles.

Trumble ended his phone call and turned toward us with a smile. "Can I help you?"

Marco put his ID on the counter. "I'm investigating Lori Willis's death and hoped

167

you might be able to provide some helpful information."

Trumble leaned across the counter to see if anyone was standing nearby, then said in a low, angry voice, "If you're any kind of investigator, you know Willis caused my wife's death. Why on earth would I want to help you?"

"I understand your feelings about the deceased, Mr. Trumble," Marco said, "but —"

"You *can't* understand unless it happened to you, too, so don't insult me by pretending you do."

"Regardless of how you feel about the deceased, an innocent person is being targeted by the police for her murder," Marco said. "I'm doing what I can to make sure he's not wrongly accused. Surely you can understand wanting to help a friend in trouble."

The pharmacist took a deep breath and let it out slowly. "I appreciate what you're trying to do, but I can't help you."

"Just ten minutes of your time," Marco said.

Trumble slammed his fist on the counter. "I don't care if Lori Willis is dead. She killed my wife! Her carelessness ruined my life and took my son's mother from him. Do you know what she said to me when I arrived at the hospital after Dana was pronounced dead? That Dana was better off because she would've had brain damage! Can you imagine a nurse saying that to a grieving husband after *her* mistake caused his wife's death?"

Even after five years, the man's pain was raw and right below the surface. His helpless fury resonated with me. I wondered if I could tap into that to change his mind.

"We're sorry for your tragic loss," I said, stepping up to the window beside Marco. "My dad almost died because of a mistake a surgeon made on the operating table. And even though he lived, he lost the use of his legs. So I can understand your anger, Mr. Trumble. But all we want to do is make sure there's not a killer on the loose. I'm certain you want a safe community for your son. So why not see if you can help us catch a murderer?"

A customer got in line behind us, giving Trumble an easy out. "I think it's time for you to leave," he said quietly.

"We'll come back tomorrow," Marco said. "Maybe you'll think of something by then."

"Wait," Trumble said before we could step away. He leaned over the counter and said in a low voice, "I usually stop at the Daily

Grind coffee shop after work. If you want to talk, I'll be there after ten."

CHAPTER TEN

After we were back in the Prius, Marco leaned over to kiss me. "That was good work, partner. You struck just the right tone with him. With a little more experience, you'll be able to handle cases alone."

"Thanks, but why would I want to handle cases alone?"

"I'm just saying."

It was what he *wasn't* saying that bothered me. Nothing like spoiling my cheery mood.

Marco checked the time as he pulled out of the pharmacy parking lot. "It's not even eight o'clock, so I'm going to head back to Down the Hatch. Do you want to come with me or would you rather I drop you off at home? I can handle the meeting with Trumble."

"I'm sticking with you, Salvare." My cell phone rang, so I dug it out of my purse, checked the screen, and flipped it open. "Hello, Jillian."

171

"No, it's me, Claymore," came a whisper. "Jillian's in the kitchen eating raw beef, and I'm afraid it'll make her sick."

"It sounds like she's already sick."

"You have to convince her that she's not turning into a vampire. She'll listen to you."

Jillian had never listened to me in her entire life. I doubted she even listened to Claymore unless he was holding a new credit card in his hand. Poor Claymore. He was fussy, snobbish, and high-strung but ultimately a nice guy who was too timid for the likes of my cousin.

"Wait," Claymore whispered. "I just heard the door slam." He covered the mouthpiece while he called, "Jillian? Dearest? Are you there?"

I heard footsteps, and a door opening and shutting, then a few seconds later, Claymore said, "Abby, she left, and she didn't take her car keys with her."

"Maybe she went for a walk," I said.

"She had beef blood dripping down her chin. She'll frighten the wits out of anyone who sees her."

"Drive around and see if you can find her. Call me back if you can't."

I slipped my phone back inside my purse and said to Marco, "Claymore said Jillian is now eating raw meat. He's worried because she left the house and didn't take her car keys."

"Do you want me to drive over to their place?"

"No. Jillian is certainly not herself, but she's Claymore's problem now. I'm done handling her crises. I did that for way too many years."

Famous last words.

Everything was humming along quietly at Down the Hatch. The bar was full, though women still dominated the counter, drawn by the charismatic Vlad, who was one of three bartenders for the Saturday night crowd. Fortunately, a college basketball game featuring the New Chapel Chargers was playing on the TVs at each end of the bar, drawing most of the male customers' attention.

As we looked for a place to sit, Marco noticed Kyle seated in a booth by himself. "What do you say we have a chat with him?" Marco asked me.

"I'd say it's efficient use of our time. Plus there's nowhere else to sit."

"I'll open with small talk. Then you have a go at what you do best."

"You want me to be sexy for Kyle?"

"I meant nosy. Not that you're *not* sexy . . .

to me anyway."

"I think you should stop right there."

"You got it."

It wasn't that I didn't appreciate Marco's confidence in me, but I wasn't thrilled that he thought my *best* was being nosy.

Marco stopped at the end of the bar to order beers for us; then he ushered me toward Kyle's booth. "Hey, buddy, got room for two more?"

Kyle had been reading a book but upon hearing his name, he glanced up. "Sure! Have a seat."

"We're not interrupting, are we?" Marco asked, nodding at the thick book.

In reply, Kyle closed the book and slid it to the far end of the table as we settled in across from him.

Marco put the crutches on the floor. "We can't stay long. Just stopped in to check on the place."

"Don't worry. I'm keeping an eye on things for you," Kyle said with a wink.

"What are you reading?" I asked.

"It's a textbook. I'm studying for an exam. Have to keep current on things. Licensing regulations and all. What have you guys been up to?"

"Just hanging out." Marco nodded toward the television. "What's the score?"

"Ten to seven, our favor," Kyle said.

Gert stopped by with our beers and a bowl of peanuts. "There ya go, lovebirds. Can I get you something else, Kyle?"

He checked the bottle in front of him and saw half an inch left. "I'm good, thanks."

"Bring him another one," Marco said, "on the house."

"Thanks, man," Kyle said.

"It's the least I can do for a friend," Marco said. He glanced around, then said quietly, "Any word on whether the coroner established a time of death?"

Kyle finished his beer and set the bottle aside. "I haven't heard, but I'll find out for you."

"How about that copy of one of the coroner's photos?"

"Gosh, I'm sorry. I've been studying so hard I totally blew it off. Look, I'll get it tomorrow, okay?"

Or would he conveniently forget then, too?

"No problem." Marco gave my knee a little squeeze, which I took to mean that it was my turn at bat . . . or hoop. Whatever.

"That looks like a serious medical book," I said, nodding toward the tome he'd pushed aside. "Are the exams really tough?"

"They're so easy, it's embarrassing," he said with a self-deprecating laugh. "I just like to refresh my memory."

If they were easy, why was he studying so hard? "How long have you been an EMT?" I asked, taking a handful of nuts.

"Several years now," he said, and turned his attention to the TV, clearly signaling that he was more interested in the game.

"Do you like being a paramedic?" I asked.

He had to drag his eyes away from the TV screen to answer. "Yeah, I like it. It doesn't pay all that well, but I get a lot of satisfaction out of helping people." He glanced up as Gert put a fresh bottle of beer in front of him. "Thanks."

"Have you always wanted to be a paramedic?" I asked.

Kyle turned his head and gave me a long look, as though puzzled by my interest — or annoyed by the interruption. "Paramedic or whatever, as long as it was in the medical field."

A cheer went up as the Chargers scored. I let Kyle watch the action for a while; then I said, "Ever thought of going back to school to become a doctor?"

"Nah. It takes too much money and too many years of study." Kyle raised the bottle to his lips and drank half the beer from it. Then he and Marco sat forward as a player made a rim shot. Another cheer went up from the crowd when the ball went in.

"How about a nurse?" I asked.

Kyle's eyes darted to my face. "What?"

"A nurse," I repeated. "I thought I heard that you started out in nursing."

He put the bottle down with a *thunk,* his face turning red. "That was a long time ago."

I pretended to be confused. "Not that long, was it? A friend of mine was in a program about three years ago and said she remembered you."

Wow, I *was* getting good. That idea came out of nowhere.

"Maybe it was three years," Kyle said testily. "It just seems longer because I've moved on since then."

For the next five minutes, Kyle sat with his back against the booth and a scowl on his face. He didn't cheer, and wouldn't make eye contact with me, as though he was pouting. Then he slid to the end of the bench and said stiffly to Marco, "I've got an early shift tomorrow. Thanks for the beer."

"Hey, man," Marco said, as Kyle stood up. "Hold up a minute. Did we offend you?"

Kyle sat back down, hands gripping the edge of the table. "I don't appreciate being grilled about my past."

"I'm sorry if you thought I was grilling

177

you," Marco said.

"It was her." Kyle nodded at me, giving me a glare.

Uh-oh. Maybe I wasn't as good as I thought.

"You mean Abby?" Marco asked, pretending surprise. He put his hand over mine and said to Kyle, "She wants to learn how to be a private investigator, so I've been teaching her how to do interviews. She's trying some of her new skills on you, that's all. Don't be offended by it."

Marco was smooth.

Kyle sat back with a thoughtful frown, as though mulling it over, then gave me an apologetic shrug. "I'm sorry I snapped at you, Abby. I thought you'd heard about some trouble I had when I was in the nursing program. I guess it's still a sore subject with me. The Willis murder must have brought those old wounds to the surface. I hope you'll forgive me."

I'd forgive, but I wasn't going to forget his reaction.

"I should have explained what I was doing," I said. "But since you mentioned it, would you mind if I asked what kind of trouble?"

"The nursing instructor accused me of stealing drugs." Kyle picked up his beer bottle and swished the liquid around, watching it swirl for a moment before answering. "The accusation was false, of course, and I was cleared, but I didn't get back into the program."

"Why did the Willis murder bring that up?" I asked, playing dumb.

"Because Lori Willis was my instructor," Kyle said, not quite managing to keep the bitterness out of his voice.

"Why didn't you reapply to the program?" I asked.

Kyle tapped beats on the table with his thumb in an obvious attempt to control his anger. "Because Willis was the instructor and she had it in for me. She knew I was innocent when she brought the charges against me."

"Then why did she do it?" I asked.

"I've always wanted to ask her that," Kyle said. "Guess I'll never have the chance now."

"That was revealing," I said to Marco, after Kyle left. "Did you see how fast his mood changed when I brought up the nursing program? I was going to ask him about his whereabouts Tuesday evening, but after that outburst, I thought better of it."

"I'm glad you didn't, Abby. No sense provoking him."

I sat back and sipped my beer, thinking about Kyle's reaction. "He sure had issues with Lori. That's just the type you have to watch out for, an ordinary guy who can slip under the radar until he reaches a breaking point and then — *snap*."

"I'm not sure I'd go that far, but he won't slip under our radar. I'll stop by the County Council office in the morning and ask the secretary for his time sheet for last week."

"Can you do that?"

"Kyle is a county employee. All county employee records are open for inspection. In the meantime, Kyle is off our list as a source. If he brings us any information, we'll have to recheck it elsewhere, just in case it's been doctored." Marco got out of the booth. "I have a few things to wrap up in the office. It should take ten minutes max. Want to wait here or come with me?"

I glanced over at Vlad, who was currently unoccupied behind the bar. Maybe now would be a good time to talk to him. "I'll wait here. Would you ask Gert to stop by the booth?"

"I'll send her over."

Marco paused to talk to Gert, then headed toward his office. Gert bustled toward me, her pad in hand. "What can I get you, doll?"

"Would you ask Vlad to come over here

when he's got a free minute?"

She hurried off again, motioning for Vlad to bend down so she could whisper in his ear. He straightened and looked at me with those piercing wolf eyes. I gave a little wave, and he signaled that he'd be right there.

Right here? Yikes! I hadn't prepared what to ask him. I had to think of something quick because spontaneous questioning didn't always work out well for a person with a tact deficit.

So, Vlad, how well did you know the dead woman before she was, well, dead?

Talk about tacky! I wasn't usually nervous questioning people. In fact, I pretty much had nerves of steel. What was the matter with me?

Quick, Abby, think. He's almost here.

Small talk. Of course! That was the way to start. But small talk about what? Surely I could come up with something more stimulating than the weather.

Vlad stopped at the booth and smiled. "How is New Chapel's finest florist this evening?" His houseplants! That was the answer. "Fine, Vlad. Thanks for asking. I have some news about your order. Do you have time to sit?"

He glanced over at the bar to see how busy his fellow bartenders were, then slid in across from me. "Has there been another delay?"

Did he have to look so incredibly, disarmingly, damnably handsome right now? "Not a new one, but I couldn't remember if I'd told you the *reason* for the delay." I shrugged, as if to say, *No big deal.*

Vlad gazed at me in a way that made me think he knew my lame ruse was just that. My face felt so hot that I knew it was flushed, which always made my freckles stand out like bran flakes in a bowl of milk. I hoped he didn't think I was flirting with him behind Marco's back.

Where was Marco anyway? Couldn't he show up about now and spare me further embarrassment? Couldn't *someone* show up? Please?

I had no choice but to forge ahead. "It turns out my supplier is having difficulty getting your voodoo lily. But everything else should be in on Monday." I gave him a sheepish shrug.

Vlad leaned forward, his hands folded together on the table. "Are you all right, Abby?"

As right as a train wreck could be. "Of course. Did you know Lori Willis?"

Damn that missing tact gene!

Vlad's gaze never wavered. "No. Is there a

reason you thought I might have?"

No reason I was willing to admit to. "I got to thinking about her murder and wondered if she'd ever come into the bar and, you know, maybe introduced herself to you, because you have a lot of admirers up there, Vlad, and she could have been one of them. Maybe you even saw her with a guy or noticed something unusual about her behavior — or something else useful."

I was babbling like a fool. Someone please shoot me now!

"If she was here, she didn't introduce herself," Vlad said calmly.

I shrugged again. It was starting to feel like a twitch. "Then never mind."

Shrewd wolf eyes searched mine. "Are you sure everything's all right?"

My shoulders were on their way up when Gert butted in. "Abby, someone at the door wants to see you."

Dear God, it was about time someone stopped me.

I turned to see who it was, and there stood Sergeant Reilly in his police uniform.

Reilly had to be the someone?

He motioned for me to hurry. Yeah, right. On crutches.

Vlad instantly sprang into action, pulling out the Evil Ones, helping me get balanced, and shepherding me to the door.

"Thanks," I said with a sheepish smile, feeling guilty now for questioning him. If Vlad had met Lori, he would have mentioned it to Marco as soon as her murder was announced.

"Abby, would you come outside with me for a moment, please?" Reilly said, ignoring Vlad.

"Why?" I asked.

"Just come with me," Reilly said. "Alone."

CHAPTER ELEVEN

"I'll get your coat," Vlad said. "Thanks, but I shouldn't be long." I waited for Reilly to open the door, then hastened outside. He pointed toward his patrol car, where I saw Jillian sitting in the backseat. "Oh, my God! You arrested her?"

"No. I should have, though. Wait till you see her."

Reilly strode to the car and opened the back door so I could talk to her. I hung on to the crutches and leaned in. "Jillian, for heaven's sake, what did you do?"

She turned her head toward me. Her lips, chin, and neck were stained red. She had on a black trench coat and no makeup, making the red juice stand out in stark contrast to her pale skin. Her beautiful copper hair hung straight down around her face, and her eyes were bleary, with dark purple circles underneath.

"What time is it?" she asked, as though in

a daze. "I have to get home before dawn."

"Jillian, stop that!" I whispered. "You're not a vampire."

"Why won't you believe me?" She started to cry and covered her face with her hands. She was wearing black nail polish and still had traces of blood on her fingers.

I turned back to Reilly. "Where did you pick her up?"

"Outside the Happy Dreams Funeral Home. She was ringing their private doorbell, scaring the bejesus out of Delilah and Max. Good thing they weren't having a viewing this evening. People might have thought someone had come back from the dead."

"Did you ask Jillian why she was there?" I asked.

"She said she wanted to buy a casket."

"I want to go home," Jillian said through her tears.

"I'm not releasing her in that condition," Reilly said. "She looks like Vampira. I tried to call her husband, but he didn't answer."

"He's out searching for her." I leaned into the car. "Why do you want a casket, Jillian?"

"So I can sleep," she said, sniffling. "The light keeps me awake."

"Can't you turn the light off?"

"It's the sun, Abby!" She dug in the

pocket of her coat for a tissue. "Vampires sleep during the day. Duh."

"Okay, that's it, Jill. I'm ending this vampire nonsense. Reilly, I'll be right back."

I knew the only one who could convince Jillian that she wasn't a vampire was Vlad, so I hopped to the door to catch his attention. But he was mixing drinks and had his back to me.

Marco came striding through the bar carrying my coat. "Vlad said you needed this. What's going on?"

"Jillian is sitting in Reilly's squad car," I said, as Marco helped me don the coat. "He picked her up trying to buy a casket at Happy Dreams. I need Vlad to go out there and tell her he's not a vampire and didn't bite her."

"Not a good idea. It would be demeaning for Vlad. I'll talk to her."

Marco acknowledged Reilly with a nod as he strode to the squad car. Then he crouched down beside the open door and had an earnest conversation with my cousin.

I phoned Claymore and said, "Found her! She's outside Down the Hatch in the backseat of a patrol car. Sergeant Reilly picked her up at Happy Dreams Funeral Home."

"Is she all right?"

"She's definitely *not* all right, Clay. Take

her to a doctor and have those bites tested."

"I'll call for an appointment tomorrow. Tell Jillian to sit tight. I'm two minutes away."

Marco came over to me just as I put my phone away. "Problem solved," he said. "We'd better head over to the coffee shop. It's almost ten o'clock."

"What did you tell Jillian?"

"That if she was actually turning into a vampire, she'd have fangs. She checked her teeth in her compact and they looked fine. As I said, problem solved."

When it came to Jillian, nothing was ever that simple to resolve.

"My car is parked right around the corner," Marco said.

"The coffee shop is only four blocks up Lincoln. I can walk it."

"Are you sure you want to do that, Abby? Crutches can rub the underarm area raw."

"I'm wearing a coat. It won't be a problem. But I need to say good-bye to Jillian first."

"I'll wait up the street," Marco said, as I veered toward Reilly's car.

Jillian's head lay against the back of the seat and her eyes were closed. "Hey, Jill," I said. "Claymore is on his way to get you. Go home and get some sleep, okay? See the doctor tomorrow. And no more raw meat."

Jillian lifted her head to gaze at me through heavy-lidded eyes, then let her head fall against the seat again.

"Thanks for your help, Reilly," I said. "Jillian's husband will be here in two minutes."

"Before you go," he said quietly, "I know Marco's not happy that I'm investigating his friend, so would you pass along a message for me? Tell him I didn't ask for the assignment."

"Sure."

"One more thing. Is Marco running his own" — Reilly glanced around, as though he didn't want anyone to overhear him — "investigation?"

I pretended to be shocked. "Where would he find the time? He's leaving in less than two weeks, if you remember."

Reilly narrowed his eyes at me, but said nothing.

"Here comes Claymore now," I said, pointing to the silver Jaguar gliding up behind the patrol car. Then I navigated up the block to where Marco was waiting.

"What did Reilly want?" Marco asked, as we started up the sidewalk together.

"Ow, ow. He wanted you to know he didn't ask for the assignment."

"He didn't turn it down either."

"Could he have? Ow."

"He could have said he had a conflict of interest. They would've assigned someone else to the case."

"Oh. Ow."

"Crutches rubbing your underarm?"

"I've got a coat on. It's not possible. Ow."

"I told you we should have taken the car."

I gritted my teeth and finished the walk in pained silence.

Ahead was the Daily Grind, now back to its original name. It had been La Journalier Routine several weeks back. That was when the town square had undergone a frenzied renovation caused by the arrival of a local TV celebrity who brought with him the starlet he was dating, plus television reporters from all the major stations.

The hysteria created by their arrival had been compounded by a homicide. But once the case had been solved, with my help, normalcy had eventually returned, and shop names were slowly reverting to their familiar forms.

Inside the brightly painted coffee shop, with its mismatched wooden tables and chairs, soft lighting, and crowds of university students, we found a table in a corner at the back where my crutches would be out of the way. I glanced around for Jerry Trumble, but he hadn't arrived.

"What would you like?" Marco asked.

"Dark hot chocolate, please. Large." Nothing like a big dose of dark chocolate to take my mind off my burning armpits. I settled into a chair while Marco placed our orders.

"Trumble just walked in," he announced, returning with two steaming mugs.

"How do you want to handle his interview? Should I do what I do best?"

"We're going to need tact, Sunshine."

Well, that left me out. "Then I'll enjoy my cocoa and watch the show."

"Feel free to jump in at any time. Just be —"

"Tactful. Yes, Marco, I get it."

Jerry Trumble stopped at the counter to pick up a cup of coffee, then headed toward our table. He had on a black baseball cap, a blue satin baseball jacket, and black jeans. With his broad neck and shoulders and slim hips, he looked more like a professional athlete than a pharmacist.

"Thanks for meeting us," Marco said, indicating a chair.

Trumble sat down, unzipped his jacket, and lifted his cup to take a sip, studying us over the rim. Beneath the jacket, he had on

191

a blue-and-green-striped polo shirt that was snug enough to show off a trim waist.

"Do you work out?" I asked, then remembered I wasn't supposed to be nosy. I gave Marco a quick apologetic glance.

"Jujitsu," Trumble said. "Purple belt."

"Congratulations," I said, storing away that bit of information.

Trumble leaned back and folded his arms over his chest, a classically defensive posture. "Let's cut to the chase, okay? My babysitter leaves at ten thirty. Explain to me why you think I can help you."

Marco also leaned back, but left his hands on the table, and said with an easy confidence, "I've learned in my years of investigative work that people often know things they don't realize are important. I'd like the chance to see if what you know about the deceased might help us."

Trumble answered with a tilt of his head, as though to say, *Give it a whirl.*

"I'd like to ask you some questions to help us build a portrait of Willis's life," Marco said.

Trumble shrugged, as if it really didn't matter.

"I know this will be painful," Marco said, "but can you recount the events leading up to your wife's death?"

Trumble glanced casually around the room, then took a slow drink of coffee and placed the cardboard cup just so in front of him, turning it so he could see the logo on the front. I suspected he needed time to gather his thoughts.

"Dana and I had just returned from a trip to Australia. It was a long flight, and she'd complained of leg pain during the last several hours, but once we were home and she'd taken aspirin, she said it felt better. That evening her pain intensified, and nothing helped it. Her leg was swollen and hot to the touch, too, making me think she'd developed deep-vein thrombosis. I rushed her to the hospital, where she was diagnosed with DVT and admitted.

"Willis was the nursing supervisor on Dana's floor, and took control of my wife's case. I knew Willis as a regular customer at Dugan's and thought Dana was in good hands. But that night, Willis injected Dana with heparin in a dose ten times what the doctor had prescribed. The heparin caused her to have a massive stroke —"

Trumble broke off. He dropped his head and shaded his eyes, as though he didn't want us to see him tearing up. Marco picked up his coffee and took a swallow. I swirled the chocolate in my cup, mixing in what had settled on the bottom, giving him time to pull himself together.

When the pharmacist looked up again, he wore an expression of sadness, yet he was dry-eyed. "Dana died before I could get to the hospital. I didn't even get to say good-bye." He sighed heavily, as though still burdened by grief. Then I saw him turn his wrist to check the time, a gesture that struck me as being at odds with his emotions.

Immediately my antennae went up. Was his grief genuine or an act? Still, at the thought of him not being with his wife at the end, *my* eyes filled with tears. All I could think of was how I'd feel if I got a call saying that Marco had died in battle far away. "How do you deal with your grief?" I blurted.

"I have a seven-year-old boy to raise," Trumble said, as though reciting facts.

Between working at the pharmacy, jujitsu training, and late-night coffee stops, when did he find time to raise his son?

"Was it proven that Willis injected the heparin?" Marco asked.

"She was Dana's night nurse," Trumble said tersely. "She was responsible for Dana's care. The hospital was more than willing to settle. I'd call that an admission of guilt."

He was wrong. I knew from working as

Dave Hammond's law clerk that a more likely scenario was that the hospital had decided it was cheaper to settle the suit than to waste a lot of time and money fighting it in court. Surely Trumble's lawyer had advised him of that.

"Was it a fair settlement?" Marco asked.

"I received a lot of money," Trumble said. "It'll take care of my boy's schooling. All in all, I'd rather have my wife here."

"That's perfectly understandable," Marco said. "Were you satisfied with the outcome?"

"Satisfied? Are you kidding? My wife is dead. How do you satisfy that?"

Killing the nurse who attended her would be one way.

"I tried to make it a condition of the settlement that the hospital fire her," Trumble said. "Unfortunately that wasn't something they were willing to do. I'll never understand why they protected that woman. If Willis were my employee and had caused a customer's death, she'd be terminated. It wouldn't matter how good she was. The last thing I'd do would be to let her keep ministering to patients."

Maybe the last thing Jerry Trumble did for Willis was to make sure she *was* terminated.

"Here's the real irony," Trumble said.

195

"She not only kept her job at County, but she ended up with a better position at Parkview. How's that for justice?"

"Isn't it possible Willis earned that position?" Marco asked. "My research indicates she had an unblemished record until the tragedy involving your wife."

"Forget your research. Lori Willis did *not* get to be director of nursing on her merit."

"How do you know that?" Marco asked.

"After my wife —" The next word seemed to catch in his throat. Trumble shook his head and started again. "After I lost Dana, someone from the hospital came forward to tell me things about Willis."

"Such as?" Marco asked.

"That she wasn't opposed to elbowing coworkers aside or using blackmail to get where she wanted to go. So if you're looking for a person with a motive, start with her coworkers."

"Are you talking about a doctor? A nurse? An aide?" Marco asked.

Trumble toyed with his cup, as though deciding whether to cooperate. "A nurse from County introduced herself at Dana's funeral. She's the one who tipped me off about the heparin. I didn't know anything about the error until then."

"Why do you think she tipped you off?"

Marco asked.

Trumble shrugged. "She didn't say, but I got the feeling she wanted to see Willis go down in flames."

If Trumble was telling the truth, then somewhere out there was a tattletale nurse with her own ax to grind. She must have been delighted when Trumble filed the lawsuit, then ultimately disappointed when Lori Willis wasn't fired. And when Lori took a better position at Parkview, who knew what that could have sparked?

"Do you believe this nurse wanted you to sue?" Marco said.

"She *encouraged* me to sue." Trumble sat back, looking pleased with himself.

"Will you give us the nurse's name?" Marco asked.

Trumble finished his coffee, then crushed the cup in one hand. "I don't care to have it get out that I was your source."

"It won't go any further than the three of us sitting here," Marco said.

Trumble glanced at me. I caught myself before making the motion of zipping my lips and gave him a single nod instead.

He studied Marco for a long moment, as though debating. "Her name is Diane Rotunno."

It was one of the names Nikki had given me.

Marco took out a notepad and wrote it down. "I'd like to ask you a few personal questions now. They won't take long."

"No problem." Trumble crumpled the crushed cup into a wad. "I don't have anything to hide."

Whenever anyone said that, I always suspected the opposite was true.

"What's your educational background?"

"Degree in pharmacology from Purdue."

Marco wrote it down. "Any other medical training? Lab work, CPR course?"

Trumble scratched his chin. "Nope."

He seemed to have forgotten his job with a veterinary clinic.

"Did you learn how to draw blood in your pharmacology program?" Marco asked.

"No."

"Have you ever drawn blood?" Marco asked.

Trumble glanced at his watch, then looked at Marco as though distracted. "I'm going to have to cut this off now. But to answer your question, pharmacists don't draw blood."

Except that wasn't Marco's question.

That made two lies you told, Purple Belt.

Kind of odd for a man who claimed to have nothing to hide.

CHAPTER TWELVE

"My babysitter's due to leave shortly," Trumble said, pulling out his car keys.

"Just one more question and we're done," Marco said. "What were you doing Tuesday evening?"

The pharmacist smiled as though it amused him. "Ah! The alibi question. I figured you'd get around to that eventually. Let's see. Tuesday evening, I worked at Dugan's until ten o'clock. Then I stopped here for my coffee and went home to my son, same as every night. You can check with any clerk at Dugan's or the barista over there, or my babysitter."

"And Friday evening?"

"Same answer. My life is very routine, Mr. Salvare." I saw a slight smirk on his face as he stood up, as though he had put one over on us, so I made a quick decision to try to rattle his cage.

"I have a question," I said. "Were you and

your wife happily married?"

"Absolutely."

I raised one eyebrow to show my doubt. "Are you sure?"

Trumble's expression turned to stone. He sat down and leaned toward me, saying in a harsh whisper, "Yes, I'm sure! What the hell kind of thing is that to ask?"

"Okay, that'll do it," Marco said, standing. "Thanks for taking the time to talk to us."

Trumble gave me a dark look, then got up and strode toward the door, dropping his mashed cup in the trash can on his way out.

Marco sat down and put his notepad and pen away. "I'm curious. What was the point of that last question?"

"I was testing him."

Marco folded his arms and leaned back. "Did he pass?"

"No, for several reasons. I'll start with the smirk on his face after he presented his well-rehearsed alibi. And I don't know about you, but I wasn't totally convinced by his portrayal of a grief-stricken husband. As for his babysitter verifying his whereabouts, he said she leaves at ten thirty. If Lori was killed after that, who's going to verify his alibi? His sleeping son?"

"But he admitted he got a fair settlement.

Why would he go after her three years later?"

"That's where my question about his marriage comes into play."

"I'm not following you."

"For Trumble to kill Lori three years after the fact, she would've had to learn something recently that made her a threat. For instance, that he was selling drugs on the side or that he killed his wife. And since Lori was there when his wife died, I'd opt for the second reason."

"Whoa, Sunshine. That's a big leap. You just turned Dana's death into a homicide."

"Before you discount it, Marco, go back to when Dana was admitted to the hospital with a blood clot. What if Jerry had just learned that Dana was about to leave him? What if he was the kind of guy who couldn't let go? It'd be easy for a pharmacist to get his hands on heparin, and he'd know what size dose would do the trick."

"Your theory hinges on trouble in their marriage, and we don't have any proof of that."

"We can talk to Dana's friends and family and see what they say. Maybe Lori had suspected that Trumble murdered Dana, but just discovered a way to prove it. Maybe she was blackmailing him, and he was finally

202

tapped out. Killing her would solve his problem."

Marco pursed his lips, thinking. "We'd have to find out if it was proven that Lori injected the Heparin. I'm assuming there's some kind of sign-off a nurse has to do after administering a drug, but I don't really know how that works."

"If you think it's worth pursuing, I'll see if Nikki can find out."

"I think you're making it more complicated than it needs to be, but since you raised the question, I'll let you locate the right people to interview. Fair enough?"

"Fair enough. And something else I noticed about Trumble is that he's really ripped. He wouldn't have any trouble subduing a woman Lori's size. Then there were his lies about not having any other medical training and never learning how to draw blood. I'm surprised you didn't call him on them."

"I wanted to keep the first interview friendly. No doubt we'll have to question him again, and when we do, I'd like to catch him off guard. That's when I'll turn up the heat." Marco tapped the side of his head. "It's a good tactic. Store that away."

He stopped short of saying *for the future,* but it was implied. "I appreciate all these tips, Marco, but you don't need to keep reminding me to memorize them."

Marco reached for my hand and traced the lines in my palm with his thumb. "You don't get it, do you?"

"Apparently not, but I'd like to."

"Teaching you the tricks of the trade helps me, Abby. It makes me worry a little less to know there's a plan in place."

"That's thoughtful, Marco, but you don't have to make plans for me. I have Bloomers."

"Stores go under all the time. You can't count on that."

Nothing like giving me a new reason to worry.

"Listen to me, Sunshine," he said, gazing into my eyes. "I'd like to think that if something happened to me, you'd be fine."

He was upsetting me now. If something happened to him, there was no way on earth I'd be fine. I'd just make do. Why did he have to keep talking about it?

"I want you to apply for a PI license."

That came out of the blue. "Why?"

"It would be something for you to fall back on — just in case."

Just in case my flower shop folded? Just in case Marco died? Just in case the earth collided with the sun?

I pulled my hand away, blinking angry tears from my eyes. "Nothing is going to happen, so let's stop talking about it. I need to go home now. My ankle is throbbing."

Translation: I'm scared to death and it's your fault!

I had horrible dreams that night of being chased through a big house with a maze of connecting rooms, never seeing who was after me but knowing I was in mortal danger, and of losing my way home. I woke sobbing and was immediately pulled into Marco's strong arms.

"What is it, baby?" he said, his lips against my hair.

"Nightmares." I snuggled against him, my head on his chest, where I could hear the steady beat of his heart. "How many days do we have left?"

"Don't think about that. Today is Sunday, and we have the whole day to spend to-gether."

He was right, of course. It wasn't fair of me to rain melancholia on both of us and spoil the days we had left. I sat up and reached for a tissue. "What should we do today?"

"Here's a thought." Marco moved back against the padded headboard. The blanket was pulled up to his waist, and his six-pack abs rippled as he made himself comfortable. I practically devoured him with my eyes. He looked totally hot and handsome, even with his hair sticking up on top of his head like a little boy's.

"I read in the newspaper yesterday about a new exhibit on the ancient Egyptians at the Museum of Science and Industry. We could take the train in to Chicago after lunch, spend the afternoon there, have dinner downtown, and come home in the evening."

I loved anything having to do with ancient Egypt, but I was surprised that Marco did. He was always more interested in trucks and tanks and wars, typical guy stuff. "That's perfect."

"I thought you'd like that. And how about a mess of eggs Italian style for breakfast?"

My stomach growled at the thought. "I'll make coffee and toast to go with it."

I started to reach for the crutches, but Marco took my hand and pulled me back. "I just had another idea of something to do today."

"Okay. Tell me!"

He lifted the covers and patted the bed. "Slide in over here and I'll *show* you."

Show-and-tell — my favorite sport.

■ ■ ■ ■

Late that afternoon, I was sitting in a wheelchair in front of tiny three-dimensional models of the great pyramids of Giza, listening to a museum docent explain their significance to a small gathering, when Marco whispered in my ear that he had to make a phone call.

"I'll meet you back here," he said, then strode toward the door marked with an EXIT sign.

Marco still hadn't returned when the guide finished his spiel, so I wheeled out of the exhibit room to see what was keeping him. I glanced around the wide balcony, trying to spot his black leather jacket and blue jeans among the throng, then proceeded to the railing to look down on the main floor. I spotted him near the reception counter talking to a beefy security guard. Was there trouble?

I rode the elevator down, then propelled myself through the crowd as fast as I could go. But as I drew near, I saw Marco and the guard laughing as though they were old friends.

"So how long has it been since you've seen Vlad?" I heard Marco ask.

"Oh, man, I'll bet it's been three months," the guard said. "Maybe more."

Marco was questioning the guard about Vlad? Why had he told me he had to make a call?

Not wanting to be caught eavesdropping, I hid behind a thick column.

"No kidding," Marco said. "We'll have to remedy that. Maybe we can meet sometime at our old hangout — you, Danny, me, Vlad —"

"That place is long gone, bro," the guard said.

"Man, that's a shame," Marco said. "We had some good times there."

I felt a tap on my shoulder and looked around to see a girl of about six years of age holding a model of a sarcophagus in one hand and wiping her nose on the back of the other.

"Want to see my casket?" she asked loudly, thrusting the toy at me.

"No, thank you," I whispered, "and it's a sarcophagus, not a casket. Now go find your mommy before you get lost."

"Why are you whispering?" she asked.

I held my index finger to my lips to warn her to be quiet. "I'm listening to someone."

She wiped her dripping nose again, this

208

time on her sleeve. "Who are you listening to?"

Clearly she didn't understand the finger-to-lip gesture because her voice was just as loud as before. "My boyfriend," I whispered, deciding not to use *fiancé* in case that prompted more questions.

"You have a boyfriend?" she asked at a decibel high enough to make ears bleed. She wrinkled up her stubby face. "You're too old to have a boyfriend."

And you're too old to use your sleeve for a tissue.

She sneezed, spraying mucus all over herself and catching me in the process.

"Go find your mommy *now*," I snapped, pointing in the opposite direction. "It's not safe to talk to strangers."

"Are you a stranger?" she asked, using her sleeve again. "Are you going to hurt me?"

A woman scuttled up and grabbed the girl's hand. "What are you doing to my child?" she screeched, proving where the girl had inherited her lungs.

I wheeled backward, feeling my face heat up as people turned to see what was happening. "I didn't do anything except tell her to go find you."

But the damage was done. The security guard was headed straight for me. And with

209

him came Marco, whose eyes were so wide they nearly met in the middle.

The guard stepped between Screeching Mom and me. "What's the problem?"

"This woman was bothering my child!" the mother charged, jabbing her finger at me.

What? "Excuse me? Your child was bothering me."

Marco said something to the guard, who glanced down at me in surprise. Then he said to the irate woman, "Would you come with me, please?"

"Why me?" the woman shrieked, as the guard led her and the child away. "She's a perv."

The guard glanced at Marco over his shoulder and touched his hand to his forehead, as though saluting. Marco returned the gesture, then took control of the chair and pushed me away from the gawkers. "Had your fill of ancient Egypt?"

"Make that an emphatic yes. Did you get your phone call made?"

"I'll explain about that after you explain why you were hiding behind the column." He stopped in front of the coat-check counter and handed the attendant a plastic ticket.

"I wasn't hiding. I didn't want to intrude

on your conversation. Who was the guard?"

"Ed Quinn, an army buddy." Marco took my coat from the man, then helped me put it on and get balanced on the Evil Ones. "Let's go have dinner. We can talk about it in the cab on the way to the restaurant. What are you in the mood for?"

"Italian sounds good."

"I know just the place," he said, shepherding me through the glass doors.

We found a taxi van waiting at the stand and climbed in. Marco gave the cabbie the name of the restaurant as we settled onto the middle bench, the crutches on the seat behind us.

"Okay, Buttercup, tell me again why you weren't hiding behind the column."

"Since you'd said you had to make a phone call, I assumed you didn't want me to know you were talking to your army buddy about Vlad."

"I did make a phone call. To Rafe. Then I went to find Ed, or Eddy Q.T., as he was known back then."

"What does the *Q.T.* stand for?"

"Ed could sneak up on anyone without being heard. He was always on the Q.T."

"So you, Ed, and Vlad were in the same unit together?"

"Yep."

Hmm. Things were starting to add up. "Did you suggest coming into Chicago so you could talk to Ed about Vlad?"

Marco put his arm around me. "My top priority was to spend the day with you, sweetheart. I just thought that I could kill two birds . . . Wait. That didn't come out right."

"Why didn't you just call Ed from home?"

"I didn't have his new phone number. Look! There's the Trump Tower. That's where the old *Sun Times* building used to be."

Diverting my attention. How original. "Marco, did Vlad use Ed as his alibi when he told you he took the train to Chicago on Friday?"

Marco paused to scratch his ear, the "reluctant to answer" signal. "Yes."

"And Ed said he hadn't seen Vlad for months."

"Yes."

"Then Vlad lied."

"Vlad told me he took the train in to see Ed. He didn't say he *saw* Ed."

"You're splitting hairs."

"Vlad wouldn't lie to me unless he had a good reason."

"Are you going to ask him the reason?"

"I'll mention that I ran into Ed and let

212

Vlad take it from there."

We had a *delicioso* meal at Volare, an Italian restaurant in the Streeterville area of Chicago, then took a cab to the train station and rode home, pulling into the Dune Park station at nine o'clock that night. Back at the apartment, I found Nikki wrapped in a green and purple comforter, sacked out on the sofa, watching the end of *Casablanca* with a pile of wadded tissues on the floor below her.

"Hey, guys," she said, casting a brief glance toward us.

"Where's Greg?" I asked, hopping over to a chair as Marco hung up my coat.

"Commercial coming up in a second," she warned, her eyes glued to the television.

She'd only seen the movie a dozen times. Simon crawled out from under the sofa and came over to rub against my leg. "Why was Simon hiding?" I asked Nikki.

"He hates to see me cry," she said, then motioned for me to be quiet.

Simon spotted Marco coming down the hallway and galloped out to greet him.

"Okay, commercial break. Now I can talk," Nikki said. "Greg isn't here because he had to leave early to prepare for a big trial that starts tomorrow. How was the exhibit?"

"Fascinating. Did you know a pharaoh would start his pyramid as soon as he became the ruler so it would be finished by the time he died? And that a pharaoh's son was forbidden to build a pyramid taller than his father's? But the sons would get around that by building —"

"Stop," Nikki said, as the movie resumed. "The ending is coming up next."

I went into the hallway, where Marco was crouched on the floor giving Simon a belly rub. Seeing me, Marco got to his feet. "I'm going to head down to the bar, Sunshine. Rafe is going to meet me there so I can show him a few things to do tomorrow while I'm out. Don't forget to ask Nikki about the procedure for administering drugs."

"Will I see you later?"

"I hope so." He kissed me, ruffled the fur on Simon's head, then let himself out of the apartment.

I returned to the living room to find Nikki whispering the lines with the actors. She blew her nose and sighed. "Is that a great love story or what?" She scooped up her pile of tissues and headed for the bathroom, calling, "What did Marco want you to ask me about?"

"We need to know if there's a certain procedure that hospital nurses have to follow when they administer a drug to a patient."

"Is this for the Willis case?" she asked.

"What else?"

"I can answer that for you." She came back into the room and stretched out on the sofa, pulling the comforter around her. Simon jumped up and rubbed his nose against her chin, then kneaded the comforter into submission, flopped down, and began to wash his face.

"The procedure is very simple," Nikki said, scratching the cat behind the ears. "Anytime a nurse administers a drug, she records the time and dosage on the patient's medication sheet. That way, the next shift, as well as the patient's doctor, always knows what was given."

"So there would be a medication sheet for the patient that Lori Willis is blamed for killing."

"There should be. It was probably an exhibit for the lawsuit."

"So if I understand the procedure," I said, "a nurse, or anyone with access to the drug, could accidentally give an incorrect dose, mark down the normal dose, and no one would be the wiser unless the patient had a serious reaction."

"Right. The system relies on the competency of the nursing staff. I've also heard about cases where a nurse forgets to mark the medication sheet, and then there's a shift change, and the next nurse assumes the dose was missed and administers more."

"Have you ever heard about a case where someone purposely gave the wrong dose?"

Nikki gave me a puzzled look. "Are you saying Lori wanted the patient to die?"

"In this case, maybe the patient's husband did."

Nikki's mouth dropped open. "Do you have any reason to suspect him?"

"Too soon to tell. But I got bad vibes when we were talking to him yesterday. He's a pharmacist at Dugan's."

"A pharmacist? Definitely check him out. Talk to his wife's friends. They'll know what kind of husband he was. By the way, I asked around as to whether Lori was seeing anyone, but no one knew. All they said was that she loved to gamble at the casino boat."

"And one more thing." Nikki got up and went to the answering machine on the table beneath our picture window. "Tara left a message for you."

She hit the PLAY button: "Aunt Abby, you need to go to that awful Web site — HOW

216

TO KILL A VAMPIRE.COM — and scroll down to the bottom to the photos. They're bad!"

Nikki brought my laptop to me, then watched over my shoulder as I typed in the URL. When the Web site opened, I scrolled down until a photo appeared. It was a view through a gap in drapes hanging at a window, and showed what looked like half of an oak casket sitting in the middle of the room. It had a shiny brass handle at the end, brass embellishments at the corners, and an arched lid. Beyond it, I could see the arm of a chair or sofa. Beneath the photo was a caption that read: THIS IS WHERE THE VAMPIRE SLEEPS.

"Could that have been taken at Vlad's apartment?" Nikki asked.

"I don't know. I've never been inside. I have a feeling, though, that this was staged."

I scrolled down farther to find a grainy black-and-white photo of a parking lot filled with cars, with the Calumet Casino River Boat in the background. The caption below that photo read: WHO IS THE VAMPIRE AFTER NOW?

In the photo was a tall figure in a black trench coat walking among the cars. He'd been caught in profile and had glowing white skin and black hair combed away from his forehead.

"Can you read the time stamp on the second photo?" I asked.

Nikki clicked the magnifying glass icon. "It's dated last Wednesday night. Didn't you tell me Vlad worked that night?"

I felt my stomach twist. "No, Nikki. He was off that night."

CHAPTER THIRTEEN

I phoned Marco at the bar and told him about the photos, but he sounded busy, so I didn't keep him on the line. Instead, I did an Internet search on Trumble's deceased wife, Dana, and discovered that her My-Space page was still up. Her profile didn't reveal any personal information, but she'd posted pictures of herself with Jerry and her son, pictures of herself with two girlfriends, and several pictures of just her little boy.

Fortunately Dana had labeled her photos, so I was able to find her friends' pages and learn that they lived in New Chapel. I spent an hour trying to track down phone numbers, and in the end sent friend requests to them, with a message saying I wanted to do something in Dana's memory and thought they might have ideas. I kept it vague and, I hoped, nonthreatening.

By the time I crawled into bed, I still hadn't heard from Marco, and when I woke in the morning, I was alone. Assuming he hadn't forgotten about driving me to work, I showered, dressed, and played hide-and-seek with Simon. I skipped breakfast because on Mondays Lottie made her egg-skillet breakfast, a tradition she'd started when she owned Bloomers.

At seven forty-five I had already made my way down to the front door to wait when Marco pulled up. I watched through the glass pane as he got out of the car. He looked so masculine in his black jacket and slim jeans, his dark hair shining in the sunlight, that my heart swelled with love. Our last days together were slipping away too fast.

Marco caught sight of me and pushed away from the car, striding up to the door to hold it open. "Morning, Beautiful."

I stopped to give him a kiss. "Good morning yourself, Salvare. I missed you."

"Missed you, too, babe." He opened the car door and tossed the Evil Ones in the backseat. "But I had a productive evening. I'll tell you about it on the way to Bloomers."

"I had a productive evening, too," I said as he started the engine. "I found out what the hospital's procedure is for administering drugs, and you wouldn't believe how easy it would be for someone with the know-how to give a patient a lethal dose and make it look like the fault of the last nurse to administer it."

"You're referring to Trumble? Okay, explain the procedure for me."

I gave him Nikki's information, then waited as he mulled over my theory.

"I can't deny that it's possible," Marco said, "but I've learned that it's best to start with the most logical explanation, which is that if Trumble killed Willis, he did so because of her error. Always test the most logical first."

At least he hadn't told me to store it away for the future. "I also found a MySpace page for Dana Trumble and found two of her friends right here in New Chapel. I sent friend requests as a way to make contact in case we want to talk to them."

"Good idea. I'll let you handle that."

"Thanks. So tell me about your evening."

"Well, surprise of surprises, Rafe is actually hanging in there. He sat down with me last night to learn how to keep track of inventory and figure out how much to charge in order to see a profit. I was afraid it was way over his head, but he didn't lose patience or give up in frustration. He seems genuinely eager to learn the business. I was proud of him."

"That's fantastic, Marco. Rafe's finally starting to mature. I think being here with you is the best thing for him. I hope you complimented him."

"I did. He said he wants to keep up the lessons."

And there went our evenings together.

Marco tweaked my chin. "Don't worry. We're going to meet *before* the bar opens."

"I wasn't worried."

"Buttercup, I can read your face like a book."

I swiveled toward him. "Really? What is my face saying now?"

Marco waited until we reached a STOP sign, then glanced at me before driving again. "It's saying" — here he switched to a falsetto voice — " 'How did I ever get so lucky in finding the man of my dreams?' "

He glanced at me again. "Now it's saying, 'How should I show that man how much I missed him last night?' "

"You're incorrigible."

"I try. And what's more, I talked to Vlad last night about his trip to Chicago."

"Seriously?"

"He did go into Chicago to see Ed, not knowing that Ed was off that day, and also not in possession of Ed's new phone number. So Vlad saw the exhibits, had lunch at a nearby restaurant, and rode the train back home late in the afternoon. He said I could call Ed and check with him to verify that he was off work that day."

"Are you going to call Ed?"

"I don't feel the need." Marco glanced at me. "I will if you want me to."

"If you're okay with it, Marco, I am, too."

Okay, am not. Didn't Marco realize that if Ed was off that day, he wouldn't know whether Vlad was telling the truth? But Marco trusted Vlad, and if I kept tearing down Vlad's explanations, it might seem as though I didn't trust Marco.

"What did you think of the photos posted on the HOW TO KILL A VAMPIRE Web site?" I asked.

"They're bogus. Vlad said he's never been to the casino boat. Whoever put up that site faked the photo to cast suspicion on him. And a casket in the living room? That's just stupid."

I didn't want to point out the obvious — once again we had only Vlad's word on it. But it seemed that was going to have to be good enough.

"The service provider won't give me the Web site owner's information, so I put in a call to a computer-savvy friend of mine and asked him to find out who's behind it."

"Do you think the person who put up the site is Lori's killer?"

"It's possible they're linked. It's also possible that someone's taking advantage of the murder to torment Vlad."

Marco simply refused to consider the third option — that Vlad *was* the killer.

"I'm going to meet with the nurse who was fired over her affair with Dr. Holloway at a quarter past nine this morning," Marco said.

"Darn! I wish I could be there."

"Your wish is my command. We're meeting at Bloomers."

"Thank you! Except how do I explain this meeting to Grace and Lottie?"

"If they ask, we're working on a new case and you don't have any of the particulars."

"But I told them you weren't taking any new cases."

"You'll think of something, Gabriella. By the way, I tried to get you off the hook for that interview with Holloway, but he wouldn't consent to see me. All it took was one mention of Willis's name and that was the end of our conversation."

"I don't mind being on the hook."

"I don't know, Abby. The idea of you pretending to be French doesn't sit well with me."

"You're adorable when you're in caveman mode. Don't worry. I can handle it. You know how I love a challenge."

Marco pulled up to the stoplight and leaned over for a kiss. "So you missed me last night?"

A horn honked behind us. I kissed him quickly. "Marco, you have the green light."

The horn sounded again, more urgently this time. "Yeah, yeah, I see the light," Marco said to the unknown driver as we pulled away. After a third and much longer honk, Marco glanced in the rearview mirror, then put on his turn signal and looked for a place to pull over.

"What's wrong?" I asked, swiveling for a look.

"I don't know, but I think we should find out. It's your mom."

"Oh, no. Something must have happened," I said as we parked the car. "Hurry, Marco, go see!"

"Too late. Here she comes. Your side."

I rolled down my window as my mom came briskly up to the car. Not one strand of her bobbed honey brown hair was out of place, thanks to a heavy coating of hair spray. She had on a tan wool coat and comfortable brown flats — her teacher

225

shoes, as she called them. And she was smiling. Clearly, it wasn't an emergency.

"I'm so glad I spotted you," she said breathlessly, leaning through the window to give me a hug. "Saves me from having to lug the box to your shop myself."

"What box?"

"Hi, Marco. How are you?"

"Just fine, Mrs. Knight."

"And your mom? I haven't spoken to her in a while."

"She's fine, too," Marco said.

"What box?" I asked again.

"How is your ankle?" she asked me. "When do you see the doctor?"

"Ankle is fine. I see the doctor this Wednesday. What box?"

Mom checked her watch and frowned. "I'd better hurry. School will be starting soon. Marco, come with me, please."

Marco hopped out of the car to follow.

"It's my new piece of art," Mom said moments later, as Marco slid a large cardboard box onto the rear seat. "You'll be able to set it up this morning instead of waiting for me to bring it after school."

Yippee?

She shut the back door and leaned in the front window to kiss my cheek. "There you go, honey. Be careful when you unload it.

It's fragile. I'll see you later." And away she went.

"What's inside?" Marco asked, glancing at the box through the rearview mirror.

"Whatever it is, it's not going to bite you," I said, laughing at his expression. I cut the laugh short when I heard something shift inside the box. Maybe I'd spoken too soon.

"What's in the box?" Lottie asked, after Marco had deposited both me and Mom's box inside Bloomers.

"My mom's latest art project," I said. "Do you want to open it now or wait until after breakfast?"

"Eggs are all ready," Lottie said. "You decide."

Within minutes the three of us were seated at the narrow strip of counter in the galley kitchen at the far back of the shop, chowing down on Lottie's eggs. She'd used organic brown eggs, asparagus tips, feta cheese, mushrooms, and chopped tomato, cooking them lightly in olive oil, with sea salt and black pepper added at the end.

"Delicious," I said, shoveling in a large forkful. I stopped for a swallow of Grace's coffee, made with a touch of cinnamon and hazelnut today, then started off our morning meeting by announcing that Marco and

227

I were going to see new clients in the parlor later that morning.

Next, Lottie reported on shipments due in, and Grace filled us in on her hunt to find an automatic door opener for under five hundred dollars. So far, she hadn't had any luck.

"With all the business we've had lately," Lottie said, "I think we should just bite the bullet and get one ordered at the best price. They're not going to get any cheaper."

"You're right," I said. "Let's do it. Grace, would you order one from a local retailer?"

"I know just the fellow. Perhaps I can persuade him to come down a bit more, too."

I glanced at my watch. We were fast approaching nine o'clock. It was time to deal with the box. After taking a few deep breaths, we headed into the parlor to unpack it and see what wondrous new objet d'art Mom had thrust upon us.

"Looks like the spines of an umbrella," Lottie said, as I held up the first part out of the container. It consisted of eight curved wire spines painted a shiny bright red, joined at the top and fanning out in a circle.

"With a brass ring on top," Grace pointed out. "Perhaps it's meant to be a chandelier."

Lottie removed the next layer of newspaper and found eight brass hooks. She hung them from loops at the ends of the eight curved wires.

"It looks like a mobile," I said.

"A mobile?" Grace asked, pronouncing it "mo-*bile*." "For above a child's bed?"

"No, a cell phone," Lottie said, rolling her eyes. "Of course a child's mobile."

"Someone is cross today," Grace said to me under her breath.

"If you'd had to listen to four boys rehearsing their brass instruments for their band competition till midnight," Lottie retorted, "you'd be cross, too."

"I'm sure you're absolutely right, love," Grace said. "However, keep in mind the words of Marcel Proust." She cleared her throat and took hold of the edges of her lavender cardigan sweater. " 'Let us be grateful to people who make us happy; they are the charming gardeners who make our souls blossom.' "

Lottie stared at her. "Did you miss the part about them rehearsing till midnight? The only thing blossoming in my house was a big fat pounding headache."

"Hello," I said to them. "My arm is going numb. Could you see what else is in the box, please?"

Lottie looked at Grace and they both said,

"Someone is cross."

Lottie pulled out a bundle of newspaper and unwrapped it. We gasped in horror.

"It's a bat!" Grace said.

She held up a brown bat made out of clay, with its wings partially unfolded, its beady black eyes staring straight ahead, as though focused on snatching up its next bug, and its mouth open, revealing tiny pointed fangs. To think I'd told Marco it wouldn't bite.

Lottie unwrapped another bat. This one was cobalt blue, its wings folded against its chest, its eyes closed.

We unwrapped six more, all in different colors: neon yellow, bright orange, fuchsia, lime green, bright red, and royal purple. Each was in a different position and half of them displayed teeth. We fastened the critters to the wires, and then I held the object up, trying to figure out the theme.

"I've got it. It's my mom's version of the Batmobile."

Lottie stood with her hand over her mouth. Grace whispered something that might have been a prayer.

"What are we going to do with it?" Grace asked.

"I'm telling you right now," Lottie said, "no mother is gonna hang that thing above her kid's crib. The poor child would never recover from the nightmares."

"I promised Mom I'd put it in a prominent place," I said sheepishly.

Both women gazed at the mobile as though waiting for it to turn into something else. Or fly away. "Could we hang it in a corner?" Grace asked.

"As long as it's not near the window," Lottie said. "We'll scare away customers."

We trooped into the shop to take a good look around. No one said anything for several moments, then I said, "I'll put it in the workroom until we find a place for it."

"I'll take it there for you," Lottie said, and swept it off my lap and through the curtain.

As soon as we opened the shop, the parlor filled with our regular customers coming in for their morning java fix and gossip exchange, keeping Grace busy serving coffee, tea, and freshly baked plum scones. I'd been a little concerned that she might overhear my meeting with Marco and our interviewee, but as I took a seat at a back table, I realized the loud buzz of conversation would cover anything she might pick up, if she even had a chance to listen.

At ten minutes after nine, a strikingly attractive young woman walked in with Marco, chatting animatedly. She had pale blond hair that fell in loose curls around her shoulders, lively, sparkling eyes, and a figure that would turn any male head. She was wearing a beige belted jacket over green nurse scrubs and rubber-soled tan shoes.

Marco spotted me and ushered her into the room where I waited in the wheelchair.

"Courtney Anne O'Keefe," Marco said, "this is my fi— partner, Abby Knight."

If the word *fi-partner* puzzled her, Courtney Anne didn't show it, but she did cast a discreet glance at my bandaged foot. She held out her hand. "It's nice to meet you, Abby."

"Same here." I lifted my right foot. "In case you're wondering, I sprained my ankle."

"I'm sorry. Sprains can be extremely painful."

"Would you like to sit down? We have plum scones today" — I pointed out the basket in the middle of the table — "and gourmet coffee or tea, whichever you'd like."

"Coffee, please." She thanked Marco as he pulled out a chair for her. She sat and unbuttoned her belted jacket as she glanced around. "I love your flower shop. It's so pretty and cheerful."

"Thank you. Are you on your way to work?"

"I work the afternoon shift," she said, "but I wanted to do some shopping while I was in town. I knew I wouldn't have time to go back home and change, then make that long drive to Chicago. That is one killer commute."

Grace bustled up with a coffeepot in one hand, a teapot in the other. "Three coffees," I told her.

Marco, seated across from me, waited for Grace to leave before he took out his notepad and pen. "Thanks for coming in on such short notice. As I explained on the phone, we're looking for information on Lori Willis to help with our investigation."

"I'm not a suspect, am I?" Courtney Anne asked, a flicker of fear in her eyes. I figured her for about my age, but she seemed much younger.

"We're just hoping you'll be able to point us in one direction or another," Marco said.

Good answer. I'd have to note that for the fut— Oh, rats! Now I was doing it.

"Have you been contacted by the New Chapel police department?" Marco asked.

She shook her head, her soft curls swaying with the motion. "No."

"Would you tell us what led to your being

fired from County Hospital?" Marco asked.

Her cheeks flushed a soft pink. "It's a little embarrassing. I was a new hire at County, assigned to the floor where Nurse Willis was supervisor. I followed her orders. I was kind to our patients. I never missed work." She shrugged. "But for some reason she took a dislike to me."

I was betting the reason was jealousy. Judging by Lori's photo, she was trying to look like what Courtney Anne already was — young and beautiful.

Courtney Anne held up her index finger, signaling a break. "Sorry. I have to try this yummy-looking scone."

"Take your time," Marco said.

She chewed and swallowed a bite, then sighed. "Wow. It's wonderful! I'm sorry. I couldn't resist. Anyway, one day Dr. Holloway introduced himself to me in the cafeteria and asked if he could join me. As if I would mind! A handsome, sophisticated cardiovascular surgeon? Be still, my heart!"

If anyone would know how to pluck heartstrings, it would be a cardiovascular surgeon.

"We talked for hours, and there was instant chemistry," she said. "I found myself telling him all about my life, even about how Nurse Willis was treating me."

"I don't mean to interrupt," Marco said, "but what was Dr. Holloway's reaction to that?"

"He was completely understanding. He said he'd talk to her if I wanted him to, but I told him I'd rather he not because it might cause more problems. Anyway, after that, things just sort of happened. One day we're having lunch in the cafeteria. The next we're meeting in a supply closet." She blushed a deep red. "That sounds terrible, but it's true. We were madly in love.

"Then one day Nurse Willis walked in on us." Courtney Anne brushed crumbs off the table. "It was terrible. I've never seen anyone get so angry, and not just at me. At Dr. Holloway, too. Nurse Willis called us vile names and said I was suspended until further notice, then stormed out of the closet."

"What did Dr. Holloway say about it?" Marco asked.

"He said not to worry. That Nurse Willis suspended me because she was in love with him and couldn't stand it that we were together. He promised to talk to her and said that everything would be fine. Then she called me at home the next day and fired me.

"I cried for an entire day. I thought Dr.

Holloway had let me down, but then I heard what she did to him . . . Getting an official reprimand is devastating to a doctor's career. At least I found a new position within two weeks, but he's had to live with his humiliation. And then his wife dragged him through the courts . . . It was a horrible mess."

"Did you have any contact with Nurse Willis after you left County?"

She shook her head.

"Have you seen Dr. Holloway since you left?" I asked.

"Only once, right after I was fired," she said with a sad sigh. "We met at a coffee shop. I thought maybe he'd contact me after his divorce was final, but I haven't heard a word. I guess he's moved on."

Many times, no doubt.

"At the coffee shop," Marco said, "did Dr. Holloway express any feelings about Nurse Willis's actions?"

At that, Courtney Anne balked. "Look, I don't remember it all that well, and I really don't want you to think poorly of Dr. Holloway. He's a good guy."

A good guy who cheated on his wife and compromised a young nurse's career?

"What you tell us will not cause an innocent party to become a target," Marco

236

told her. "We have several strong suspects already. We just don't want to leave any stone unturned."

She gave Marco a grateful smile, as if he was the most understanding man on earth. "Thank you. It was a horrible time in my life. I've tried to put it behind me, but Nurse Willis's death brought a lot of it back."

"Tell us what you remember about your last meeting," Marco said.

Courtney Anne stared into the distance, as if trying to recall their conversation. "He was very concerned about me and promised to contact someone he knew to help me get a new nursing position. That's how I got my job, as a matter of fact. I asked him how he was coping with having to work with Nurse Willis every day — but I shouldn't have brought it up. He got ugly about it. I'd never seen him be anything but charming, so it was rather unsettling to hear —"

Her face drained of color. She reached for her cup and held it to her mouth with trembling hands.

"What is it?" Marco asked.

"Maybe Dr. Holloway wasn't such a good guy after all."

CHAPTER FOURTEEN

Marco gave me a look that said, *This is your department.* So I put my hand on Courtney Anne's shoulder. "I know this is rough. You probably think you're betraying his friendship, but trust me, you'll feel better if you get it off your chest."

She nodded, blinking back tears. "Dr. Holloway said he told Nurse Willis she was insane if she thought he'd go for a dog like her, and if she ever came near him again, there'd be some bloodletting." She put her hands over her mouth, as though she couldn't believe she'd told us.

"Did Holloway explain what he meant by that?" I asked.

"I'm sure he was just blowing off steam." She glanced at us, seeking reassurance.

"Guys talk tough when they're angry," I said.

"I knew him intimately, you know?" she said. "I would have sensed something if he was a . . ." She let her sentence die, unwilling to utter the word *murderer.*

Not to burst her happy bubble, but Marco had once told me that anyone was capable of murder under the right circumstances. But I said I agreed with her, and that seemed to ease her mind.

I knew Marco hated snap judgments, but I was ready to cross Courtney Anne off our list. For his sake I would withhold my opinion until we'd interviewed all of our suspects.

"I have just a few more questions," Marco said. "At your present job, do you change shifts or are you always on the afternoon shift?"

"I'm permanently on afternoons."

He jotted down her answer. "What time do you start and end?"

"I start at three o'clock, end at midnight. Then I have to commute home."

"Do you drive, carpool, or take the train?"

"I usually take the train, but today I'm driving in."

"How did you get to work last week?"

"I took the train."

"Do you ever go to the casino boat at the Little Calumet River?"

She shook her head. "I don't have money to waste on gambling."

"Were you seeing anyone at the time of your affair with Dr. Holloway?"

"No. I was between boyfriends."

"Last question," Marco said. "Is there someone I can contact at the hospital who can verify your employment information and work schedule?"

Courtney Anne gave Marco the information, then reached for another scone. "These are heavenly. I'm going to have to buy some to take with me to the hospital. The other nurses will go crazy over them."

"I'll have a dozen packed up for you," I said. "On the house."

"Thank you! You're so sweet." She leaned over to give me a hug, then sat back and smiled at Marco. "You're right. Abby *is* gorgeous."

Snap! Not guilty by reason of flattery.

After Courtney Anne left, Marco and I sat at the table to reconnoiter and eat scones. The second part was my idea. After watching Courtney Anne devour hers, I was so ready.

"What did she mean when she said you were right about me being gorgeous?" I asked between bites.

"I met her coming into Bloomers, so I introduced myself and said you were waiting in the parlor. I told her to look for the most gorgeous woman in the room."

What could I say to that? "Thank you."

He shrugged as though it was no big deal. Little did he realize how much that meant to a girl who'd never even been asked to a high school dance. "What do you think about Courtney Anne?" Marco asked, breaking off a chunk of my scone and popping it in his mouth.

"I don't think she killed Lori Willis," I said, placing a fresh scone in front of him, "and yes, that's a snap judgment, but I didn't get any negative vibes from her. I'm pretty sure she still has feelings for Dr. Holloway, but I didn't sense any malicious intent toward Lori. It felt like she was able to move past that part of her life."

Marco sat back, tapping his pen on the table as he studied his notes. "What are your thoughts about Lori Willis now?"

"Lori was definitely jealous over Courtney Anne's affair with Holloway, and when she found them together, she decided to punish them."

"So far I agree with you one hundred percent. And Holloway?"

I loved it when we were on the same page. "Your typical egotistical surgeon who thinks he's God's gift to the earth. And I say that as someone with brothers who are surgeons. That's why I've made it my duty to keep them humble."

Although flunking out of law school wasn't the method I would have preferred.

"I also think Holloway had plenty of motive. Courtney Anne might have been right about him just blowing off steam, but it was a bit too coincidental that he'd used the term *bloodletting*."

"There's no sense speculating about Holloway's guilt until we've had a chance to interview him. You see him tomorrow, right?"

"Yep. Two p.m."

"Are you okay going to that appointment alone? I'll be happy to go with you."

I toyed with the top button of my shirt. "I can't very well work my feminine wiles on him with you there, can I?"

Marco leaned toward me until we were practically nose to nose. "If he lays a hand on you —"

Ever my hero, ready to jump to my defense.

"— belt him with your crutch." With a little grin, he got up. "I'll be back at noon for that trip to the casino boat."

"Good meeting?" Lottie asked, when I

wheeled into the shop. She was standing behind the cash counter, filling out a phone order form. The coffee parlor had pretty much emptied out.

"That young nurse was quite lovely," Grace said, coming out of the parlor.

They both smiled at me, hoping I'd share a tidbit of information with them. They didn't know how much I wished I could. I missed our lively discussions. Instead, I pointed toward the curtain. "I'll be in the back working on orders until Marco picks me up at noon."

I rolled through the curtain and turned to find Grace behind me. "Abby, love, I believe I've found a place to hang your mum's mobile."

"Where?"

"Behind the new dieffenbachia."

"Behind it? Won't it be obvious to my mom that we're hiding it?"

"Not if I shift the tree over a few feet before it's time for Mum to arrive."

"That'll work."

Grace started toward the curtain, then paused and turned back. "You do know that bloodletting could be considered exsanguinating, don't you?"

Damn Grace's supersonic hearing! "Yes, I do. But thank you anyway."

When I didn't say anything more, she said, "Well, then, I'll just go hang that bat mobile."

Said Batwoman to Girl Blunder.

I plucked an order from the spindle. It was for a table centerpiece for a thirty-fifth wedding anniversary celebration, so I pulled out my handy anniversary guide, which told me my theme colors should be in tones of coral and jade. The closest I had to true coral was orange-red roses. After that, I'd have to make do with orange lilies, Gerberas, and carnations, so I pulled a mix of all four, plus green carnations. For a base, I eyed the collection of containers stacked on top of the cabinets and realized I couldn't reach any of them.

Frustrated, I decided to find a way. I wheeled over to the counter along the back wall, dragging a wooden stool with me, and then, balancing on my good foot, I climbed onto the stool, got onto the counter on my knees, and carefully raised myself up. Once I felt balanced, I stretched my hand as high as I could reach . . . only to miss the mark by several inches.

"Abby, good Lord!" Lottie exclaimed, rushing over. "Why didn't you call me?"

I slumped down onto the counter. "I thought I could do it."

"You can't do everything you used to do, sweetie," she said, helping me down.

"I hate being so dependent."

"I'm sure you do, but sometimes you've just got to accept your limitations. Now tell me which vase you want."

Accepting limitations was a skill I had never mastered. Five minutes later, however, I was back at the worktable, my supplies laid out in front of me, ready to bury myself quite contentedly in my new design. I started with a round glass vase, then fastened a flat glass plate onto the top so that it looked like a cake platter. I placed my wet foam in the center of the plate and used orange-colored sisal to cover the foam and add texture.

Since I wanted some of the floral stems to arc downward, I used long, curving lime twigs, then added pale green eucalyptus and pieces of Nandina domestica. For my base, I used Hedera colchica "Sulphur Heart," a leaf that mixed light and dark green, reminding me of the veins in jade. Then I began to arrange my blossoms — pale green "prado" carnations, orange-red roses, orange lilies, pale orange carnations, and then five orange Gerberas of differing heights standing upright in the center. I added the last stem, then turned it in a circle to view it from all sides. Perfect!

Grace came through the curtain with sticky notes lined up in a row on her sweater sleeve. "Oh, how absolutely lovely, Abby! Bravo, dear. Well-done. Your clients will adore it."

"Thanks, Grace."

" 'A thing of beauty is a joy forever.' "

I'd created a thing of beauty. Grace never disappointed me.

"That was Keats, in case you're curious."

Make that Keats who hadn't disappointed me. Of course, I always felt on top of my game when working with flowers. Who would have guessed that a redheaded, freckle-faced tomboy would fall in love with designing floral arrangements?

Grace plucked the first sticky note off her sleeve. "The automatic door opener will be installed this coming Friday, and I was able to get the price dropped another fifty dollars."

"Bravo yourself, Grace."

"Also," she said, removing another square from her sweater, "the bats are hanging safely behind the dieffenbachia." The third note she read silently, then sighed as she said, "Jillian asks that you call her as soon as possible because Claymore is trying to kill her."

He probably wasn't the only one.

"You don't think Claymore would actually . . ." She made a slashing motion across her neck.

"No."

Grace breathed a sigh of relief. "I didn't think so."

I finished wrapping the arrangement and stowed it in the cooler before I returned Jillian's call. "Hey, Jill, what's up?"

"You have to help me," she whispered. "Claymore is trying to poison me."

"Don't be ridiculous. Claymore loves you, Jillian."

"He loved the old Jillian. I can't help what I've become. I didn't seek it. I couldn't stop it from happening. Why won't he accept that I've become a creature of the night?"

"Did you go to the doctor?"

She whispered, "The doctor is conspiring with Claymore. That's who gave him the poison."

"Is Claymore there?"

"He just walked out of the room, but he'll be back any minute. He thinks I took the poisoned pill, but I hid it in my cheek and spit it out when he looked away. Oh, no. Here he comes." The line went dead.

A few minutes later, Claymore called. "Abby, I'm sorry Jillian bothered you. Did she say I was trying to poison her?"

"Yep, and that the doctor is in on it."

He sighed heavily. "The doctor thinks she was bitten by a spider. He said she's got a blood infection from scratching the bites and he prescribed an antibiotic. But she won't believe me. She said he's lying and that we're antivampiristical."

"If she's making up words, she can't be too ill."

"She needs to take her meds, Abby," he whispered. "She puts them in her mouth, but I don't think she's swallowing them."

"She's not. She told me as much. You're going to have to trick her. Can you mash one into her favorite dish?"

"All she's eating is red meat. Maybe I can put the meat and the pill in the blender."

A raw meat shake. Yum. "Okay, Claymore, whatever it takes."

Lottie stuck her head through the curtain. "Marco is out front."

Was it time already? "I've got to run, Clay. Good luck."

Run. Ha. If only! I took my coat from the back of my desk chair and wheeled into the shop. Lottie helped me get onto the Evil Ones, Grace got me out the door, and Marco got me situated in the car. Thank goodness for my village people.

■ ■ ■ ■

One deck above the gaming room of the Calumet Casino boat, three men sat before a bank of television monitors in a U-shaped area, their eyes fixed on the activities going on below. And although it was only half past twelve, it seemed by their intense concentration that there was a lot of it to watch.

We were standing just inside the doorway of the darkened security room with Paul Van Cleef, the chief of security. Paul was a large, friendly man in his sixties who looked like a throwback to a Western cowboy of old. He had a full white mustache and goatee, and heavy sideburns down his deeply lined face. He wore a fringed leather vest over a blue twill shirt, with blue jeans and cowboy boots.

Van Cleef introduced us to the three men, who murmured a response without taking their eyes off the monitors. We were shown to an open station to view a digital video taken in the main gaming room on Tuesday evening. Our primary goal was to make sure Vlad was nowhere on the tape, but we were also hoping to learn whether Lori Willis had come to the boat that evening, and if so, whether she'd left with anyone.

"I brought you bottles of water," Van Cleef said. "It can get pretty warm up here. I'll be in and out, so if you need anything else, holler."

Marco handed me his notepad and pen, and I recorded the video's date and starting time. Then he fast-forwarded through long parts of the tape until we saw Lori arrive. She was wearing a pair of navy patent high heels, a slim navy skirt, a white blouse that she'd unbuttoned far enough to reveal a glittering gold chain with what appeared to be a yellow daisy pendant hanging from it, and a matching pair of yellow earrings. She carried a small red clutch purse in one hand.

"Six thirty," Marco said.

I wrote it in his notebook: *6:30 p.m. Lori Willis arrives. No sign of Vlad.*

We skimmed through the tape until the time stamp in the corner showed that it was nine o'clock, at which time Lori got up and walked over to the hostess outside the Tumbling Dice Restaurant. They talked briefly; then Lori returned to a different slot machine.

9:00 p.m, Lori talks to hostess at restaurant. No sign of Vlad, I wrote. "Lori must have been checking to see if her dinner date had arrived."

"We need to find out what she said to the

hostess," Marco said.

"Didn't Grant Gambol tell us that neither party had shown up for dinner?"

"I think he said neither party had dined there. Would you make a note on that, though?" Marco turned to Van Cleef, who had come back into the room and was seated nearby. "Would it be possible for us to bring one of the restaurant hostesses in here to view this piece of video?"

"I can arrange that. Who do you want?"

Marco pointed to the young woman on the tape. "I don't know her name."

"That's Caryn. I'll see when she works next." He got up and left the room.

We continued to watch the tape, which showed Lori playing the slot machines. No one stopped to speak to her and it didn't seem as though anyone was watching her. She gambled for another half hour before checking back with the restaurant hostess. Marco paused the video when Van Cleef returned.

"Caryn will be here in about ten minutes if you want to talk to her," he said.

"Thanks," Marco said. "Appreciate it."

He hit PLAY, and the video resumed. After another ten minutes of it, I rubbed my eyes, feeling the strain of staring at a bright monitor in a dark room.

"Someone wanted to see me?" I heard.

In the doorway stood a young raven-haired woman in a long, shimmering blue dress.

Marco stood up. "Yes. Over here."

He made the introductions, then explained what he needed. "If you'd care to sit down, Caryn, I'll show you the woman in question." Marco reversed the video, then paused it at the point where Lori walked up to the hostess. "Do you remember this woman?"

Caryn leaned closer to the monitor. "Can you zoom in?"

Marco found the icon to magnify the image. "Sure, I remember her," Caryn said. "She's the one who was murdered, right?"

"Right. Her name is Lori Willis," I said.

"Creepy how she was killed, wasn't it?" Caryn said to me. "Like a vampire attack."

A muscle in Marco's jaw twitched, but he didn't comment. Instead, he directed Caryn's attention back to the video at the point where Lori was speaking to her. "Do you remember what she said to you?"

"She wanted to know if anyone had asked for her. I said no, then asked if she had a reservation. She said she had one but not under her name. Then she said she'd be back later."

"Did she tell you the name of the other party?"

Caryn shook her head. "Not then, but she did the second time she checked. She said the reservation was under Vlad Serban."

I glanced at Marco and saw that jaw muscle working hard, but he let Caryn continue without interrupting.

"So I said to her, 'Are you talking about the vampire?' And she just smiled like it was supposed to be a secret." Caryn rubbed her arms, as though shivering in delight. "I *wish* he'd shown up! How exciting would that be?" She turned toward me. "Are you into vampires?"

"No, I like normal, red-blooded men, not men who drink red blood."

"Whatever floats your boat," Caryn said, and giggled. "We say that a lot here."

I noticed Marco giving me a look that said, *Can we get on with this?* So I said, "I think my partner has a question for you."

"Oh, sorry," Caryn said, turning her attention back to Marco.

"How many times did Lori check with you?" Marco asked.

"Just twice. Then she sat down at a slot machine where she could see the front of the restaurant."

253

"Did her date ever show up?" Marco asked.

"Not that I was aware of."

"Did anyone ask for Lori at any time during the evening?"

"No. Sad, isn't it? First the woman gets stood up, then killed. Talk about bad karma."

Marco thanked Caryn for her time, and Van Cleef escorted her out.

"Someone wanted Lori at the boat that night," Marco said. "But why use Vlad as the lure? I'm not seeing the connection."

"Did you see Caryn's reaction when you mentioned Vlad? A lot of women are into the vampire craze, Marco, and therefore highly attracted to Vlad. Lori must have been one of them. Maybe a coworker or someone at the bar overheard her talking about Vlad."

He pointed to the screen. "Let's see if Lori leaves with anyone."

We started the video again, skimming through as much as we could, stopping so I could write: *1 a.m. Lori left boat alone. Still no sign of Vlad.*

We ran through another hour's worth of the video; then Marco turned to Van Cleef, who was working at a desk nearby. "Can we see the surveillance video of the parking lot for the same Tuesday evening?"

"If you give me about thirty minutes," he replied.

I glanced at my watch. "I've got to get back, Marco. The orders are probably piling up. Why don't you take me home and then come back?"

"Let's make it in one hour then," Marco told Van Cleef.

I asked Marco to call me as soon as he'd viewed the video; then Team Bloomers swept me into the shop and off the crutches so Grace could take her lunch break. Because of my limited mobility, Lottie took parlor duty while I helped customers in the shop. We weren't as busy as the week before, primarily, I thought, because of a police presence on the block to keep away the vigilantes.

Once we were fully staffed again, I headed toward the purple curtain, then noticed that the dieffenbachia was standing several feet away from the corner, with nothing behind it.

"Lottie, what happened to the bat mobile?"

"It sold. Can you believe it? Two college kids were in here for coffee and scones at lunch and happened to spot the bright colors swaying behind the dieffenbachia leaves. They bought it for their dorm room."

"Fantastic! Mom will be thrilled."

Smiling happily, I rolled into the workroom to whittle down the stack of orders, only to discover a measly two waiting for me. I pulled the first, then wheeled over to the giant coolers to gather my stems. I heard a scratching noise coming from somewhere near the back of the room, so I went to investigate. By the time I got there, however, it had stopped.

I started to move away, then heard it again, but this time it seemed to be coming from the kitchen, so I wheeled through the doorway and paused to listen. Now it sounded like it was coming from the back door.

I maneuvered the wheelchair through the narrow galley kitchen to the landing. To my left was the thick fire door that exited onto the alley. To my right was the steep wooden staircase that led to the basement, a chilly old dungeon of a place that I visited as infrequently as possible. In my current condition, that meant not at all.

There it was again.

I wheeled to the back door and put my ear against the metal. It was coming from the other side, as if an animal in the alley was scratching to be let in.

"Lottie, would you come here a minute, please?" I called.

"What is it, sweetie?" she asked, huffing as she hurried toward me.

"It sounds like something is scratching at the back door. Do you think we should open it?"

"I'm game. But you'd better move back. No telling what's out there." She gave the big handle a hard turn, put her shoulder against the door, and pushed until she could peer outside.

"Oh, Lordy!" she exclaimed.

"What is it?"

"Not what. Who." She opened the door wider and said to the unknown who, "You'd better come in."

A wraithlike figure in a hooded black cloak slipped inside. In the dim light of the overhead bulb, I saw white eyeballs with dark circles beneath them and only a partial outline of a face, the rest hidden in shadows. A puffy red hand reached out of the cloak and pushed back the hood, revealing shimmering copper hair.

"Hide me!" Jillian whispered.

CHAPTER FIFTEEN

"Jillian!" I cried in alarm, only to have her put a trembling finger to her blue-tinged lips.

"Sh-h! I might have been followed."

"Jillian, sweetie," Lottie said, "you don't look good. Let me see if you have a fever."

Jillian cringed and moved away from her. "I'm fine! I just need to talk to my cousin for a moment." She faked a smile.

Lottie raised her eyebrows at me, so I nodded that it was okay.

"If you need anything," Lottie said to me, "just call."

Jillian waited until she was gone, then knelt in front of me. "I think she's in on it."

"Jillian, no one's in on anything. You've got a bad infection that's affecting your thinking."

She rose and paced the length of the kitchen, arms folded, and said in a brittle voice, "Or so Claymore wants everyone to believe!" She opened the old refrigerator, scanned the contents, found the egg carton, and pulled out one of two remaining eggs, cracking it and emptying it directly into her mouth. Good thing they were organic.

Giving a shudder, she wiped her mouth with the back of her hand, disposed of the shell, then sighed, as if she felt better. "Got any raw beef?"

"No! Come on, Jill, you're not a vampire."

She pointed to one of her eyeteeth. "Look at this! Do you need more proof?"

"What am I looking at?"

"Fangs, Abby! I'm growing fangs!"

"Your tooth is the same length it's always been."

She shook her head sadly. "You're going to have to face facts, Abs. Your gorgeous, talented cousin — the Knights' own bright light — has become a night fright."

An endowment that included a penchant for verse, obviously.

"If you're a vampire, what are you doing out during the day?"

"Why do you think I wore this cape? I had no choice if I wanted to escape."

I narrowed my eyes at her. "Are you rhyming on purpose?"

She fanned her face. "Why is it so hot in here?"

"Abby?" Lottie called from the workroom. "Marco is on line one, and Claymore is on line two."

"One minute." I glanced at Jillian. "What do you want me to tell your husband?"

"You haven't seen me." She glanced around like a desperate animal, saw the doorway to the basement, and scurried toward it.

"Jillian, no! Don't go down there. It's cold."

"Good. I need to cool off." She descended a few steps, then called back, "You don't happen to have a coffin down here, do you?"

"What do you think?"

I heard footsteps going down, then from the bowels of the basement, "How about a pullout sofa? I think I might camp out here for a while."

I picked up the receiver from the wall phone in the kitchen and hit the button for line one. "Marco, I've got a minor situation with Jillian on my hands. Can I call you in a few minutes?"

"Sure. I'm on my way back from the boat."

"Okay, I'll call you in a few minutes." I punched line two. "Claymore?"

"Abby, Jillian's missing again."

I heard a clatter of clay pots coming from

below. "Actually, she's in my basement."

"What is she doing down there?"

"From the sound of it, making a mess. She wants to camp there."

"I'll be right over."

"Hey, Claymore, bring her antibiotics."

I hung up, then called Marco back. "Sorry. Jillian showed up. Despite your heart-to-heart with her, she's certain that her eye-teeth have grown longer and that Claymore is trying to do away with her. She just went down to the basement to hide."

Marco groaned.

"Hey, your relatives are nothing to brag about," I said. "Tell me about the video."

"How about some good news first? My computer-savvy friend was able to track down the HOW TO KILL A VAMPIRE Web site owner. I contacted him and explained the situation, and he promised to take it down. He said he was hired to design and manage the site and was sent the materials for it by a John Smith, who paid in cash through the mail. John Smith is an alias, so we don't know who was actually behind it, but at least it's down."

"John Smith? That's original. So what was on the security video?"

"Let me get my notes. Okay, here we go. At twelve forty a.m., a male in a black trench coat, with black hair and light skin, can be seen moving among the parked cars in the lot. It's obvious the person is dressed to look like Vlad."

"Just like the photo I saw on the HOW TO KILL A VAMPIRE Web site."

"The figure heads in the direction of Willis's vehicle, then steps behind a large gray van that's parked beside her car and isn't seen again. At one a.m., Willis leaves the casino, enters her vehicle, and drives away alone. So whether the person in the trench coat had anything to do with her disappearance is not proven by that video, but he sure as heck wanted it recorded that Vlad was in the parking lot that evening."

"The trench coat man could have broken into Lori's car and hidden in the backseat."

"It's possible. It's also possible that the person in the trench coat had nothing to do with Willis's abduction. The driver of the gray van is seen leaving the casino ten minutes after Willis and driving out of the lot. There's no way to tell if he has company or is alone. But I did get a license plate number and will have that run down.

"The bad news is that the video seems to implicate Vlad, and the police will be looking for just such evidence to prove their case. They already have digital copies, so it's just a matter of time until they view that particular video and spot the figure in the black coat. That may be all it takes for the chief prosecutor to file a murder charge against Vlad."

"We need to find a better suspect fast."

"Are you prepared for your meeting with Holloway?"

"Got my outfit all picked out."

"You'd better prepare more than that. Once Holloway finds out you don't have a heart problem, *Gabriella,* you'd better have a really good reason for being there."

Oops. I hadn't thought past getting through the door. "I'll work on it later. Clay is on his way over here, and somehow we've got to get Jillian to swallow a pill."

"Will I see you at the bar at five o'clock?"

"If you're a good boy. Actually, make that a bad boy."

I hung up and wheeled to the landing to listen. When I didn't hear any sounds coming from below, I called, "Jillian?"

Silence.

"Jillian, could you cough so I know you're alive?"

"Am I alive?" came a faint reply. "Or am I now one of the undead?"

With a sigh, I went out to find Lottie. But by the time I got to the front, Claymore had arrived with two giant Neiman Marcus shopping bags.

"What did you bring?" I asked.

He began to disgorge the contents onto the table. "Chinese meditation CD and portable player, Italian red satin pj's, Scottish cashmere socks, Swiss skin caviar, Icelandic cloud face cream, French rose water mist —"

The United Nations would be proud.

"— retainer —"

Jillian still wore a retainer? I'd have to store that away for future ammunition.

"— white silk sheets, and, of course, one of Jillian's special pillows. She's very picky about where she puts her head."

"Right now, I'd guess her head is resting on a pot, so don't be too sure about that."

After he repacked the bags, I led the way to the back stairs. "She's down there."

Claymore carried the bags down the steps, calling, "Jillian? Darling? It's me, your beloved husband. I brought your *accoutrements de nuit.*" At the bottom, he called, "Abby, where's the light switch?"

"It's an old basement, Claymore. It doesn't have switches. You have to pull the chain hanging from the ceiling."

He grumbled until he found it. I heard footsteps as he moved about the dusty concrete floor; then he said, "Darling, here are your — Jillian! What are you doing back there?"

What *was* she doing? Darned sprained ankle! I wanted to go downstairs, too.

I heard a faint raspy voice; then Claymore came up gnawing his lower lip. Already the jittery type, he now looked positively distraught by his wife's latest antics. "She made a fort out of bags of potting soil and big clay pots and barricaded herself inside. I can't get to her without taking down a wall, and she said if I try to come near her, she'll chuck a pot at my head. What should I do?"

"I don't know, but she shouldn't stay down there. It's damp."

"Tell *her* that. She insists she's going to stay until her transformation is complete."

Oh, brother. How were we going to get her upstairs and talk her into taking a pill before that infection raging through her body did some real harm? Could I use a lure? The old Jillian would have run barefoot through the snow to see the latest pair of Jimmy Choos. Not that I could have afforded a pair anyway, but I doubted such a ploy would interest Vampira in the least now. All she was interested in was red meat.

"Claymore, did you bring her medicine?"

He held out an amber-colored plastic pill bottle with a pharmacy label on it.

"Good. I have an idea. Will you go to Adagio and get a takeout order for me?"

"You want to eat first?"

"It's for Jillian. Adagio is the only restaurant in town that serves steak carpaccio. It's sliced thin, so we can roll up a sushi-sized bite and hide a pill inside."

"I'll be back as soon as I can." Claymore gave me a hug. "You're brilliant!"

Huh. Claymore's brother had pretty much decided the opposite was true. I felt the diamond ring on the chain beneath my shirt and smiled. Being dumped by Pryce Osborne had been the second-best thing that had ever happened to me. Meeting Marco was the first.

Once Claymore was gone, the workroom was quiet again, so I returned to the flower arrangement I'd started before Jillian showed up. Then I heard what sounded like chirping birds and tinkling chimes, with a waterfall in the background. I paused to listen. It was coming from the basement.

Jillian's meditation CD. Strangely enough, I found myself inhaling and exhaling slowly, feeling the tension drain out of my body. Ah. That was actually quite relaxing.

"Yoo-hoo! Abigail!" I heard my mom call.

266

No rest for the wicked.

Mom swept back the curtain and came into the room, followed by a young woman who couldn't have been a day over twenty. "Here you are," Mom said. "I want you to meet my new student teacher, Chelsea Dunaway. Chelsea, this is Abigail."

"Just Abby," I said with a smile.

"Nice to meet you, Abby," Chelsea said, shaking my hand. "Your mom brags about you all the time."

Really?

Chelsea had long honey brown hair caught up in a low ponytail, then twisted and fastened on the back of her head, so the tips of her hair fanned out at the crown. She had straight bangs and long pieces of hair that fell in front of her ears, making her look both cute and sexy at the same time. She also had big blue eyes and a pretty smile, and she appeared quite stylish in her black peacoat, tan wool pants, and black boots. Hmm. Was she single?

I glanced at her hand as she pushed a strand of hair away from her face. No ring, pretty, polite, smart, and single. Possibly the perfect girl to mend Rafe's broken heart.

"How is your ankle, honey?" Mom asked.

Not much different from when she'd questioned me that morning. Luckily, I was spared having to answer when she turned to Chelsea and said, "Abigail fell off a spike heel and suffered a nasty sprain." She added in a whisper, "I think she learned her lesson."

Yes, I did. If I ever sprained my ankle again, I wouldn't tell Mom how it happened. "Did Lottie give you the news about your bat mobile?"

"No, Lottie is helping a customer."

"It sold!"

Mom's face flushed with joy. "So soon? You only had it, what, six hours? That has to be a new record. Oh, Chelsea, I'm so sorry you didn't get to see it. It was something, wasn't it, Abigail?"

"Yes, it was." Something.

"The way you described it, Mrs. Knight, I can imagine it would sell quickly," Chelsea gushed, clearly knowing how to get on Mom's good side. No one could hear a true description of that mobile and think it would sell in a million years.

"It's probably already hanging over some lucky child's bed," Mom said, pressing a hand to her heart.

I could hear the screams now.

"I'll just have to get the next one finished tonight," Mom said.

Wait. What? The *next* one?

268

"Nothing succeeds like success, as Grace always says." Mom gave me a hug. "We're off, honey. I promised I'd show Chelsea around town. This is her first year in New Chapel and she never gets off campus except to come to my school."

"I adore your flower shop," Chelsea called, following Mom through the curtain.

"Wait, Chelsea," I said. "How old are you?"

She stuck her head through the curtain. "Twenty-one, why?"

"Seeing anyone?"

She shook her head.

"Then there's someone I'd like you to meet. Are you free for dinner tonight?"

Twenty minutes later, Claymore returned with a white cardboard carryout carton. We removed one of the rare beef slices from the box, cut it into strips, placed antibiotic capsules inside two of them, then rolled them up and fastened them with floral picks. We rolled up a few more strips to make it look authentic, put them back in the box, and then I called downstairs, "Jillian! I've got raw steak for you. It's from your favorite restaurant, Adagio."

I heard scraping sounds, as though clay pots were being moved, but there was no answer. "Jillian?" I called.

Still no answer. "You'd better go check on her, Clay."

He crept down the steps. "Jillian? Sweetheart?"

Moments later Claymore came pounding up the steps. "Her accoutrements are there, but she's not."

"She has to be there. She didn't turn into a bat and fly away, did she?"

Claymore stared at me in horror, as if such a thing were possible.

"Stop it, Clay! Did that spider bite you, too? There are plenty of places to hide in that old basement. She probably found one of them." I glanced at my watch. It was nearly closing time. "Why don't you go home and let me work on her? And leave the bottle of pills. I'll call you as soon as I have news, okay?"

"Are you sure she'll be safe down there?"

"What's the worst that can happen? She's already been bitten by a spider. Now go!"

After he left, I called downstairs, "Jillian, Clay is gone now. You can come up."

From far away I heard, "No."

Fine. If she was going to be difficult, then she could just cool her heels in that dank old basement all evening. "Jill, I have to leave in a little while to meet Marco at the bar. I'm going to put your food in the fridge. I'll be back after dinner to see how you're doing."

"Do we dare close up the shop with your ailing cousin down there?" Grace asked, startling me.

"When Claymore tried to get her to come up, she went deeper into hiding. I can't get down there unless I scoot down on my rear, so if you'd care to try to convince her, be my guest."

"In that case, I'm sure she'll be perfectly fine until you return." With a nod of affirmation, Grace said good night.

At five fifteen, as Chelsea and I headed up the sidewalk toward Down the Hatch, I gave her the important details on the Salvare brothers — *important* meaning nothing that might scare her away from Rafe, such as his ill-fated engagement to a nineteen-year-old Hooters waitress whose father owned a striptease club and whose mother had been a dancer there. Instead I focused on the Salvare men's positive qualities, of which there were many.

There was still a heavy police presence around the square, along with more people carrying antivampire signs and walking in a continuous loop. They weren't bothering anyone, simply exercising their constitutional rights, which I'd done a number of times myself for animal rights causes. Plus, they were on public property, so the police couldn't chase them off. Still, their presence worried me.

The protesters didn't seem to faze Chelsea. "I can't wait to meet Rafe," she said, holding the door open. "Thank you so much for inviting me."

The first thing I did upon entering was to make sure Rafe was there. He was. My next task was to make sure Vlad had arrived without harassment from the protesters. He had. I spotted Marco already seated at our booth in the far back and paused to point him out to Chelsea. "That's Marco."

Marco lifted his hand in greeting. I'd already filled him in on my plan and surprisingly he'd agreed to it right away. We would order drinks and have Rafe deliver them to the table, at which point I'd introduce Chelsea. Then Marco would invite Rafe to take a short break to join us. Hopefully, sparks would ignite and the rest would fall into place.

"And there's Rafe," I told her. But Rafe chose that moment to duck behind the counter to get something from a lower shelf. "Correction, there *was* Rafe."

"Here's my girl," Marco said, standing up to give me a kiss. He offered his hand to my guest. "Chelsea, right? Marco Salvare."

She shook his hand and then we sat down. The Evil Ones were stowed; drinks were ordered; and the curtain on my little drama began to rise. As the orchestra struck up the overture, Chelsea exclaimed, *"O-M-G!"* and lifted herself up off the bench to watch as Gert carried our order up to the bar. "Is that *him?*"

Marco and I both followed the direction of her gaze. Rafe had popped up again and was mixing drinks, looking young and dashing. I saw Gert give him our orders, point at us, and pass along the message that he was to serve our drinks. He glanced our way, so I waved.

"Yes, that's him," I said. Let the play begin.

"I can't believe it," she squealed. "I'm actually seeing the vampire in person!"

What? I glanced at Marco and he shrugged, as though to say, *Nice try.*

"Everyone in my dorm is talking about Vlad." She pulled her cell phone out of her purse and slid out of the booth, her eyes wide with excitement. "The girls will *not* believe this. I have to get his picture. Thank you *so* much for inviting me!"

I watched in dismay as Chelsea surged into the crowd just as Rafe pushed through from the other side to deliver our beers. He set three bottles on the table, then gave Marco a vexed look. "I was busy. Why did I have to bring them over?"

Marco propped his chin on his hand and gazed at me. "Yes, Abby, why did Rafe have to bring them over?"

I pasted on a smile. "Because . . . I haven't had a chance to congratulate you, Rafe. Marco says you're doing a terrific job."

"Yeah, well, it kind of goes unnoticed when I'm working next to the superstar." He indicated Vlad with a nod of his head. "That reminds me, bro, while you were out this afternoon, Vlad's attorney stopped by. Dave Hammond, right? He said he couldn't reach Vlad by phone so he was hoping to find him here. I passed the message to Vlad, just so you know."

"Is it me," I asked, "or does it seem like no one can reach Vlad during the day?"

Marco ignored my question to ask Rafe, "Did Dave say why he needed Vlad?"

"Nope. Just when I saw Vlad, to make sure he called ASAP because he had news."

"I hope it was good news," I said. "We could use some of that."

"By the look on Dave's face," Rafe said,

"I wouldn't count on it."

A hush fell over the room. I glanced around to find out what had caused it and saw all eyes on the television screens, where a photo of Lori Willis was being displayed.

"Turn up the volume," one of the men called.

"In area news," the anchor said, "New Chapel police are close to making an arrest in the murder of director of nursing Lori Willis."

At that, every head in the place turned toward Vlad, who was busily mixing a drink.

"Willis was last seen early Wednesday morning leaving the Calumet Casino," the anchor continued. "Her body was discovered in a garbage bin behind Down the Hatch Bar and Grill. Police are asking for anyone with information to call their tip line."

I heard low murmurs coming from several groups of men near the front and felt a new tension in the air. I glanced at Marco and saw his sudden alertness. He sensed it, too.

"Sit tight," Marco said quietly, as he got up and made his way toward the bar.

CHAPTER SIXTEEN

The rumblings ceased when Marco took the remote and clicked over to a sports channel. There was a watchful silence as he and Vlad headed toward Marco's office, but as soon as they were out of earshot, a buzz of conversation began.

I caught snatches of whispers from people around me: *"Is Vlad going to be arrested?" "Could he be guilty?" "Why is Marco letting him work here?" "Is Marco being duped?"*

When Marco returned to our booth ten minutes later, Rafe and Evan were busy mixing drinks and taking payments, Gert and another waitress were delivering food and beverages, and customers were drinking, eating, and talking as though nothing had happened. Only the women at the bar seemed to have been affected. With Vlad gone, their numbers had decreased sharply. Chelsea, however, was still there, and seemed to be flirting with Rafe.

"Where's Vlad?" I asked Marco quietly.

"I told him to take a break. I gave him the opportunity to go home, but he didn't want to."

"Do you think that news report was about him?"

Marco sighed heavily. "I don't know, but I don't have a good feeling about it. According to what Dave told Vlad, the casino's surveillance videos are now a part of the prosecution's evidence against him. Vlad is going to meet with Dave at seven this evening to discuss strategy."

"Dave never meets clients in the evenings."

"Apparently he makes exceptions."

For vampires?

Gert stopped by our booth, tablet in hand. "You kids gonna eat tonight?"

"I'd like a big green salad and a bowl of French onion soup, please." After handling that raw steak, I was craving something as far away from red meat as I could get.

"Salad and a burger," Marco said. "Thanks, Gert."

"I thought we were gonna have trouble there for a while, boss," Gert said in a low voice. "Things seem pretty calm now, but the Garlic Party idiots are back across the street."

"Thanks for letting me know," Marco said. After Gert was gone, he said to me, "I think I'd better stick around here again this evening, Sunshine. Want to keep me company?"

So much for our dwindling number of evenings together. "Of course I do. I just need to check on Jillian. She's hiding in Bloomers' basement because she thinks Claymore and her doctor are conspiring to poison her. She even wants to sleep down there."

"Is this the same woman who won't put her head on anything but a silk pillowcase?"

"The very same. I told you she's sick. And we can't get her to take her medicine."

"Maybe spending a night in the basement will convince her she needs help. I've got blankets and a cot here. If you'd like, I'll carry them down after we eat."

Not a bad idea. If I made Jillian comfy down there, and she got hungry in the night, she'd eat her medicine-laced steak roll-ups. "I think I'll take you up on that."

Marco walked me to Bloomers carrying his folded cot and blankets, studiously ignoring the bunch across the street. One of them stepped forward and yelled, "Vampire lover! If the killer strikes again, it's on your head, buddy!"

"Did you say good-bye to your mom's student teacher?" Marco asked.

I eyed the protesters warily, admiring Marco's calm. "Yes, I said good-bye, but she barely noticed because she was busy flirting with Rafe."

Marco locked the shop's front door behind us, then stood at the window for a moment watching the marchers.

"I don't know how Vlad stands it," I said, switching to the wheelchair. "I'd be on the next train back to Chicago."

"I know the strain is getting to him. Still, he told me if he leaves now, those people across the street will think they've won, and everyone else will believe the rumors about him. One thing about Vlad, he isn't the kind to give up without a fight. The shame of it is that he likes it here. It's just idiots like them" — Marco hitched a thumb at the marchers — "who ruin it for him."

He turned away. "Let's get your cousin set up."

I preceded him to the kitchen. At the landing, I called downstairs, "Jillian, I have a cot and blankets for you. Marco is going to bring them down."

There was a sudden scuffling sound as Marco started down the steps. At the bottom, he pulled the cord to turn on the light, then called up to me, "I don't see her, Abby."

"She's hiding. Just leave everything by the Neiman Marcus bags. She'll find it."

He set up the cot, turned out the light, then jogged up the steps. "She has a place to sleep now."

"Jillian?" I called. "Did you hear that? You've got a bed now, plus food and water up here in the fridge. If you don't speak up, I'm going to lock you in the shop for the night. You can always call me, of course, but I'm leaving right now. This is your last chance."

"Go away," was her raspy reply.

I gave Marco a shrug. "Let's go. I'll call Claymore on the way and give him an update. If Jillian isn't better by morning, I'm going to call an ambulance and have her taken to the hospital."

We returned to Down the Hatch but ended up sitting in Marco's office because the place was packed. Vlad was back at the bar performing for the women as though the news report had never happened. So we took the opportunity to go over all the notes we'd made so far and to discuss the upcoming interview with Dr. Holloway. Marco was still a little nervous about me seeing him alone, so I assured him I had a plan.

"Want to elaborate on that?" he asked.

"I'm going to play to Holloway's ego. Self-centered people love to talk about themselves, and thinking that someone came all the way from Paris to see him is going to put him in an agreeable mood."

"Holloway's going to figure out your French persona is a sham. Why not be straightforward with him? Tell him you're investigating a murder and you need his input."

"Did straightforward work for you?"

Marco didn't answer.

"Don't worry. I've got it under control. If he catches on — *when* he catches on — I'll swap out one story for another, and he'll have no choice but to believe it. Who would lie twice?"

"And if your second story doesn't work?"

"O ye of little faith."

By nine o'clock the protesters had departed, so Marco felt comfortable leaving head bartender Chris, along with Evan, Rafe, and Vlad, tending bar, giving us a few precious hours to ourselves. But before we returned home, I asked Marco to make a quick stop at Bloomers to check on Jillian.

I unlocked the front door and Marco held

it open for me, but inside, I didn't hear the familiar beeps of the security system. "Is someone here?" Marco asked, glancing around.

"It could only be Lottie or Grace, and they would turn on a light. I must have forgotten to set it when I left."

I switched to the wheelchair; then we made our way to the kitchen, where I found an empty plate on the counter. "Marco, look! Jillian ate the meat with the pills in them. I'd better call Claymore and tell him the good news."

"Wait, Abby." Marco bent down and picked up something off the floor. "Are these her pills?" He showed me two familiar-looking capsules. Just to be certain, I got the amber-colored plastic container from the fridge and opened it. Yep. Same pills.

"That does it. I'm going downstairs and force these pills down her throat. She's going to get better whether she wants to or not."

"No, you don't," Marco said, standing in front of my chair. "You'll fall."

"I'll scoot down on my rear. You don't know where the hiding spots are."

He frowned at me, and when that didn't work, he said, "Stay there until I get your crutches."

Carrying the Evil Ones, Marco headed to the basement and waited at the bottom while I came down the old wooden steps one at a time. Luckily, I wasn't wearing light-colored pants. Once balanced, I saw the cot Marco had set up and noticed that Jillian's white silk sheets had been spread out on it and all of her various creams had been lined up on a shelf nearby. I went through the warren of rooms, checking a few tucked-away places, finally reaching the furnace room way in the back, where I had once hid from a murderer. But Jillian wasn't there.

"I told you she wasn't here," Marco said.

"She must have left the building while we were eating. That's why the alarm was turned off. I'll bet she memorized the security code when she worked here. I'll have to remember to change the code."

I headed for the steps. "I'd better alert Claymore that Countess Jillian von Dracula is on the loose."

It had been a busy, productive, yet ultimately frustrating day, so by the time I slid under the bedcovers, I was ready for a good night's rest. Lying in Marco's arms, drifting off to sleep, I heard him murmur, "I like having you as my partner."

I snuggled closer to him and said drowsily, "And I like *being* your partner."

Then, just as my eyelids fluttered closed, he said, "I'm meeting with Dave tomorrow to finalize my will."

It took a few minutes for his words to sink into my semisomnolent brain.

My eyes snapped open. *His will?*

I didn't get restful sleep that night, not only because I was worrying about my cousin but also because of that little bomb Marco dropped about his will. I figured he was merely being cautious, not wanting a probate court to decide what to do with his assets if, God forbid, something were to happen to him, but still, did I want to know about it?

Now that I did know, though, I was curious as to why he had told me. But he didn't mention it the next morning, so I hated to bring it up. It wasn't exactly a pleasant way to start the day.

"Hey, Gorgeous," Marco said, coming up behind me as I stood in front of the bathroom mirror. I had propped myself against the sink to put on my silver earrings.

I smiled at his reflection as he slid his arms around my waist. "Hey, yourself, Salvare."

"You look way too sexy in that sweater and skirt to meet a doctor who's hot to trot. I'd better come with you."

"Don't worry. I know how to handle frisky men."

"Do you now? Want to show me?"

I turned to wind my arms around his neck and smile at him. "You bet, but let's save that show for tonight. I'll be late for work if we don't leave right now."

"Spoilsport." He handed me the crutches and helped me into my coat, then, before we left, stooped down to scratch Simon behind his ears. Simon rubbed his face against Marco's hand, then gazed adoringly at him and meowed.

"Is he hungry?" Marco asked me.

"No, he's had his breakfast. He's just saying, Don't go! Stay and play with me."

"Sorry, buddy," Marco said. "The boss says we have to go." He pretended to whisper to Simon, "You know what an iron will she has."

Iron will . . . Will . . . Last will and testament.

No, I was *not* going to ask about it. Not. Going. To. Ask.

"We're leaving you in charge, Si," Marco said, rising. "You're the man of the house now. Guard it well."

Well . . . Will . . . Oh, hell. "Marco, why did you tell me you had your will drawn up?"

He opened the front door for me. "Because you're in it."

I was in his will? I waited for him to enlarge on that, but he didn't. So that was how I left it — hoping that I would never need to find out the details.

On the drive to Bloomers, I phoned Claymore to see if Jillian had turned up, but he didn't have any news. "I'm frantic with worry, Abby. The police won't help until she's been missing for two days. I've been driving all over town, hoping to spot her, I've got her parents out searching, and I've even alerted her favorite shops and restaurants in case someone sees her."

"I doubt she'd be dining out or shopping in her condition. Does she have her credit cards with her?"

"She should have them. She took her purse."

"I'll bet she checked into a hotel."

"Good thinking. I'll call around. Thanks, Abby."

"Call me the minute you find her, Clay."

Marco gave my hand a squeeze. "Jillian will turn up. Don't worry. This town isn't so big that a sick woman in a black cape can walk around unnoticed."

Grace and Lottie were standing at the window watching for me, and when they saw Marco's car out front, they sprang into action. Within five minutes, I was in the wheelchair sitting in the parlor with a cup of coffee in front of me, filling them in on Jillian's escape.

"Claymore has a posse out looking for her," I said. "So far no reports."

"Maybe this will explain her whereabouts. It was by the cash register this morning." Lottie handed me an envelope that was marked in capital letters: TO A. KNIGHT FROM J. KNIGHT-OSBORNE, FORMER WARDROBE CONSULTANT.

I opened it and unfolded the piece of Bloomers stationery inside. In a spidery hand, Jillian had written:

I've gone to be with my own kind.
I know you think I'm out of my mind,
But thanks for the meat on which I dined.
Your cousin Jillian has this note signed.
P.S. I never expected you to try to poison me, too.

Grace and Lottie read it over my shoulder;

then Lottie said, "Why would she think you tried to poison her?"

"I hid antibiotics in her food and left it in the fridge, but it didn't work. She found the pills and left them behind."

"Does your cousin always rhyme her notes?" Grace asked.

"She never did before. Jillian always hated poetry. Mother Goose rhymes used to give her fits. When Jill tumbled down the hill after Jack, Jillian took it personally."

"Her own kind," Lottie mused. "Would that be delusional rich people?"

"If Jillian truly believes she's turning into a vampire," Grace said, "she might check herself into a hospital, mightn't she?"

"Or a bat cave," Lottie offered.

Hmm. Where *would* Jillian go? I didn't have a clue. But I knew someone who might. All I needed was a reason to drop by and see him.

"What I'd like to know," Lottie said, "is how Jillian got out of here without setting off the alarm."

"That puzzled me, too," I said, "but I think I've figured it out. Remember when Jillian was helping out here while I was investigating the clown's murder during Picklefest? I gave her a spare key and never asked for it back. She was usually with me when I set the alarm at night, so she probably memorized it. She has an uncanny memory for numbers — phone numbers, dates, bank accounts, you name it."

"She sure has your mom worried," Lottie said. "She and your dad helped Jillian's parents search until late in the night."

"You talked to my mom this morning?"

"She dropped off another mobile," Grace said. "Lottie and I have already unpacked it. You'll find it hanging safely behind the dieffenbachia."

Right. Like there were any safe spots when it came to Mom's art.

Lottie was tapping her chin thoughtfully. "I was just thinking about something. You heard there was another so-called vampire sighting last night, didn't you?"

"No. Where?" I asked.

"People coming out of the movie theater reported seeing someone in a long black hooded cape running out of the bushes and disappearing behind the building," Lottie said. "And Jillian was wearing a black cape with a hood when she showed up here. Do you think it might have been her?"

"I'll let Claymore know so he can search there," I said.

"It sure started up the rumor mills again," Lottie said. "The radio was full of people reporting sightings. Then the leader of that so-called Garlic Party phoned in and put out a call to arms. This vampire hysteria is out of control. I feel sorry for Marco's friend."

"If I were Vlad," I said, "I'd be hopping a train to Chicago."

"By the way, love," Grace said, "the plants you ordered for Vlad are in."

"The dandelions, too?"

"Yes, two flats of dandelions. That's what you ordered, wasn't it?"

And there was my reason!

"What the heck does he want with so many weeds?" Lottie asked.

"Maybe I'll find out when I deliver them."

"*You're* going to deliver them?" Lottie glanced at my wheelchair. "I don't think so."

"My two weeks are almost up," I said. "I should be able to take my bandage off so I can put on a shoe and drive."

"That's a bad idea, sweetie," Lottie said, as I unwrapped the mile of Ace bandage around my ankle and foot. "I'll deliver the orders. You stay put."

"I agree with Lottie," Grace said. "There's no need to test your ankle when she can make the deliveries. You can't rush the healing process."

290

I knew they were looking out for my best interests, but delivering those houseplants to Vlad was an opportunity I couldn't miss. I tossed the stretchy bandage aside and examined my lower leg. Other than my ankle being a tad on the scaly side, it didn't look that bad. The swelling was completely gone.

I braced my hands on the arms of the chair, putting first my good foot and then the bare one on the floor. Then I rose to test my weight and — voilà! It worked. I was standing without help. Boy, did that feel great.

I held out my hands. "See? I'm fine!"

"Oh, Lordy, she's gonna fall," Lottie said, covering her eyes.

"Don't worry," I said. "I'll still use the crutches to keep the weight off my ankle."

"How do you propose to carry the arrangements up to the customers' doors?" Grace asked, handing me the Evil Ones.

Rats. Another obstacle. Obviously I needed help, but I couldn't use one assistant and leave the other alone. Who could I get to go with me?

"I think I have a solution," I said, hop-stepping toward the curtain.

CHAPTER SEVENTEEN

"Do you have your other shoe," Grace called, "and sock?"

Yet another obstacle to overcome. Good thing I loved a challenge. I rummaged through cabinets in the workroom and found an old pair of yellow rubber rain boots. Not the most fashionable footwear to complement my pencil skirt, but they'd have to do.

I propped the crutches beside my desk and sat down to phone Rafe at the apartment he shared with Marco. "Hey, Rafe, are you busy later this morning?"

"I'm supposed to meet with Marco at ten o'clock to go over bar stuff. Why?"

Another obstacle? "Never mind. You answered my question. Oh, and, Rafe? You did not get this call."

"I'm cool with that."

I thought about my delivery dilemma as we opened Bloomers and settled into our normal routines. Business had definitely dropped off. I counted only six orders on the spindle. At least I'd have no problem finishing them by midmorning so I could have a good hour for deliveries before lunch — if I could find a ride.

Before I started working on the first order, I logged onto my MySpace page and found answers from Dana Trumble's friends, whose Web site identities were Becky Delight and Alison St. J. Both wrote that they thought we should meet in person. Becky had included her phone number, so I gave her a call to invite them to come to Bloomers for free coffee and scones.

"That's very kind of you," Becky said in a cautious tone, "but before we accept, I have to ask what you're planning and whether Jerry is going to be included."

"I hadn't actually gotten around to planning anything yet," I told her. "I was waiting to hear from you."

"Well, just so you know," Becky said, "if you want Jerry included, we're out of it."

That was interesting. "I'm fine with that, Becky, but may I ask why?"

"We'll tell you at the meeting. Will five o'clock this afternoon work?"

"That would be perfect. See you then."

I pulled the first order and went to work.

The client wanted a luncheon arrangement using the colors of a vegetable salad, so I wheeled to the first cooler to pull the appropriate stems.

To represent yellow peppers, I selected brilliant yellow Gerbera and solidago; for tomatoes, a rose called Rosa Etoile de Holland; freesia for the softer yellow of summer squash; white narcissi for the onion; and purple sage and hosta leaves for the greens. For texture and scent, I decided on oregano and basil, but someone had beat me to them, so I used feathery dill and the pine-needle-like rosemary instead.

Later I asked Lottie about the missing herbs.

"They should be there, sweetie," Lottie said. "I put a new batch in the cooler Monday morning and haven't touched them since . . . although I did see some oregano leaves on the counter by the envelope that Jillian left this morning. Is it possible she took them?"

"I can't think of why she would," I said.

"My granny used to treat infections with oregano leaves," Lottie said. "She swore by her home-brewed basil tea, too. Said it would clean out a body's poisons."

"This is Jillian," I reminded her. "The closest she's ever come to a home remedy is gargling with salt water for a sore throat."

"Speaking of Jillian," Grace said, "has there been any word?"

"None. I think I'll give Claymore a call."

I went to my desk in the workroom and dialed Claymore's cell phone. He answered anxiously, "Yes? Hello?"

"Clay, it's Abby. Have you heard from Jillian?"

"No," he answered wearily, "and I'm desperate. I checked all the hotels in the area, as well as the hospitals, but no luck. She could be dying somewhere, Abby. I tried to go to work, but I can't concentrate. I feel like I have to keep looking for her."

The proverbial lightbulb went on. "Are you driving around now?"

"Yes."

"In that case, would you like to help me make a few deliveries? I could really use some assistance and we can look for Jillian at the same time."

There was a long pause, and then he asked gingerly, "Do I have to drive your minivan?"

Even in a desperate state, a blue-blooded Osborne couldn't bring himself to sink to such depths. "If you want to use your BMW, Clay, that's fine. It has a big trunk, right?"

"Of course."

"How soon can you be here?"

■ ■ ■ ■

It was a new experience making deliveries in Claymore's big black BMW. More than a few customers' mouths fell open when they opened their door and saw it parked at the curb. And they didn't know what to make of the man in the expensive suit who handed them their arrangements.

After the sixth stop, Claymore got behind the wheel with a big smile on his face. "I can see why you like your work. Everyone is delighted to get flowers."

"It's the best feeling in the world," I said.

"Five more stops?" Claymore asked, as we drove away.

"Actually, only one. The rest of the plants are going to the same place. The Casa Royale Apartments."

"Isn't that where Marco's friend Vlad lives?"

"That's who the plants are for."

Claymore tightened his grip on the steering wheel. "I don't think I should make that delivery. I might be forced to punch him in the nose."

I glanced at Claymore's skinny frame. If he tried to punch a soldier trained in the martial arts, he'd be the one who would end up with a bloody nose. "Clay, Vlad did not bite Jillian."

"But Vlad is the reason she thinks she's a vampire. If anything happens to her, I shall hold him personally responsible."

"Listen, Clay, all I need is for you to carry the box up to Vlad's door. Then you can return to the car and wait for me there. You don't even need to see Vlad."

"Good," he said grimly. "I'm not fond of having to use my fists against another human being."

It took Claymore two trips to get both long boxes containing the plants to the door of Vlad's apartment, and then he stood there squeezing his hands together, as if being near Vlad made him anxious. "Are you certain you want me to leave you here?"

"Yes, Clay. I'll be out as soon as I instruct Vlad on how to care for his plants." And do a little harmless reconnoitering. Of course, that all hinged on Vlad being home. I'd tried to phone him earlier, but he hadn't answered.

"Then I'll meet you at the car," Claymore said, and practically sprinted to the elevator.

I waited until the elevator had ascended, then raised my hand to knock, only to have the door open suddenly. I squinted to see inside, but it was pitch-black. "Vlad? Are you there? I brought your plants over."

Vlad stuck his head out and glanced up and down the hallway, causing me to look, too. What or whom was he checking for?

"Okay. Come inside." He stepped back so I could walk in. "Where are your crutches?"

"I left them in the car. Why is it so dark in here?"

"I'll tell you in a minute." He dragged the boxes inside, then shut the door and locked it, leaving me unable to see my own hand in front of my face.

I shivered from the chilly temperature in the apartment. A fan was running somewhere, sending currents of cool air into the room, carrying with it the fragrance of some kind of herb. I sniffed. Was he making a pizza?

I could hear him moving around behind me, but I couldn't tell what he was doing. Then I heard old hinges squeaking, as though a lid was being opened. My first thought was of the photo of a casket on the HOW TO KILL A VAMPIRE Web site. Then the skin on the back of my neck prickled, as though someone was standing nearby. I shivered again and rubbed my arms. My ankle was starting to throb, too.

"Vlad? What's going on?"

"Come with me." His voice was a husky whisper near my ear. He took my arm and led me through the apartment. The smell of herbs was overpowering now, as though Vlad had doused himself in them.

"Where are we going?"

"To my bedroom."

I swallowed hard. "Why?"

"There's something I need to show you."

That sounded like a line from a bad movie. *Come with me, little girl. I have something to show you. Thwack!*

Calm down, Abby, my voice of reason said. *Vlad is Marco's trusted friend. Do you really believe he would hurt you?*

It was that kind of thinking that got people killed in every horror movie I'd ever seen. I wondered if I should pull my arm free and bolt for the door. Then I remembered my ankle and decided not to try it. Instead, I slipped my free hand into my purse and felt for my cell phone.

"Listen, Vlad, let's do this another time. I'll come back with Marco and you can show both of us."

"That won't work."

Correction. It wouldn't work for *him*. It most definitely would work for me. "The thing is, Vlad, Claymore Osborne is waiting

for me in the car and if I don't come out
—"

"Claymore is outside?"

Vlad didn't sound pleased, which was exactly the reaction I'd hoped for. Now he knew that someone else knew that I was in his apartment. He'd have to let me go. "Yes, Claymore Osborne. So if you'll show me the way out —"

"You can't leave." He was insistent and his grasp was solid.

My heart started to gallop in apprehension. My fingers fumbled over my wallet. Where was my cell phone? "Why can't I leave?"

"Abs?" a raspy voice called. "Is that you?"

I knew that voice. "Jillian?" I turned toward where I thought Vlad was, catching the barest glimmer of the whites of his eyes. "My cousin is here?"

"She collapsed outside my door. I brought her inside, and she was shivering so hard from a fever that her teeth were chattering. So I put her on the bed, covered her with blankets, and made her tea. She's been sleeping for hours."

"Abs?" Jillian called again.

"Could you turn on a light?" I asked Vlad. "Jillian said lights hurt her eyes."

"She'll survive."

Vlad turned on a wall sconce that threw out a very weak light. I glanced behind me and saw that he had steered me past a doorway and was leading me down a wide hallway that had three more doors in it. I assumed the one we'd just passed led into the living room. The apartment seemed to be built in the European style, where each room could be closed off by a door.

"Are you sure you should be walking without crutches?" he asked.

"My ankle is fine." Although it did feel a bit puffy.

Vlad led the way, carrying a black mug in one hand. I passed an open doorway on the left, glanced into it, and saw a refrigerator and range, obviously the kitchen. On my right was a closed door with a strange blue light emanating from beneath it.

"That's my plant room," Vlad said. "I'll show you that later."

He passed another closed door, but offered no explanation, coming to a stop at the end of the hallway. "She's in here." He stood back and allowed me to enter his bedroom. In the dim light from the hallway, I could just make out my cousin's form under a pile of blankets.

"Could I have a little more light?" I asked.

Vlad crossed the room to a window covered by heavy wooden Florida blinds and opened the slats just enough to allow in a bit more light. I saw Jillian lying on a massive bed that had a dark wooden headboard that reached almost to the ceiling. It was carved with scrolls and swirls and seemed like something out of a Gothic horror movie.

The bedroom was large for an apartment, and had a high vaulted ceiling and a palladium window that was covered by a pleated room-darkening shade. Against the wall opposite the bed was an enormous armoire made out of the same dark wood. Tucked in one corner was a cozy armchair and ottoman, with an arc lamp behind the chair, making the perfect reading corner.

"Abs," Jillian said, making an effort to raise her head. "You came! You *do* care."

"Of course I care, silly. But you shouldn't have bothered Vlad."

"I was compelled to," she said, then let her head fall back onto the pillow.

"She was seeking her own kind," Vlad said with a hint of humor. "You know how we vampires like to stick together." He moved past me to sit on the side of the bed. "Jillian, I brought you more herbal tea. Would you like to sit up and drink it?"

She nodded.

I watched in astonishment as Vlad put his arm behind her and raised her far enough to sip the tea. "Is it my oregano tea?" she asked.

"Yes. Drink it all. You're still dehydrated."

She did as she was told, draining the cup. Then she sighed. "That tasted good."

Vlad propped the pillows behind her so she could sit up. "Now you can visit with your cousin while I brew more." On his way out, he whispered in my ear, "You didn't happen to bring her medicine along, did you?"

I reached into my purse, found the small cylinder, and slipped it to him.

"I'll be back with more tea," Vlad promised her.

As soon as he was gone, I sat down on the bed and took Jillian's hand. It felt cool and as dry as paper, not the soft, moist hand of a young woman. "We've been worried about you, Jillian. Claymore, your parents, my parents — we've been searching all over town for you."

She motioned for me to come closer. I leaned in and she whispered, "Tell me you're not really wearing yellow rain boots."

"You're hallucinating."

"Thank God," she said with a sigh, and closed her eyes.

She couldn't be that sick if she was worried about my boots. I dug deep into my purse and pulled out my cell phone. *Sure. Now I find it.* "We need to let Claymore know you're here so he can pass the word along to your parents."

"No!" she cried, and grabbed the phone from me, clutching it to her chest. "Claymore wants to kill me."

"Jillian, stop it. Claymore loves you!"

"He brainwashed you, Abs. Can't you see that?" Her eyelids fluttered closed. "Whatever happens, I forgive you for trying to poison me."

Then she fell silent. Alarmed, I felt her wrist for a pulse and found it beating healthily. I watched her for a moment, but she seemed to have slipped into a deep sleep, so I tiptoed out of the room and started down the hallway only to see Vlad coming toward me carrying one of the boxes.

"I've got tea brewing. It should be ready in ten minutes."

"Vlad, we need to let Claymore know Jillian is safe. He's frantic with worry."

"If you want to, that's your choice, but I promised Jillian I wouldn't call him until she gave me the okay, and I don't break promises."

He opened the door to a room that glowed

with an eerie blue light. "Come in."
    Said the spider to the fly.

CHAPTER EIGHTEEN

The room that I entered was filled with exotic plants lit only by the blue-white glow of overhead plant lights. All around me were stands holding species I'd seen only in catalogs. Fascinated, I circled the room, admiring the strange but beautiful blossoms, while Vlad unloaded his new plants, placing each one in a carefully chosen spot. Oddly, what I didn't see was dandelions. Not a single weed. He'd told me his supply was low, but still, what had he done with them?

He brushed off his hands and rose. "These are great additions, Abby."

I noticed that the flats I'd brought were not in the room. "What about your new dandelions?"

"Well . . . they're for a different project."

"What kind of project?"

"You'll find out soon enough." He smiled. Were his teeth actually glowing or was that the blue light?

"What kind of violet is this?" I asked, pointing to a specimen that was a deep rose color at the center blending to burgundy on the edges. "I've never seen anything like it."

"It's called Vampire's Kiss. The petals in the center resemble fangs. Appropriate, right?"

I didn't know what to say.

"The African violets are my favorites," Vlad said. "I developed a fondness for them while I was with the Rangers. We trained in some pretty exotic locations."

"That must be where Marco got his love for them," I said.

"You know about that? He made me swear not to tell anyone. Marco must trust you deeply." Vlad glanced down, as though embarrassed. "Well, of course he does. You're going to be married. Shame on me for suggesting otherwise."

"He told you about our engagement?"

Vlad studied me for a long moment, as though wondering why I needed to ask. "Marco trusts me, too."

I felt my face get hot. "I know he trusts you, Vlad. Shame on me."

"I wish you trusted me." He held up his hand before I could reply. "It's okay. I know I'm different. It's hard to trust people who are different."

"It's not that I want to mistrust you. I just don't know you well enough to have the confidence in you that Marco has."

"Then I suppose you have to decide whether you can trust Marco's judgment."

When he put it that way, how could I argue?

"I should get Jillian's tea now." Vlad started out of the room, calling over his shoulder, "I made it from the oregano and basil leaves she brought with her. I was surprised she had knowledge of such a remedy."

"Me, too." I followed him across the hall into his kitchen, where he turned on a light, although again, not a bright one. The kitchen had black appliances, black granite counters, medium oak cabinets, and tan walls — a beautiful look, if a bit dark.

"My assistant Lottie told me her grandmother used herbal tea to treat infections," I said.

"That does work, but not fast enough for people nowadays. My parents use folk remedies all the time. They're in their sixties, have perfect health, and still take daily hikes in the mountains."

"Do they dress like you?" As soon as I said it, I pressed my lips together, cursing that missing tact gene.

Vlad smiled. "You mean in black clothing? As far as I know, only for funerals."

"Forgive me for asking, but why do you wear black clothes? You know it feeds the rumor mill."

Vlad crossed his arms over his chest. "Marco was right. You are nosy."

"I'm sorry. Sometimes my curiosity gets the better of me."

"Don't worry about it. You're brave. I admire that. I wear black because I like it, because I don't have to think about what to wear, and because it sets me apart from other men. Except for one time when I was in the military, it hasn't been a problem — that is, until recently."

"You could start wearing regular guy clothes. You'd fit in better."

"I could." His eyes crinkled at the corners. "If I wanted to fit in."

"You like being thought a vampire, don't you?"

Vlad poured tea into the black mug from a ceramic pot, then gave me a smile. "Let's go poison our patient."

He was joking, right?

When we returned to the bedroom, Jillian immediately raised herself on her elbows, already showing improvement, no doubt from being rehydrated.

"Here you go," Vlad said, sitting beside her.

Jillian drank thirstily, stopping for air after every few gulps. Then she sighed contentedly and leaned back against the pillow. Vlad met my gaze with a look that said, *Success!*

I was beginning to like the guy.

Jillian handed me my phone. "You can have it back now. I texted Claymore to let him know I was safe and not to worry."

"Did you tell him where you were?"

"No, I just told him you'd give him all the details later. Happy now?"

"You told Claymore *I'd* give him the details? Then he knows where you are, Jillian."

"No, he doesn't."

"Yes, he does. Claymore brought me here."

As if on cue, there was a hard pounding on the front door. Jillian's eyes grew as round as golf balls; then she pulled the blankets over her head.

"That'll be Claymore," I told Vlad.

He strode out of the room, so I followed, hoping to intercede on his behalf in case Claymore tried to avenge his wife's honor. Up ahead, I saw Vlad open the door, then be thrown back as Claymore pushed it open

310

and barged inside. Two paramedics followed, carrying their medical bags. One of
them was Kyle, who gave me a nod. A col-
lapsible gurney waited just outside.

"Where is my wife?" Claymore demanded,
his slender fists clenched as though ready to
punch.

"Claymore, calm down," I said, putting
myself between him and Vlad. "Jillian is fine.
She's resting in the bedroom."

"She's in *his* bedroom?" Claymore said,
nearly choking on his words.

"I'll show you the way," Vlad said to the
two paramedics, and started toward the
bedroom. They followed, taking the gurney
with them.

I grabbed Claymore's sleeve before he
could go after them. "Listen to me. You owe
Vlad a big thank-you. Jillian showed up here
in the night and collapsed in the hallway
outside. Vlad took her in and was able to
get liquids in her, which probably saved her
life. And just now he got her to take her
antibiotics."

Claymore was breathing hard, but as my
words sank in, he began to calm down.

"Jillian didn't think she could trust any of
us, Clay. She trusted Vlad precisely because
she thinks he's a vampire. She made him
swear he wouldn't tell where she was, and

he kept his word. That's why we didn't know. It was just good luck that I dropped those plants off and found her."

A loud screeching sent us both scurrying toward the bedroom. I turned the corner and found Jillian engaged in a blanket tug-of-war with the EMTs. "I won't go! You can't make me!"

"We just want to take you to a nice quiet room at the hospital," Kyle said. "No one will bother you there, and you'll be able to say who can visit you and who can't. How does that sound?"

Jillian didn't have the strength to keep fighting, so she reached out to Vlad. "Help me."

Vlad took her hand and sat on the bedside. "Jillian, do you trust me?"

She nodded.

"Then go with these medics to the hospital to be checked out. I will send your herbal tea mix with you so you can continue to get your strength back. Okay?"

She nodded again.

Vlad placed her hand on the bed. "I'll put the tea in a cardboard take-out cup. Let these men help you onto the cart."

Jillian watched the medics roll the gurney to the opposite side of the massive bed. Vlad left the room to get her tea, so Claymore moved up to his spot. "Jillian?" he said softly.

She glanced at him, then turned her head away. He stared at her, crushed, then left.

I followed him into the hallway.

"Clay, give her time," I said "Once her meds have fully taken effect, she'll be her old self again."

"I hope you're right." He glanced toward the kitchen. "Before I leave, I suppose I should apologize to Vlad for my rudeness."

"That would be a good idea. But don't leave without me. I'll need a ride back to Bloomers." I patted his arm, then watched as he headed down the hallway. I went back into the bedroom and found Jillian lying docilely on the gurney while the medics tucked the sheet in around her and prepared her for the trip to the hospital.

As they rolled her out of the room, Kyle said to his partner, "Go on ahead. I'll be right there."

He stepped back into the room, took an envelope from inside his jacket, and handed it to me. "That's the info Marco wanted."

"Thanks." I stared at the envelope for a few moments, tempted to open it, then stuck it in the side pocket of my coat. There'd be time for that later. I didn't want to miss my ride.

I started down the hallway and realized that the throbbing in my ankle had stopped. In fact, I couldn't feel the lower part of my leg at all.

With a feeling of dread, I lifted my leg and saw what appeared to be a big skin-colored balloon inside the rubber boot — the balloon being my ankle. I probed the swelling and set off a cascade of pain that started in my toes and ran up to my thigh. I knew then that I wasn't going anywhere without my crutches.

I glanced up and saw Claymore step outside the apartment with Vlad. "Hey!" I called. "Wait!" I hopped toward him, using the wall for balance, dislodging my purse on my shoulder in the process. It fell to the floor, but I had no time to stop.

"Hey," I called again. "A little help here, please."

Vlad turned to look first, his gaze instantly traveling to my ankle. He reached me in two strides and swept me effortlessly into his arms. "I was afraid of this."

I'd never been that close to Vlad before, and I had to admit, it wasn't such a bad experience.

Okay, Abby. Stop thinking like that. "Claymore, if you'll bring my crutches —"

"No need for that," Vlad said. "I'll carry

you out to the car."

"I'll pull my car around front," Clay said, and took off.

Nice of them to ask what *I* wanted to do. "Before we go, I dropped my purse back there."

"No problem." Vlad carried me back through the hallway, lowered me so I could retrieve the purse, then straightened — all without breaking a sweat. For a tall, slender man, he had amazing strength. He smelled good, too, like fresh herbs.

"Thanks," I said, "and not just for that. You were kind to take my cousin in and care for her. Jillian can be a handful on a good day."

"It wasn't so bad," he said, his light gray eyes quietly assessing me. "After all, it brought you here, and that gave us a chance to get better acquainted."

"That's true."

"So," he said, "let me show you my casket."

There I was, in the arms of the alleged vampire, with no witnesses in sight, being carried to the room that contained his coffin. Why did I feel like I was living that horror movie?

Vlad managed to open the door and hit a

315

light switch that turned on a table lamp without dropping me. I did a quick survey of the room but didn't see a single coffin in sight.

He carried me into a cozy living room and put me down on a caramel brown suede sofa. In front of the sofa was a beautiful old wooden chest with an arched lid and brass trim. "This is it," he said, nodding toward the chest. "My casket."

"That's not a casket."

"According to the HOW TO KILL A VAMPIRE Web site, it is, although I prefer the term *blanket chest*. But who am I to say?" Vlad smiled again, clearly finding humor in the rumors being spread about him. I, on the other hand, felt like an idiot. I'd been completely willing to believe he had a coffin in his living room.

"Have you considered putting up your own Web site to counter the rumors? You could post a photo of the chest to prove it's not a casket."

"If I do that, Abby, I give the creep behind that Web site validity. The best thing is to ignore the rumors and let people judge me by what they see — a friendly guy mixing drinks behind the bar."

"You're right, but it angers me that some-one is able to get away with spreading lies."

"It's why we live in the United States, isn't it? To have such freedom? Anyway, I have every confidence that Marco will find out who it is and handle the problem."

My cell phone rang. I took it out of my purse and saw Claymore's name on the screen. "Hi, Clay. I'll be right down."

"That's not a good idea," Claymore said. "There's trouble out front."

"Do you have a window that looks out in front of the building?" I asked Vlad.

He carried me to one of the windows in his bedroom. We lifted a slat and peered through.

A big white van sat at the curb, and as we watched, a panel door in the side of the van opened and a group of angry, baseball-bat-wielding large men jumped out. They were all wearing T-shirts that said GARLIC PARTY VAMPIRE SQUAD.

"Kill the vampire!" one of them shouted.

"Kill the vampire!" the others repeated, slapping their palms with the bats. Then they headed straight toward the building.

CHAPTER NINETEEN

"Tell Clay to go around to the alley behind the back parking lot," Vlad said, as he carried me to his front door.

I relayed the message to Clay and put my phone away. Vlad stopped to take a black leather man bag from a drawer in a table by the door and hand it to me. "Hold it for me, please."

He carried me out of the apartment, down the hallway to a flight of steps, and out the back door. I didn't know how he did it, but he wasn't even breathing hard.

Vlad checked carefully before leaving the building, then carried me through the parking lot and straight toward the black BMW idling in the alley. He opened the passenger door and put me inside, took the leather bag from me, then shut the door and patted the window. "Go!"

"What about you?" I cried, rolling down

the window. "You can't go back. Come with us."

"I can take care of myself. Now go!"

I turned to watch as Vlad disappeared behind the garage, then buckled myself in as Claymore sped away. "I hope he'll be all right."

"I called the police. They're on their way. Do you want to come with me to the hospital and have your ankle X-rayed?"

"No, thanks. Icing it should work." I hoped it would, anyway. I had to interview Dr. Holloway at two o'clock. No way did I want to be stuck in the ER all afternoon. "But please call me later and let me know how Jillian is."

"I can't thank you enough for helping us, Abby. If I can ever return the favor, just ask."

I tucked his offer away. It might come in handy one day.

Claymore wasn't familiar with Operation Abby, so he watched in amazement as Lottie and Grace swooped out of Bloomers, got me onto my crutches, and had me inside the shop in two minutes flat. I had just enough time to glance up the block and see that there weren't any protesters across the street. My ankle, however, was protesting a lot.

"Lordy, would you look at that?" Lottie cried, after I'd peeled off the yellow boot. "Didn't I tell you unwrapping your ankle was a bad idea?"

"I've got to make it all better so I can keep my two o'clock appointment. Marco will be here to get me in less than two hours."

"Your doctor's appointment is today?" Grace asked.

"Yes," I said. Stretching the truth wasn't considered a lie, was it?

"I don't think the doctor will be pleased to see the damage you've inflicted on your ankle," Grace said.

"I'll get you some ice," Lottie said, starting toward the kitchen. "We've still got a few of those old metal ice cube trays filled with water in the freezer, don't we, Gracie?"

"Last time I checked," Grace said. She had a look on her face that made me suspect she was on the verge of lecturing me. She took hold of the edges of her crisp navy blazer, clearing up any doubt as to her intentions.

"I'm reminded of the words of Thomas Fuller, a physician in the early seventeen hundreds, who said, 'Health is not valued till sickness comes.' I believe we can safely say you've proved him correct, can't we? And, of course, we shouldn't forget —"

"Gracie, would you give me a hand?" Lottie called. "The trays are frozen to the freezer."

We shouldn't forget to thank Lottie for her timely interruption.

By the time Marco came to pick me up, the swelling had gone down, my ankle was back in its Ace bandage, and Grace and Lottie had promised not to mention my mishap to anyone.

"Hey, Honeypot," he said, coming into the workroom. "How's it going?" He kissed me on the cheek, then pulled up a stool and sat down at the table with me, watching as I tied a satin bow around a bouquet of callas and roses.

"Good news. We found Jillian, and she's now in a private room at Parkview Hospital being treated for her infection and dehydration."

"Where was she?"

"At Vlad's apartment. She thought since he was a vampire, he would give her refuge."

Marco groaned. "Poor Vlad."

"He didn't seem to mind. Anyway, one of the EMTs who came to pick Jillian up was Kyle, and he gave me something for you.

It's in my jacket pocket." I pointed to my jacket hanging on the back of my desk chair.

Marco opened the envelope and pulled out a piece of paper. On the paper was a four-by-six-inch scanned photo of Lori Willis taken shortly after she'd been brought into the morgue. It showed her lying on her back on a stainless-steel table, dressed in a white blouse and a navy skirt, both badly stained and wrinkled, no doubt from the time spent in the garbage bin. Her shoes were missing. Her blond hair had been pulled away from her face, and her head turned away from the camera so that two pinhole-sized marks were visible on one side of her throat.

"Do you have a magnifying glass?" Marco asked.

"In the desk drawer."

He got it out and took a closer look. "Whoever drained her blood must have known exactly what to do. There are two puncture marks on her neck but no blood-stains." He moved the magnifier slowly across the image. "I'm not seeing any ligature marks. I would expect to see some kind of restraint, since she was held for several days, but maybe it's the poor quality of this copy. I'll have to have this enlarged and sharpened. There may be other things we're not seeing."

"Or maybe there aren't any ligature marks because Lori was locked in a basement or a storage shed — or even a barn. There are lots of abandoned barns scattered around the county."

"She would have tried to get out and her nails would show it. It doesn't look to me like her nails are broken."

I took the magnifier and held it over the photo. "It looks like they were just manicured."

"Her killer must have used drugs to subdue her. Somehow I've got to get a copy of the tox screen."

I studied the photo again. "In the casino video, Lori was wearing a yellow flower pendant and earrings. Where did they go? Her purse was intact, so is it likely that her killer would steal her jewelry but not her wallet?"

"Could've been taken as a souvenir, although that's more typical of a serial killer, and I don't think that's the case here."

"When I get home, the first thing I take off is my jewelry so that it doesn't snag my clothes. My rings and necklace are also the last things I put on in the morning. So maybe Lori was getting dressed for work Wednesday morning, or had just come home Tuesday night, when she was abducted."

"Good point. We'll have to talk to her neighbors." He glanced at his watch. "We should get going now so you won't be late for your appointment with Holloway. After supper, if everything is quiet at the bar, we'll head over to Willis's neighborhood and see what we can dig up."

We were in for a busy day. But at least we'd be together.

Sebastian Holloway's office was on the second floor of a private medical clinic across the street from County Hospital. In contrast to the old hospital building, the clinic was new and modern, with lots of windows and skylights and comfortable waiting areas. Surprisingly, when we reached Holloway's office, there were no other patients in sight.

"Still feel comfortable meeting Holloway alone?" Marco asked, after I'd signed in at the desk.

"Mais oui."

"Gabriella La Cour?" the nurse called from the doorway.

"That was fast," I said to Marco, as he helped me get balanced on the crutches. "When was the last time you saw a doctor that quickly?"

"Maybe he doesn't have many patients. He did suffer a blow to his reputation. And remember, I'll be right here if you need me."

After having me fill out a consultation form, a nurse took me into Dr. Holloway's office and asked me to sit in one of the chairs facing the doctor's desk. "Doctor will be in as soon as he finishes up with his patient," she promised.

She closed the door and left me alone in the office. I glanced around, noting the expensive oil paintings, the beautiful black cherry furniture, the overstuffed chairs, and built-in cabinets filled with leather-bound books, marble sculptures, and framed photographs.

I could hear a man talking in the next room and assumed it was Holloway, so I decided to do a little snooping. I hopped to the bookcase by holding onto the backs of furniture, then examined the photos. Some were of Holloway being presented awards. A few had been taken with political figures, the governor and a state senator among them. There was also a photo of a much younger Holloway with an attractive woman and two small children. Next to it was a shot of an older Holloway with two teenaged children, minus the woman.

I was studying the photograph of Holloway with his children when I realized the talking in the next room had stopped. Quickly, I put the frame back on the shelf and turned just as the door opened and Dr. Speedo himself stepped in. He still had the dashing appearance of George Clooney, but with more girth around the middle and the start of a sagging jawline.

"Bonjour, mademoiselle," he said with a smile, checking out my sweater and skirt. He finished that off with a lustful stare at the cleavage showing where I'd left the top two sweater buttons undone. *"C'est un plaisir de faire votre connaissance,"* he said, finding my face at last.

His accent was deplorable, but he got the French right.

Gabriella, ma cherie, *if he speaks* Français, *you're in trouble. He'll know right away you're a — how you say — fraud? In which case he won't be as pleased to make your acquaintance as he thinks.*

Holloway came toward me with his hand outstretched, his white physician's coat flapping open, revealing a white shirt and blue silk tie, with tan pants that matched his ostrich-leather shoes. He caught sight of my crutches lying beside the chair and came to a stop. "I didn't realize you were injured. *Qu'est-ce que s'est passé?*"

I was going to have to go to Plan B sooner than expected.

I let him help me into my chair, then, as he made his way around the desk, I crossed my legs so that my good foot swung free and my wrapped ankle was hidden. Naturally, the first thing he did when he was seated was stare at my bare knee. I wondered how many swings of my foot it would take before he was hypnotized.

I leaned forward and said with a sheepish smile, "You caught me, Doctor."

With a convincing show of modesty, he said, "Did I now?"

"You knew right away I wasn't French."

He shook his finger at me. "Many have tried to fool me, but few have succeeded."

"You were going to go along with my act because your curiosity got the better of you, didn't it? Shame on you for trying to fool *me!*"

"Well, it appears that now *I've* been caught." Holloway put on a good front but was unable to stop a blush of embarrassment from spreading up his neck, not because he believed he'd outsmarted me, but because he knew he hadn't.

We had a laugh; then he sat back and

studied me, or rather, my breasts. "So why are you here, Miss La Cour?"

"I'm working on an article entitled 'Brilliant Surgeons Who Give a Damn,' for a national magazine. I'm not at liberty to reveal the name of this publication just yet, but you would be exceedingly pleased." Not that any magazine editor would ever see such an article.

Holloway's gaze was focused on my face now. He was not only intrigued but also flattered. "I'm a little puzzled as to why you couldn't have told me this at the outset."

"You weren't supposed to know about the piece until after it was written. That's to ensure that the surgeons I interview don't treat me any differently than a real consult."

"I think my patients would tell you that I treat all of them very well, Miss La Cour."

What patients? "I'm sure they would. Unfortunately, I can't use you now because you know why I'm here."

He tapped his fingers on the desk for a moment, then shrugged and stood up. "Well, I'm sorry it didn't work out."

Damn. He wasn't falling for it. *Think, Abby. Stroke his ego!*

I reached for my crutches and got to my feet as he walked toward his door. "Ironic, isn't it?" I said. "The other surgeons will be in the piece because they're not as smart as you."

He stopped, his hand on the doorknob. Then he turned. "Unless . . ."

I waited.

"I don't believe we've met," he said, coming toward me with his hand outstretched. "I'm Dr. Sebastian Holloway. And you are?"

A genius.

CHAPTER TWENTY

"So," Holloway said, leaning back in his chair, "how can I help you, Miss — La Cour, was it?"

Unbelievable. Holloway was actually enjoying the charade. It made my work so much easier. Continuing the ruse, I took out my notebook and pen. "As I told your nurse, I'm interviewing doctors for my *employer*. He's seeking a second opinion from the top cardiac specialists in the world, but he's asked for a dossier on each candidate first."

A dossier. Wow. I'd pulled that right out of the air. Marco was going to be blown away. I only wished he could have been there to watch me work.

Holloway gave me a conspiratorial wink. "I understand. What would your employer like to know?"

"I already have the names of your schools, the hospital where you did your internship, et cetera, so could you tell me of any honors or awards you've received?"

Holloway was in his element now. He laced his fingers behind his head and rattled off the information, while I jotted notes furiously to make it look real.

After ten minutes of writing, I flexed my fingers to get rid of the cramps. "Very impressive, Doctor. Now tell me a little about your personal life. Children, marriages, that sort of thing."

"Okay," Holloway said with a little less enthusiasm. He went straight into a spiel about his kids, noting how they were taking after him by excelling at science and math. He got up to show me the photo of them, remarking how they also took after him in looks, then sat back down, clearly pleased with himself.

"Are you married or divorced?" I asked.

He gave me a distinctly lecherous smile. "Let's just say I'm available."

Like that was any different from when he was married. It was all I could do not to make gagging sounds. "I'm going to have to get a little more personal now, Doctor. I've found that it helps to explore some of the more painful moments in life to expose the human side, something that patients don't often get to see in their physicians."

"Okay," he said warily.

"I came across a reprimand that you received a few years back —"

Holloway smacked the top of his desk with his open hand, making me jump. "That should never have happened!"

He stood up, pushing his chair away from his desk so hard it hit the window behind him. "I was the victim of a vicious, vindictive —" He cut himself off and shook his head, as though he were about to say something revealing. "A vindictive act."

Had he stopped himself from naming Lori Willis?

"Would you clarify that for me?" I asked.

He chose his words carefully, pacing with his head down and his hands clasped behind his back. "I suppose you could call it retaliation by a person who wanted to discredit me."

"Was this person a patient?"

"It's really not pertinent, Miss La Cour."

"What was the reprimand for?"

Holloway shrugged, as if it was no big deal. "An infraction of hospital policy. Nothing that would warrant what happened."

"Which was what?"

"To start with, my reputation was tarnished and I nearly lost my hospital privileges. It also caused my marriage to fall apart and almost ruined me financially."

"That must have been quite an ordeal."

"It was a living hell, Miss La Cour. A. Living. Hell."

I could see that he was enjoying the role of martyr, so I played up to it. "What would cause someone to seek retaliation against such an esteemed surgeon as yourself?"

"Jealousy," he said, as though it should be obvious.

"Over your success?"

"Of course. Among other things."

"Such as?"

"Let's just say everything that comes with success."

"There have to be other skilled surgeons at County Hospital who have had great achievements. Have they been targets, too?"

Holloway smiled. "Just yours truly."

"Because of your success."

"Yes."

Somehow I had to get him to admit that Lori was behind it. "Excuse me for saying so, Doctor, but I'm not buying it. Someone targeted you alone, and that smacks of more than jealousy. That sounds like retaliation for something much more personal. Am I right?"

He continued to walk back and forth.

Finally, he looked at me, his head at an angle. "Why are you so interested in this?"

"Can't you see how this will play out on the written page? Think about it, Doctor. There you are, a prominent surgeon, attacked and nearly brought down by a vindictive — colleague?"

He smiled cagily. "Perhaps."

"Wounded professionally, cast adrift emotionally, you rose above it all to be where you are today, one of the preeminent cardiac surgeons in the *world*."

If that didn't get to him, nothing would.

"Cardio-thoracic," he corrected.

I made a show of amending my notes. "And you did it in spite of this *colleague* who wanted to destroy you. What a great human-interest story. The readers will eat this up."

"And it's all true," he said, nodding sagely.

"All because you rejected this colleague's, what, advice? No, that's not it. I can tell by your expression. You rejected this colleague's — ah, of course — advances."

Holloway paced for a few more moments, as though gathering his thoughts, then stopped by the window to gaze out toward the hospital across the street. "You're very shrewd, Miss La Cour. And you're right. She was a woman in desperate need of power. A woman who would do anything to get ahead. What she saw in me was a way to have more authority and prestige."

"By having an affair with you?"

Holloway turned, his arms wide-open. "What else?"

"While you were married?"

"The fact that I was married didn't matter to Lor—"

He'd said it!

Holloway pressed his lips together and turned to stare out the window.

"Lori? Is that her name?" I asked, pretending to scribble more notes.

He waved it away. "Names aren't important."

"How did Lori hope to gain prestige and authority if your affair was to be kept secret?"

"Her name wasn't Lori," Holloway snapped, turning to give me a fierce glare. "*My* name is the only one you need to be concerned about. *My* name! Understand?"

"I am so sorry, Doctor. Yes, I understand, and you're one hundred percent correct. This piece is about you. We'll simply refer to her as a colleague, then. So let me rephrase my question. Can you explain how your colleague planned to reap any benefits from the affair if it was clandestine? Through blackmail?"

"No, of course not," Holloway said irritably. "None of this matters anyway because I made it perfectly clear to her that I wasn't interested in any kind of relationship. After that, she left me alone, or so I mistakenly believed. But all the while she was biding her time, and when she saw an opportunity to bring me down, she grabbed it. Fortunately, neither my patients nor the hospital deserted me, nor did I keel over from the shock of what I went through, which is a tribute to my strong constitution."

"It must have been a bitter pill to swallow," I said. "What helped get you through it?"

He turned back to stare out the window. "Careful planning."

As in, planning a bloodletting? "Would you share that plan with the readers? Something they can take away with them?"

He rocked back on his heels, his hands clasped behind his back. "How does one plan anything, Miss La Cour? A vacation, for instance. You pick your destination, determine the best way to get there, arrange your accommodations, and hope for no bad weather."

"What was your destination in this case,

Doctor?"

"Redemption."

I waited for Holloway to elaborate, but he continued to stare out the window, so I said, "Would you like to explain how that worked?"

"It's self-explanatory."

Okay then. "From what you've told me, the reprimand put you in a tailspin. People often seek solace from traumatic situations by engaging in unhealthy habits. Did that happen to you?"

He turned to give me a puzzled look. "Unhealthy habits? Are you asking if I became an addict?"

"There are many types of addictions. Drinking, drugs, gambling . . ."

"I don't believe in polluting my body with excessive alcohol or recreational drugs, Miss La Cour, and I don't have the time or interest for gambling. In fact, I opposed legislation allowing casinos to operate in this state."

I jotted that down. "This is going to make a fascinating in-depth piece on you, Dr. Holloway. I appreciate your granting me this interview. All I need now is a way to end it. Clearly you've moved on with your life. What of your colleague? Do you ever see her? Have you had any contact with her

337

since the reprimand?"

"Does it matter? I'm here, aren't I? I survived it."

But Lori didn't, I wanted to say. "That's true, Doctor. However, what I meant was —"

"I know what you meant."

I glanced at him uncertainly. He couldn't possibly know.

He smiled coyly. Was he going to accuse me of lying? Demand to know my real purpose for being there? Have me thrown out? Should I grab my crutches and make a run for it?

If only I could.

I uncrossed my leg and leaned down for my purse. No sense delaying the inevitable.

When I straightened, Holloway was coming toward me. I watched warily as he turned the chair next to mine so it was facing me. He sat down, the tart men's cologne he had bathed in that morning washing over me like a lemon tsunami. He took my pen, stuck it in the pocket of his white coat, then picked up my hand and began to stroke the palm with his thumb.

"The magazine article is a ruse, isn't it?"

My face instantly got hot. "Why would you think that?"

"All these questions about my personal

life — whether I'm married, whether I've moved on — they have nothing to do with my being a preeminent surgeon. The simple truth is that you've been wanting to meet me."

He couldn't be serious. "I'm sorry if you somehow got that impression from my questions, Doctor, but —"

"Call me Bastian."

What a coincidence. I was thinking of calling him something very similar to that.

Holloway stroked my wrist, making little circles with his thumb. "Let's be honest, Miss La Cour. We both know the primary reason you chose me for your article is not because I'm a brilliant surgeon — not that it didn't help, of course."

Let's be honest indeed. I forcefully removed my hand from his. "You're wrong."

He placed his hands on the arms of my chair. "I'm never wrong. I'm an expert at reading women's desires. And I have to say, your little cat-and-mouse game is quite a turn-on."

"Okay, I'm going to have to end this now. Would you give me my pen, please?"

He leaned toward me, his gaze fastened on my lips as he said seductively, "We needn't end anything, *Gabriella.* This is our beginning."

Fearing that his next move would be to kiss me, I quickly felt alongside the chair for one of my crutches, intending to follow Marco's advice and smack him with it. Before I could lay my hand on it, however, there was a quick rap on the door.

"What?" Holloway snarled, turning just as the door opened and his nurse stepped inside. She was followed by Marco.

I breathed a sigh of relief. The cavalry had arrived.

The doctor erupted in a fit of temper. "What's the meaning of this?"

Steely-eyed, Marco instantly calculated Holloway's close proximity to me to assess my immediate danger, then started toward us. I gave him a quick shake of my head to let him know that my safety hadn't been breeched, and then I saw him visibly relax. The nurse had disappeared.

"Who are you?" Holloway bellowed, jumping to his feet. "How dare you barge in here!"

Keeping his gaze fixed on the surgeon, Marco said to me, "Let's go."

As I packed up my notebook and slid my purse over my shoulder, Holloway charged toward the door, bellowing for his nurse. Marco stepped into his path, shutting the door so the doctor had nowhere to go.

"I demand to know who you are!" Holloway raged, backing away from Marco's hard stare.

Balancing against the chair, I wedged the crutches under my arms and hop-stepped toward Marco. Without a word, he opened the door to let me through, then followed me out and shut the door behind him. We started down the hallway together, saying nothing. As I passed the reception desk, I caught Holloway's nurse covering her mouth, trying to hide a grin. I gave her a smile and continued on.

"That was exciting," I said, as we left the clinic.

"Did you get your questions answered?"

"Most of them, until Holloway decided I was lusting after him."

"So much for being able to handle frisky men," Marco said, helping me into the car.

"Trust me. Holloway wouldn't have gotten far." I gave Marco a playful punch in the arm. "But I'm glad you showed up anyway. And you would have been proud of me. I got Dr. Wonderful to say Lori's name. He told me she tried to ruin him for rejecting her advances, just as Courtney Anne had said. And get this — when I asked how he'd handled the crisis, his answer was 'by careful planning.' "

"Did he explain that?"

"He would only equate it with planning a vacation. So I asked what his destination had been and he said *redemption.* I tried to get him to clarify that, but he wouldn't. Maybe all he meant was that he had a financial plan to pull himself out of debt, but if that were so, you'd think he would've told me. If he hadn't gone all Lusty Louie on me, I might have gotten more out of him."

"Next time we talk to him, we'll use the direct approach."

"Next time? Holloway wouldn't talk to you before, Marco, and he's certainly not going to talk to either one of us now."

"I think he will. His nurse was nice enough to tell me where he hangs out after hours. Tonight, eight o'clock, we're going to be there."

"And where is that?"

"The casino boat."

"He told me he's opposed to gambling."

"According to his nurse, blackjack is his game."

"So Dr. Speedo lied to me twice."

"Yep. He and Jerry Trumble are now two for two."

"Speaking of Jerry, I almost forgot. I'm

meeting with his wife's two friends at closing time today."

"When did you set that up?"

I thought back over the past two days. "So much has happened, I can't remember. This morning, I think."

"Do you want me there?"

"It'd be better if you weren't."

At ten minutes to five, Grace came into the workroom to report that a pair of women were in the coffee-and-tea parlor asking to see me. By the time I grabbed a pen and notebook and wheeled into the parlor, Grace had poured them coffee and put out the last two scones of the day, along with a bowl of clotted cream.

One of the women had already spread cream on her scone and was nibbling at the end, while the other stirred sugar into her coffee. Both appeared to be in their midthirties, one a pleasant-looking woman with short, curly brown hair that framed her round face, the other a lean woman with the physique of a runner, her brown hair in a high ponytail.

I introduced myself, and at their curious looks, explained about my ankle.

"I sprained my ankle once," the runner said, "but all the doctor did for me was tell me to stay off of it. I'm Alison, by the way."

"I'm Becky," the other woman said with a sweet smile, shaking my hand.

"Thanks for coming over." I noticed Grace hovering, so I said, "Would you close up shop, please? We might be a while, so I'll see you and Lottie in the morning."

I waited until Grace had left the room, then said, "Before I explain what I want to do for Dana, how do you happen to know her?"

"We went to college with her," Becky said. "We shared an apartment for our last two years at school."

"Until she met Jerry," Alison said drily, "and he talked her into moving in with him." She glanced at Becky and they shared a private look.

It seemed pretty clear that they didn't like Jerry, but I hated to assume it and end up offending them. I had to be tactful. "You mentioned on the phone not wanting to be involved in anything if Jerry was included. Would you mind telling me why?"

The two again shared a look; then Alison said, "Because he murdered Dana."

And I'd been worried about being tactful.

CHAPTER TWENTY-ONE

I glanced from Alison to Becky. "Jerry murdered his wife?"

They nodded in unison.

"Do you have proof?" I asked.

"No," Alison said, "but in the last months before she died, she told us that if something happened to her, we should tell the police Jerry did it. So we told them, and they acted like we were airheads. Turns out both detectives we talked to knew Jerry through the pharmacy."

"Everyone thinks Jerry's Mr. Nice Guy," Becky said. "He's an expert at hiding his true personality."

"Except in front of us," Alison added. "He hates us. He did everything he could to keep Dana away from us. We'd steal her away from work at lunchtime so he didn't know."

"Dana went along with that?" I asked.

"She was scared every moment," Becky said, "but she went along with it."

"Did he physically abuse her?" I asked.

Alison tapped her temple. "He played mind games with her. He'd be sweet for a few days. Then he'd accuse her of having affairs, of turning their son against him, of hiding money so she could leave him —"

"While he was actually the one being sneaky," Becky finished. "When Dana found out, she confronted him. It caused a big fight that ended with her telling him she wanted a divorce. The next thing we heard, they were taking a trip to Australia to fix their marriage."

I saw Alison roll her eyes, so I said, "You don't believe that?"

"Dana wanted out," Alison said. "Their marriage was beyond repair. The only reason she would have gone was to let him down gently."

"Then Dana got a blood clot on the way home and ended up in intensive care," Becky said sadly, "giving Jerry the perfect setup."

"How conveniently it all worked out for Jerry," Alison said.

"You don't think it's possible that the nurse gave her too much heparin?" I asked.

"Sure, it's possible," Alison said, "but it's more probable that Jerry knew Dana wasn't going to stay with him and planned a way to kill her that would make him appear innocent."

She'd just voiced my theory. "Do you think Jerry is one of those guys who can't stand the thought of Dana being with anyone else?"

"With Jerry, it would be about the money," Becky said.

"He was a control freak," Alison said. "He watched every dime Dana spent. He'd go berserk if she bought a new lipstick before the old one was gone."

"Are you absolutely sure Dana was going to leave him?" I asked.

"That's how she was talking before they left," Becky said. "After she got on that plane for Australia, we never heard from her again, so there's really no way to know what she was thinking then."

"Of course she was going to leave him," Alison said to her friend. "She told us so."

"She could have changed her mind," Becky argued.

"No way," Alison retorted. "She was determined to get away from him."

Both women took sips of coffee, as though they needed to calm down.

"I think it's time to tell you why I wanted this meeting," I said.

Over the last of the coffee, I explained the

investigation into Lori's murder. Neither Alison nor Becky was offended by my ruse, and both were delighted that Jerry was finally being investigated.

"Do you think Lori found something that proved Jerry murdered Dana?" Becky asked.

"That's the only way it makes sense for him to kill Lori now," I said. "We're going to interview Jerry again, so I hope I can get him to let something slip. And that reminds me. You mentioned that Dana caught him sneaking around. Do you know who the woman was?"

"He wasn't having an affair," Becky said.

"That we know of," Alison amended. "Dana found out he was gambling again. He'd gotten them into deep financial trouble about six months earlier and had supposedly sworn off gambling. But a few weeks before Dana died, someone she worked with saw Jerry at the boat."

At the word *gambling,* my ears began to buzz. "Do you know which boat?"

"The Calumet Casino," Alison said.

That was quite a coincidence.

"Then she found out he'd been going there on a regular basis," Alison said. "He had been able to hide it because he handled their finances. Once Dana looked into it, she found out they were up to their ears in debt again."

"Do you know whether Jerry took out an insurance policy on Dana before she died?" I asked.

The women glanced at each other. "No, but we've wondered that for years," Becky said.

"Even if he didn't," Alison said, "with the settlement he received from that lawsuit, he has to be set for life. First thing he did after the case was over was to get himself the biggest, fanciest truck money could buy. For a guy supposedly grieving over his wife, Jerry has been one happy camper."

As soon as Alison and Becky were gone, I called Marco. "I've got great information on Trumble. I'll tell you about it when I see you. Is it okay for me to come down by myself?"

"No vigilantes in sight, but I'd still rather come get you."

"Is Vlad there?"

"You want *him* to come get you?"

"No, silly. I was just checking to make sure he hadn't had a problem getting to work."

"Are you referring to the incident with the men in the white van carrying baseball bats, which you somehow forgot to tell me about?"

"I'm sorry, Marco. There's too much going on. I can't keep track of it all. I guess it was Vlad's story to tell anyway."

"Luckily it had a happy ending. I'll be right down."

As I kept pace with Marco, I told him about my meeting with Dana Trumble's friends, their strong beliefs about Jerry being responsible for Dana's death, their surprising revelation about Jerry's gambling at the Calumet Casino, and our speculation as to whether he might have used both the insurance money and the settlement money to pay off his gambling debts.

"I'll see what I can find out about that," Marco said. "And we'll need to watch those security videos again, to see if Jerry was there Tuesday night. I'll call the casino and see if we can go in at lunchtime tomorrow."

"We'd be cutting it close. I have to see my foot doctor at two. Can you make it later?"

"Are you sure you want to take all that time off, Abby? I can watch the tapes. I'll head over there as soon as I drop you off at Bloomers in the morning."

"You're right. I've been gone a lot. I'd better stick close to the shop."

Marco had saved the back booth for us, so as I made my way through the crowd ahead of him, I caught Vlad's eye and smiled. He winked. Two women sitting at the bar thought he had winked at them and nearly fell off their stools.

I glanced to the left and saw Kyle at a nearby booth watching our progress. He lifted a hand in greeting.

"How's it going?" Marco called to him.

I eased into the booth, making sure not to bump my tender ankle, while Marco went to put in our food orders and bring back beers. I saw his head bartender pull him aside to tell him something, so when Marco returned with our drinks, he said, "One of my distributors phoned and needs to talk to me. I'll be right back."

Marco headed toward his office, and a moment later, Vlad sat down across from me. Every female in the place swiveled to watch as he leaned toward me. "How's your ankle?"

"It's back to its normal size. Thanks for not mentioning it to Marco. No sense stressing him over nothing, right?"

Vlad gave me a nod, his cool gray gaze saying, *Don't worry. I know how to keep a secret.* Which was why I still didn't feel safe in taking him off the suspect list.

"I feel like an idiot," Vlad said. "I didn't pay you for the plants this afternoon. Okay if I stop by the store tomorrow?"

"Sure."

"Have you heard how Jillian is?"

"She's better. Claymore texted a little while ago that the antibiotic is working, and she's giving everyone at the hospital a hard time."

"Is that good?"

"It means she's becoming her old self again."

"Give her my regards," he said, rising.

"Will do."

Vlad did a visual sweep of the room before starting through the crowd, as though checking for danger. It was something I'd seen Marco do many times, a vestige from his Special Ops training, he'd told me. As Vlad made his way to the bar, I saw more than one woman slip him a business card. I also saw Kyle frowning as he watched Vlad.

Marco slid onto the bench beside me. "Got it all straightened out," he said, reaching for his beer.

"Do women give you their business cards?"

Marco gave me a puzzled look. "What?"

"I saw several women give Vlad their cards, so I wondered if it happens to you."

"All the time."

"What?"

"All the time." Marco leaned toward me until our foreheads were touching. "And I throw them all out."

"Nice save."

He unfolded a piece of paper and turned it to face me. "Look what I picked up today. A copy of Kyle's time sheet."

"Just so you know, Kyle is sitting at the front booth."

"I know. See this? He was on duty last Tuesday from three until midnight, and back on duty Wednesday morning at eight. He could have easily made it to the boat before Lori left Tuesday night. His alibi doesn't hold up."

"Then why isn't he being investigated?"

"You know how it works. The chief prosecutor is looking for a quick arrest and a simple conviction. Vlad's practically got a target on his back. All we need is one damning piece of evidence on one of our suspects, Abby, and we can make it go away."

"Dinner's served," Gert said, setting plates of pulled pork sandwiches and potato salad in front of us. "Need anything else?"

"This will do. Thanks, Gert." Marco picked up the big sandwich with both hands, while I tried to attack mine in a more ladylike fashion, cutting bites with my fork and knife.

"Anyway," Marco said, "I got to thinking about that photo of the Vlad look-alike taken in the casino parking lot. There had to be two people involved — one to take the photo and one to pretend to be Vlad — so my first thought was that Kyle might have enlisted the help of one of the other EMTs. So I checked the time sheets, got the name of the paramedic who worked with Kyle last week, and arranged a meeting for tonight at the Daily Grind."

"How did you convince him to come?"

"I told him I had evidence that linked him to the murder investigation. It was a long shot but it did the trick. So we'll visit Willis's neighbors first, then hop over to the casino at eight o'clock to catch Holloway, then return to meet with the paramedic."

I yawned, thinking about the late night. "Sounds like we'll be busy all evening."

"We need to get this investigation moving, babe."

"I'm not complaining."

"Yes, you are."

"Yes, I am." I leaned my head against his shoulder. "I really wanted us to have free time together this week, Marco. But that's okay. I understand this is important."

Marco put his arm around me. "It *is* important, Sunshine. I appreciate your understanding. Who knows? Maybe we'll find that piece of evidence tonight."

Lori Willis had lived in a neighborhood of bungalow houses just west of County Hospital. The houses were small and affordable and therefore popular among the hospital's huge nursing and administrative staff. Lori's white aluminum-sided house sat on a corner, with her backyard abutting the yard of the gray-shingle house whose occupants had decorated their lawn with plastic geese and spotted fawns, along with half a dozen bird feeders.

We canvassed the neighbors on Lori's street first, and none reported seeing or hearing anything unusual Tuesday night or Wednesday morning. But a woman in the gray-shingle house told us that a nurse living two doors away on the other side of her had visited Lori on Wednesday morning, blowing our theory that she had been abducted from the casino.

"Are you sure this nurse visited Wednesday morning?" Marco asked.

The neighbor, Mrs. Green, a ferretlike woman who kept blinking her eyes as though they were itchy, said in a loud voice, "It was Wednesday, sugar. Wednesday morning is garbage pickup day. I may be a senior but I'm not senile." She wiggled her hips. It was quite startling. Then she went back to watering pots of newly emerged sweet peas that bordered her patio.

"Do you know the nurse's name?" I asked, as Marco took out his notebook.

She shut off the hose, casting me an annoyed glance. "It's Diane."

"Last name?" I persisted.

"Diane the tuna is all I know. That's how she introduced herself."

"Diane Rotunno?" Marco asked.

"Could be, sugar. I don't hear so well." She smiled at him, revealing dentures that hadn't seen a good cleaning in quite a while.

"How did you see Diane visit Lori from your house?" I asked.

She pointed to a sliding glass door that opened onto her patio. "You see that door? I sit in front of it all morning with my coffeepot and my bagels, watching the birds come to the feeders. It's more entertaining than those inane morning talk shows, that's for sure."

She sniffed indignantly and hitched up her blue stretch pants, which were having a hard time staying up on her scrawny frame. The pants matched the blue-and-green-flowered knit top under her white sweater. "Everyone cuts through these yards. Diane and Lori used to go back and forth between their houses all the time. Nowadays, not so much. But Wednesday morning I saw Diane cut across my yard and go right up to Lori's back door. Then Lori let her inside."

"Are you positive it was Wednesday?" I asked. "Not Tuesday?"

"Do I look like a moron to you?" she shot back, glaring at me, one hand on her hip.

Okay, I was done asking her questions.

"How long did Diane stay?" Marco asked.

Naturally, Mrs. Green wasn't as harsh with Marco. "Now, that I can't tell you. Phyllis always calls right about that time. Talks my ear off for an hour every morning. Talk, talk, talk, and never says nothin' interesting. I didn't see Diane leave, is what I'm telling you."

"Do you know if Lori had any visitors Tuesday evening?" Marco asked.

Mrs. Green shook her head. "Can't help you there, either. Lori's house was dark when I went to bed. I usually watch the ten o'clock news, then hit the hay."

"Do you know whether Lori went to work on Wednesday?" Marco asked.

"I guess she did. When I walked to the other corner at nine o'clock to wait for the geezer bus, her car wasn't parked at the curb like it usually is. Next thing I knew, the TV news people were reporting her missing. She was a good neighbor, Lori was."

"How long has Lori lived there?" Marco asked.

She scratched her belly. "Oh, gosh, maybe eight years? She moved in about a year after Diane did. Lots of nurses live around here. I always say if I keel over one day, my husband won't have to look far for help."

Marco handed her his business card. "If you remember anything else about Lori's movements on Tuesday or Wednesday, would you give me a call?"

She pinched his cheek. "You bet your sweet behind, sugar." She stuck her tongue out at me, then went back to watering her plants.

"Unpleasant little ferret woman," I said, as we headed toward the sidewalk.

"She's harmless. Let's see if Diane's home — if you're up to the walk."

I took one hand off the grasp bar of my crutch and showed Marco the impressive callus that had developed on the heel of my palm. "I'm tough. I can do it."

"That's my girl. I like my women — sorry, *woman* — tough."

"You're getting good at those saves, Salvare."

"I get lots of practice."

Diane lived in a tidy tan bungalow with brown shutters. It had a small front yard and a long backyard with a giant weeping willow tree in it. So as not to alarm her, we'd decided I should make the introductions, so I knocked on her front door while Marco waited at my side.

"Diane Rotunno? I'm Abby Knight — from Bloomers Flower Shop."

"Just a minute." Diane opened the door, leaving the chain in place, so all I saw was an eyeball and a slice of blue clothing. "Can I help you?"

"I'm here with a private investigator. We're talking to people in the neighborhood about Lori Willis's murder. This is Marco Salvare." I stepped aside so Marco could show her his license.

"I've already given a statement to the police," she said.

"Unfortunately, that doesn't help our investigation," Marco said. "We don't have access to their files. That's why we're hoping you'll share whatever information you have about Lori with us to help us narrow down our suspect list." He kept his gaze on the eyeball. Even one-eyed, she would surely be susceptible to his charm.

"If you're a private investigator, who's your client?" she asked warily.

"I'm not at liberty to say," Marco said.

"It's not Sebastian Holloway, is it?" she asked.

"No," Marco said. "Not Sebastian Holloway or anyone associated with him."

"How do you know Dr. Holloway?" I asked.

"I work at County Hospital. So is Holloway on your list of suspects?"

"I'll answer your question if you'll answer ours," Marco said.

The eyeball moved to me, then to my crutches. Apparently deciding I couldn't do her much harm, she unchained her door and opened it halfway. She had on a blue jogging outfit and was perspiring, as though she'd just been out for a run. She appeared to be in her midforties, brown hair tied back, no makeup, and attractive in a wholesome kind of way. "What do you want to know?"

"Why you asked about Dr. Holloway," Marco said.

"Because if you're serious investigators, you'd have to be looking at him as a suspect. The police didn't want to hear what I had to say about him. All they wanted to know was whether Lori was seeing that vampire guy, and if I'd seen him around here."

"And your answers were?" Marco asked.

360

"No to both questions. That didn't make them too happy."

"How did the police get your name?"

"They were canvassing everyone in the neighborhood," Diane said.

"Would you tell us what you know about Dr. Holloway?" Marco asked, pulling out his notepad and pen.

She opened the door wider. "You might as well come inside. I have nosy neighbors."

We stood in her foyer because she didn't ask us to sit.

"Like I said, I work at County. I can't avoid Holloway."

"I was under the impression that you worked with Lori at Parkview," I said.

"I did for a while. Then I moved back to County."

I was waiting for Marco to pick up on that line of questioning, but instead he moved on.

"Tell us why you think Dr. Holloway should be a suspect," he said.

"Because he hated Lori," Diane replied. "Because I've heard him brag that he knows ways to kill people that would never be detected. And because if you dig deeper into his alibi than the police did, you'll find he was lying."

"Can you be more specific than that?"

Marco asked, writing down the information.

"That's about as specific as I want to be."

"Do you know what Holloway's alibi is?" I asked.

Diane used a terry-cloth towel to wipe her forehead. "Medical conference in Phoenix."

"He didn't go?" I asked.

"Oh, he went, all right. But like I said, dig deeper."

"So he went to Phoenix," I said, "but not to the conference?"

"You're half right," she said. "And that's all I'll say on it. I like being employed."

"How do you know this information?" Marco asked.

She smiled. "I can't tell you that. But I have it from a reliable source."

"Did you see Lori Wednesday morning?" he asked.

"Not Wednesday, no. I went to Lori's place Tuesday morning. I'll bet Mrs. Green told you Wednesday, didn't she? That old busybody. She's half off her rocker and always sticks her nose into everyone's business."

"Every neighborhood has a Mrs. Green," I said.

Diane took another look at me. "Do we know each other?"

"Possibly. Do you ever buy flowers at Bloomers?"

Diane's mouth dropped open. "You're the florist who's always helping catch criminals!"

"Not *always*," I said modestly. "A few times, perhaps. Well, okay, ten."

She leaned against the door and crossed her arms. "You're such a little thing. How do you do it, and on crutches yet?"

Marco cleared his throat. He was growing impatient.

"The crutches are temporary," I said, then put my hand on Marco's arm. "And he's how I do it." Then I turned the floor over to my intended before he started pawing the ground.

Marco pulled out the photo of Lori. "Would you mind looking at this?"

Diane took it from him, saw what it was, and turned her head away with a grimace. "You should have warned me."

"I know it's difficult," Marco said, "so try to look only at the clothing, see if it looks familiar."

Diane closed her eyes for a moment, steeling herself. Then she took a long look at the photo and handed it back. "That's the outfit Lori was wearing Tuesday morning."

"Are you certain?" Marco asked.

"She had a matching blazer when I saw her, but it's the same skirt and blouse. She called it her power suit. She was also wearing a shiny yellow flower pendant, kind of Art Deco style, with a white center, and matching earrings."

"What kind of flower?" I asked.

Marco glanced at me as if to say, *What difference does it make? A flower is a flower.*

"It wasn't a daisy," Diane said. "It had lots of thin petals, like a dandelion."

A flower was definitely *not* a flower when it was a weed that a certain vampire lookalike had a thing for.

"Why did you visit Lori Tuesday morning?" Marco asked.

"To get my hibachi back," Diane said. "I leave it on my patio. Every time Lori decides she wants to grill, she takes it. But that's how Lori is — was. Whatever she wanted, she took."

Including someone else's promotion. Diane had just opened the gate for us. That must have been what Marco was waiting for.

"I understand you and Lori were up for the same position a few years back," Marco said.

Diane's nostrils flared, as though the thought of it still stank. "Yeah, until she

364

went behind my back to sabotage my chances of getting it. Then she couldn't understand why I didn't want to be friends anymore."

"Being stabbed in the back is hard to take," Marco said.

"I was furious for a long time," Diane said. "I went to Parkview before Lori did and helped her get hired. Then she sabotaged me. I couldn't even stand to be in the same room with her after that. But I ended up with a position at County that I like even more — and she ended up dead — so it all worked out." She smiled wryly.

Macabre sense of humor. I liked her.

"Were you at County Hospital when the wrongful-death lawsuit was filed against Lori and the hospital by a patient named Jerry Trumble?" Marco asked.

"Sure was," Diane said.

"Do you know how Mr. Trumble learned about the dosage error?" Marco asked.

"I sure don't."

"Did you have a conversation with Jerry that might have tipped him off?" Marco asked.

She looked confused. "Are you asking if I told Jerry that Lori gave his wife the overdose? No!"

"Did you say anything to him at his wife's

funeral that might have led him to believe Lori had a hand in Dana Trumble's death?" Marco asked.

"No! Jerry asked *me* if I knew that Lori had given his wife the heparin. All I said to him was that I didn't know anything about it and I was sorry for his loss. I only knew them through the Lamaze class I taught when Dana was pregnant."

"Would you have said something to Jerry to get back at Lori?" I asked.

"Get back at her for what? Dana died while Lori and I were still at County, well before the director's position became available. Look, even if I had known something about Dana's death, I wouldn't have told Jerry about it. I'd have gone to my supervisor."

Marco wrote it down. "Last question, and this is just a formality. I know you've already given a statement, but would you tell us where you were last Tuesday night?"

"I spent the night at my boyfriend's place. We had dinner with another couple and spent the evening playing the Wii. I didn't come back here until after work on Wednesday. I'll be glad to provide names and numbers so you can check."

Marco took down the information, thanked her, handed her his card, and told her to contact him if she thought of anything else.

"I vote for crossing Diane off the list," I said to Marco as we headed for his car. "She doesn't strike me as a vengeful person, and her motive is weak."

"First we need to give her friends a call to check out her alibi. Remember, verify everything."

"Diane also denied what Jerry told us about her encouraging him to file the suit. So why would he tell us something that could be disproved?"

"That's Diane's version, don't forget. That's why we —"

"I know. Verify everything. What do you think Diane was hinting at when she told us to dig deeper into Holloway's medical conference?"

"Someone must have told her he showed up for the conference but didn't attend the sessions. My guess is he was engaged in an activity that would get him — or whoever he was with — into trouble."

"Such as having an affair with a co-worker?"

"Or gambling, meeting a lover, flying home to commit murder. Someone else knows what he was doing."

"How do we find out who it is? Diane's

not going to give up the name."

"Maybe we won't need the name. Maybe all we'll need to do is make Holloway believe we know who it is."

Marco helped me into the car, and then we headed for the casino to try to catch Dr. Speedo in his lie.

CHAPTER TWENTY-TWO

My ankle was aching after hobbling around Lori's neighborhood, but during the half-hour drive, I felt better. In fact, I was eager to confront Holloway, especially with the plan Marco and I had devised. I couldn't wait to see the doctor's face when he saw us again.

It was worth the effort. Holloway was seated at one of the blackjack tables looking quite pleased with the play he'd just made when I took an empty seat at the table. Holloway glanced at me, then did a double take.

"Doctor," I said with a nod.

Before he could react, Marco clamped a hand on his shoulder, causing Holloway to turn with a jerk. Instantly, his face darkened in fury. "What are you doing here?" he asked, keeping his voice low.

"We could ask you the same thing," I said.

"We need to talk," Marco said.

Holloway did a quick survey of the others

at his table, as though to see if anyone was watching him, then said out of the side of his mouth, "What about?"

Marco bent down near his ear. "Lori Willis's murder."

"I have nothing to say to you."

"Pick your spot, Doc," Marco said. "Here or at the bar." He patted Holloway's shoulder, giving the impression to anyone observing their exchange that they were buddies.

"You have no right to question me," Holloway said in a furious whisper.

"Here, then," Marco said, and looked around for a chair.

"I'll report you to security and have you tossed out."

"You do that," I said, "and I'll report you to the hospital administrator for putting the moves on me." I held up my cell phone. "Amazing what these smart phones can do. Take pictures, record conversations . . ." Not that I had a smart phone. Not on my salary.

Holloway threw down his cards and got up, making a beeline for the bar. Marco helped me get settled on my crutches; then we followed him to where he'd perched at the end of the long polished-walnut counter. The only other patrons, two women who were on the lookout for available men, and

370

a drunk who had his elbows propped on the wood to keep from falling onto his shot glass, were well outside of hearing range.

"I should have you arrested for harassment," Holloway ground out, as we sat on the next two stools.

"Two ginger ales," Marco told the bartender.

"Sir?" the bartender said, waiting for Holloway's order.

"Vodka gimlet," Holloway grumbled. Without looking at Marco, he said, "I can't tell you anything about that woman's death. What business is it of yours anyway?"

Marco opened his wallet to show his ID. "I'm investigating her murder. I'd like to ask you a few questions."

Holloway looked at it askance. "So you're a private eye? Big deal."

"Did you kill her?" Marco asked.

"Of course not! I had no reason to kill her!" Holloway said, raising his voice. That got everyone's attention, including the drunk, who sat upright and tried to focus on us. He gave up after a minute and went back to leaning on his elbows.

"That's not the impression you gave me," I reminded Holloway. "You told me Lori nearly ruined your career. You said she caused you deep humiliation, financial problems, and a divorce."

"It all adds up to a powerful motive," Marco said. He waited while the bartender delivered our drinks, then said, "That leaves just means and opportunity, Doc, and I'm betting you're up to speed on knowing how to do some bloodletting. Isn't that the word you use for exsanguination?"

"Who told you that?"

"Let's talk about your alibi," Marco said.

"My alibi is sound!" Holloway dropped his voice to a whisper. "I was out of town attending a medical conference last Tuesday and Wednesday and didn't get home until late Wednesday evening."

"Try again," Marco said.

"I beg your pardon?"

Marco took a drink of his soda. "Try again."

"Check with the cops if you doubt me," Holloway said. "Or call the American Heart Association. They'll tell you I was at the conference."

"The only thing the AHA will tell me is that someone signed you in at the conference registration desk on Tuesday."

"You want a handwriting sample? Here. I'll provide one for you free of charge." Holloway pulled a gold pen out of his chest pocket, scribbled his name on his cocktail napkin, and shoved it toward Marco, who folded it and tucked it away without looking at it.

"Even if the signature matches, Doc, can you prove where you were when you were supposed to be in those sessions?"

"I don't know what you're talking about."

Marco leaned closer to him. "I know a person who knows what I'm talking about, and I think you know that person, too."

It was a good bluff. The muscles in Holloway's face tensed. He drank half his gimlet and signaled for another. "What do you want from me?"

"Proof that you didn't kill Lori Willis."

Holloway studied Marco as he toyed with the olive spear in his drink. Then, as though he'd made a decision, he turned away, ate the olives, finished the drink, and pushed the glass aside. A sly grin played at one corner of his mouth.

At the same time, Marco glanced at me long enough to give me a wink, as though he was certain the doctor was about to come clean. I wondered if he'd seen Holloway's grin.

"I can't prove it," Holloway said.

Marco didn't say a word. I knew he'd been caught off guard.

The doctor shrugged. "So what now? Call

the cops and have me arrested?"

This time it was Marco's jaw that tensed. Holloway had outsmarted us. He obviously felt confident that whoever our purported source was, he or she couldn't do the doctor any harm, just as Holloway knew there was nothing we could do to him either. He threw a twenty-dollar bill on the counter, picked up his fresh drink, slid off the barstool, and sauntered toward the blackjack table, leaving Marco stewing.

"Looks like we're going to have to find that source," I said.

"Unless we can positively rule him out." Marco got up. "I think I know how to do it. I'll be right back. I'm going to make a phone call. Sit tight."

As I sipped my soda, waiting for Marco to return, I noticed the drunk staring at me. He saw me glance his way and gave me a lopsided smile. I looked away. Next thing I knew, he was clambering down from his stool and staggering toward me. Great.

I reached for my crutches, but Marco beat me to it, helping me down from the stool just as the man reached us. "Hey, buddy," the drunk said, "I (hic) saw her first."

Although I'd always dreamed of being fought over by two men, this wasn't exactly how I'd pictured it happening.

374

Marco ignored the guy and ushered me away. "We've got an hour before our meeting at the coffee shop, so the security guards are going to let us use the upstairs room again to review Tuesday evening's video. I asked to start with the parking lot tapes. This time we're looking for two men — Holloway and Trumble."

We proceeded up to the second floor and sat at the same monitor, where a cooperative security guard got us set up. Marco fast-forwarded through the video as much as possible, slowing it down only when someone approached or exited the boat.

At six fifteen, we saw Jerry Trumble get out of a small car, glance around, then move swiftly through the parking lot and up the ramp into the boat. Marco handed me the notepad and pen, and I wrote down the time. We watched as the parking lot filled up and people made their way to the boat, but none of their faces was familiar.

Just after nine o'clock, an emergency rescue van pulled up to the ramp; then the paramedic riding shotgun got out and walked into the casino. Marco stopped the tape, then zoomed in. "Who does that look like?"

"Kyle."

Marco studied the image a moment

longer. "Note the time and that the emergency lights weren't activated."

Three minutes later, Kyle exited the boat, got into the van, and then the vehicle left.

"Why would a rescue van stop at a casino if they weren't responding to an emergency call?" I asked.

"I don't know, but if they were responding to an emergency, they'd have had lights going."

"Could Kyle have been looking for Lori?"

"Maybe Kyle's partner can answer that one." Marco started the video again, fast-forwarding and pausing, checking everybody who entered or left. We were well past the midnight mark and Holloway still hadn't appeared, nor had Jerry Trumble left the boat. Once again we saw the figure in the black trench coat enter the picture, head toward Lori's car, then vanish behind the gray van parked beside her.

Marco checked his watch and stopped the tape. "We'd better quit so we can make our meeting. I'll come back in the morning to watch the rest. With any luck, Trumble will stop at the coffee shop tonight, and we can have another chat with him."

Marco parked around the corner from the Daily Grind, then turned up his collar and took a cap from the glove compartment. "Wait here. I'll be right back."

I watched in the side mirror as he donned the cap, then walked to the corner and peered around it, as though scoping out the front of the coffee shop. He returned a few minutes later to help me get balanced on the crutches.

"The EMT's name is J.C. He's sitting against the back wall. You can't miss him. He has red hair. Tell him I'm looking for a parking space."

"Where are you going?"

"I want to watch the shop for a while, make sure Kyle doesn't show up."

"Are you expecting him to?"

"J.C. and Kyle are partners and may be good friends, in which case Kyle will know about our meeting and may try to disrupt it. Also, Kyle may have told J.C. how to answer our questions. Remember, whenever you interview a suspect's friend or family member, anticipate lies. An investigator's job is to dig under the lie to find the truth."

"I don't know if I'm experienced enough for that, Marco."

He cupped my face with his hands. "Sure you are, sweetheart. You're a natural."

Was that a synonym for *nosy?*

Marco kissed me, then walked me to the

corner and glanced around it. "There are two people walking toward the shop. They should reach the door in time to open it for you. Go!"

The paramedic was easy to spot. He had light red hair worn short and a square face covered in freckles. He had on a blue Windbreaker, jeans, and athletic shoes, and appeared to be physically fit.

I maneuvered to the counter to order a hot dark chocolate drink, then asked to have it delivered to my table. Then I headed for the table.

"J.C.? I'm Abby. My partner, Marco, called you to set up this meeting."

"Hi," he said, jumping up to pull out a chair, clearly surprised by my appearance. "Have a seat."

"Thanks. Marco will be in as soon as he finds a parking space."

"How'd you hurt your foot?"

"Actually it's a sprained ankle. I fell off my high heel."

J.C. shook his head. "I keep telling my girlfriend she's gonna hurt herself on those tall heels, but she never listens to me."

I waited while the barista delivered my cocoa. J.C. already had a coffee drink loaded with whipped cream. "Thanks for meeting with us so late. We're helping investigate the Willis murder, and at the same time do our day jobs. It gets hectic at times."

"I hear you on that." He tried to come off as friendly, but I noticed that his smile was tight and one of his knees bobbed. "So how does your investigation involve me?"

I blinked at him. I hadn't planned anything because I thought Marco would be handling it. "Well," I said, stalling, "we were told that you responded to a call at the Calumet Casino boat last Tuesday evening and wondered if you'd noticed anyone out of the ordinary hanging around the parking lot."

That was lame, Abby.

J.C. sipped his coffee, regarding me with narrowed eyes, as though he didn't believe me. So I played dumb, something else that came naturally. "I've got the date right on that call, haven't I? Tuesday? Around nine o'clock in the evening?"

"Yeah, I think it was Tuesday. We got a nine-one-one about a possible heart attack. Turned out to be a false alarm. But as for seeing anyone out of the ordinary, what are you looking for?"

"A person in a black trench coat, with very white skin and black hair worn slicked back.

There were reports of him being seen in the parking lot that evening."

"It sounds like you're looking for the New Chapel vampire."

I smiled. "If there is such a thing."

J.C. took a drink of coffee, then licked cream off his lips. "I wish I *had* seen the guy. My partner keeps telling me to stop by Down the Hatch to take a look at him."

"Who's your partner?" Me playing dumb again.

"Kyle Petrie."

"Oh, sure. I know Kyle from the bar. He's a nice guy, but he's got it wrong. The man he told you about isn't a vampire."

J.C. shrugged, as though to say, *Whatever.* "Kyle's convinced the guy killed that nurse."

"What makes him think that?"

"The way the woman was murdered. Bite marks in the jugular vein. Blood drained from the body. Who else would do that?"

"Maybe a guy who wanted it to look like the work of a vampire?"

J.C. sipped his coffee. I could tell he was turning the matter over in his mind.

Marco came up to the table and tossed his car keys down. "Hey, J.C.," he said, sticking out his hand. "Marco Salvare. Thanks for coming down."

They shook hands, and Marco sat next to

380

me and put his arm around my shoulders. "I found a parking space right around the corner. No problem." He tapped on my shoulder with his thumb on the last two words. I took it to mean he hadn't seen Kyle.

I could sense that J.C. was uncomfortable being there with us, so I decided to speed things up and at the same time make Marco aware of the groundwork I'd laid. "J.C. just told me he didn't notice anyone matching our suspect's description in the casino parking lot last Tuesday evening. And he also verified that he made an emergency call there on Tuesday evening."

Marco nodded, as though absorbing the information. "Do you get a lot of calls from the casino?"

"No, not really. And that one turned out to be a false alarm. I wish we had more of those and fewer genuine heart attacks."

"So, even though it might be a false alarm," Marco asked, "is it SOP to respond as though it's a life-or-death situation?"

"Sure."

"Does that mean carrying in your emergency equipment?" Marco asked.

"Of course. We can't waste time running back to the van when seconds count."

Marco took a sip of my cocoa. "Do you

always work in pairs?"

"Yes, we do."

"So how does that work? Does one of you go into the building with the emergency equipment while the other stays with the ambulance?"

"Not usually, not unless there's a reason for the other partner to remain in the vehicle, and then it should only take a few minutes."

"What kind of reason?"

"Calling in to HQ to report that we had arrived on the scene, or to get additional instructions or equipment." J.C. shrugged, as though he couldn't come up with another reason.

"But at least one of you would take in some kind of medical equipment, just in case."

"That's how we operate."

Marco's brows knitted. "That puzzles me, J.C. I watched a surveillance video that shows Kyle going into the casino alone Tuesday evening, but he didn't take anything with him, not even a medical bag."

J.C.'s face turned so red, his freckles seemed ready to jump ship. He cast me a furious glance, obviously angry because I hadn't told him about the video. I picked up my cocoa and sipped it, avoiding his angry stare.

"What are you trying to prove?" J.C. asked Marco.

"I'm just trying to understand why Kyle went into the casino without equipment for an emergency call," Marco said.

"Sometimes when a person calls nine-one-one, he or she isn't certain whether there's a real emergency situation. So in that case one of us might go inside to check it out first."

"You're sure about that?" Marco asked.

He shifted positions. "I said we might do that."

Marco looked doubtful. "So if I called nine-one-one right now and reported that someone in this coffee shop might be having a heart attack, one of the responding paramedics would come inside without any medical bag or equipment to check it out first?"

J.C. chewed on the inside of his cheek. "As I said, he might."

"And if I posed the same question to the responding EMT, he'd give me the answer you gave me?"

The nervous paramedic shrugged.

Marco pulled out his phone. "Let's test it and see."

CHAPTER TWENTY-THREE

Marco punched in 9-1-1, put the phone to his ear, then said, "I think someone at the Daily Grind coffee shop might be having a heart attack. That's right. At Lincoln and Morgan."

J.C. tried to grab his phone, but Marco snapped it shut and slid it into his pocket.

"Listen, man," J.C. said, clearly agitated, "you'd better call again and say it was a false alarm. They'll send responders if you don't."

Marco took out the phone and opened it, but stopped short of making the call. "What was the real reason you and Kyle stopped at the casino that night?"

"Are you kidding me?" J.C. said angrily. "You're gonna let them come out here for nothing? You'll be arrested!"

"Answer the question and I'll call it off," Marco said.

J.C. slouched back in his chair with an

exasperated sigh. "I don't believe this. What if a real emergency comes in and they're on their way here?"

"Then you'd better answer fast," Marco said.

"Kyle stopped at the boat to make a payment, okay? He owes the casino money. The emergency call was Kyle's cover story. He asked me to use it in case anyone questioned me about the stop. So that's what I did."

"How much money?" Marco asked.

"Look, I'm only telling you what Kyle told me," J.C. said, sweat beading on his upper lip. "I didn't question him. It was none of my business. Now would you make the call?"

"You and Kyle are friends, yet you didn't talk about him being in debt?" I asked.

"We work together. We're not friends. All I know is that he had to stop there to make a payment. I don't gamble. What do I know?"

Marco closed the phone. "Calm down. I didn't make that call. No one is coming."

The EMT's face turned red. "Why did you do that to me, man? I came here to help you."

"Lying doesn't count as help," Marco said.

"Look, I'm sorry! I didn't think Kyle would want it to get around that he owed money."

It was Marco's turn to slouch back with an exasperated sigh. "You're still lying."

J.C. threw his hands in the air. "You know what? I don't need this crap. You want me to take a lie detector test? Because I will if you want me to."

"Did you tell Kyle you were meeting with us?" Marco said.

"Yeah, I told him. Why shouldn't I? It was something to talk about while we were on duty."

"Did he seem upset about the meeting?" I asked.

"No, just annoyed," J.C. said, rubbing his eyes.

"Why was he annoyed?" I asked.

"I'm not his shrink," J.C. said tersely. "Kyle *seemed* annoyed. I didn't ask him if he *was* annoyed. I listen to only about half of what Kyle says anyway because so much of it is pure bull. To hear him tell it, he picks up a different girl at the bar every night."

That certainly wasn't the nerdy guy I knew. "Does Kyle date?"

"He says he does, but I've never seen him with a woman."

"Now that everything is out on the table," Marco said, "let's go back to last Tuesday night. You finished your shift at midnight.

386

Then what?"

"We parked the vehicle in the lot behind the hospital. Kyle and I logged out. Then we got into our cars and went home."

"Are you certain Kyle went home?" I asked.

J.C. gave us a look of disbelief. "I don't know what he did. Am I reading this right that you think Kyle might have murdered that woman?"

"At this stage in our investigation, we can't draw any conclusions," Marco said. "We're merely trying to rule Kyle out as a suspect. So anything you can tell us about his movements Tuesday night, Wednesday morning, and Friday night will help accomplish that."

J.C. kept shaking his head, as though he didn't know what to say. "Why didn't you tell me that at the outset?"

"You might have felt the need to protect your partner," Marco said.

"Look," J.C. said, "we're not friends. Kyle doesn't let anyone get close. So you want to know about Wednesday morning? Kyle showed up for work on time and we had a normal workday. Friday night? My girlfriend and I went to a movie. I don't know what Kyle did."

"Did he say anything about the murder?"

J.C. rubbed his palm over his short hair as he thought about it. "Every time we heard a news report about the murder, Kyle would say he couldn't understand why the vampire hadn't been arrested. 'How much more evidence do the cops need?' he'd ask. And I'd always say, 'More than they've got.' "

"Did Kyle express a fear of vampires, or a fascination with them?" Marco asked.

"It never came up until the murder," J.C. said. "No, wait. That's wrong. Kyle started talking about the guy at the bar a couple of days before the woman was abducted, because the day after she made the news, he said something about it being the work of the vampire."

"In what context did he talk about the so-called vampire?" Marco asked.

"Kyle couldn't understand why all the women were attracted to him. He kept trying to analyze it. I told him women obviously found vampires sexy and to please drop the subject."

"Did he ever talk about the murdered woman?" Marco asked.

"He said he knew her from the bar. I said it was a shame about her death, and he agreed."

"How tall are you?" Marco asked.

J.C. ran his hand over his hair again. "Six

388

feet two."

"Ever dress up in a Dracula costume?"

J.C.'s face flushed but he didn't reply, merely looked down at his lap.

Marco leaned toward him. "Did you dress up as Dracula to help Kyle stage a photo in the casino parking lot?"

"Kyle said it would be funny to make people believe there'd been another vampire sighting. I did it as a favor, that's all."

"Are you aware that the photo was on a Web site called HOW TO KILL A VAMPIRE?" Marco asked.

"No," J.C. said, shaking his head.

"Did Kyle put that Web site up?" Marco asked.

J.C. sat back. "Honest to God, I don't know any more than what I've told you. I meant what I said before. Give me a lie detector test."

Marco looked into my cup. "Ready for another cocoa?" He made a slight motion with his head in the direction of the counter. I glanced around and saw Jerry Trumble waiting to pay. I also noticed that the shop had pretty much emptied out.

I finished the last swallow and gave him the empty cup. "I am now."

"Okay, J.C., we're done," Marco said, and offered his hand. "We appreciate your honesty. Our conversation won't go any further than this room, just so you know."

The paramedic looked relieved. "What do I tell Kyle if he asks about this meeting?"

"Tell him what I told you," Marco said, standing. "We're trying to rule him out."

As soon as J.C. was gone, Marco said, "I'd like you to question Trumble on the information you got from his wife's friends. I'll interject when I have a question."

As Marco headed for the counter, I ran quickly through the conversation I'd had with Alison and Becky, picking out things to ask. I saw Marco speak to the pharmacist and then Trumble stiffened. I guessed Marco had just informed him that we'd seen him on the casino's surveillance videos. Marco ordered another hot chocolate and headed back to our table. Trumble picked up his coffee and followed.

"You remember Abby Knight," Marco said to him, taking his seat.

Trumble didn't sit down, but he did lean over to say to us in a low voice, "I'm going to tell you this once more. I did not kill Lori Willis. Despite what you think you saw on that video, I didn't see Willis at the casino last Tuesday night. I didn't know she even frequented the place. If you keep harassing me, I'll get a restraining order against you.

Is that clear?"

"What isn't clear," Marco said, "is why you didn't tell us about your evening at the casino. If you didn't know Willis was there, why lie about being there?"

At that, Trumble pulled out a chair and sat. "Okay, look, I had a gambling problem at one time, and after Dana died, her parents made an issue of it. They called it an addiction, like it was an ongoing problem, so they could get custody of my son. That's why I didn't say anything. If it gets out that I've been to the boat, my in-laws will try to take my boy away from me."

"How often do you go to the boat?" Marco asked.

"Maybe once a week. There's not much fun in my life anymore, so I look forward to an occasional night out. Can you understand that?"

If I hadn't spoken to Dana's friends, I would have felt sorry for Trumble. But I kept replaying their conversation in my mind. "How did Dana feel about your gambling?"

"She didn't like it. That's why I stopped going. I hated to upset her."

I wanted to stick my finger in my throat to show what I thought of his lie, but I refrained. "Have you ever been in debt because of your gambling?"

"A long time ago," he said. "I'm in control now."

I gave him a dubious look. "You haven't lost money in the past six months or so?"

"Who could stand to throw away money in this economy?" He smiled, trying to make light of it.

"What was the trip to Australia for?" I asked.

"Dana and I went through a rough patch," he said, trying to look embarrassed, "the kind of thing that happens in every marriage from time to time. So we decided to take a second honeymoon to repair our marriage. It was supposed to be the trip of a lifetime." He looked down, shielding his eyes with his hands, as though trying to hide tears. "I never in a million years thought it would be the end of Dana's life."

I glanced at Marco and raised my eyebrows. Why wasn't I buying Trumble's grieving-husband act? Maybe because it felt like an act? Somehow I needed to shake him up, get him off his rehearsed pity party. I decided to let my tactlessness work for me.

"Was Dana going to divorce you?"

He lifted his head and opened his eyes wide in a fair imitation of shock. "No! Where did you get that idea?"

"Someone close to your wife told me," I said.

The pharmacist's look of shock was replaced by one of fury. He pressed his lips together so tightly that if the air in his lungs had tried to escape, it would've blown a hole through the top of his head. "You talked to Alison and Becky."

"Was Dana going to divorce you?" I asked again.

"No!"

"Wasn't the purpose of your trip to talk her out of divorcing you?" I asked.

He hit the table with his fist. "She had no intention of divorcing me! She never would have left me!"

"Because you wouldn't let her?"

Marco pressed his knee against mine, signaling for me to back off. But I felt like I had Trumble on the ropes now and I didn't want to lose the momentum.

"I think Dana was going to divorce you on her return from Australia," I said, "so you killed her."

The pharmacist was so angry the cords in his neck stood out like strands of spaghetti. "I don't care what you believe! It isn't true!"

"How much did you collect on Dana's insurance policy? Enough to pay off your gambling debt?"

Trumble's mouth opened, but only a choking sound came out. He was almost to the point of cracking. With a little more effort . . . Marco pressed my knee harder, but I forged ahead. "Lori Willis found a way to prove you injected Dana with the heparin, didn't she? So you had to kill her, too."

Trumble lunged across the table, hands outstretched, going for my throat. I froze. I hadn't seen that coming. Luckily Marco had. Because of his lightning-fast reflexes, he was able to block the attack, and in a matter of seconds, the pharmacist was on the floor on his stomach, arms pinned behind his back, Marco straddling him.

The few customers in the shop had fled their tables and were behind the coffee counter with the barista, who was on the phone, no doubt calling the cops. But the best I could do was to sit there shaking all over, trying to regain my composure. I'd been too cocky. I shouldn't have pushed Trumble that far.

By the time I got my wits about me, Marco was dragging Trumble to his feet.

"We're going outside," Marco said to me. "Wait here."

No problem. My legs were trembling too hard to stand anyway. I couldn't begin to imagine how I'd balance on crutches now.

The barista came over with a cup of coffee. "This should help steady your nerves. The cops are on their way. What a jerk that guy was." Shaking her head, she went back to the counter.

What an idiotic thing I'd done was more like it. And what had we learned from it? Nothing. On top of that, I knew I'd disappointed Marco. I sipped the coffee and let it warm me from the inside. I glanced at the window, but it was too dark to see what was happening outside.

When Marco finally returned, he didn't seem angry at all. "Ready to go?"

I gazed at him in surprise as he picked up my crutches. "Don't we have to wait for the cops?"

"Trumble decided he'd rather keep the cops out of it, so I explained to responding officers that it was a misunderstanding, and they let him go."

"Where's Trumble now?" I asked, as we headed toward the door.

"On his way home is my guess. He got into his car and drove off."

"I'm sorry, Marco. I should have paid attention to your warning."

He didn't say anything. We left the shop and walked around the corner to his car, not speaking. It wasn't until we were pulling away that I asked, "Are you angry with me?"

"I was — for about a minute, but only because you put your safety in jeopardy."

"I shouldn't have goaded him. I really messed up."

"You made a judgment error, Abby. I made my share of them when I was starting out. It's called experience. If you ever feel that you have to push someone like that, make sure you have somebody there to watch your back. I was there, so it turned out okay."

"If only something useful had come from it."

"Something did. We learned that Trumble can be pushed to violence pretty quickly. By the way, good job with J.C.'s interview. I don't think you'd have any problem handling an interview like that by yourself."

Like I'd want to. But I accepted the compliment graciously. "J.C. had some pretty revealing things to say about Kyle. It's clear to me that Kyle is jealous of Vlad, which makes me think he's the one behind the HOW TO KILL A VAMPIRE Web site."

"I agree. When I go out to the casino tomorrow, I'll look into this debt Kyle claims to have. If he lied about that, too, he moves to the top of my suspect list."

"We've got three suspects and all of them lied, so why does Kyle move to the top?"

"For one thing, I think Holloway is playing coy with us because he knows he's not guilty. My guess is that a woman is involved, someone he spent time with in Phoenix, maybe a colleague, or a hospital executive, and neither one wants news of their liaison to get out. I don't think he's our killer, but I won't move him off the list yet either.

"So that leaves Trumble and Kyle in a dead heat. I'm hoping what I find out at the casino will tip the scales one way or the other. If that doesn't do it, then we'll have to look at the next layer of the investigation. Where would each suspect keep a woman hidden for three days?"

"And why would he keep her hidden for three days?" I added.

Marco leaned over and kissed me. "If all is well at Down the Hatch, what do you say we forget about this for the night and go home?"

Alone time! Music to my ears. Wait. That was Marco's cell phone.

"Salvare," he said, pressing it against his ear. "Yeah, Rafe. When? Okay, I'll take care of that in the morning. Everything good there? Terrific. Abby and I are retiring for the evening."

"What was that about?" I asked when he ended the call.

"A message on the answering machine back at my apartment. Nothing urgent."

"Good, because I want you all to myself."

At the next red light, Marco took out his phone and shut it off. "That makes two of us."

After a blissful night with the man I love, I woke up on Wednesday feeling optimistic. Marco and I were going to find the killer, clear Vlad, make our announcements about our engagement and Marco's possible deployment, and then, the very next day, Marco was going to get a letter from the military saying he wasn't being recalled after all.

That seemed a bit much to hope for, but the way I felt, all things were possible.

We left my apartment earlier than usual so Marco would have plenty of time to get me safely installed at Bloomers, then start working on the items on his to-do list. First on that list was a stop at his apartment to check the message that had come in for him. After that, he would pick up the enlarged photo of Lori Willis, head out to the casino to watch the rest of the security tapes, and arrive back at the bar in time for

398

Rafe's next business lesson. After a quick lunch, we'd be off to see my foot doctor.

I got to Bloomers half an hour before Grace and Lottie were due to arrive, so I pulled an order from the spindle and was about to collect my supplies when the phone rang. I picked it up at my desk, noting the caller ID. It said: PARKVIEW HOSPITAL. My first thought was that Jillian had taken a turn for the worse.

"It's me, Abs," Jillian said in a scratchy voice.

"Jillian? Are you okay?"

"Yes, thanks to my guardian vampire."

"What are you talking about?"

"I'm talking about Vlad. He was here during the night."

"Why would Vlad be in your hospital room?"

"To watch over me. We even have a secret code. At least I think that's what he said."

She was hallucinating again. "Do you still have a fever?"

"A tiny one. Would you thank Vlad for watching over me when you see him? He left before I woke up."

Slight fever and hallucinations. "Sure, Jillian. Has the doctor been in to see you?"

"Yes, about half an hour ago. He said if my fever is gone, he'll release me today."

Not if I alerted him to the hallucinations. "Will you call me when you're home?"

"Okay. Gotta go. They finally thought to bring me breakfast." She covered the phone to say to someone, "Would you take that back and bring me an espresso? Make that a double. With room for cream. Is that supposed to be an omelet?"

My phone beeped, so I said, "Jillian, I have another call."

"Abby, can you believe they don't have espresso? What kind of hospital is this?"

At least she had her attitude back. I clicked over to the other line. "Bloomers Flower Shop. How can I help you?"

"Hey, Abby, it's me," Marco said. "I'm just leaving my apartment now. Change of plans, babe. It looks like I'm going to have to make a trip down to Grissom Air Base this afternoon."

My stomach did a nervous flip. "Why?"

"I don't know. It wasn't on the message. All I know is that I have to report by four o'clock."

I swallowed a lump of dread. "The letter said you had to report in three weeks. We're supposed to have another week together."

"I know, sweetheart, and that's still possible. We'll have to play it by ear. In any case, I should be able to get everything on my list accomplished this morning, and then I'll stop by to discuss what I found out with you."

"Can we have lunch together at least?"

"We'll have to play that by ear, too. The army base is on Eastern time, an hour ahead of us, and I still have to get everything wrapped up at Down the Hatch, just in case, so it'll be tight."

Just in case? How could three words feel so threatening?

"And don't worry about your doctor's appointment. Rafe will drive you."

That was the least of my worries. I said good-bye, hung up, and sat there frozen, stuck on the words *just in case.* When my assistants arrived at eight o'clock, I tried to pretend nothing was wrong, but at our morning meeting, I couldn't swallow a bite of Grace's raspberry scone.

"What is it, sweetie?" Lottie asked. "You're not with us this morning."

I took a deep breath and tried to get it out in a rush. "It looks like Marco has to report to the army base today. He doesn't have any more information than that, so it might be nothing to worry about. Or he might be leaving."

On the last word, tears welled in my eyes. I picked up my coffee cup and tried to take a drink, but my hand shook and coffee sloshed over the rim. I grabbed a napkin to wipe up the spill. "We were supposed to have another week."

"Oh, sweetie," Lottie said, and leaned over to give me a hug. "I'm so sorry."

"Let's think good thoughts for Marco, shall we?" Grace said, taking her turn with a hug.

Good thoughts didn't work for me. Only by immersing myself in my flowers was I able to keep my stomach from tying itself into a pretzel. I worked like a fiend all morning, and by eleven o'clock I'd completed all but the last order on the spindle.

It was a bright, joyous arrangement of pink roses, stems of green spray chrysanthemums, red Hedera helix berries, and orange Gerberas, finished off with the greenery Heuchera "Stormy Seas" and Phormium leaves. I gazed at it for a long time, taking pride in my work.

I had just wrapped it when the curtain parted. I glanced up and there was Marco. He gazed at me for a moment, and as always happened when I saw him, my breath caught in my throat. Then I saw the look on his face and felt dark clouds moving in.

He'd come to say good-bye.

CHAPTER TWENTY-FOUR

"Come on, green-eyes, don't be sad," Marco said, putting his arms around me. "Maybe I'm just needed down there to sign off on something."

"I'm sorry, Marco. I'm trying to think positive, but why would they make you drive all the way down there unless they wanted you to report for duty? They could mail papers to be signed."

Marco didn't say anything for a moment, just gazed into my eyes, brushing a lock of hair off my face. "You'll be okay, Abby."

How did he know that? And why did he have to say it as though he knew he wasn't coming back? Now I was truly frightened. But I couldn't let Marco leave home worrying about me. He had enough on his plate. I forced myself to smile back. "Of course I'll be okay. It's not me I'm concerned about, doofus."

"You can't be worried about *me*," Marco

said, as though he couldn't believe anyone would doubt his ability to take care of himself.

With my chin trembling, I said, "I thought we'd have more time."

Marco held me close for a long moment, then kissed me passionately. And all I could think about was what if this was the last time I ever saw him?

He ended our kiss, then pressed his lips to my forehead. "I wish we had all day together, sweetheart, but I've got to get going."

I hugged him hard, breathing in the scent of his skin, committing the feel, the taste, the touch of him to memory. Just in case.

Marco leaned back to gaze at me. "I hate to talk business now, Abby, but I have to bring you up to speed on the investigation. If I'm — delayed — for any reason, you have to do your best to make sure Vlad is cleared."

All sorts of protests ran through my mind, but all that came out was, "I'll try."

"You'll do it. You love a challenge."

"Okay."

"That's my fireball."

More like a pile of wet ashes.

"All right. On to business matters." He pulled up a stool and sat beside me, removing an eight-by-ten blowup of the photo of Lori Willis from an envelope he had with him. "Take a good look and tell me what you notice."

I noticed she looked as dead outside as I felt inside. I took a deep breath and forced myself to focus. The enlarged picture showed the puncture wounds more clearly, but it also showed a red mark like a pinprick just beneath her jawline. I pointed to it. "Was she stuck with a needle?"

"That's what it looks like to me. Remember when I told you she might have been drugged? I think we're looking at the entry point for an injection. The tox screen would tell us whether there was a large amount of sedative in her system, but we can't count on Kyle for help now. Whether he's our killer or not, I'm sure he's upset that we're looking at him as a suspect. I was going to stop by the coroner's office to see whether I could coax one of the staff to give me the results, but the best time to do that is early, around seven in the morning, and I probably won't be here."

"Do you want me to go?"

"It's worth a try. Rafe knows the situation and will be available to take you."

I swallowed the lump in my throat. "Okay."

"Now, on to the casino report." Marco took out his notebook and read from his notes. "There was no sign of Kyle in the parking lot other than when he stopped with his partner around nine o'clock. Jerry Trumble, on the other hand, exited the boat at twelve thirty and walked through the lot until he was beyond the range of the camera. After that, there's no further sign of him. As we know, Willis exited the boat at one a.m.

"So Trumble may have parked off the lot to hide his car from his prying in-laws. It's also possible he circled around and came up on the far side of Willis's car, where the camera couldn't catch him, broke into the car, and hid in the backseat. Another possibility is that he got into his car and followed her home. And here's another point. Trumble played at the same roulette wheel all evening, from which he had an unrestricted view of Willis at the slot machines."

Marco turned the page. "Here's where it really gets interesting. I talked Van Cleef into doing a little checking for me, and he found out that Kyle does not and never did have a tab. There is no debt in his name, so it begs the question of why he lied to his partner. Remember when J.C. said that Kyle asked him to use the emergency call as his cover in case anyone questioned him about the stop? That tells me Kyle was expecting J.C. to be questioned. And again, why? What made him think he'd be investigated?"

"So Kyle made up a cover story — for his cover story?"

"Something like that."

"So his stop at the casino might have been to see if Lori was there so he'd know to come back later. Marco, I'm beginning to think we found our murderer."

"Maybe not. Remember Jerry Trumble telling us he'd had only a minor gambling problem years ago, which his wife's friends disputed? Her friends were right. According to what Van Cleef uncovered, five and a half years ago, Trumble racked up a two-hundred-fifty-thousand-dollar debt at the casino that he paid down by fifty thousand shortly after Dana died."

"He blew two hundred fifty thousand dollars?" My mind boggled at the thought.

"That's right. And I'm betting he got the fifty thousand from Dana's insurance policy. From that point, Trumble made minimum monthly payments on the loan until three years ago, on April twenty-first, when he paid it off in full. My guess is that he used the settlement money from the lawsuit."

"So Trumble benefited twice from Dana's death. If he hadn't received all that money, he'd be up to his eyeballs in debt."

"Or he'd have filed for bankruptcy by now. Unfortunately, whatever agreement was reached in the lawsuit is a private matter."

"I know a clerk at the courthouse who might be willing to help us out."

"It's a long shot, but go for it." Marco turned the page. "Next item, Holloway. I checked with hotel management and security in Phoenix, where Holloway was registered for the conference, and learned that he was there both late Tuesday night and early Wednesday morning. I also checked flights from Phoenix to O'Hare, and given the arrival times, there's no way he could have flown to Chicago, driven an hour and a half to New Chapel, abducted Willis, and flown back to Phoenix to finish the conference.

"Just to be sure, I tracked down another doctor who attended the conference. He said it was well known that Holloway slipped away with another conference attendee, but he declined to name her. As for Friday night when the body was dumped, Holloway was called in for emergency surgery at nine o'clock and was there until three Saturday morning. That pretty much eliminates him as a suspect."

Marco flipped to the next page. "Regarding Diane Rotunno, I spoke with her boyfriend and friends and they all gave the same story she did, confirming her alibi. So I'm ruling her out, too. And finally, my source at the BMV tracked down the license plate number of the gray van that was parked next to Lori's car. It's a dead end. The van belongs to a senior citizens' residence. Tuesday night is seniors' night at the casino.

"That leaves Kyle Petrie and Jerry Trumble in a dead heat, as far as I'm concerned. Both men lied several times. Both had the means, motive, and opportunity to kill Willis, but we still don't have that smoking gun."

"So what's our next step?" My stomach knotted. "I mean my next step, after I visit the clerk's office and the coroner's office?"

Marco turned to another page. "This is Kyle's address. He lives over his mother's garage on Napoleon, two blocks north of Lincoln. You'll need to talk to neighbors to see whether they've noticed any suspicious activity at his house, and set up a surveillance on the garage to see who comes and goes from it, what's inside, and where Kyle goes when he's not working or at home. You can direct and Rafe can do the legwork. He knows where my camera is."

"Are we looking for a place where Kyle might have held Willis?"

"Yep. And this is Jerry Trumble's address. He has a home on Lafayette Street, seven blocks north of the square. Follow the same procedure with him. And one more thing — I want your solemn oath that you'll have Rafe or Vlad or someone trustworthy with you during any kind of investigative work."

"It's not like I can do much on my own anyway."

He lifted my chin and gazed into my eyes, the corners of his mouth lifting in that endearing way of his. "Sunshine, I know you. If there's a way, you'll try. You have to promise me you won't."

I let out a breath. "Okay. I promise."

"I've also arranged for you to have company in the evenings when Nikki is at work."

"Don't tell me you lined up Reilly to babysit again, because that didn't work last time you tried it."

"It's not Reilly."

"Oh, please tell me it's Rafe and not my parents or your mom."

"Your parents. My mom is your backup person."

"You told my parents that you're leaving?" Worser and worser. I was shocked they hadn't called. "Marco, I'll be perfectly fine on my own. I don't need sitters."

"It's just a precaution." He leaned in to press a kiss against my lips. "I hate like hell having to leave you. All I can do is try to ensure that nothing happens to you."

"I wish I could do the same for you."

Marco kissed me again, then closed the notebook and handed it to me. "Do you have any questions?"

Just a few million, such as, how was I going to manage without him? "Will I be able to call you if I need advice?"

"I hope so, but I don't know what my circumstances will be. I'll try to call you later today to let you know what's happening, but in any event, you let me know as soon as you have any information. If I don't answer, leave a message."

I nodded. What if there was nothing to tell?

"Don't worry. You'll do fine. I've been preparing you for this."

For investigating perhaps. There was no way to prepare for Marco's leaving. On top of that, he was putting a lot of trust in me. I hoped I wouldn't let him down.

He sighed and stood up. "I need to get down to the bar and start wrapping things up. I'm riding down to the base with another

Ranger from my unit so that Rafe can use my Prius."

I gazed at Marco in dismay. This was it, then.

He took me in his arms for one more kiss that didn't last nearly long enough. A year wouldn't have been long enough. Marco hugged me fiercely, promised that when he got back, we'd make plans for our wedding. And then he was gone.

And just like that, my optimism vanished.

"This is Abby Knight. I'd like to speak to Mr. Morgan, please."

"What is the nature of your call?"

I was not in the mood for the games his uppity secretary liked to play. "The nature of my call is personal. The mood of my call is dark and dangerous, so unless you want me to come across the street and show you exactly how dark and dangerous —"

"Hold, please."

A few seconds later, Greg came on the line. "Hey, Abby. What's going on? My secretary said you threatened her."

"And you believed her? Boy, are you gullible. Listen, Greg, I need a tiny favor."

"If it involves Marco's friend Vlad and/or the Willis murder case, no can do. I don't know why you're even bothering to ask after what happened to me last time."

"You still have your job."

"That's not funny."

"I wouldn't bother you except Marco asked me to handle something for him. Then he got a call last night ordering him to report to army headquarters today."

"Sorry to hear that. I thought Nikki said he had another week."

"That was the original plan."

"Well, you know how those Special Ops Rangers operate."

As if Morgan knew. The only uniform he'd ever worn had been for Little League.

"What's the favor?"

"Get me the tox screen results on the Willis case."

"I can't risk it, Abby. I wish I could, but no. Now, if there's anything outside this office I can help you with, feel free to ask."

I thanked him for the offer and hung up. Wonderful. Now I'd have to get up extra early to visit the coroner's office.

Lottie came into the workroom and pulled up a stool. "How are you doing, sweetie?"

I shrugged. "Okay, I guess. Trying not to think about Marco."

She patted my knee. "You'll get through it. My Herman went to Vietnam right after we got married. He was gone for a year, and I survived. There are a whole lot of families out there who have a loved one overseas. All you can do is get up in the morning, put one foot in front of the other, and keep going."

In my case, I had only one foot to put down.

"Here's something that'll make you smile," she said. "We sold the new bat mobile. Seems that college student who bought the first one started a trend. Another girl in her dorm bought the second one, and she brought orders for five more."

"Holy cow! Mom will be thrilled."

"You want to give her the good news? She called while Marco was here."

I hesitated. If I called Mom now, she'd inundate me with questions about Marco, and I was still hurting too much to deal with that.

Lottie patted my knee again. "You know what? You've got enough on your mind. I'll make that call as soon as school is out. Do you want to take the first lunch shift?"

"Sure." Since I had no appetite, I'd use the time to go to the clerk's office.

After Lottie left, I flipped idly through Marco's notebook. How was I ever going to accomplish everything on his list? *When* was I going to do it? I glanced at my watch and decided I'd better get started. One foot in front of the — well, whatever.

Those crutches were going to be my Waterloo. Given all the cracks in the sidewalk, the uneven lawn, the wide steps, and the bouquet of callas sticking out of my shoulder bag, it was a miracle I survived the trip to the courthouse. Then I had to go through the security line and ride the ancient elevator to the basement, my heart in my throat at its every groan and shudder. At least the crutches made me a sympathetic figure, so the clerk was more than willing to listen to my reasons for needing to see the agreement, especially after I gave her the bouquet.

"Well, aren't you sweet?" Janine the friendly clerk said, admiring the flowers. "But I'm afraid I can't give you a copy of the agreement."

Rats. My first solo assignment, and I'd blown it.

"I remember this lawsuit," Janine said. "One of the women who worked here then was a friend of Dana Trumble's, and she was convinced that Dana's husband had done her in. Said he was an abusive jerk. What a shame he ended up making a pile of money from her death." The clerk sighed sadly. Then she gave me a determined look. "You said one of the things you need is the date the agreement was recorded? Wait here."

She was back in a few minutes and handed me a piece of paper on which she had made a note. With a shrug, she said, "It's the best I can do. Maybe it'll help a little."

I paused outside the office to glance at the paper. On it Janine had written: *Settlement recorded three years ago on April 11th.*

Marco had said that Trumble paid off his debt on April 21, ten days later — just the amount of time it took for a big check to clear the bank. Added to his hatred of Lori, the lies he'd told us, and his presence at the casino the night Lori disappeared, we had a convincing case for him being Lori's killer.

Yet what nagged at me was the timeline. If Jerry had killed his wife five years ago, what could Lori have found on him recently that would have gotten her murdered? I just couldn't make it work. The more I thought about it, the less likely it seemed that Jerry was our man.

Rafe drove me to my two o'clock foot doctor's appointment, where the doctor examined my ankle and scolded me for not following his orders.

"So you got busted, huh?" Rafe asked on the way back to Bloomers.

"Ten more days on crutches." Yet another disappointment.

"Hey, you know the dinner at the country club Friday night? Your mom invited my mom and me to it, so I was wondering if anyone would mind if I brought a date."

I smiled at him. "You met someone?"

"Your mom's student teacher, Chelsea. I didn't know you brought her down to meet me the other night. I got to talking to her later and we just seemed to hit it off."

"It wasn't like I didn't try to introduce you, Rafe. So you really like her, huh?"

He nodded shyly. "It was like an instant attraction. So is it okay to bring her?"

"More than okay." In fact, it was perfect. Rafe and Chelsea would take some of the heat off me.

"Awesome." He pulled up in front of Bloomers and came around to help me out. "What time do you want me to pick you up? Five o'clock?"

"That'll work. I'll see you then."

I moved through the day like a zombie, waiting for the phone to ring and, when it did, praying that it'd be Marco on the other end. But it didn't happen, and with each call I grew more dispirited. What if he was sent overseas without being able to contact me? What if I never heard from him again? I knew such fears were unfounded, but they were, after all, *my* fears.

I saw Lottie's and Grace's concerned glances but pretended I didn't. I knew I was sinking into a black hole of depression, but there didn't seem to be a way to stop it.

Until I got a call from Rafe.

"Abby," he whispered frantically, "the cops are here to arrest Vlad."

Oh, no. My heart began to pound. "Is Vlad there?"

"No, but he's due in anytime now. It's almost five o'clock. Should I call and warn him?"

Should he? I couldn't think. My brain felt as though it was moving through mud. "Better not. Marco wouldn't want you to interfere with police business."

"You really think Marco would let Vlad go to jail without a fight?"

Of course he wouldn't. What was wrong with me? *Get a grip, Abby! What would Marco do?*

I needed to pace, but I was stuck in the wheelchair. "Can you get Vlad's number from Marco's computer without the cops knowing?"

"I'll find a way."

418

"Okay, call me back as soon as you have it, and I'll phone Vlad. I don't want you getting into trouble. Is Reilly there?"

"Yeah, he's here."

"Put him on."

A moment later, Reilly said, "What is it, Abby?"

"You're seriously going to arrest Vlad?"

"Yes, we're going to arrest him."

"Based on what? New rumors?"

"Based on the evidence we found in his apartment."

Oh, crap. It was more serious than I thought. "What kind of evidence?"

"You know I can't answer that. All I'll say is that it was enough to convince a judge to issue an arrest warrant."

"Come on, Reilly. At least tell me what prompted the search, or is that a big dark cop secret?"

He sighed impatiently, then said in a hushed voice, "We got a tip that items belonging to the deceased were in the apartment."

"A tip from whom?"

"Don't do this to me, Abby."

"Can't you tell me a little more? Like what kind of items? Her shoes or —"

"Abby, stop it."

Immediately, I thought of the missing

necklace and earrings. "Was it her jewelry — a big yellow multipetaled flower and —"

I heard a muttered curse. Then he hung up on me. It had to be the jewelry.

I replaced the receiver, my mind spinning wildly. How would Lori's jewelry have gotten to Vlad's apartment unless he'd put it there? More dandelions for his collection, perhaps?

"Abby, love, the shop is all set for morning," Grace said, peering through the curtain. "Is there anything we can do for you? Shall we wait here until your ride comes?"

I was so preoccupied, it took a moment for her words to sink in. "Oh, no, thank you, Grace. I'll see you both in the morning."

Lottie peered through, too. Both of them stood there gazing at me as though I was about to expire. My cell phone rang, so I said, "I need to take this call. See you tomorrow, okay?"

I checked the screen, hoping it was Marco. But it was Rafe.

"I've got the number," he said quietly. "Vlad hasn't arrived yet, so maybe you can catch him before he shows up, because the cops are still here waiting for him."

I grabbed a pen and took down the number. "Thanks, Rafe. I'll call you back as soon as I reach him."

But then I sat there with the phone in my hand, wondering if I was making a huge mistake. If Vlad was indeed the killer, wouldn't I want to have him arrested?

A memory surfaced: Marco and me in front of Bloomers, his hands on my shoulders as he gazed into my eyes. *I need to help Vlad, Abby. If I don't get involved, the police investigation will stall right on his head. Then the media will catch the fever, and we'll have a three-ring circus on our hands. Vlad wouldn't stand a chance for any real justice. That's not how I want to leave things. I won't leave things that way, and I need you to be on my side on this, Sunshine.*

When it came to Marco, I was always on his side. And if there was one thing I believed in with my whole heart, it was justice. Whether I thought Vlad was guilty or not, I had to make sure he got a fair shake.

I took a deep breath and punched in Vlad's number, counting the rings as I wheeled through the curtain and went to the front window to look out. Down the street, three patrol cars with lights flashing were parked in front of Marco's bar, already drawing a crowd.

The call went to voice mail, so I left a message. "Vlad, the cops are at the bar to

421

arrest you. I don't know if you've been home yet, but they searched your apartment and found something belonging to Lori. I thought you should know."

I hung up and called Marco, but that, too, went to voice mail. Frustrated, I left him a message, then phoned Dave Hammond at his law office. Luckily, he was still there, so I told him what was going on.

"I hope I didn't get myself in trouble, Dave, but I thought it was only right to alert Vlad."

"Don't worry about it. I'm just glad you called me. This has certainly taken me by surprise. The prosecutor should have given me a heads-up. I'll phone Darnell right now and ask him to explain. If you talk to Vlad, have him contact me at once."

"I'll do that. Thanks, Dave." I hung up and phoned Rafe, watching the activity down the street from the bay window.

"Abby, I can barely hear you," Rafe said. "I hope you don't need a ride home anytime soon. It's insane here. We're swarming with news reporters, protesters, cops, customers . . . Now it looks like one of the detectives is getting set up for a press conference outside the bar. Is that legal? What should I do?"

"Channel Marco, Rafe. Take charge of the

422

bar. And don't give any interviews. I'm coming down."

I hung up and scrolled through my address book. Time to call in that favor Claymore had promised.

CHAPTER TWENTY-FIVE

An angry redhead on crutches was a force to be reckoned with. I made my way through the crowd on the sidewalk, elbowing people when I had to, until I was close enough to see who was giving the press conference and find out what was being said.

It was portly Al Corbison, his chest puffed up with importance, announcing to the row of microphones in his face that, due to diligence, good detecting, and a complete examination of the evidence, they had solved the murder and were ready to make an arrest.

I had worked my way to the front of the crowd, and at his last statement I called, "What kind of good detecting ignores three prime suspects to pursue a mythical character?"

A murmur went through the people standing around me. The reporters turned their microphones in my direction.

"Excuse me?" Corbison said, looking for the speaker. His eyes locked on me and his gaze narrowed to an icy slit. "We pursued every possible lead, Ms. Knight. You don't know beans about this case."

"Obviously you don't either," I said, generating more murmurs, "or you would have uncovered a physician who vowed to get even with the victim by doing some bloodletting."

"You're wrong!" Corbison said, red-faced, as the mics swung back to him and the murmurs grew louder. "We followed many leads and interviewed numerous persons of —"

"Did you interview the person who believes the victim was responsible for his wife's death?" I called, as the mics were aimed at me. "A man who has the skills and equipment to drain a person's blood? What about the man who felt he was wronged by the victim after she falsely accused him of selling drugs and kicked him out of a nursing program? Did you follow that lead, Detective?"

"Get her out of here!" Corbison bellowed, as people began to yell things, such as "Is that true?" "What kind of police work is that?" "Is that justice?" and even "Spare the vampire."

Two cops moved in front of me, blocking my view of Corbison and the reporters. But my speech had done the trick. I saw the news reporters hustle across the street to their vans, cameramen in tow, to tape reports to send back to their stations, while newspaper reporters were trying to dodge the cops to ask me more questions. I'd stirred the pot. Hopefully, the detectives would have to take another look at their persons of interest now.

Corbison stepped between the officers and shook his fist at me. "You're going to be sorry you did this. If it wasn't for your dad being a cop, I'd arrest you for interfering with a criminal investigation."

"If it wasn't for my dad being an honest man," I said, "I wouldn't be here demanding justice."

Photographers were clicking away as I hop-stepped through the crowd. Several people congratulated me, but a few booed as I headed to the corner, where Claymore waited in his BMW. He jumped out to help me into his car, then got back in and pulled away.

"Thanks, Clay. I appreciate this. You wouldn't believe what's going on back there."

"Yes, I would. You've already made the

news." He turned up the volume on the car radio, where a reporter was recapping the exchange I'd just had with Corbison. The reporter ended with, "We are told we'll have a statement from Chief Prosecutor Melvin Darnell within the hour."

Claymore turned the volume down. "An earlier report said they were ready to make an arrest because of something found in the suspect's apartment. I'm assuming the suspect is Vlad, so do you think it's possible Vlad did murder the woman?"

How I wished I could say positively that he didn't. "Does Vlad strike you as a killer?"

"If you'd asked me four days ago, I might have said yes, but not after meeting him, or after what he did for my wife. I know Jillian would say he's innocent. She's convinced Vlad is her guardian angel. She swears he was protecting her in the hospital all night."

"She told me that, too, but she must have been dreaming. Why would Vlad be in her hospital room? Is she doing better, by the way?"

"When I left, she was lying on the sofa at home, reading fashion magazines. She'll be on antibiotics for another week, but otherwise, she's back to normal. Oh, and I'll need to pick up her accoutrements. Let me know when it's convenient to come by the shop for them."

"Do you need them tonight? Because I really don't want to go back into that crowd."

"Tomorrow should be fine. Jillian buys double of everything . . . well, except for her special pillow, but I'm sure she can get along without it for one night."

"In that case, do you want to pick me up at seven o'clock tomorrow morning?"

I thought I would be spending the evening moping around, missing Marco and hoping he would call. Instead, I spent the first fifteen minutes listening to messages on the answering machine and returning calls from my assistants and family members who'd seen me on the news and wanted to be sure I'd made it home safely.

I also had messages from reporters wanting to know if I was certain Vlad Serban wasn't the killer. I deleted them. What could I say? That Vlad was Marco's army buddy and therefore innocent? I didn't know whether Vlad was innocent. All I knew was that I had to make sure the police arrested the guilty man.

Even Nikki called during her evening break to lecture me.

"Abby, are you crazy?" she whispered. "I

just saw the news report in the nurses' lounge. What were you thinking when you talked to those reporters? You practically spelled out the names of your suspects. I can't imagine what their reactions will be. You'd better make sure the lock is double bolted and the chain is on — and keep the lights out until I get home."

"Nikki, you're overreacting. Our suspects are going to lie low. They're not going to do anything to draw attention to themselves now. Besides, they don't know Marco is gone."

"Are you brain-dead? Everyone at Down the Hatch has to know. It's a bar! What do people do at bars besides drink? They gossip. By midnight, half the town will know that you're home alone."

I shivered. "My parents are coming over to keep me company, Nikki. I'll be fine."

"Maybe you should ask Reilly to keep an eye on you, too."

"Now *you're* brain-dead. I practically called every officer working on the case a moron for not doing their jobs. I don't think Reilly is going to be too eager to help."

"Don't be silly. He's still your friend. Oops. I've got to go. Be careful!"

I checked the locks, then called the bar to get an update from Rafe.

"It's still a zoo down here," he said. "Did you ever reach Vlad?"

"No, but I left messages for him."

"There are two cops posted outside, waiting for Vlad to show up, but he must have figured it out and gone into hiding. Let me know if you hear anything, okay?"

I'd barely hung up when the door buzzer went off. I hobbled to the intercom and pushed the button. "Yes?"

"Abigail, it's Mom and Dad. Buzz us in, please."

A few minutes later, I admitted my mom, who was carrying a green-handled bag stuffed with groceries, which she immediately began stashing in my refrigerator.

"Why did you bring food?" I asked her.

"Because it's time you had something for dinner besides a grilled cheese sandwich."

"I eat salads, too."

My dad followed in his wheelchair, with two duffel bags on his lap.

"What would you like for supper?" Mom asked. "Pasta or meat loaf?"

"Meat loaf. What's in the duffel bags?"

"Our pajamas," Dad said. "Until the killer is caught, we'll be sleeping here."

Wow. Corbison was right. He said I'd be sorry.

■ ■ ■ ■

Having my parents spend the night on the convertible sofa in the living room of our small apartment wasn't easy. Toss in a cat who liked to race down the hallways as if he were high on catnip and a father who snored, and it wasn't what anyone would call a restful night. However, there were benefits to having them there. I didn't worry about being attacked; I got a big home-cooked breakfast in the morning; and I didn't have to clean the kitchen afterward.

My parents were early risers, so when I dragged myself out of bed at a quarter to six, they had already made up the sofa and had breakfast under way. Simon was perched on my dad's lap, eating scraps of turkey bacon from his hand, having apparently decided Dad was an acceptable male. Mom was frying eggs, and a fresh pot of java was brewing in the coffeemaker.

"Why are you up so early?" Mom asked, as I reached for a glass of coconut juice on the counter. It was part of their new healthy living plan. I tasted it and decided it was pretty good.

"I have to go to the courthouse to pick up some information for Marco."

431

"How are you getting there?" Mom asked.

"Claymore is picking me up."

"Claymore has his hands full with Jillian. I'll take you," Mom said.

"But he has to pick up Jillian's things."

"No buts. I'm taking you. He can pick them up later."

She used her teacher voice. There was no arguing with her now. I grabbed my cell phone and sent Clay a quick text message to let him know I wouldn't need him.

"You'd better look at this," Dad said, and showed me the front page of the *New Chapel News.* There I was in full color, standing in front of Down the Hatch, mouth open, crutches wedged under my armpits so I could shake my fist. The headline read: FLORIST FAULTS COPS FOR FINGERING WRONG MAN. Beneath that, in smaller type: SAYS SHE KNOWS WHO KILLED NURSING DIRECTOR.

Nothing like advertising it to the killer.

The article provided a full account of the murder, as well as my exchange with Corbison. It concluded with a statement by the DA that he was there to make sure justice was served, that the good citizens of our county had voted him into office because they trusted him, and that he wouldn't let them down. It was pure political pap.

I saw my parents scowling at me. "I didn't say I knew who the killer was. I just mentioned the suspects that the cops overlooked."

"You really stuck your neck out for Vlad," Dad said. "I hope your confidence in him isn't misplaced."

"Marco's the one with the confidence in him, Dad. You taught me to stand up for what's right, and that's what I did. When we realized that Vlad was being railroaded, Marco and I did our own investigation and found three suspects with the means, motive, and opportunity to kill Lori Willis. If the detectives knew about those suspects, then they purposely ignored them. If the cops didn't know about them, then they weren't doing their jobs."

"Where is Vlad now?" Mom asked.

"I don't know. I haven't been able to reach him."

Dad gave me a skeptical look. "So he's missing? Maybe on the run? Does that sound like an innocent man to you?"

Nikki stumbled into the kitchen, rubbing her eyes, her blond hair sticking up all over.

"Did we wake you, Nik?" I asked. "I tried to be quiet."

"No, I smelled bacon."

Mom put her arm around Nikki and

433

ushered her to the table. "I've got all the bacon, eggs, toast, and coffee you can handle. I've even set a place for you."

She handed Nikki a glass of coconut juice. Nikki sniffed it, decided it was okay, and took a sip. She licked her lips and said to me, "Can we invite your parents more often?"

Mom pulled the van up to the rear of the courthouse and helped me get situated on the crutches. "I'll circle around the square and meet you back here," she said.

"You don't have to wait. I just have to cross the street when I'm done here."

"A lot can happen between here and there," she said, using her teacher voice again.

A thick fog swirled through the van's headlights as Mom bounced up over the curb and drove away. The sky was overcast, and a storm was brewing off to the west. I hoped it stayed there. I didn't have an umbrella with me and wouldn't have been able to manage one anyway.

A nice-looking guy about my age saw me coming and held the door open. "I don't mean to be presumptuous, but most offices don't open until nine."

"I'm going to the coroner's office," I said.

Eyeing my obviously inconvenient mode of travel, he said, "Well, then, maybe I can save you the hassle of getting to the lower level. I work at the coroner's office. Is there something I can help you with?"

Wow. That was the second time the Evil Ones had worked in my favor. I gave the guy a smile. "Actually, there is."

Ten minutes later I hobbled out of the courthouse with a document in my hand. My mom hadn't returned, so I stopped on the sidewalk below the steps and hit speed dial number two — Marco's number — hoping against hope that he would answer so I could tell him the news. But it went to voice mail again. All I could do was leave a message and hope he got it.

"Marco, I just left the coroner's office, and guess what. You were right about Lori being drugged. She had enough insulin in her system to keep her in a coma for days. And we know who has unlimited access to insulin. So I wanted to let you know that I'm going to poke around Trumble's house and talk to his neighbors to see what I can find out. I'll call you later with an update. Oh, and Vlad is still missing. I hope he's in contact with you, because it's beginning to look like he's on the run. And, Marco, I miss you. I wish I could talk to you."

I hung up and searched for Mom's van, but there was no sight of it on the streets around the square. I finally called her cell phone to find out where she was.

"Abigail, I'm stuck a block away, on the other side of the train tracks. The longest freight train I've ever seen is coming through at about five miles an hour."

"That's okay, Mom. I can make it across the street. Go on home."

"I'm so sorry, honey. Call me as soon as you get inside."

I dropped my phone in my pocket and headed across the courthouse lawn to Franklin Street. Dawn had broken, but there was still no sign of the sun through the thick rain clouds gathering overhead. Luckily, there was almost no activity on the town square at that time in the morning, so I went straight to Bloomers' front door without encountering a soul.

The shop was dark when I let myself in. The only illumination came from the twenty-four-hour security light in the workroom that right now was making the purple curtain glow an eerie plum color. I locked the door, phoned Mom to tell her I was safely inside, then dropped my purse on the front counter. But when I went behind the counter to shut off the alarm, I realized it hadn't beeped when I'd opened the door. I checked the keypad and saw that the green light was on. It wasn't armed.

Hadn't I set it before I left the shop yesterday? I glanced around the room, but nothing seemed to have been disturbed. I knew the alarm hadn't been deactivated by Lottie or Grace because they would have turned on the lights. It had to be my fault. Maybe I'd been so intent on getting down to that press conference that I'd forgotten.

Oh, wait! It was probably Claymore. Jillian must have sent him for her things. She had a key and knew the code. With a sigh of relief, I switched to the wheelchair and stowed the crutches behind the counter. I heard a rapping on glass, and backed around to see Kyle outside the door. He wore his navy EMT jacket and pants, and had a piece of paper in his hand.

He motioned me over and said through the glass, "I saw you coming out of the courthouse, so I thought I'd drop this off. It's the tox screen I promised to get for you."

Instantly, my antennae were up and quivering. His being there felt wrong. Was it by chance that he was around when I had come out of the courthouse? Thank goodness the door was locked, because I suddenly felt vulnerable. I decided against telling him that I'd already obtained a copy.

"Put it through the mail slot," I said, then smiled. "Thanks."

He stuck the paper through the slot and watched as I turned it over. I was looking at a line graph with a bunch of chemical names and symbols on it. It didn't look anything like the document I'd picked up. I held up the paper and said, "I'll give it to Marco."

"I thought I heard Marco was out of town."

"He'll be back. I've got to start the coffee now. My assistants are due in anytime."

Kyle gave me a puzzled look. "Sure. No problem." He turned and walked away.

I waited until he was out of sight, then let out a breath of relief and rolled toward the curtain. The phone rang, so I continued into the workroom to answer it at my desk. I picked up the receiver with, "Bloomers Flower Shop. How can I help you?"

There was a click on the other end as the line went dead. My heart thudded heavily as I put the receiver back. I tried to tell myself that it was just a wrong number, but that panicky little voice inside kept whispering, *It might be the killer. Call Reilly.*

But what would I tell him? Someone hung up on me? On the other hand, having him know I was at the shop alone might have been a wise move.

I dialed his cell phone and got voice mail. "Hey, Reilly, it's Abby. It's almost seven thirty and I'm at the shop alone. Just wanted you to know."

As I hung up, I heard a slight sound from the front. I paused to listen, but it had stopped.

Okay, Abby, it's an old building, and old buildings make lots of strange noises.

I turned on the computer to check for orders and heard another sound from the front, like something scraping against the window. Old building or not, I didn't like it. As I started toward the curtain to investigate, I heard a loud bang and then glass shattering. My first thought was that someone had thrown a rock through the window.

But when I parted the curtain, I saw a hand-sized hole in the door pane adjacent to the lock, with broken glass on the floor below. The door was shut and no one was standing outside. Someone was in the shop.

I immediately backed up and turned to go for the phone, but my chair was spun around and I found myself facing Kyle.

He held up a syringe. "I almost forgot to leave this."

I swallowed, trying to find my voice.

"What for?"

"You know what it's for."

My chest tightened in fear. "My assistants will be here any second. You'd better get out."

He glanced at his watch. "We've got time. They won't be here for another twenty-five minutes. Grace, maybe twenty."

He could only have known that if he'd been watching the shop. Quickly, I snatched a pair of clippers I'd left on the worktable and threw them at his head, then backed up and snatched the handset off the base. But before I could dial 9-1-1, he grabbed the phone and tossed it through the doorway into the kitchen.

"Come on, Abby! That doesn't even work in the movies."

I backed away, my gaze darting around for something else to use as a weapon. All I saw was my floral knife at the far end of the worktable — too far for me to get to it before Kyle did. I'd have to stall, and hope one of my assistants arrived early. "Why do you want to hurt me? What did I do?"

"What did you *do?*" He shook his head as though he couldn't believe I was asking. "Besides telling the cops to investigate me? Besides telling the whole friggin' world that I got kicked out of nursing school? *What did you do?*"

"I didn't name anyone. No one knows who . . ." I drew in my breath as Kyle swept his hand across the worktable, sending a glass vase crashing to the floor.

"Those questions you asked me at the bar the other night, they were intended to belittle me. Don't deny it! I know you, Abby Knight. You're just like Lori. You're two of a kind."

I edged closer to my desk, where I had a heavy ceramic pencil cup in the shape of a cat. "Why would I want to belittle you? I barely know you."

"You know me well enough to stick it to me about being kicked out of the nursing program. It was a bad time in my life, and you took great pleasure in making me relive it."

"Kyle, I only asked you —"

He kicked over a basket I'd set beside the table. "What did I ever do to you to make you treat me like that? Wasn't I always polite? Wasn't I a nice guy to everyone? Good old Kyle, always ready to help a friend?"

"You're not going to get away with killing me, and you certainly won't get away with Lori's murder. Marco's got all the evidence he needs to —"

"Stop it!" he cried, spittle flying as he hit his head with his free hand. "Stop. Lying. To. Me!"

My heart was racing so fast, I was light-headed. "Okay, Kyle, calm down and think about what you're doing."

"Liar!" he shouted. "You're a *terrible* liar. We both know there's not one shred of evidence that points to me. It all points to that *idiot* . . . that *buffoon* who likes to parade around as a friggin' vampire! He wants people to think he kills for blood, so why shouldn't he pay the price?"

"Because he's not the killer," I managed to say.

"Of course he's the killer! Ask anyone in town. Do you understand how easy it is to convince people that there's a murderous vampire on the loose? A few rumors, a Web site with some phony photos, some vampire sightings, and then the pièce de résistance — a body drained of blood. The absolute stupidity of the people in this town! I mean, really, a police-led vampire hunt? The *Garlic* Party? I couldn't have asked for a better setup. It was just too good to pass up."

I tried to calculate how much time had passed, but it was impossible. It felt as though we'd been there for hours and yet I knew it was minutes. "You must have been planning to kill Lori for some time."

"I've thought about it for years. Dreamed of it, in fact. But I didn't seriously consider it until she put the moves on me at the bar. And then, just like a prayer answered, Vlad moves to town." He wiped his damp face with his sleeve. "Can you believe an old hag like Lori going after a stud like me? And the irony of it? She didn't have a clue as to who I was. I was just another hot guy."

And I thought Jillian was delusional.

"That woman ruined my life," he said with a sneer, "and she didn't even *remember* me."

"Maybe Lori did remember you, Kyle. Maybe she was attracted to you and figured what happened was in the past. Let bygones be bygones."

"No," he said, as though explaining to a slow child, "she did *not* remember me. Not until I reminded her. But by then it was too late. I had the syringe in her throat."

I was almost within reach of the pencil cup. "Why did you put her in a coma? Why didn't you kill her right away?"

"Correction. *Vlad* killed her. But to get people to buy that, I had to build up the vampire myth first. Then, to keep the myth growing, I drove her car to the parking lot behind Vlad's building, held Lori for a few days to up the drama, then bled her in a way that looked like bites." He curled his fingers to look like fangs, then touched them to the side of his throat. "Weren't those marks on her neck convincing?"

"Where did you hide her?"

"Abby, really. You're not going to need this knowledge. Why do you care?"

"Come on, Kyle. Indulge me. It was an ingenious plot."

"It was ingenious, wasn't it?" He pulled a stool out and sat down in front of me, as though preparing to be interviewed. "And you don't know the half of it."

"I know you told J.C. you had to stop at the casino to make a payment so you could be sure Lori was there. And I know you returned later and hid in the backseat of her car."

"Wrong! How stupid would that be? I followed her home and she welcomed me in. I didn't want to risk any nosy neighbors seeing me carry her out, so I invited her to come back to my place. She was so hot for me, she went willingly."

"You killed her at your apartment?"

"You know the saying 'Nosy people don't live long'? You're trying to prove it, aren't you?"

He was acting cocky now, clearly sure of himself. If I could keep him talking, there was a good chance Lottie or Grace would arrive. "At least tell me how you disposed of the blood."

"I bagged it up and stowed it somewhere safe. Soon it'll be in the hospital's blood bank, helping those in need of a few pints. Lori was type O positive, a universal donor. I figured it was a way for her to give back to the community. Generous of her, wasn't it?"

I doubted he'd be able to simply slip it into the blood bank, but I congratulated him again on his ingenuity. "You took quite a gamble, Kyle. A lot of things had to fall into place for your plan to work."

"I did my homework. I knew that once Lori started playing the slots, she'd be there until one, two o'clock in the morning. All I had to do was find a patsy to blame the murder on. And then along comes Marco's fanged friend."

Kyle snickered. "What a fool. I figured I'd have to break into his place, but then your cousin got sick and gave me the perfect excuse for being there. You'll have to thank her for me. Oh, wait. I guess I'll have to do that. You won't be around."

I heard my cell phone ringing in the other room. Was it Marco? Reilly? My parents? When I didn't answer, would they know I was in trouble? "So you took Lori's jewelry and planted it in Vlad's apartment when you picked up Jillian? Then tipped off the cops?"

"Clever, wasn't I? Vlad was so perfect. Dressing like Count Dracula. Drawing in all the women. You know, that really bugged me. When Vlad was around, none of us guys had a chance. But with him out of the way, the playing field will be level again. And now that he's on the run, it'll be easy for people to believe he killed you, too."

I grabbed the ceramic cup and hurled it at his head, hitting him squarely in the center of his forehead. Then I turned the wheelchair and raced toward the other end of the table. I had to get to my knife.

CHAPTER TWENTY-SIX

Kyle bellowed in pain as he ran after me. He grabbed the handles of my wheelchair and jerked back with enough force to send me tumbling to the floor. I scampered under the worktable, my ankle throbbing from the pressure I was putting on my foot. I forced myself to ignore it as I tried to stay out of his reach. I had to stop him long enough to make a run for the front door.

I shook with fear, watching for my opportunity, as Kyle circled the table. Then I noticed a stack of five-pound bags of potting soil on the floor near the far end. Quickly, I crawled over to the stack, and when he came around the end, I pushed with all my might, sending them tumbling against his legs. As his knees buckled and he lost his balance, I scrambled out from under the other end of the table and dashed through the curtain.

When I was just yards from the front door,

Kyle grabbed a fistful of my hair and yanked me off my feet. Tears of pain blurred my vision as he dragged me toward the back of the shop, threw me down, and straddled me, pinning my hands to my sides as he squeezed with his knees.

"See how things just seem to fall into place for me?" Kyle said, as I struggled to free myself. "Marco is called away, you show up here early, and Vlad gets cold feet."

He readied the syringe, pushing up with his thumb until a bead of insulin appeared on the tip. "I wish I could be here to see the look on that wimpy *vampire's* face when he finds out he killed again. My only regret is that I didn't have a chance to waste that coward myself."

There was a rustle of fabric behind me. Kyle glanced toward the curtain, his eyes widening and his mouth dropping open. He nearly fell backward onto my legs as he struggled to get to his feet. Quickly, I twisted around and saw the outline of a tall man dressed in black, his shape backlit by the glow of the red security light. The curtains on either side of him formed a wine-colored cape that seemed to flow off his broad shoulders, making him look like a vampire.

Kyle was trembling so hard, he couldn't

speak. A dark stain spread down the front of his navy pants. He took another step back, shaking his head in disbelief.

The curtain closed behind Vlad as he moved silently into the room, a larger-than-life presence. He smiled at Kyle, his long eyeteeth looking sharp and deadly. "Who's a coward?"

Kyle screamed shrilly as Vlad lunged and took him down. Within seconds, Kyle was on his stomach on the floor pleading for mercy, with Vlad's knee in his back.

"Did Lori beg for her life before you stuck her in the neck, Kyle?" Vlad sneered, pulling Kyle's arm up farther behind his back, making him sob in agony.

"Please don't hurt me," Kyle cried. "Lori was an evil woman. She needed to die. I did everyone a favor. I'm begging you! Let me go!"

"Do you have any rope?" Vlad asked me, ignoring Kyle's pleas.

"I'll get some twine." Biting my lip against the pain, I pulled myself into the wheelchair, then rolled into the workroom and cut a long length of twine. Vlad wrapped it around Kyle's wrists and tied it tightly. Then he bound Kyle's ankles and used another piece to fasten his ankles to his wrists. It was done quickly and efficiently.

After pulling Kyle to the back of the shop, Vlad motioned me aside and crouched in front of me to look at my bandaged leg. "How badly is it hurt?"

"I don't know, but it's swelling up fast."

"I'm sorry you had to go through that, Abby. I had to let Kyle keep talking to get his full confession. I wouldn't have let him hurt you." He held out a small cell phone. "Take this. I recorded his confession on it."

I put the phone on the chair beside me. "How did you get in?"

He stuck his hand in his pocket and pulled out a brass key. "Here you go. I took Jillian's key from her purse when she was in the hospital. She gave me the alarm code, too, although she probably won't remember. By the way, that was nice of you to leave a cot in your basement. I needed a safe place to hang out last night."

"You stayed here last night? Did you know Kyle would show up here?"

"I wasn't sure Kyle was the murderer, but after that press conference yesterday, I figured there was a good chance the killer would come after you." He smiled. "I had your back, Abby. Never fear."

Now I understood why Marco had said there was no one else he'd want guarding his back. "You saved my life."

"And now you're going to save mine. Make that call to the cops. I'm going out the alley exit."

"Vlad, don't run. Once the cops know that Kyle murdered Lori, you'll be cleared."

"You know they'll lock me up until the warrant is pulled, and who knows how long that will take? Don't worry. I'll arrange for Dave Hammond to turn me in. There's something I need to do first."

"What do I tell the police?"

"That I changed into a bat and flew out the door."

"Wait, Vlad. Have you heard from Marco? He promised to call me, but he hasn't, and I'm worried."

"You'll hear from him as soon as he's able to contact you."

"What do you mean?"

Vlad gave a small shrug. "It's Special Ops, Abby. Make that call now."

Reilly was first on the scene. He had called my cell phone to check up on me, and when I didn't answer, he'd started for Bloomers when the emergency call came in. After that, more cops arrived, followed by an emergency response team, Lottie and Grace, and crime scene investigators. The media camped outside to photograph and interview everyone they could, and the curious public gathered in groups across the street to watch the spectacle.

The rest of the morning was one long blur. Lottie and Grace parked me in the parlor and kept me supplied with cups of Grace's special blend of tea, guaranteed to be both bracing and calming, while I answered endless questions. When there was no more I could tell anyone, the detectives left, and my assistants went to begin the cleanup process. Only Reilly stayed behind. He sat down across from me at the table. "I'm glad you're okay."

"Thanks. I'm glad you responded to my message."

"I wish I'd caught it sooner." Reilly leaned closer and said quietly, "Listen, if you have any idea at all where Vlad is, you should let me know. He's better off turning himself in."

"I understand that, Reilly, but I honestly don't know where Vlad is. Besides, he didn't kill anyone. Don't scowl. He promised he would give himself up soon."

"I hope you're right." Reilly glanced down, turning his hat in his hands. "I heard about Marco being called up early. I just want you to know you can contact me anytime you need me."

"Thank you. I really appreciate it, Reilly. I hope when Marco returns, the two of you can be friends again."

"Me, too." He stood up, put on his hat, adjusted his thick leather belt, and strode out.

The news of Kyle's capture and arrest spread quickly. By that afternoon, we had more customers than we could handle. Reporters tried to get in, but my self-appointed guardians kept them out. First it was Rafe at the door, and later it was Tara and her friends, who had stopped by to take my photo for their Facebook pages. My parents came by to make sure I was okay, and Jillian also made it to the shop to collect the belongings she'd left behind.

"Are you fully recovered?" I asked her, when she came up from the basement with her Neiman Marcus bags. "No more red meat cravings?"

"I'm not turning into a vampire, Abby. I realize it was an infection and that you, Claymore, and the doctor weren't trying to poison me. But I still wonder about Vlad being a you-know-what. There has to be a reason I couldn't get his photograph."

"That reminds me." I wheeled to my desk and picked up her key, dangling it in front of her. "Vlad wanted me to return this to you, but since it's mine, I'm keeping it."

"How did he get it?"

"He took it from your purse when you were in the hospital. You gave him the code to my alarm, too."

"I did not! I would never give that out."

"It's okay, Jill. I know you didn't do it on purpose. You thought you were sharing secrets with your guardian vampire."

"Whatever," she said, waving it off. "Where is Vlad? Shouldn't we be giving him a medal for catching the murderer?"

"He said he had something to do, but he promised to come back."

Jillian sighed dreamily. "That is such a heroic thing to say." She patted her shopping bag. "Thanks for taking care of my *accoutrements de nuit.* I'll see you at the country club tomorrow night. And that reminds me." She dropped her voice to a whisper. "With Marco gone, you're not going to announce your engagement, are you?"

I touched the ring hiding beneath my sweater, checking to make sure it was still there. "Yes, I'm going to announce it."

Jillian gave me a sorrowful shake of her head. "Don't do it, Abs. It's not right to do it alone. Hold off until Marco gets back."

"I don't know how long that will be.

Besides, you're the one who insisted I make the announcement tomorrow."

"That was then. This is now." She patted my shoulder. "But whatever you decide, I'm good with it."

I was not in the best of moods on Friday. My ankle was suffering the aftereffects of the punishment it had taken the day before, and I was suffering from an aching loneliness. I hadn't heard from Marco, and I feared it was because he'd been shipped overseas immediately. I felt his absence keenly, but I followed Lottie's advice and plodded forward. Luckily, I had Bloomers, my oasis in the desert.

I dreaded attending the family dinner, but there just wasn't a good way out. Rafe offered me a ride, so I accepted, feeling a little more cheerful, being with bubbly Chelsea. She kept us entertained on the way there with stories from her student-teaching experience. I was so pleased that she and Rafe had hit it off. I had a hunch she'd be a stabilizing force in his life.

Rafe dropped us in front of the country club, then went to park the car. Seeing him drive off in the Prius, looking so much like his older brother, brought on a sharp pang of sadness. I turned away, leading Chelsea into the sprawling one-story brick building.

"This is beautiful!" she said, gazing around. We were standing near the lounge, with its grouping of plush chairs and sofas, baby grand piano, and thick Oriental carpet. "Don't you love coming here?"

I decided not to dampen her enthusiasm by admitting I felt about as comfortable there as I imagined a queen would feel dining at a 7-Eleven. Next to my skilled surgeon brothers and their socially adept, fashionably dressed wives, I was always the fish out of water. Tonight was just especially difficult.

I pointed to the left and told her about the enormous banquet rooms, where a wedding reception was in progress. Downstairs were the clubrooms, pro shop, and exercise rooms. The dining room ran along the back of the facility, its long stretch of windows and French doors facing the extensive flower gardens and the golf course beyond. And on the far right side of the dining room was a doorway to a private room, which my brothers had reserved for the dinner.

"We're back there," I said, pointing to the doorway.

"I hope they like me," Chelsea said, giving me a nervous smile. "Rafe tried to prepare me for, um" — she shrugged apologetically — "his mom."

"Don't let Rafe scare you. Mrs. Salvare is a warmhearted lady. She just gets a bit enthusiastic at times. And you've met my dad, right? You know he's a great guy. And the rest of the gang you don't need to worry about. They'll be busy picking me apart."

My mom was watching for us from the doorway, and as soon as she saw us, she hurried out to give us hugs. "Chelsea, I'm so glad you could make it. Abigail, how's your ankle?"

"It's okay," I said, attempting a carefree shrug. I could hear lots of chatter and laughter coming from the room and suddenly didn't feel ready for it. "Why don't you take Chelsea inside and introduce her? I need to use the ladies' room."

Mom hooked her arm through Chelsea's and led her into the lion's den. I turned and steered toward the hallway, wanting to put off my entrance for as long as possible.

Rafe came through the double glass doors and called, "You're going the wrong way."

"I've decided to crash the wedding reception." At his puzzled frown, I pointed toward the ladies' room. "That's where I'm headed."

"Gotcha."

In the ladies' room I stood at the black

457

granite counter and stared at my reflection in the mirror. Did I really want to go into that back room? But what was my alternative? Sit at home with Simon and watch TV? Maybe I'd try Marco's number again. If I could hear his voice, I might have the courage to face the family.

I dug out my cell phone to see if I could reach him, but I wasn't getting a strong signal, so I left the building and walked to the other side of a brick column, under the wide portico just outside the glass doors. I hit speed dial number two and listened, but the call went to voice mail. Damn!

Where are you, Marco?

"Aren't you coming inside?" Rafe called from the door.

"In a minute." With a sigh, I slipped the phone into my purse. "I still can't reach Marco."

"Why do you need to do that?"

"Because, Rafe," I said impatiently, turning, "I —"

It wasn't Rafe. It was Marco.

He was wearing army fatigues and brown boots, and had a brown canvas bag slung over his shoulder, as though he'd come straight from the base. He strode toward me with open arms and hugged me against him, lifting me off my feet. My crutches fell to the sidewalk with a clatter and I squeezed him tight. "You're here! How did you get back? Where have you been? Why didn't you call?"

"Whoa, Sunshine. Take it easy," he said, getting me back onto the crutches. "I wasn't able to call until just a few hours ago, and then I decided to wait and surprise you. I'm sorry, babe. I would have phoned if I could have. But I did get to hear your messages, and Vlad told me what happened with Kyle when he picked me up today."

So that was why Vlad hadn't stuck around.

Marco shook his head. "I don't know what to say except that I'm extremely thankful you weren't hurt."

"Vlad had my back, Marco. I understand now why you've had so much faith in him all along."

"If there was anyone in the world I could trust to keep you safe, it was Vlad."

I glanced around. "Where is he?"

"He said he had to go see Dave Hammond."

"Dave doesn't meet clients at ni— Oh, right. This is Vlad."

"He's a man of his word, Abby. And wait — he gave us a gift." Marco opened his brown bag and pulled out a wine bottle with a homemade label on it. He held it up so I could read the label. It said: VLAD'S DANDE-LION WINE.

"It's our engagement present," Marco said. "I've got one more in my bag. They're his last two bottles. He'd been saving them for us because the new batch won't be ready for months."

"He wanted all those dandelions to make wine?"

"It's one of his hobbies. We can open one tonight, just the two of us, and celebrate. How does that sound?"

"Like a dream come true. But does that mean you don't have to go back?"

"I can't promise I won't ever be called back, but I'm done for now."

"Oh, Marco —" I couldn't hold back my tears any longer. He put his arms around me and held me while I wept in relief.

"Hey, sweetheart," he murmured, "I told you everything would be okay."

I wiped tears off my cheeks. "I'm just so thankful you're safe. Can you tell me why they needed you?"

"I had to accompany someone on a quick trip to South Korea." He shrugged enig-matically. "A little security matter."

"Just you? Not your Ranger unit?"

"A few of us from the unit."

"Who did you accompany?"

"I'd tell you, but then I'd have to kill you." His mouth curved up at one corner. "Does it matter? I'm here, aren't I?"

I smiled at the man I loved with my entire being. "Yes, you're here, and that *is* what matters."

I'd get the details later.

"What's Vlad going to do after he's cleared?" I asked. "Is he still going to work at Down the Hatch?"

"No. He said he had a lead on a bar for sale in Chicago. I think he's had his fill of New Chapel."

"Are you still planning to sell your bar?"

"I'm thinking about hanging on to it and letting Rafe manage it for me."

The best of both worlds. I knew Marco would never be able to totally let it go. "That's a great idea, Marco. Rafe brought Chelsea tonight, by the way. They hit it off after all. Wait till you see them together. They're such a cute couple."

"Speaking of couples, we have an announcement to make."

"Then let's go inside and make it."

"First, there's something we need to do." Marco unfastened the chain around my neck and removed my engagement ring. "Time to start showing off this baby."

He held me so I could let go of the left

crutch; then he slid the ring onto the fourth finger of my hand. I held it up so we could admire it. "It's beautiful, Marco." I smiled at him. "I'm so happy right now, I could burst."

"Don't burst yet. We've got a room full of people inside who are going to want to know when we're getting married."

"Oh, no! We haven't even talked about a date."

"I'm still partial to September."

My head started spinning with all the plans I'd have to make. "I don't know if I can pull a wedding together in five months. I have to find a dress, a caterer, reserve a room —"

"There's always the elopement option." He gave me a mischievous grin.

"September it is."

That earned me one of Marco's rare full smiles. "Ready to share the news?"

"You bet I am, Salvare."

I started to hobble toward the door, but Marco said, "Not that way," and swept me into his arms. "This way."

We hope you have enjoyed this Large Print book. Other Thorndike, Wheeler, Kennebec, and Chivers Press Large Print books are available at your library or directly from the publishers.

For information about current and upcoming titles, please call or write, without obligation, to:

Publisher
Thorndike Press
10 Water St., Suite 310
Waterville, ME 04901
Tel. (800) 223-1244

or visit our Web site at:

http://gale.cengage.com/thorndike

OR

Chivers Large Print
published by AudioGO Ltd
St James House, The Square
Lower Bristol Road
Bath BA2 3SB
England
Tel. +44(0) 800 136919
email: info@audiogo.co.uk
www.audiogo.co.uk

All our Large Print titles are designed for easy reading, and all our books are made to last.